EVERLASTING
QUILTS

a novel by
Ann Hazelwood

C&T PUBLISHING
Another Maker Inspired!

Text © 2017 by Ann Hazelwood
Artwork © 2017 by C&T Publishing, Inc.

Executive Book Editor: Elaine H. Brelsford

Copy Editor: Chrystal Abhalter

Graphic Design: Lynda Smith

Cover Design: Michael Buckingham

Cover quilt: *Bow Tie Quilt* by Martha Dellasega Gray (2007). 62″ × 78″. Hand pieced and hand quilted.

Published by C&T Publishing, Inc., P.O. Box 1456, Lafayette, CA 94549

Library of Congress Cataloging-in-Publication Data

Names: Hazelwood, Ann Watkins, author.
Title: Everlasting quilts : a novel by / Ann Hazelwood.
Description: Paducah, Kentucky. : American Quilter's Society, [2017] |
Identifiers: LCCN 2017014711 (print) | LCCN 2017020360 (ebook) | ISBN
  9781604604290 (eBook) | ISBN 9781604603934 (pbk.)
Subjects: | GSAFD: Mystery fiction.
Classification: LCC PS3608.A98846 (ebook) | LCC PS3608.A98846 E94 2017
  (print) | DDC 813/.6--dc23
LC record available at https://lccn.loc.gov/2017014711

POD Edition

DEDICATION

I'd like to dedicate this book to my incredible readership that continues to encourage me with compliments and personal experiences as they read my novels. It has made my journey a real pleasure! I will always be grateful. Thank you.

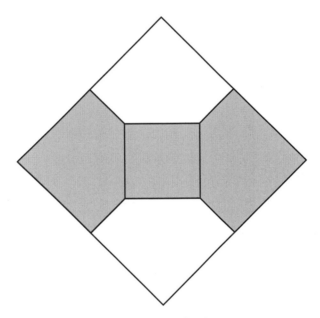

Bow Tie block

CHAPTER 1

How was I supposed to respond to the three magic words that most people long to hear? That was my dilemma last week when Clark McFadden said, "I don't think I have told you that I love you!" When someone professes their feelings in that way, is it necessary to respond with the same words? Did Clark make this admission to test or tease me? Am I making too much of the situation? It's just that I haven't heard anything akin to that from a man since my husband was killed several years ago. I just assumed I would never hear a romantic profession of love again, nor did I plan on saying those words to any other man in my lifetime. The whole situation has left my mind and emotions spinning at hyper-speed.

I must admit that Clark has been more than a casual friend. We became good friends when he did all the cabinetry work at my historic house here in Borna. This handsome artist is a confirmed bachelor that keeps his life as private as he possibly can, despite his artistic fame. When I arrived in Borna, he seemed to understand my pain as I tried to recover from the loss of my husband, Clay. Clay's alcoholic lifestyle was the reason he was killed in a car accident. It was during my grief that I inadvertently discovered Clay's infidelity. It felt like someone twisting a knife in my broken heart. This horrible discovery left me feeling so alone and betrayed. With Jack, my son, living in New York, I knew I had to find my own way through the grief that was forced unexpectedly upon me.

My hometown of South Haven, Michigan, was special to me and it was where I lived many happy years. It was where Clay and I reared Jack and where we made our lives. Clay worked in the family lumber business. It was in South Haven that I thought I would spend the remainder of my days. When I unexpectedly inherited a house and property in Borna after Clay's death, I found friends, charm, and purpose. It was the perfect place to start a new life. In so many ways, it was Clark who helped me adjust to this small Missouri town.

As time passed, I felt less and less as if I needed to protect myself emotionally. I eventually found myself open to the idea of enjoying the company of the opposite sex. I allowed Maggie, my best friend in South Haven, to fix me up with an older gentleman on my last visit home. It was pleasant, but was definitely not a match I chose to continue. Surprising myself, I also took an unexplained liking to my downstairs neighbor in the condo I purchased on Lake Michigan. I knew he was way too young for me, but I was fascinated with his career as a travel writer and the fact that he found me attractive. Both encounters had been safe, leaving me to fully pursue my newly achieved independence.

Clark was different, somehow. Perhaps he had been at the

right place at the right time. His aloofness was a challenge to me at times. I liked his attention and willingness to listen—a quality I found to be unique in a man. I also knew there were times when we were on the cusp of turning the relationship into something more intimate. So, when Clark used the L word for the first time, I didn't know how to act. I simply snuggled into his embrace and whispered, "How sweet." Perhaps that wasn't a good response to his confession. As our evening continued that New Year's Eve night, I became aware that my words had been interpreted as a sign of rejection. Men don't like being rejected in any way, shape, or form. I was smart enough to know that. They assume women long to hear those three little words to make their life complete. I am not one of those women. Perhaps it was my fault and I pondered whether I had sent false signals that I was ready for the next step in our relationship. When Clark took me home that evening, I didn't invite him in. Somehow, I knew we had vastly different thoughts on our minds.

CHAPTER 2

Clark knew I was leaving this week to visit South Haven. He also was planning to go away for a medical checkup and to visit his gallery in Springfield, Missouri, where he sold his work. Clark had shared his experience with prostate cancer with me awhile back, but he kept most of the treatment details a secret by simply leaving town, which he frequently did. There were times that he would just leave town without telling me. I tried not to make it a big deal because I was determined to respect his privacy.

As time passed, I tried to not be hard on myself for not responding the way Clark may have wanted me to when he told me he loved me. For all I know, Clark may have been relieved that I did not repeat the same three words.

On this trip, I was going back to South Haven to help my longtime friend and housekeeper, Carla. I owed her big time for taking Clay's dog off my hands when I moved to Borna. Sadly, she had recently been diagnosed with breast cancer and I didn't want her to go through it alone. She had been there for me all the years I was married to Clay. I don't know what I would have done without her.

I was so happy with my decision to sell our big home and buy a condo on Lake Michigan to have a place to stay when I came back to visit. It was also convenient for Jack when he came back to what he still called home. He is engaged to Jill Moore, the daughter of my friends Maggie and Mark. Jack and Jill getting together was a dream come true. As parents, we watched the two of them grow up together and had often hoped they would become attracted romantically some day. The wedding date had not been set as yet, but the mere thought of it happening was delightful.

Leaving my business, Josephine's Guest House, to go on a trip wasn't as easy as just leaving home. My place was well looked after by Susie and Cotton. I hired Cotton when I first arrived in Borna to do the grunt and yard work as I prepared getting 6229 Main Street ready to put on the market. Susie was great at cleaning houses, so it was a win-win situation. When I decided to live in Borna and turn my property into a guest house, I found that Cotton and Susie looked forward to enjoying some of my guests' breakfast food when they arrived in the mornings to do their work. The highlight of that meal is typically my famous blueberry muffins which have become my signature menu item. One couldn't live in South Haven and not be influenced by its fame as the Blueberry Capital of the World, so I brought a little bit of South Haven to Borna with my delicious muffins.

In Borna my friend Ellie next door kept an eye on my guest house when I was gone. Ellie and I met the very first night I arrived. She saw my light on and offered me a place to stay while I did the necessary work that my house needed. Her darling little house and her genuine friendship were very endearing. It didn't take me long to fall in love with Borna and make the decision to make it my permanent home.

Not everyone was happy with my plans to make the home my permanent dwelling. When a creepy realtor found out that I had changed my plans, he became nasty and broke into the house to attack me. Clark came to the rescue, for which I am eternally grateful. As I think back, I realize I could have been raped or killed. My brother-in-law, James Meyr, also became belligerent when I refused to sell him the property, something he felt he was entitled to. He was hoping to use the property to pay off his debt with East Perry Lumber, located here in town. Needless to say, this conflict ended my relationships with the Meyr side of the family.

Eventually, everyone began to realize I was settling in and becoming part of this small community of just over two hundred people. I quickly became a member of a wonderful group of women called the Borna Friendship Circle. Ellie took me to a meeting as a guest even before I decided to move here. There were eleven of us until recently when precious Emma passed. She was the oldest member and a delightful soul that captured my heart.

I had a list of things to accomplish before I could leave on this trip back to South Haven. One of them was to make sure things were progressing for my Aunt Mandy. She had visited at Christmas and decided to move closer to me and make Borna her new home. Through much excitement and the help of my friends Ellen and Oscar, we helped her arrange plans for the building of an octagon-shaped cottage on the wooded property behind my house. She went back to Florida to arrange her move, and we agreed that she would return as soon as I got back from South Haven. It was exciting to think about having a relative living nearby to share my life with, but it was a big step for all concerned.

Another chore before I could leave was to take down my antique feather tree, still set up from Christmas. My large, real tree had been taken down before New Year's Eve. Aunt Mandy purchased the unique tree for me from Imy's Antique Shop down the street. Imy was another one of those friendly people that made my transition to a new town so easy. Clay never wanted antiques in our big new home in South Haven, so when I purchased 6229 Main Street I filled it up with a lot of antiques from Imy's shop.

My first Christmas here was amazing. For Christmas dinner I entertained Aunt Mandy, Jack, Clark, and Rock, Clark's brother who was visiting. It was nearly perfect until I reluctantly agreed to go to Ellie's New Year's Eve party with Clark. Ellie owns the charming Red Creek Winery, located on top of the highest hill in East Perry. Neither Clark nor I were much for crowds and noise, so once at the party we ventured outside to stand by the fire pit. It was so inviting. It was perfect for a nice snuggle on a cold winter's night. That was when Clark said those three little words that frightened me to the core.

CHAPTER 3

"Are you sure this trip isn't turning your life upside down, Kate?" Carla asked when I called her to confirm my arrival date.

"Not at all," I assured her. "I have thought of everything and I should be there to take you to the hospital. Everything will be fine."

"I'm not so sure," she said quietly. "What if it has spread to my lymph nodes?"

"We aren't going to think about that right now," I soothed. "We'll take one day at a time." When we hung up, I had to admit that I was indeed worried about what we may be told after her surgery. This was uncharted territory for both me and Carla.

I checked the forecast on my phone another time and it was going to be clear but very cold. I needed to make my list for Cotton and then call Ellie and confirm with her about my departure tomorrow. That left one last thing on my list, which was my communication with Clark. It just wasn't right the way we had left things between us. Clark was never much for telephone conversations or texting, so I knew I would have to be the one to break the ice. He liked to drop in unannounced once in a while, but that wasn't likely to happen anytime soon. Dropping in without calling first was a common practice with folks around here, which almost never happened in South Haven. Gathering my nerve, I took a deep breath, pulled up my big girl panties, and called his number. It rang and rang. It was about to go to voicemail when he answered.

"Yeah, Clark here."

"Oh, Clark, I'm glad I reached you," I began, as if nothing were wrong. "I want to touch base with you before I leave tomorrow." I paused. "Is this a bad time to call?"

"I'm about to pull over to gas up, so hold on a minute," he instructed. He obviously was driving.

I waited and waited.

"Thanks," he said finally.

"Where are you?"

"I'm near Springfield," he reported. "I just have about thirty more miles to go."

"Oh, I didn't know you had left," I replied, not able to disguise the disappointment in my voice. Another pause followed. "Is everything okay?" I asked, feeling at a loss for words.

"Sure. And you?" he asked casually.

"The weather is still promising, so I'm leaving for South Haven tomorrow," I said, feeling foolish. "I just wanted you to know."

"You know I'm not good about those things," he mumbled.

"Are you upset with me?" I asked bluntly.

"No." Then he repeated my question. "Are you upset with me?"

ANN HAZELWOOD

"Of course not," I conceded. "I surely hope things go okay for you. I'm going to miss you." I probably shouldn't have said that.

"It sounds like you'll be fine, going back to your old stomping grounds and seeing your friends."

"Will you let me know when you plan to return home?"

"We'll see how it goes," he said, avoiding my question. "Be safe and we'll catch up later. Take care now."

"You too," I said, feeling a surge of disappointment as I hung up.

I sat at the kitchen island and wondered if this was Clark's way of ending his relationship with me. If he really did love me like he said, how could he give up on me so easily? I then called Ellie to tell her I would be leaving first thing in the morning. She knew by the tone in my voice that I was not myself.

"Look, Kate, I'm about to leave to go to work," she explained. "Why don't you come on out to the winery and have a quick bite to eat?"

"Oh, I don't know," I said, confused. "I finally just talked to Clark and I can't figure out what may have happened. He's already in Springfield and he didn't even tell me he'd left."

"I didn't think we'd seen him around lately," she mused. "Come on out and we can eat a bite together. Your refrigerator is likely bare since you're leaving."

"You're so right there," I agreed. "Okay, I'll see you later."

The thought of seeing Ellie was what I needed to perk me up. I started wrapping each antique ornament in tissue paper as I took them off the tree. They were all so delicate. I couldn't help but wonder about their history. The process also gave me time to think. My cell phone rang as I finished the task.

"I have some good news, honey," Aunt Mandy's voice said cheerfully when I answered. "My lease here has been purchased, so that's a load off my mind. Now, I can begin packing."

"That's wonderful!" I responded. "I'll let you know when I'll be back here in Borna. I don't want you arriving until I'm here."

"So, have you seen any action in my neck of the woods?" she teased, chuckling at her own insinuation.

"Yes, I see some orange-colored stakes where your cottage will be and they are clearing away some of the forest," I reported, hoping to steer her toward a new subject.

"I hope they are careful and avoid the trees we wanted to keep."

"Oh, they will be. Not to worry," I assured her. "It's a dandy spot. I envy you being all tucked away from Main Street."

"Well, you can camp out there anytime you want," she kidded.

"I'm leaving here in the morning, and I'll bet we will be surprised at the progress made by the time we both return," I speculated.

"Splendid!" she said, excitement in her voice. "Now you be safe and have a nice trip."

"Thanks, Aunt Mandy. I will."

"I'll look forward to seeing you, the handsome Clark McFadden, and the Friendship ladies when I return," she said just before our conversation ended. Little did she know, but Mr. McFadden might be a no-show.

CHAPTER 4

It was good to sit down and relax with Ellie. When either of us needed to talk, she would wisely steer us to an area of the winery that provided more privacy. The gas fireplace was going, so we settled on a table near the warmth.

"So, have you heard from Carson since his New Year's Eve visit?" I asked cautiously. Carson, a wine salesman, had captured Ellie's heart before he decided to get divorced. Seeing Ellie so vulnerable was concerning, but she claimed to know what she was doing. She felt confident that he had truly filed for divorce.

"I have!" she answered happily. "I think he'll be back next weekend." She paused before asking, "So, I take it you and Clark are out of sync again."

"That's a good analysis," I responded with a grin. "New Year's Eve ended out of sync, actually."

"What do you mean by that?" Her face registered surprise. "You looked like you were having a good time!"

When I explained the chain of events of the evening and Clark using the L-word, her face went from joy to confusion.

"Honestly, I don't think the two of you will ever be on the same page. Timing is everything. When one is hot, the other is not." Ellie shook her head in disbelief.

"I guess you're right," I nodded. "Perhaps it will never happen. I think I've come to that conclusion and I may be okay with it."

"Well, aren't you wise, my friend," Ellie teased as she filled my wine glass. "Now, let's enjoy this food!"

Like always, we laughed and gossiped as Trout, the bartender, added his two cents worth once in a while. Before I left, I purchased bottles of wine for Carla and Maggie and some to have in my condo. This visit was just what I needed before leaving Borna.

Coming back to the guest house, I marveled at all the changes that had happened since I moved here. Actually it was Clark who first suggested that I turn my home into a guest house. Borna had no place for people to stay. When I added a large sunporch to the house, he said it would be perfect for guests and an excuse for me to bake my blueberry muffins. I talked it over with Ellie and the guest house became a reality. It also gave purpose to my life in Borna. For now, I went up to my bedroom suite and finished packing.

My house had been adapted to include one guest room on the first floor that was once Doc's office. I called that room The Study. On the second floor were my suite, a bedroom called the Wildflower Room, and another called the Forest Room. The third floor was named Josephine's Attic Suite, which was sizable and had a nice view of Main Street. I liked to think I was living here alone in the house, but I knew there was a spirit of some kind, which I had assumed was Josephine. I felt a connection to her when I found a disturbing quilt left in the house that she had made. The more I learned about Josephine, the more I didn't know. For some reason, however, I felt connected to her. Doc Paulson and his wife had no children. It was rumored that Doc drank too much and chewed tobacco even as he was seeing his patients. People recall never seeing Josephine when they saw Doc, so Ellie and I assumed she spent a great deal of time in the attic. I was continuing to research her life in little bits and pieces. The Heritage Museum in Dresden was somewhat helpful, but there didn't seem to be a single picture of her anywhere. How odd, I thought.

CHAPTER 5

It was very dark when I left Borna the next morning. I made certain to leave early in order to get a good start. I had traveled to South Haven several times by now, so I knew the route well. I usually stopped at the same places for gas and food. The drive was a good time for me to escape both worlds and plan ahead for my upcoming visit.

I called Maggie to confirm my travel plans, and she invited me to have dinner with her this evening. I knew I would be tired, so I begged off and agreed to meet her in the morning at the Golden Bakery, a favorite practice of ours. Their blueberry scones were the best in the land. It was inspiring how the entire town promoted blueberries every chance possible and celebrated with a blueberry festival in August of each year.

As I got closer to South Haven, there were still a few Christmas lights left here and there. When I crossed the popular drawbridge I smiled, knowing I had arrived in the town I loved. The next landmark was the red lighthouse on Lake Michigan which was the signature piece of South

Haven. With touches of snow and ice still present, it made a beautiful and welcoming winter display.

As I drove into the parking lot of my condo, I wondered if John happened to be in town. I hadn't received a text from him since New Year's Eve. When I got to my building his place was very dark, except for our porch lights.

When I opened my door, the place felt stuffy and empty. Jack had visited here last. Carla checked on the condo every now and then, but it was clear that no one lived here full-time. Before I went to get another load of things from the car, I opened the doors leading to the deck to get some fresh air circulating inside. My covered lawn furniture reminded me of happy times on this deck as I drank wine and gazed at the lake during warmer weather. It was where I had been when I first heard John's classical music floating up to my floor. We had hit it off immediately. On our first visit, John had been impressed with my description of Borna and I was equally impressed with his travel and writing skills. In the end, he came to visit Borna for Thanksgiving and wrote a lovely article about Borna in *Scenic America* magazine. He was a frequent contributor to the magazine, and the article had been awesome exposure for all of us.

I walked around the condo, pleased to see that Jack had covered his bed with the lighthouse quilt I made for him as a Christmas gift. I looked in the refrigerator and saw plenty of beer left from his visit. I grabbed a frozen pizza from the freezer which would easily suffice as a late-night dinner.

While I waited for the pizza to bake, I went up to the loft where I kept a laptop and a sewing machine. The room really needed some attention. I still had to purchase a daybed that overnight visitors could use. When I finished eating, I called Carla to see if she wanted to join Maggie and me at the Golden Bakery the following morning.

"No thanks, Kate," she answered firmly. "I have a few last-minute things to do. Are you still okay with checking on Rocky? I don't know how frequently you need to do that."

"Of course," I assured her. "I would bring him here except they don't allow pets." Then, wanting to focus on her upcoming surgery, I added, "At the most, they will just keep you one night, don't you suppose?"

"Let's hope so," Carla responded. "Can you be here as early as six in the morning?"

"I'm used to getting up early so that's no problem," I assured her.

After I hung up, I realized I had one free day before taking on the role of nursemaid.

CHAPTER 6

After breakfast with Maggie, I was hoping she would go with me to Cornelia's Quilt Shop. I wanted to pick out a quilt pattern for Jill and Jack's wedding quilt. I also wanted to look for a simple idea for my East Perry Fair block.

Another topic on my list of things to do was to contact my niece, Emily. Since there was no funeral service after her mother had committed suicide, I'd had no communication with Sandra's three children. I would also try to contact Sandra's housekeeper, Noreen. She was the one who called me right after Sandra had taken a knife to her wrists.

My mind was on too many things as I tried to go to sleep. Perhaps I should be thinking about those big blueberry scones waiting for me in the morning! I hadn't fallen into a deep sleep for very long before I heard something that sounded like someone slamming a door. I jumped, wondering for a second where I was. Because I'd once had an intruder in my home, I remained pretty jumpy when hearing strange noises. I quickly realized that the noise had to be John coming home. I smiled, pleased to know I would see him on this visit.

The next morning I slept until eight thirty, that was late for me. I had agreed to meet Maggie at nine, so I jumped into action. When I left the condo, snow flurries were coming down. Welcome back to South Haven, I told myself. I pulled my hood over my head and cleared off the windshield, missing the luxury of a garage at the condo. I was nearly there when Maggie sent a text asking if I would be arriving soon. She knew I was never late. Perhaps she knew me well enough to know I had overslept. Minutes later, I arrived.

"Sorry I'm late," I said, brushing snowflakes from my coat. "I overslept and had to clear my windshield. Some of us don't live in the Hamptons." Mentioning the Hamptons was an inside joke between us. She just laughed as I gave her a long overdue hug.

We took our scones and coffee to the same booth that we considered ours for many years. It was as if our names were engraved on it. It didn't take us long to start giggling when Maggie told me about Mark talking in his sleep.

"Did you decide if you can go with me to the quilt shop?" I asked, hoping she would come.

Maggie shrugged her shoulders. "Are you sure making them a quilt won't jinx the whole thing?" Maggie teased.

"Oh! I never thought of that!" I said with a chuckle. "I just thought that if I'm going to do this, I need to get started. My friend Ruth Ann did a great job quilting Jack's quilt, so I'll give it to her to quilt."

"How in the world am I going to top you when you give them a quilt?" Maggie asked, shaking her head. "What can I do?"

"You can make them a quilt, too," I suggested. "You and

I do totally different work. You are such an artist. You could make them a really nifty wall quilt. They will have walls to decorate, and Jill has always been fond of your work."

"You don't think it's too personal?" Maggie asked, resting her head on her hands.

"Heavens, no," I protested. "Make it about something they both love, like Lake Michigan, for example. If they live in New York, they will love the reminder of their home."

"You're so smart and creative. I'll give it some thought." She paused. "Mark and I want to treat you to dinner at the country club before you leave," Maggie stated as the waitress refilled our coffee cups.

"Oh, no," I responded. "You are not going to trick me into seeing Max again."

Maggie burst into giggles. "We won't!"

"I just don't know if I'm ready for the country club scene," I admitted. "It brings back too many memories. I want to see how Carla recovers before I commit to my own activities."

"Of course, but she won't object to you having a dinner out with us. Remember how much you love their crab cakes?"

"Using food is not fair," I joked. "I am curious about their new renovation, so we'll see, okay?"

"Deal!" Maggie cheered.

We each ordered some scones to go and headed to the quilt shop.

CHAPTER 7

Cornelia was overjoyed to see me and greeted me with a big hug. The place looked as bright and beautiful as ever with so many new samples to catch my attention. Cornelia introduced me to Penny, her new employee. She was young, thin, and pretty. It was hard to think of her behind the cutting counter. She looked like a model ready to walk the runway.

I told both of them what I was seeking. "I hate appliqué," I complained. "I didn't think I would ever get Jack's quilt done."

"Well, you could go traditional and make a Double Wedding Ring quilt, but it's not easy," Penny suggested. "Quilters are doing some pretty innovative things with that pattern these days."

"I don't think I could bear to make that," I said, shaking my head. "I don't even like that pattern."

Penny laughed.

"Well then, let's look around," Cornelia suggested. "What are the colors in the wedding?"

"I have no idea," I said, shaking my head once again. "I guess I'm getting a little ahead of myself."

"You should make something you like, too," Penny suggested. "If you're going to spend a lot of time making something, you should enjoy doing it."

"Good thinking," I said agreeably. "I'll just browse around for a while." As I looked at a pattern rack that had a sign advertising new patterns, I thought I heard a familiar voice. An elderly woman whom I believed to be Noreen was looking at the thread rack. I put down the pattern in my hand and approached her immediately.

"Noreen, how are you?" I greeted.

"Why, Miss Kate, how nice to see you," she said softly.

"I didn't know how to get in touch with you," I explained. "I felt so badly for you after Sandra's death."

She looked down, her expression fallen. "All mighty sad, mighty sad," she whispered.

"Did I miss a service?" I asked as Maggie listened.

"No ma'am. She was cremated right away, but I visit her grave once a week."

"You do?" I asked, surprised. "Where?"

"Her children took her ashes and had them buried at Lake View Cemetery," she revealed. "Emily was nice enough to call and tell me. I think it really bothered the children that there wasn't a funeral."

"That was all James's idea, of course," I stated bluntly, and was immediately sorry I had spoken the words.

"Oh, sure enough, Miss Kate," Noreen said. "He treated her so poorly. It broke my heart when she took to the bottle. You would think after she passed that he would show some respect."

"I just arrived here last night. I'll take some flowers to the gravesite. She always had such pretty flowers in her garden."

"Put flowers on in the dead of winter, Miss Kate?" she asked with a smile. "But she did love her flower gardens, even to the end."

"Yes, indeed," I nodded. "Can you tell me where I might find her marker in the cemetery?"

"Well, once you enter, stay to the right," she described. "It's close to the road, but I don't know if you noticed that it's snowing out there!"

"I know," I nodded with a smile. "How are you doing, by the way?"

"I didn't go back to work after Miss Sandra died. The Meyrs were pretty generous to me over the years, so I'm okay."

"I'm glad to hear that," I said before telling her good-bye. I had lost all interest in looking for a quilt pattern and so had Maggie. When we exited, I asked Maggie to go with me to find Sandra's grave.

"Well, on this snowy day, it's not what I had in mind, but I'll go with you," she quipped. "What are friends for?"

"We have to stop at the Rose Shop first so I can get some roses. Leave your car here and I'll bring you back."

"Yes siree, girlfriend," she teased. "You never stop telling me what to do."

We laughed together. It was wonderful to be with Maggie again.

CHAPTER 8

I purchased a lovely bouquet of red roses that would show up nicely in the snow. Maggie thought I was nuts to visit the cemetery in such snowy weather. However, Maggie would remember how disturbed I was when I got the word about Sandra's suicide. I'll never forget the day. Maggie and I were having lunch at the Taste restaurant when Noreen called to tell me she had found Sandra bleeding from self-inflicted cuts. By the time I rushed to the hospital, James had her taken away to the funeral home to be cremated immediately. As we entered the cemetery, I drove slowly as I tried to remember Noreen's instructions.

"Oh, my goodness! Look how old and elaborate some of these gravestones are," Maggie exclaimed. "It is so picturesque against the starkness of the white snow. I feel badly that I haven't come here very often to visit my parents' gravesites."

"Some families just don't practice the ritual and my family was one of them. I think we need to park here and look around. I'm not sure we'll find it because of the snow."

We got out into the bitter cold and soon found that our task was impossible. It was somewhat daunting to stand there and think about all the cold bodies underground. We stood there in silence taking in the quiet scene until the driver of a car going by gave us a suspicious look.

"Okay, Kate, we'd better return another time," Maggie suggested as she hastily got in the car.

"I agree. I'm freezing!" As we took the curvy road toward an exit, I wondered if Sandra knew we were there.

"Oh! What about your roses in the back seat?" Maggie remembered.

"They will do nicely for Carla," I suggested. "She will love them."

"I'll certainly keep her in my prayers tonight," Maggie said, sounding concerned. "She needs a break."

"Well, it's weird, because she's not really sick."

"She will be in the future if she needs chemo."

"Let's not jump ahead of ourselves," I cautioned. "I want to keep things as positive and upbeat as possible."

"Do you want me to sit with you tomorrow?" Maggie offered with a sigh.

"No, that's not necessary. I'll call you as soon as I know something."

Maggie gave me a big hug when I dropped her off at her car. Before I went back to the condo, I stopped by the grocery store to get some things. I wanted to make Carla some of my blueberry muffins. It was also a way of calming my nerves for what may be ahead. When I got back to the condo, I had to make a couple of trips to get all my bags inside. On the second trip, John pulled up next to me as he parked his car.

"Hey, beautiful!" John called out. "Welcome back."

He was so darn cute when he smiled. He got out of his car, gave me a hug, and took the bags from my hands.

"Thanks. How are you?" I said as we walked toward our condos.

"Good! It appears you'll be staying awhile from the looks of all this food."

"I hope I don't, but I only have beer in my refrigerator right now," I joked. "Carla's surgery is tomorrow, which is why I'm here, so I hope it goes well."

"I do too! So, what are you doing tonight?" John asked when we arrived at my door.

"Nothing. Just getting settled. I feel like I have a lot to do."

"So, how about I cook some dinner for you?" John offered as he put the groceries on the counter.

"That's not necessary," I said, shaking my head. "First, I have to get these roses in water and then I bought food that I can make for my dinner."

"Okay, we can do this," he persisted. "I'll cook us something simple and when it's ready, I'll call you to join me. When you're finished, you can head upstairs to do your chores and get a good night's sleep."

I had to chuckle at his determination. "Okay. It's a deal, so now get out of here!" I said, pushing on his chest. He was pleased!

"I'll give you a call," he said, going out the door.

As I unpacked the groceries, I checked my phone. Ellie had sent me a text asking me to call her. How did I miss that? I poured a glass of orange juice and sat on the couch to make the call. "Ellie, is everything okay?"

"I think so," she answered. "I was hoping you would call me when you arrived. Has Carla had her surgery?"

"No, that's tomorrow."

"I almost called last night, but I didn't want to alarm you unnecessarily," she added.

"What are you saying? Should I be alarmed?"

"Well, when I came home from the winery last night, your bedroom windows were lit up like it was daylight!" Ellie explained.

I didn't respond so she could continue.

"So, Kate, when you first moved in, didn't you tell me about some light that appeared in your bedroom? Is that what I saw?"

I took a deep breath. "I suppose so," I said, giving her questions some thought. "I don't know why this would happen with no one home. Occasionally, guests would say something, but this happening while the house is empty is puzzling."

"It bugged me all night," Ellie complained. "I suppose I should have gone in to check but frankly, I was too scared."

"No. I'm sure everything is fine, Ellie."

"It's Josephine, right?" Ellie asked.

"It's Josephine or Doc," I stated with a chuckle. "When she moved all those quilts around after I moved in, I figured she was the active one in the house."

"I don't know how you take this so calmly. Aren't you ever scared?"

"I actually feel very safe there for some reason. Check again tonight and see if it happens."

"Oh, I will! I'm sorry to bother you with this, but I thought you should know. By the way, Sharla Lee and her staff came to the winery yesterday for lunch, and she told me that she has some news for you when you get back."

"It must be information about Josephine," I said, feeling excited about the prospect of knowing more about Josephine. "I may have to call her while I'm here."

"Well, I have to go, but hurry home, okay? Give Carla my best!"

CHAPTER 9

After Ellie's phone call, I kept wondering what news Sharla Lee had for me. Why had I agreed to have dinner with John? I had muffins to bake and other details to attend to! A text from Jack came up on my phone.

> Hope all goes well with Carla tomorrow. Let me know ASAP about her results. Tell Maggie and Mark hello. XOXO, Jack.

It was just like Jack to be so thoughtful. I quickly changed my clothes before John called. I was putting on lipstick when my cell phone rang.

"Cocktails are being served on the first floor, and I don't want you to miss out," John teased.

"You were supposed to call when dinner was ready, not cocktails!" I teased back.

"Sorry. I already poured the wine."

"I'll be right down!" I said, hanging up.

When I walked into John's condo, I was even more impressed than last time. His table was elegantly set with lit candles which sent a signal of romantic expectations.

"How lovely, Mr. Baker," I observed as he handed me a glass of wine.

"To happiness and good health for all," John toasted.

I thought of Carla.

"Hear, hear," I cheered, raising my glass. "What's for dinner? It smells so good."

"It's my quick Swiss and American steak. It's one of my fastest go-to dinners to accommodate you and your tight schedule."

"Awesome! Are there mashed potatoes?" I inquired playfully. "You have to have mashed potatoes. It's the German way!"

"Of course," he grinned.

"Seriously? Yum! Let's eat!"

"Can't you just relax for a minute? I want to hear all about your aunt's house and any other news from Borna before we chow down."

I was more than happy to catch John up on the news from Borna. I knew he sincerely loved his visit there, and I enjoyed hearing about his travels and what he was writing. I felt a bit envious of his career, and when he talked I felt I was traveling with him. As the conversation progressed, dinner was served and the hours passed by swiftly. The food was delicious and John's love for cooking showed.

I looked at my watch and it was already nearly ten. "I must go, John. I hate to leave you with all this to clean up, but I still need to bake muffins. If you let me go, I promise to share some of them with you for tomorrow's breakfast."

He gave me that magic smile. "I was hoping so. You make the best muffins around! Please go ahead and get your preparations done, but if I start smelling something delicious, I may have to come up and check it out!"

"Don't you dare!" I warned. "Thanks for an awesome dinner." I blew him a kiss and headed up the stairs to my place.

Once there, I turned on the TV for company and changed my clothes. After the two glasses of wine that I had enjoyed earlier, I had to work to stay alert. Once I got started with the process, I realized that I could make these muffins in my sleep.

John did not knock on my door, but I could hear some of his classical music floating up the stairs as I settled into bed. It made me smile. I prayed for Carla and drifted off to sleep that night with positive thoughts.

CHAPTER 10

When I awoke at five the next morning, I showered and gathered what I might need for the long day ahead. I packed a basket of muffins for Carla and a sealed container of muffins to leave at John's doorstep.

Carla was somber and ready to leave when I arrived to pick her up. We both knew from previous experience that neither of us was very talkative in the mornings. Registration at the hospital desk was slow despite Carla being preregistered. When they finally called her name, I stood to accompany her.

"Kate, you need to stay here," she stated firmly. "I'll be fine. Just the thought of knowing you are here will be all the comfort I need."

"Are you sure?" I asked, feeling hesitant. "You be very brave and know I'll be praying for a good outcome. Whatever the result, we will face it together." She nodded and we shared a tearful hug. I gathered my emotions and got a cup of coffee, much like the others in the waiting room. No one was talking and I surmised that most of us were praying. I wondered about all the people waiting and what various circumstances had brought all of us together into this room at this time. I checked my phone for emails and texts. Everyone knew where I was today. The only email was from a distant relative of Josephine's who said he would be visiting Borna sometime soon. I'd had a phone call from him back inquiring about the house. His visit would be interesting. I quickly emailed him back telling him the time of my return to Borna was uncertain, but I would let him know my schedule when things were clearer.

Almost three hours passed and there was still no word about Carla. I went to the nearby snack bar and purchased a container of yogurt. I felt it was time to give Maggie an update. When I called Maggie, she was on pins and needles had and offered to come to the hospital and sit with me. She also had known Carla forever and wished her a better and healthy life.

"Don't you think by now you need to go let Rocky out?" Maggie asked, concerned. "I would be glad to do it for you, but I don't have a key."

"Oh, my! Yes, I should," I responded. "I'll go see how much longer it will be. Perhaps I can run to her house and be back here before she comes out of surgery." I finished my yogurt and checked on Carla's progress at the nurses station. A red-haired nurse barely looked up from her keyboard and said Carla should be out soon but explained that she'd be pretty groggy. I told her I'd return very soon.

"Well, honey, no hurry," she began to explain. "Dr. Yeager will be the first one to visit with her when she comes around and then she'll come speak with you, okay?"

"That would be great," I said as I collected my coat.

"She ain't goin' anywhere," she added with a chuckle.

Not funny, I thought. So, off I went as fast as I could. Rocky was barking when I entered through the back door. As always, he jumped all over me as I tried to hug him. I attached his leash and he looked at me, confused. I hoped that he hadn't taken my rejection personally when I gave him to Carla. I thought he had aged somewhat, and I supposed he thought the same thing about me.

When I got back to the hospital, I went straight to the waiting room. By now, there was just one man sitting there. His head was lowered. His hands covered his face. I wasn't sure whether I should exit the room and leave him alone so he could grieve or pray or just have some time alone. Deciding that I needed to stay where I could be reached in case any report came in about Carla, I sat down quietly. He looked up.

"I'm sorry. Would you like me to give you some privacy? Can I get anything for you?"

He shook his head and straightened up in his chair. "She's full of cancer," he said simply, as if that explained everything.

I listened for more.

"How can I tell my wife that we don't have much more time together?" He stood and started pacing the floor.

"Did she just get out of surgery?"

He nodded. "It didn't take long. They closed her up right away. I had a feeling about all this. It started years ago with breast cancer and she passed that hurdle with flying colors. Then it showed up in her colon. That was harder to deal with, but she muddled through the hardship." He blew his nose as I continued to listen. "This time, there's nothing we can do but wait." He smiled and nodded at me as he turned and made a slow exit from the room.

Tears flowed down my face. How very sad to hear all of this as I waited for Carla's outcome. I said a prayer that God would help him cope with his new circumstances and once again requested that God be kind to Carla.

CHAPTER 11

"Are you Kate Meyr?" the doctor asked as she approached.

"Yes, yes," I eagerly answered.

"I'm Dr. Yeager," she said as she extended her hand. "I understand you are a friend of Carla Gonzales and that you brought her here today."

"Yes, can I see her?"

"Sure," she nodded. "She's fine and all went well. I'd like to keep her overnight, so if you come get her tomorrow, that would be better. I understand that she lives alone."

I nodded.

"Keep in mind that today she'll be very drowsy and may not even remember your conversation."

"Thanks. Where do I go?" I asked, collecting my purse.

"She's in the observation room down the hall and to the right," she explained. "Look for the sign."

I couldn't get there fast enough. I felt a huge sense of relief. When I got to the area, Carla appeared to be sleeping. I didn't want to disturb her. As I sat, I thought about the old man who had just received such bad news. No matter what kind of result Carla would have, I knew she was a fighter and would survive.

I must have been in a daydream myself when I heard Carla say, "Kate, Kate."

"Oh, my goodness!" I said, surprised. "How are you?"

Carla gave me a big grin. "Sore, but fine," she said, lifting her head to speak. "Dr. Yeager said the cancer did not spread to my lymph nodes, so that's a big relief."

"That is wonderful news!" I said as I squeezed her hand. "Our prayers worked, didn't they?"

She nodded. "I do have six weeks of radiation, but I can handle that," she continued. "No chemo, no chemo."

"You are very fortunate and you can do this!" I cheered as I squeezed her hand.

"I know I can," she agreed. "Your support by being here has really meant a lot. When I was first told I had cancer, I felt so alone."

"I can imagine," I sympathized. "You get some rest tonight. I will be back to get you in the morning. Remember how when I got down, you would always tell me that the sun would come out tomorrow?"

"Thanks, Kate," Carla said as she reached out to give me a hug. She appeared to be in pain.

As I walked out of the hospital, I couldn't wait to say a prayer of thanks. So many women seemed to be getting breast cancer. I could easily be next. It was an unsettling thought. I was feeling very melancholy, so I decided to once again try to find Sandra's grave now that most of the snow had melted. I drove the same way as Maggie and I had gone before. It didn't take long to arrive at the cemetery. All of a sudden, I recognized Emily getting out of her car. She was carrying a quilt with her, which I thought was odd. I pulled over and parked right behind her.

"Emily, Emily," I called. "It's Kate!"

She turned around and registered complete surprise. "Aunt Kate!" she exclaimed.

Without a second thought, I gave her a hug. "I'm so glad you're here," I said, releasing her. "I tried to find your mother's grave yesterday and gave up because of all the snow. I wanted to come to the funeral service, but I understand that there wasn't one."

Emily shook her head sadly. "Dad didn't want the bad publicity for her. So without consulting us, he had her cremated," she revealed with a hint of anger. "We were pretty upset because he was really the one that didn't want the bad publicity. He finally agreed for us to have her ashes so she could be buried here, which she wanted. I had talked to her once about her funeral wishes and the one thing I remembered was that she wanted to be buried with Grandma's quilt, which was special to her. She grew up with this quilt that I have in my hands. She said it was always a comfort to her. I know she had it at the bottom of her bed after she and my dad separated."

"Oh, how special," I said, feeling tears well up in my eyes.

"I know this may seem odd to you, but I bring this with me when I come to visit her. Sometimes I lay it on the ground and cover her grave with it just to show her I remembered. She would have liked that. I brought newspaper to put down today since the ground is wet." She spread the newspaper like she had done it before and then folded the quilt in quarters. "Would you like to sit for a bit or are you too cold?"

I smiled and sat down on the soft, warm quilt.

"I miss her so much, Aunt Kate."

Sensing her grief, I gave her another hug. "Oh, Emily, Emily, I am so sorry this all happened," I said. "She didn't take her life to hurt any of you. She was so depressed, which is a terrible disease you sometimes cannot control. I had lunch with her a couple of days before she died, but I didn't realize her depression was that bad. I wish I had done more that day to get her to talk about the things that were bothering her."

"Yeah, when I talked to Noreen awhile later, she told me about your visit," Emily recalled. "I'm sorry she asked you to leave. That was so rude. It's all been very hard on Noreen. Noreen did everything to help her."

"So tell me about this quilt," I suggested, hoping for a lighter subject. "Do you remember this quilt from when you were growing up?"

Emily nodded and smiled. "Mom pointed out some of the fabrics that are in the quilt, which are actually pieces of some of her dresses from when she was little. I love to run my hands over the tiny stitches. It makes it special knowing that Grandma stitched them."

"She was a wonderful quilter, as was Grandma Meyr," I added. "I have such fond memories of her. I asked Clay where all her quilts ended up and he said he didn't know. I would have loved to have had one of hers, but Clay didn't like anything antique, no matter how sentimental."

"Dad's like that, too!" she said, shaking her head in disgust. "He's still drinking too much and now has some woman attached to his arm everywhere he goes. It's pretty revolting to us kids. You would think that after Uncle Clay died, Dad would have quit drinking. It had to be so hard for Mom."

I consoled her as much as I could before I left. If Sandra had been looking down on the two of us, she would have seen a pitiful sight.

As I drove away, I felt so badly for Emily. Lacking the closure a funeral service can provide perhaps made her grieving so much more difficult. How comforting that quilt would be to Emily as she continued to live her life. That would make Sandra very happy. Emily said she was getting her degree at the local community college and that Sandra and James's house was up for sale.

CHAPTER 12

Carla was waiting in her wheelchair when I arrived the following day. Her spirits had remained high ever since she learned she didn't have to have chemo. We didn't waste any time in heading home. Carla went straight to bed for a nap after she gave Rocky a hug. I looked around the house searching for anything I could do to be helpful, including paying some attention to Rocky. I had to admit that my mind was now on Emily instead of Carla. I knew Carla enjoyed food from Tello's, so I placed an order to be delivered for our evening meal. By late afternoon, she was already hungry and begged for more of her pain medication. When I told her Tello's would be bringing our dinner, she perked up considerably. She wanted to join me for a glass of wine before dinner, but I wouldn't allow it while she was taking medication for pain. I decided to tell her about my visit to Sandra's grave in hopes of getting her mind off her pain. She kept nodding and smiling.

"That reminds me a bit of my childhood," Carla recalled. "On Mother's Day and Father's Day, we would pack a lunch, spread a quilt on the ground, and picnic by my grandparents' graves. It was our family's way to pay respect and share our memories. And yes, I heard some of the same stories every year."

"Really?" I asked, genuinely interested.

"It was our family ritual; however, we'd see others sometimes doing the same thing," she recalled. "When I moved away from home, I got away from joining them."

This practice seemed so odd and at the same time quite charming. Intrigued, I asked, "Did you have the same food and take the same quilt each time?"

Carla snickered. "Pretty much. There was always fried chicken, of course. When more family joined us, we'd just spread out tablecloths. As children, we really looked forward to it. We'd play hide-and-seek among the tombstones."

I laughed and could see the picture in my mind.

"On Memorial Day, we would place flowers on all our family graves."

"Those are good memories," I said sincerely.

The doorbell rang, signaling the arrival of our Italian food. We continued our conversation about family traditions. Carla had worked for Clay and me for many years, but I had never heard much about her family. Carla's appetite was huge, but she kept talking.

"So, how often do you visit those family graves now that you are an adult?" I asked, curious. "We just didn't do that. Perhaps my parents did, but I was unaware of it."

"I feel guilty sometimes that I haven't carried on the tradition," Carla said between bites. "My mother died when I was nineteen. I'll never forget that my dad insisted that they wrap one of her favorite quilts over her feet because her feet would always be cold at night. I thought it was sweet, but my siblings thought he was crazy and that it was a good waste of a nice quilt. I think of that quilt with her every time I visit her gravesite."

"That is so special, Carla. I think that simple gesture gave your dad great comfort. They say we should do what we can to comfort the ones left behind, not the one who is gone. Was your mother a quilter?"

"No, I don't think so, but we always had many quilts in the house," Carla noted. "I think they were mostly from my grandmothers."

I could tell that Carla was feeling tired from the meal and conversation, so I suggested she turn in early. I went out to the porch and called Maggie who had wanted an update on Carla's condition. I had every intention of heading home for the night, but something told me to stay in case Carla needed assistance. I made myself comfortable on her couch and covered myself with a nearby blanket. As I drifted off to sleep, I took much comfort in knowing I was helping my friend.

CHAPTER 13

The next morning, I was awakened by a noise in the kitchen. When I looked to see what was going on, I saw Carla making coffee! "What in the world are you doing?" I asked, incredulous.

She laughed. "I'm not sick, Kate, I just have a very sore owee!" she claimed as she held her chest. "They told me I had to start moving around when I got home, so I decided I was ready for coffee and those blueberry muffins!"

I had to admit, she was the one who knew her body better than anyone else. As we sat eating our breakfast, I went over the doctor's orders and made sure Carla had all her prescriptions. I told her I would pick up the last two prescriptions that were ready and get anything else she might need for a couple of days.

Maggie called as I was driving. I parked at the drugstore and returned her call. She made a pretty good argument for joining her and Mark at the country club for dinner tonight. I had mixed feelings about accepting. What would I wear and who might I run into? Maggie reminded me how quickly people forget and reiterated that there are now so many new young members in the club these days. I finally said I would go.

When I got back to Carla's, she was taking a nap, which pleased me. I made use of the time and made her a veggie quiche that she could heat for dinner. I also picked up some blueberry scones that she and I could share tomorrow. I was about to leave a note when she woke up. Carla was elated that I was going to go out for dinner to have a nice visit with friends. I told her I would check on her in the morning.

I rushed home, hoping I wouldn't run into John. For several reasons, I didn't want him to know I was going to the club. Maggie insisted that they pick me up. I typically felt better having my own car in case I wanted to leave at a certain time. However, I did feel it would look better if I came with someone rather than arriving by myself.

The more I looked in the mirror, the more critical I became of my appearance. I didn't have much in my wardrobe to choose from in my South Haven closet, so I settled on a little black dress, as usual. When I heard a knock at the door, it caught me by surprise. Maggie was never early for anything. I opened the door and there stood John.

"Wow! You look fabulous!" he said, following up with an appreciative whistle. "I'm a little too casual, so you don't mind if I do a quick change, do you?"

"Very funny, John, I responded, feeling awkward. "Maggie and Mark are taking me to dinner, so I'm glad you approve."

"Nice, nice," he said, looking me up and down. "Is this your first visit back to the 'the club,' as the elite refer to it?"

"I don't know what you mean by that, but yes, and I'm

feeling a little gun-shy about it. I suppose it was just a matter of time. There are folks and things I don't want to totally give up in South Haven. It's not like I'm going on a date."

He laughed. "I wish you would consider going on a date. I'd be first in line."

"You're making me nervous, so please go before they come to pick me up."

"Okay, okay, I'm leaving. Hey, when you get back, perhaps we could share a nightcap."

I smiled, closing the door. Truth be told, if given a choice right now, I would prefer to be having a nightcap with John rather than facing the dreaded trip to the country club.

CHAPTER 14

Mark and Maggie were very chatty as we traveled to the place that held so many memories. Mark reviewed the many improvements that had taken place since I was there last. He bragged about the new chef but said the crab cakes were still the same and continued to be a favorite item on the menu. When we entered, I hardly recognized the place! The beauty was over the top, as I'm sure were the membership dues. I saw a few familiar faces as we walked to the bar area. Some took double takes as if they weren't sure it was me. I excused myself to go to the powder room to check my appearance. The décor was fit for a queen and I admired every detail. As I exited, my timing couldn't have been worse.

"Well, look who's here!" James said sarcastically when he saw me. "I thought you became a country girl in that little hillbilly town." The young girlfriend hanging onto his arm waited eagerly for an introduction.

I ignored his comment. "Hi, I'm Kate Meyr, James's former sister-in-law," I stated, holding out my hand. "And who might you be?"

"Oh, you're Clay's widow," she said in a light, childish voice. "I'm Sherry."

"Well, Sherry, I'll have to share your name with my niece, Emily, who wasn't sure what to call you." I noticed that James was turning red and I believe he would have hit me if we had been in a less public venue.

"We need to get back to our table," James mumbled as he took her arm. She just grinned and I had a feeling she had no clue who Emily was. As I walked away, I felt I had scored one for Sandra. If Clay was watching, he would have turned over in his grave at my boldness.

"What are you so smiley about?" Maggie asked when I got back to the table.

"I just exchanged pleasantries with someone," I blushed. "I'll share it with you later."

"You know that Max still asks about you," Mark mentioned.

"Well, give him my best," I said, hoping Mark would drop the subject.

"He's too old for Kate," Maggie interjected.

Mark looked at her questioningly. "I don't know if you remember Carlton Hayes, Kate," Mark asked. "He played golf with Clay and me a couple of times."

I shook my head.

"He just got divorced. His wife left him quite suddenly. Carlton's done very well as a lobbyist. I think you should meet him. He asked if you were seeing anyone."

"Mark, that's exactly the kind of man I do not want to meet," I responded as nicely as I could. "I can just imagine his sad song, and if he was indeed Clay's friend, I would be very leery of him."

"Hey, wait a minute," Mark objected. "I take offense to that remark."

"Oh, I'm sorry. I don't mean you, of course," I explained.

"Who gets the sea bass?" the waiter interrupted.

"I do," responded Mark.

I knew I shouldn't have made that remark. Despite the rough start, each of us enjoyed our various choices of seafood. Mark was right about it becoming a younger crowd at the club. How could these young couples afford to belong here? Clay had a good job, but for years his father paid the dues for us to belong. The young women in attendance this evening were pencil thin and decked out in what I recognized to be very expensive clothing. I could only imagine what their lives were like.

When we left, I realized that James and Sherry were eating in another dining room. Thank goodness! I knew Maggie was dying to hear what I had experienced.

CHAPTER 15

It was only nine thirty when I got back to the condo. I immediately called Carla to see how she was doing. She was watching a movie. She said the soreness was keeping her awake, and she couldn't get comfortable. I told her I would check on her in the morning. My phone alerted me to an incoming text. It was John.

> Still up? How about an after-dinner drink? Amaretto on the rocks, right?

I smiled at the offer and it sounded refreshing after a stressful day.

> A short one would be delightful.

John arrived upstairs within minutes with two tumblers filled with ice and likely the best amaretto on the market. I turned on my gas fireplace and we sat on the couch.

"How was the club?" John asked, getting right to the point.

I grinned and shook my head. When I told him about my encounter with James and Sherry, his eyes widened and his eyebrows rose.

"You're something, Kate!" John said, raising his glass. "Here's to the newly liberated Kate Meyr!"

I smiled and took a deep breath. I was undecided about how proud I was regarding my behavior. "That's exactly how I felt," I admitted. "I felt I had scored one for Sandra. I think my conversation with Emily confirmed what a selfish and uncaring person James is."

"What conversation?" John asked innocently.

I explained about seeing Emily with a quilt at the gravesite and how touching her story was to me. When I said it was Sandra's wish to be buried with the quilt, he seemed shocked.

"Do people do that?" he asked before taking another sip of his drink.

"Yes, they do!" I assured him. "When you think about the practice throughout history, there had to be many quilts buried along with loved ones. Think of the many miscarriages and children's diseases that people endured years ago. Take going across the prairie, for instance. They wouldn't have buried someone in the cold, dirty ground. Wrapping the deceased in something of their very best would seem logical. What about during the Civil War when people were burying their prized possessions with men in the battlefields? I'll bet they used quilts for those purposes as well, don't you think?"

"Absolutely," John said with a nod. "That would make

a great human-interest story." He tilted back his head and paused to think for a moment about the newly sprung story idea.

"I'd guess that Cornelia at the quilt shop here in town could give you some interesting data on that subject. I know quilts are sometimes displayed at some wakes when a quilter passes away. At my friend Emma's wake, they had one of her quilts on display. She quilted at the church and quilts were part of her life. They seem to be everlasting, whether it's here on earth or in the ground."

"I did a story on quilts many years ago and it got a great response," John shared. "Quilts are so personal with so many people. They all have a quilt to tell you about when you just say the word quilt."

"I'm sure! I really love quilts, but Maggie knows so much quilt history. She collects crazy quilts from the turn of the century. She said that pattern was used for many home viewings and funeral homes as casket covers. I think it's a little creepy, but they wanted to show their very best and fanciest quilt and many times that happened to be a crazy quilt."

"So, it's another link to death, just as in life," John surmised as he refilled his glass of amaretto. "How very interesting it is to know the many uses of a quilt in its lifetime."

"You are so fortunate that your publisher prints whatever you choose to write about. That is such a tribute to you and your work."

He smiled like I had just given him the best compliment ever! "You are very kind, dear friend," he said, taking my hand.

"I'm fading fast, John," I said, sliding my hand from his and getting up from the couch. "I have to get an early start in the morning and check on Carla."

"How is she doing?" he asked, following me to the door.

"She's doing really well, and she's fortunate to have the outcome she had. She'll have to deal with radiation, but some say it's a piece of cake. I hope it will be for her."

"I sent her flowers," John said, surprising me. "She is a sweetheart and I'm so glad you recommended her to me."

"She will love and appreciate the flowers. Thanks for the drink," I said, handing him my glass. "This was very nice and relaxing."

"That's because it is nice," he said, kissing me on the forehead. "I hope I can see you again before you leave."

"I don't know, John, but I'll be in touch," I said, holding the door open for him.

Out the door he went. Part of me wanted him to stay longer and part of me said I shouldn't have agreed to have him bring me a drink. He was too young for me and not someone I would consider for a serious relationship. And, as far as relationships, where was Clark and why hadn't I heard from him? If he was not thinking of me at all, should I be thinking more of him? Clark and John were so different. How could I feel so close to both of them? Why would either of them find me attractive? I was too tired to analyze it all!

CHAPTER 16

The next morning, I decided to call Ellie before checking on Carla. "I'm glad I caught you this morning," I greeted her. "How's the weather in Borna?"

"Very nice, actually," Ellie reported. "I just heard the weather forecast, and they say we are going to have an early spring. I can't wait because it's been very slow at the winery."

"I'm checking the road conditions because if Carla is doing okay today, I'll leave first thing in the morning to come back."

"Well, it'll be nice to have you back because Josephine is still keeping the light on for you," Ellie joked.

"Still?" I asked in disbelief. "I surely hope everything is okay."

"Not to worry! Say, I wanted to tell you that Esther's mother passed away quite suddenly. She was just at church quilting that morning, and in the afternoon she had a heart attack."

"Oh, I feel bad for Esther," I sympathized.

"Ellen has arranged to have a floral arrangement made

and delivered from the Friendship Circle. I don't have funeral details yet. I think they had to wait for family members to get in from out of town."

"I should be back in time for the funeral. It's nice to be here, but each time I visit I feel I need to go home where I belong."

"That's a good thing! Do I dare ask about your neighbor?" Ellie teased.

"He's just fine. I don't suppose Clark is back in town, is he?"

"No sign of him," she responded. "I think this is the longest he's been gone. Isn't he communicating with you at all?"

"No, and I'm sure it's deliberate. He'll have to come back to Borna eventually."

"I'm tellin' you girlfriend, you are lettin' him get away! You may regret this someday."

"I doubt it. It should work both ways. I sometimes think we were just meant to be good friends."

"You know how the saying goes, 'If you're not growing, you're dying,'" Ellie quoted.

She was probably right. "You're so smart, Ellie," I teased. "I'll text you when I leave in the morning." I hung up, shaking my head. So many people had so many different opinions about Clark and me.

When I reached Carla's house, I saw Rocky running around in the yard. He seemed to be so happy and he had to be great company for her. I knew I made the right decision to give him up.

"So, how goes it this morning?" I asked when I got inside her back door.

"Better!" she said with a big smile. "I slept like a log last night. How was your evening?"

"I accidently ran into James and his new Bond girl, Sherry," I said sarcastically. "That was awkward, but we had a delicious meal. The whole place certainly looked different."

"I can't believe James would parade around with a floozy so soon after Sandra's death," Carla said, shaking her head. "Men are stupid. Clay had it all and threw it all away. Is it all about power, control, or ego? Look at what some of these politicians are doing!"

"Oh, Carla, I have to move on in my life, but I do agree with everything you said," I assured her. "They think with the wrong part of their anatomy, if you know what I mean, instead of using what little brains they have."

Carla burst out laughing as she bent over in pain. "Oh, it hurts to laugh," she complained as she sat down.

"When it comes to matters of the heart, look at my friend Ellie," I continued. "This smart lady has it bad for a typical ladies' man that happens to be a wine salesman! How many red flags do you need?"

"Oh, Lordy," Carla said, shaking her head. "I remember that guy at the winery when we went there for your birthday dinner. What a schmuck! Don't get me wrong, I would like a good man in my life. I have to realize my time has come and gone, and now I have this body that looks like I've been in a train wreck."

"Don't talk like that, Carla," I scolded. "No one has a perfect body. You're in good shape and your dark, gorgeous eyes and wonderful personality are very attractive—not to mention your courage and that cute little Hispanic accent you have."

She smiled. "What would I do without you?" Carla said as she started to get emotional.

"I will always be here for you," I consoled her. "If you think you're okay, I plan to go back to Borna in the morning."

"Yes, go! I'll be fine," she cheerfully exclaimed. "I so appreciate your coming, and I hope Maggie and I will get back to see you again one of these days."

"I told Maggie we should repeat our birthdays together in Borna like we did last year. I also want her to talk the Beach Quilters into coming for a quilt retreat at Ruth Ann's place."

"I'll be ready for something fun after I complete these radiation treatments."

"You will do great, my friend," I assured her with a hug. "Don't worry, say your prayers, and be thankful!"

CHAPTER 17

I left Carla's and went to the Blueberry Shop to get gifts to take back to Borna. I loved going downtown to my favorite shops; but unfortunately, some were closed for the winter. From there, I went to Cornelia's Quilt Shop to settle on a design for my Borna raffle quilt. I was pleased that I could browse alone so I could make a confident decision on a design that I knew I could manage. The design I chose was a simple front porch with a place above it to stitch in "Josephine's Guest House." I loved porches and I intended to make my front porch in Borna more appealing. I had been so focused on my back sunporch and deck that I had neglected the part of the house that provided the customers their first impressions of the guest house.

I was walking up the condo steps when John peeked out his door.

"You need some help?" he asked politely.

"No, I'm good," I replied as I got near the top landing. I leaned over the rails to see him better. "I'm leaving in the morning, by the way. Carla's doing great and I need to get back."

"Do you have any plans for dinner?" he asked with his hands on his hips.

"No, and I really can't afford to take the time."

His face turned to disappointment. "I can deliver food, if that helps," he teased. "I'm leaving tomorrow as well, and I need to finish an article tonight. I'll bet I could tempt you later with some Sherman's ice cream!"

"Now you have my attention," I bantered, warming up to the idea. "I haven't had that for some time."

"Well, they're only open on the weekends in the winter so I stocked up. How about around eight? We can have a quick dessert. Your place or mine?"

I shrugged my shoulders.

"I'll give you a ring and you come on down," he decided. "Wine or coffee?"

"It'd better be coffee. See you later, alligator!"

"After while, crocodile!"

John surely had a way of tempting me with the little things in life. Was he always in such a good mood? I guess as a writer, you see the best and worst in things. What could be wrong with a dish of ice cream?

As I packed, I nibbled on cheese and crackers. I finished a bottle of wine that only held a couple of swallows. I was getting excited just thinking about getting back home. I couldn't help but wonder what Josephine was up to with keeping the light on. The phone rang and it was John.

"You're fifteen minutes late and the ice cream is melting!" he said, a sense of urgency in his voice.

"Okay, I'll be right down," I said, hanging up. I did a quick makeup check, tossed my hair, and went out the door.

"Good, you have a fire going," I said with a shiver when I entered his condo. "I didn't wear a coat."

"I figured that eating the cold ice cream would make us appreciate a warm fire. What's your pleasure? Rocky Road or Vanilla Bean?"

"Rocky Road, for sure," I said with anticipation. "It's always been one of my favorites."

"The only thing I hate about going there are the long lines, even in the winter."

"Oh, how I remember," I said, taking my first bite of sheer delight.

We sat down at his cute dining room table and started to gobble our gigantic scoops of ice cream.

"I made these servings pretty generous. I assumed you didn't have dinner."

"It's so delicious," I said, savoring each spoonful.

"Say, I've been thinking some more about the idea of cemetery quilts," he said, catching me by surprise. "I like the contrast of being covered up underground. I've done a little research on custom burials in different cultures and religions and it's fascinating. You see them refer to a quilt every now and then. There's probably more information than I could possibly use in one article."

"Really? It's not a subject matter you hear or read about every day, so you might be onto something."

"It's a private thing, as you pointed out. Emily's story is quite revealing. Do you think she'd let me interview her? I would change her name if she preferred."

"Oh, John, I don't think you should take that approach," I warned. "She told me her story in confidence. I wouldn't want her to know I shared it with you."

"That's fine," he conceded as he thought more about it.

"I'll be happy to pass on any other information as I talk to quilters," I volunteered.

"I'd like that," he said, giving me a wink of approval. "More coffee?"

"No, I'm stuffed," I said, tilting my head back. "I can't imagine the calories I just consumed."

"A penny for your thoughts," he said, watching me.

We both moved to the couch to be more comfortable.

Relaxed now, I leaned against the back of the couch. "I was just thinking what a nice idea this was," I said with a smile. "You are always thinking about ideas and feelings, aren't you?"

"I suppose," he said, also leaning back. "I picture things and then I want to put them into words."

"Is that how it works? I journal, but that's not the same thing."

"Am I in your journal?" he asked, an expression on his face that let me know he was teasing.

"You are, but you'll never know in what capacity!"

He laughed. "You know, I thought about writing an article about you," he said, getting my attention.

I sat up.

"I could maybe call it 'The Upstairs Girl' or 'The Lady of Borna,'" he teased. "I have many titles I could use."

"John Baker, you'd better not," I warned.

He laughed some more.

"I am your friend, not your subject matter. If you do that, I will no longer be your friend."

"Point well taken," he said, employing a more serious tone.

"I have to go. It's getting late," I said, getting up to stretch. "This was another interesting evening, as always."

"When will you return?" His question had a sad tone to it.

"I'm not sure, but I'll keep in touch. I am also anxious to hear more about the progress of the quilt article."

John took my hand and led me to the door. In one fluid motion, he pulled me close and kissed me on the lips as if I wouldn't be seeing him for a long time. It happened so fast that I didn't have time to think about resisting. I pulled away and whispered blankly, "Thank you."

He gave me a wink and I turned to exit.

When I got back to my condo, I replayed what had just happened. Did he think I thanked him for the ice cream or the kiss? Thank you? What was I thinking?

CHAPTER 18

Before I left, I called Aunt Mandy to tell her I was returning to Borna so she could make her plans. She was anxious to hear about Carla and then shared that she wouldn't be arriving for a few weeks. We were curious about any possible progress on her house. I told her I would report to her as soon as I got back to see it for myself. Next, I texted Ellie to let her know I was on my way. It was a very dreary, cloudy day for such a long drive, but I was happy about not running into any snow or ice. I felt extremely good about the outcome of my trip. Carla had hopeful news and my visit with Maggie and John was wonderful.

When I got off the interstate, I pulled over to the side of the road to check on Jack. I had to leave a voicemail asking him to call me. It was nearly dark when I arrived in Borna. I looked up to see my bedroom from the front of the house and, sure enough, there was the light Ellie had told me about. How could this be?

I unloaded the car and then put it in the garage. I made sure most of the downstairs lights were on before going upstairs to check on my bedroom. I listened for noises but it was perfectly quiet. When I opened my bedroom door, the room was very, very dark! I proceeded to the other bedrooms and they were the same. My next step was to check on the third-floor suite. I turned on the light to the stairway, climbed my way up, and slowly opened the door to the suite. Everything was dark and undisturbed so I headed back down. When I got to the main floor, I turned up the heat to lift the chill. Why would Josephine light up my bedroom while I wasn't here? Was there something she was alarmed about? Why did she make it dark now that I was home?

I went to the kitchen for some nourishment and settled on a slice of frozen quiche I pulled from the freezer. Seeing my kitchen brought great memories of baking again, and I couldn't wait. I looked at the painting of the red lighthouse John gave me for Christmas which was hanging near my refrigerator. What a great way to remember my hometown. Tomorrow for breakfast I would eat the last of the blueberry scones that I had brought with me.

I sat on the sunporch to open the mail. In the pile was a pleasant surprise. It was a color postcard with a nice photograph of one of Clark's carvings. The name of the carving was Confused. The reverse side had details of a reception in Clark's honor last week at the gallery. The only personal handwritten message was, "Appropriate, don't you think?" What did that mean? Now I was confused. I put it aside and noticed that bills were coming in for Aunt Mandy. I assumed that there must be some progress and action on the property. My phone alerted me to an incoming text. It was from John.

Hope you arrived safely. I'm in Chicago. Hope to hear from you. J

I texted back the following:

I'm here. Enjoy Chicago. K

I had to smile at how thoughtful he always seemed. Would he have this kind of contact with me if he had a girlfriend? Why didn't he have a girlfriend? Maybe he did and I just didn't know about her. Maybe she lived in Chicago! I decided I needed to slow my thoughts down a bit.

Crawling into my own bed was the best part of my long, stressful day. I now had to focus on being a proprietor of a guest house. There were messages left on the phone that I hoped would become reservations. I couldn't wait to see my Friendship Circle friends again, which would likely be at Esther's mother's funeral. Soon, I would be welcoming that early spring the weatherman talked about. I can picture the buds of my red and yellow tulips popping up. Welcome home. It was a comforting feeling.

CHAPTER 19

The next morning, I awoke with a smile as I fluffed my favorite pillow and prepared to plan my day. I decided that after my coffee, I would check on Aunt Mandy's house. I was surprised that I wasn't receiving frequent updates from Ellen about its progress. I dressed in my well-worn jeans and an old South Haven sweatshirt and skipped down the stairs.

I looked at my guest house quilt on the wall and cautiously checked to see if Josephine had added any names to the quilt while I was gone. I was pleased to see it hadn't changed. I touched it gently and then opened the front door to retrieve the many newspapers that had been collecting there while I was gone. I glanced at the front porch and again thought about how I could make it more inviting. I visualized padded wicker furniture, ferns, and even a rocking chair to make guests want to stay forever. I would put these purchases on my bucket list for spring.

I was pleased to see the sun shining brightly, so I got in my Mercedes and headed down the road to check on Aunt Mandy's place. She and I would have to think of a clever name for her new digs. The first thing I saw was a couple of pick-up trucks parked along the side of the road. When I got past them, I was shocked to see wide open spaces where a foundation was built and two walls already up! Piles of lumber and equipment were everywhere. I checked the large trees we designated to keep, and they were still there despite many others being removed.

"Can I help you?" asked a man approaching me.

"Oh, I'm Kate Meyr, the owner of this property. I've been out of town, so I'm checking on the progress here."

"Nice to meet you, Ms. Meyr," he said, shaking my hand. "We were wondering why no one had been coming around."

"I can't believe how much you've accomplished!"

"We've been lucky to have had decent weather," the man explained. "After that snow around Christmas, we've been able to work. You live in Doc's house, right?"

I nodded and smiled. "Yes. Are you familiar with it?"

"Not really, but my mom knows all about it," he said with a smile. "I just know it by Doc Paulson's house and going by it most every day. I think my friend Clark McFadden did some work for you."

"You know Clark?" It was getting interesting now!

"Everybody knows Clark," he said with a chuckle. "He's the best there is. We both like workin' with wood, that's for sure. I build buildings and he makes art. Guess who gets the big bucks?" He laughed.

"Well, you're both doing what you love to do and that's the main thing. I'm sorry. I didn't get your name."

"Oh, Charles Hopfer, but everybody calls me Chuck," he said as he blushed.

Why did everyone around here have a nickname?

"That's interesting. I know another Charles and they call him Cotton."

He laughed and nodded. "Sure, I know Cotton and Susie," he acknowledged. "They're good people and work hard. I've used Cotton for some minor work, but he's just not a carpenter to speak of."

I nodded in agreement.

"We both grew up in Unionville and could be kin for all I know. I guess you've picked that up around here that nearly everybody could be kin or related by marriage."

I laughed at his true remark.

"Hey, Chuck! I need some help here!" yelled another guy as he carried some lumber.

"I'd better go. Nice to meet you, Ms. Meyr," he said, tipping his red baseball cap. "If you ever need anything or have some questions, just give me a holler. I work for myself and my phone number is on the truck."

"Thanks, and you can call me Kate," I said politely. "You'll be seeing me around here more often."

"That would be a pleasure," he said smiling, revealing a beautiful set of white teeth. "When I talked to Oscar about this job, I was under the impression that the owner here was an older lady. You don't quite fit the bill."

"That's because the house is for my aunt who is moving here from Florida," I explained. "You will love her and she's anxious to move here. I'm going to email her a photo of your progress."

"I see. Well, I'd better go or I'll get fired." He laughed at his own joke and then turned around and walked away. He was handsome, tan, and built like a lumberman. Let's just say he was easy on the eyes, if you liked the outdoorsy type.

The ground was muddy so I didn't walk around the place. I picked up my cell phone and called Aunt Mandy. "Guess where I am right now, Auntie?" I teased.

"Heaven knows, my child," she answered.

"I'm standing in front of your new house," I reported. "The foundation is in and the walls are going up!"

"Oh, my goodness," she said breathlessly. "I can hardly wait. You must email me a photo."

"I plan to. I just met the head carpenter, Chuck Hopfer. He's a looker, so you're going to want to get here quickly."

She laughed. "Now don't you move in on me before I get there," Aunt Mandy teased.

She is so darn cute. It will be grand having her here with me in Borna. We talked a while longer, but we didn't have a strong signal so we hung up. I took some photos and got colder and colder. I finally left the scene feeling excited about all the progress. It was nice meeting Mr. Hopfer. I liked him very much. Perhaps tomorrow morning I could bring the workers some blueberry muffins. After all, they were my neighbors now.

CHAPTER 20

The rest of the day, I returned phone calls and responded to a couple of guest inquiries. Most of my responses never materialized into firm reservations. I certainly noticed more traffic going down the road since the construction of Aunt Mandy's house began. It somehow added to the excitement of the project.

Ellen got word that I had returned to Borna, so she called to give me the details of Esther's mother's funeral. "I guess you noticed Chuck's great progress on the house by now," Ellen remarked.

"I did! I checked it out as soon as I could. I'm amazed at the progress. I emailed my aunt a photo and she hopes to get here as soon as she can."

"Chuck does really good work. Oscar says he's the best, so he's really in demand. You were lucky to get him. Have you met him?"

"Yes, he's a very nice man. I thought that tomorrow morning I'd take them some of my blueberry muffins, since I'm anxious to get baking again."

"They would love that, especially Chuck. He lives alone and he'll devour them!"

"He's not married?"

"No, and I don't think I've ever seen him with anyone," Ellen said with certainty. "When he's not working, you'll see him around town wearing a cowboy hat." She snickered as if the thought of it were a funny sight. "He's got a good crew and other than his mother, the work crew seems to also be his family."

"He said that he and Clark are friends. I never heard Clark mention him."

"They are, most likely. Well, I guess I'll see you at the funeral. Have a good day!"

Next on my list was to return Sharla Lee's phone call.

"Oh, honey, I'm glad you're back," she began. "Gerard and I wanted you to know that we found Josephine's and Doc's gravestones."

"You did? Where?"

"They're right under your nose on the Concordia Cemetery hill," she said with a chuckle. "They are in the flat stone section and very close to the road. I think there was only a stone or two between the two of them. Josephine's marker is beaten up a bit. Warren and Gerard got some pictures if you can't get there."

"That location makes sense. That church is where Josephine went to quilt. I'll try to go by there tomorrow. Thanks so much!"

Once again, my research team at the museum was at work. After I hung up, I wondered if seeing their gravesites would make any difference in my research. For me, it was just calming to know where their bodies were located. My thoughts were interrupted by my cell phone ringing. It was Ellie.

"I'm closing early, so I wondered if you wanted me to bring some chili by your place for supper," she offered.

"That sounds really good! I haven't been to the store since I've been back. Thanks so much. I can't wait to see you." I quickly straightened up around the house and set a place setting for two. Twenty minutes later Ellie arrived, not only with chili but also with fixings to make chili dogs. She said they prepared them once a week at the winery because they were so popular.

It felt so good to hug my friend again. When she saw the blueberry wine and blueberry-covered chocolates I brought for her, she was elated.

"Sorry, but the scones didn't survive the trip."

She gave a frown and then smiled at me. "How is Carla doing?" Ellie asked as she prepared the chili dogs.

"She's doing fine and wanted me to tell you hello," I shared cheerfully. "She's a lucky gal. Her outcome could have been a lot worse."

When we sat down, I showed her the postcard I received from Clark.

"Well isn't this all lovey dovey?" she asked with a chuckle.

"That's Clark for you," I nodded, smiling. "Can you imagine what it would be like to be married to him?"

"Have you ever thought about that?" Ellie teased as she presented my plate to me containing great aromas of spices and childhood delight.

"No, not at all, so let's change the subject," I answered in a serious tone. "Say, Ellie, can we go to the funeral together?"

"Sure. I don't have to go to the winery until later," she agreed as she took a big bite.

"We don't want to miss the delicious 'dead spread' afterwards in the church hall," I reminded her with a smile.

Ellie nearly choked as she responded to my reference. "I hear Esther's mother used to help those ladies herself. It would mean a lot for us to be there for Esther."

Happy to change the subject, I realized I had so much to tell Ellie. I started with my encounter at the country club with James Meyr. I eased into telling her about my two short visits with John.

"I think your infatuation with John keeps you from nurturing a relationship with Clark," Ellie stated, assigning me a level gaze.

"What infatuation? He's pretty real to me and I enjoy being around him. Clark and John are like day and night. I appreciate them both and feel lucky to have them in my life."

"Well, we'll see how long that arrangement lasts," Ellie quipped.

To steer her away from Clark and John, I showed her my embroidery design for the raffle quilt. She said she liked it and told me that Mary Catherine offered to make a block for her since she wasn't a quilter.

"She chose a nifty pattern that has a wine bottle design. She's going to use her machine to embroider 'Red Creek Winery' on it."

"How nice!" It was a clever idea. "I want 'Josephine's Guest House' on mine as well."

"You missed our last Friendship Circle meeting, but we decided not to have an exhibit at the county fair this year because we're doing this raffle quilt," Ellie informed me.

"I thought I heard that might happen and I agree," I said, taking my last spoonful of chili. "I have to admit, our plants-out-of-the-box project last year was pretty clever. I'll bet folks will be looking for what we do next. How is Carson, by the way?"

Ellie looked away. "We're okay, but I don't see him much. Of course, I'm always wondering what he's up to. I don't like that about me. He consumes too much of my thoughts, and I don't have time for that nonsense."

"Since he's got you signed, sealed, and delivered, he may

not feel the urgency to communicate with you," I said bluntly, realizing it may hurt Ellie's feelings, but sensing the need to introduce the idea.

"Don't tell me that," she said, taking dishes to the kitchen.

"I'm sure Carson has his good qualities," I said in an effort to soften my words. "Just please don't marry him."

"I'm not, don't worry," she said, shaking her head.

I knew from the look on her face that I may have been too outspoken. I opted to change the subject. "Have you driven down the road to see Aunt Mandy's house going up?"

"No. I didn't think they could do a whole lot until springtime."

"Well, the walls are going up, by golly. The octagon shape is so darn cute in that setting. I met Chuck Hopfer, the main carpenter. What a nice guy."

"He comes into the winery now and then, and the ladies love him," she said with a big grin. "He's the kind of guy that doesn't have a clue that he is that handsome. He's a lot like Clark, come to think about it. There's a quality of innocence about him that women are attracted to. I'd say he's about fifty or something. Working out in the weather has probably aged him. I wondered for a time if he might still be in the closet, if you know what I mean, but I've discounted that idea. He's very good to his mother. He built her a nice little home in Unionville. I think he said one time that he was an elder at Grace Lutheran Church in Uniontown. The Hopfers are a good family."

"Sounds like you may have personally checked him out," I said, teasing.

She laughed. "I guess there was a time when I thought he was flirting with me, but he wasn't," she admitted. "He's just a nice, friendly guy."

"I wish there were more guys like that."

CHAPTER 21

All of us from the Friendship Circle sat in the same pew at the funeral. Listening to the eulogy about Esther's mother made me realize how it fit the description of many of the staunch German women who raised big families in East Perry County. She didn't have a formal education and raised six children on a farm. She always tended a big garden from which she would can enough food for all her children and their families. Her favorite pastime was quilting with her women friends at church, which explained the pretty Dresden Plate quilt that was displayed on the table along with family photographs. Her casket was closed, which I thought was unusual. A large bouquet of mixed flowers was arranged on the top of the casket. As I observed the family, Esther seemed to be the most grief stricken.

After the service, we went into the church hall for an enormous spread of homemade dishes and baked goods. Elderly ladies wore pretty aprons as they kept the serving bowls filled and refilled our iced tea glasses. They all had to be sad, knowing Esther's mom was one of their own as well as a church lady quilter. Before we left, I went to give Esther a big hug of support.

"You need a haircut, my friend," Esther said, looking me over.

I had to chuckle in agreement. "I just got back from South Haven, as you well know, but if you can fit me in some time soon, that would be great."

She smiled in agreement. "Sure. What about later this week?"

"It's a deal." I paused and then continued, "It broke my heart to see you crying during the service." I slipped my arm around her waist.

"Mom and I talked every day on the phone," she shared. "She never complained, even though I knew she was hurting from this or that. She always had a remedy to suggest or a recipe to share. She never judged people, so it was always pleasant to talk to her. I'm going to miss her." She broke into more tears.

The rest of the day, I tried to remember the best memories from my own mother. I certainly didn't have some of the same memories as Esther. I mostly remembered the disappointments I provided her, like dropping out of college to marry Clay. I certainly wished we had shared those daily conversations like Esther and her mom shared.

That evening, I got everything ready to bake muffins in the morning. I had the perfect red picnic basket to carry them in. Adding a thermos of extra coffee might be a good idea. My plan would be to drop everything off and then visit Concordia's cemetery to find Josephine's gravesite. I would likely see Esther's mom's fresh gravesite as well.

My preparations done, I decided to make a fire. I had

desperately missed the fireplace while I was gone. I stared into the flames while thinking of both Clark and John. The calmness of the fire was also a reminder of how alone I felt. It made me yearn for Aunt Mandy to be nearby. Suddenly the lights in the house began to flicker off and on. The weather outside was fine so it seemed odd. If the lights went out completely, I wasn't sure I could even find my circuit breaker box in the basement. Should I call Cotton? I sat still, trying to be patient. I leaned back on the couch and prayed for peace. It wasn't long before the lights steadied. I found relaxation that put me to sleep for the night, right on my couch.

CHAPTER 22

Bright and early the next morning, I turned on the oven to create the magic of making my blueberry muffins. I sipped coffee and nibbled on toast while I followed each step. It felt good to be back in the kitchen. The butcher block Clark made for me as a Christmas present made me smile as I saw the top dusted with flour.

By eight thirty, I had a couple of batches out of the oven and ready to take to the carpenters. I wrapped them in towels to keep them warm before placing them in the picnic basket. I filled a thermos of coffee to help them keep warm throughout the day. Cotton pulled in my driveway just as I was about to leave.

"Gosh darn it, Miss Kate, I didn't know you made deliveries!" Cotton teased.

We laughed.

"I just came by to welcome you back and to see if you need me to do anything."

"I'm glad to be back, thank you," I said with a smile. "I'm just headed to Aunt Mandy's house down the road to deliver muffins to the workers."

"Well, ain't that special," he said, scratching his head. "If that's where the muffins are going, I'll be right behind you! I was curious about the goings on there anyway."

"Great," I said, getting in my car. This morning, there were three trucks parked in a row when I pulled up to park. Cotton pulled up behind me. I also noticed two more walls had gone up since yesterday.

"Holy mackerel!" Cotton exclaimed, getting out of his truck. "Hey, Chuck!"

Chuck waved and came our way. "Aren't we working fast enough? You had to bring Cotton to help?" Chuck teased. "How ya' doin', Cotton?"

"Fine. I'm just following the boss here so I can have some muffins and coffee," Cotton responded with a hearty laugh.

"Muffins and coffee?" Chuck repeated, looking surprised.

"Here you go," I said, handing Chuck the picnic basket. "I brought more coffee if you need it. There are cups inside the basket."

Chuck gave me a big grin.

"It's just a little thank you for all the progress you've been making."

"Frankly, Chuck, it's the only reason I work for the lady," Cotton teased. "Wait until you taste them!"

Chuck didn't waste any time as he placed the basket and coffee on a wide board resting on two sawhorses. He unfolded the towels and shook his head in disbelief. "How many workers do you think we have here, Ms. Meyr?" he said as he helped himself to a muffin. "There's enough to feed an army!"

"I'm Kate, remember? You can't just eat one. Cotton, help yourself!"

I took the thermos and filled a couple cups of coffee as two more guys came our way. They made cute remarks and didn't waste any time getting a muffin.

"Patrick, you'd better come get one of these muffins while you can," Chuck said to the other worker on the ladder. "Little Red Riding Hood here just brought us a basket of goodies!"

I laughed and blushed at the same time. "Clever," I responded. "I'll just leave this here and when you guys go by the house tonight, you can leave everything on my deck."

"I'll do just that," Chuck said seriously. "They really are delicious! Thanks a lot."

"She makes them every morning for her guests, so you can probably smell them going by the house," Cotton joked.

"I hate to see any go to waste, so I'll keep you guys in mind," I said, going to my car. "See you later!"

Cotton stayed behind, and I felt he was likely to ask about any work they might have for him.

I headed straight to Concordia Cemetery from there, wishing I had some fresh flowers to take to the graves. I had always admired this cemetery on the hill as I drove down this road. The scenic hill was just so typical of the hillside beauty Borna maintained. I could only imagine that those who had loved ones buried here could look up to pay their respects as they drove by.

I carefully drove up the narrow, winding road that finally led me to the top of the hill. The cemetery was probably a quarter of the size of Lake View Cemetery in South Haven. Hopefully, that would mean I could find Josephine's grave quickly. There was no place to pull my car over to the side of the road, so I just stopped the car and got out. I looked around and discovered I was totally alone in this little world of the dead. Sharla Lee said Josephine's in-ground marker had a broken corner. I looked ahead to the stones that appeared much older and were primarily engraved in German.

CHAPTER 23

As I gazed across the hillside of the cemetery, another car pulled up the hill. It was Esther. She stopped at the first curve. There was a fresh grave there which was most likely her mother's. With Josephine on my mind, I had forgotten that this was where she had been buried. Esther didn't look my way as she got out of the car. I thought she would want some privacy, so I didn't wave or try to get her attention.

A few more steps down the road, I saw a damaged stone. A corner was cracked but the stone itself was still in place. Josephine Paulson was displayed in big readable letters. Underneath her name was carved Oct. 22, 1879 - May 29, 1954. I stooped down to run my fingers across her stone. She seemed more real to me now that I knew where her body was laid to rest. So where was Doc? Sharla Lee said to look a couple of graves away.

I first went in the wrong direction but then went back to see his stone. In his stone was carved Dr. Gotthild A. Paulson with birth and death dates of March 22, 1875 - March 10, 1951. His stone had settled further into the ground but was not damaged. Were they watching? Did they know me like I knew them? I caressed his stone and was at a loss for words.

I looked down the hill and saw Esther kneeling at her mother's grave. She appeared to be crying. How sad and alone she must feel. I walked in another direction to an area where some older stones were located. I saw many of the same last names repeated over and over. So many folks were related to each other around here. The stones were getting smaller as I went down the hill. They appeared to be stones for children. One of the stones was more ornate than the others. It read:

No farewell words spoken,

No time to say good-bye.

You were gone before we knew it,

and only God knows why.

It was so fitting and could have applied to any of our loved ones who have passed.

I was getting colder and colder, so I headed back to the Paulsons' graves to take some photos on my phone. When I got in the car, I realized I couldn't turn around to try to avoid Esther's car. I had no choice but to drive to the same curve where she was parked. I parked my car near hers. She looked up when I got out of the car. She was truly in distress.

"Oh, Esther, I'm so sorry for you," I said, giving her a hug.

"I don't know what is with me today," she confessed. "I just can't stop crying so I decided to come here and talk to her."

"Well, you shouldn't feel badly about that. This is the time to grieve. The funeral was so lovely and everyone's words were so meaningful. I felt as if I knew her." Esther smiled.

"It meant a lot to me for all of you to be there," she said between sniffles. "My mom would have been so surprised to see how many came to pay their respects. Her quilting group is really taking her loss very hard. When I told them her Dresden

Plate quilt went with her to the grave, they all were pleased and some even broke into tears. One of the ladies said they would keep an empty chair where she sat during quilting."

"Oh, that is special," I said, picturing the sight. "Whose idea was it to bury her with the quilt?"

"Well, when they opened the casket for us to say good-bye, my sister Edna was holding the quilt to take home with her. She said she felt guilty taking it since it was Mom's prized procession. Edna is the eldest in the family, which was why we thought she should have it. All of a sudden, I mentioned the idea of keeping it with our mom like we decided about her wedding ring from Dad. Everyone agreed, so we placed it over her and tucked her in for a nice heavenly sleep. We all smiled and it gave us a sense of relief. I just know she would have been okay with that."

"That is so beautiful, Esther," I said, tears welling in my eyes.

"I know she's up in heaven, but it gives us comfort to know the quilt is with her body."

"Why don't we get a cup of coffee and warm up?" I suggested with a shiver in my voice. "It's almost lunchtime. I would be happy to treat you to lunch."

"Oh, no, I've been gone too long as it is. I must look a mess. I'm so glad you stopped by. Maybe I just needed to talk to someone like you. Why are you here, by the way?"

"I found the Paulsons' gravestones up there on the hill," I explained. "I can't believe they were laid to rest so close to their homeplace."

"I'll bet my mom could have told you exactly where they were buried," Esther said with a big smile on her face. "Thanks for being my friend, Kate." We hugged again and went back to our cars to go home.

CHAPTER 24

    I checked my emails when I got home and was reminded that Mr. Lottes, a distant relative of Josephine's, would be stopping by to see the house he remembered from long ago. I also had a guest arriving tomorrow who was an older gentleman that was coming to visit relatives. He would be staying only one night. The Study hadn't been slept in for some time, so it was ready to go.

    Around five, I saw Chuck pull up in his pick-up truck. I watched from the window as he placed my picnic basket and thermos on the deck. He paused and looked around as if he might find me doing some activity on the property outdoors. After a pause, he returned to his truck and left.

    I was craving vegetable soup, so I used some frozen items to make a small pot for myself. I loved having the aromas of baking or cooking wafting from my kitchen. It was also a good night for a fire so I cuddled up in my rocking chair and set to work on my raffle quilt block. It may have been wishful thinking, but it seemed that the days were starting to stay brighter longer. I replayed the events of the day and my thoughts took me to my visit with Esther. John would be interested to know I had another report of a quilt going into the ground. Had I been just ignorant of this practice until now?

I felt very calm in that cemetery. Perhaps I should visit Josephine there more often. I've always wanted to do a stone rubbing, so I decided Josephine's would be my first. East Perry County had many small and charming cemeteries that usually existed behind church properties. My curiosity about old tombstones might take me to visit each one! I was about to doze off to sleep on the couch when Maggie called.

"Am I calling too late? I figure you country folk are usually in bed by now," she joked with a giggle in her voice.

"Funny, funny," I answered. "I'm working on my quilt block, I'll have you know. I must admit that I was getting bored and was close to falling asleep. What's up with you?"

"I went to take Carla some food today instead of flowers."

"Oh, Maggie, that is so sweet of you. How is she doing?"

"Really well, I think. She'll be starting radiation next week, so she's a little apprehensive about that, of course."

"I can't say that I blame her. I'll check with her tomorrow. I had a busy day today, which included visiting Josephine's grave, by the way."

"Another trip to the cemetery, huh?" Maggie teased.

"You remember Esther from our club? She cuts my hair. She lost her mother recently so she was also at the cemetery when I was there."

"Sure, I remember her. Well, I'm sorry to hear that. Do folks around there hang out in such places on a regular basis?" She chuckled, missing my point.

"Okay, girlfriend, knock it off. You know John is writing an article about quilts and cemeteries for his magazine. He said any quilt-related topic goes over big. He was touched by my story about

Emily and her mother's quilt."

"You're kidding. That sounds pretty gruesome, if you ask me, but what do I know?"

"I think he's onto something. After my visit with Emily and her quilt, I'm convinced there are many quilts residing in the cemetery."

"Well, I guess that's what makes John such a good writer. It sounds as if you like following his interests, girlfriend."

I ignored her comment. "Did you tell the Beach Quilters that I was sorry to have missed them on this visit?"

"I did and, by the way, they are considering a road trip to Borna either late summer or early fall! Can you believe it?"

"Seriously?" I gasped. "That would be great! Maybe you can also bring Carla!"

"Carla thinks the two of us need to come for our birthdays again. As far as the quilters, there may only be five or six who can even get away to do such a thing."

"Oh, that would be so cool. Please keep working on that plan, okay? I would love that so much!"

"I will. It would be fun, for sure. Well, Mark just came home and you know how he is with me always being on the phone, so I'm hanging up now. Call you later. I love you!"

"Bye, girlfriend, love you too!"

Conversations with Maggie nearly always put me in a good mood. We could have a great time discussing just about anything. Maggie and Mark had a nearly perfect life, the way I felt life was supposed to be. The only thing wrong was that she lived so far away from me in South Haven.

CHAPTER 25

It was late in the afternoon the next day when Edwin Heartling arrived. I looked out of the window and saw a bald, heavy set older man get out of a huge Cadillac. It looked similar to one belonging to Aunt Mandy. He stood there for a while and observed the house and property before he came to the front door.

Before he could knock, I opened the door to welcome him. "Welcome to Josephine's Guest House, Mr. Heartling," I greeted.

He gave me a big smile. "You must be Josephine," he responded.

"Sorry? My name is Kate Meyr. I'm the proprietor," I corrected. "I named the house after a woman that used to reside here."

He smiled as he walked in and looked at his surroundings, visually taking in the historic home like every other visitor before him. "Well, it's a mighty nice place, I must say, Ms. Meyr."

I took him into the reception area and got him

registered. I explained about the guest book and the guest quilt on the wall. He was quite taken with the quilt after he carefully examined it, although I could see he was completely uncomfortable with the thought of actually writing on it.

"My mother made quilts for our beds but this is one for the books, you might say," he chuckled. "It's mighty nice. Did you make it?"

I shook my head. "No, I commissioned a friend to make it for me," I explained. "I was too busy restoring this place."

"Well, I'd love a tour before I leave for supper tonight," he requested.

He carefully signed the quilt on a corner block and then went over to sign the guest book. When I showed him his room, he was very pleased. From there, we went upstairs where I showed him the other rooms. As always, my room was closed off for anyone to see.

I offered him refreshments, but he declined. He requested an early breakfast because he would be in a hurry to get home the next day. That sounded fine by me. He smelled like he may have been a pipe smoker, but if he read the rules provided him, he hopefully knew better than to light up.

He went to his room and I poured myself a glass of wine before dinner. I had just turned on the evening news when he came out of his room looking very sharp and dapper.

"Would you like to join me, Mr. Heartling?"

"It looks quite inviting, I must say," he responded. He paused and then said, "If I may ask, what do you think of living in this little town?"

"I like it very much," I answered with a smile. "I inherited this property when my husband died. When I drove to the area with the plan of putting it on the market, I fell in love with it as well as the whole town."

He smiled after I finished my explanation. "I've lived alone all my life," he shared. "They're having a birthday party for my brother this evening. I haven't seen him in quite some time, so I thought I'd better show up."

"That sounds like a nice affair. I hope you enjoy yourself."

He reluctantly put on his overcoat and slowly walked toward the door before stopping and turning around. "I don't suppose you'll be up later so I can take you up on that offer of wine?" he asked shyly.

"Well, the light down here will be on, but I turn in pretty early since I fix breakfast nearly every morning."

"That's a shame," he said, looking to the floor. "You have a good evening."

When he went out the door, I thought about what a lonely man he must be. I wasn't sure how friendly to be to my guests, but I knew that after dinner I would head to my locked room for the rest of the evening.

Aunt Mandy called while I was eating. She was so excited because she had opened her email and had seen the photo of her house's construction. "I just can't believe how quickly this is happening," she said, sounding elated. "I wish I were there every day to see the changes. I still have things to do, but some things you just can't rush. I hope this isn't a burden for you, honey."

"Not at all," I assured her. "I took some blueberry muffins to the men at the site this morning," I bragged. "Hopefully we'll have some good results because of it. They were delighted!"

Aunt Mandy chuckled. "You are something, sweetie." Aunt Mandy paused. "Wilson says he is very pleased with how things are progressing."

"Wilson?" I asked, confused.

"Yes, my architect, Wilson Schumacher," she reminded me. "He's been so nice to keep me informed by phone about how things are coming along with the house."

"Well, well, well," I chuckled. "You two have really hit it off, haven't you?"

"Now, Kate, none of that!"

I could sense her blushing over the phone.

"How's Clark doing?"

"He's still out of town," I reported. "I did have a strange postcard from him, however."

"A postcard! Not a phone call of any kind?"

"Now, Aunt Mandy, none of that!" I imitated. "He had an art gallery show in Springfield, according to the card. I guess he felt I should at least know about that."

"So maybe now I'd better ask about John," she teased.

"He's in Chicago," I said, chuckling again. "Everyone's busy. I have a guest here tonight that you may have found interesting. He's driving a big Cadillac like yours."

"Well, if that doesn't beat all," she responded. "I'm glad you're finally making some money! By the way, thanks for letting me know about the passing of Esther's mother. I sent her a card."

"That's so sweet of you. Take care of yourself and get back here as soon as you can, okay?"

"I will, honey, and thanks for taking care of the men!" she said, ending the call.

CHAPTER 26

    I had just fallen into a deep sleep when I was awakened by the sound of footsteps creeping up my stairs. I looked at the clock and it was ten minutes to twelve. Was Mr. Heartling coming up the stairs? Who else could it be? I stayed perfectly quiet. The footsteps drew closer and I could feel that there was someone at the door. Surely he wouldn't try to open it! What would I do if he did?

    Finally, I heard him go back down the stairs. What was he thinking? If he had read the house rules, he wouldn't be roaming around the house. I wasn't about to make a noise of any kind or go downstairs. How could I possibly go back to sleep? I had to think of ways to keep this from happening again. Suddenly, there was daylight that Josephine provided. I welcomed the warm light because I knew I would have peace now and would be able to go back to sleep.

    My alarm went off sooner than usual because of Mr. Heartling's request for an early breakfast. As I jumped out of bed, I started to question whether I had experienced a bad dream or whether Mr. Heartling had truly been at my door last night.

A breakfast of baked pancakes, bacon, muffins, and fresh fruit produced aromas in the house very quickly. I dreaded seeing my guest, but I decided I would pretend nothing had happened.

"Good morning, Kate," Mr. Heartling greeted as he came into the kitchen.

When did he decide to call me Kate? "Well, good morning to you too," I responded as I poured him a cup of coffee. "I hope you had a good night's rest. How was your party?"

"The party was enjoyable but sleep was pretty sparse," he reported. "I could have sworn there was a dark cloud over my bed last night."

It reminded me of when Tina had stayed in that room and complained of the very same thing. "Oh my, I'm sorry to hear that," I said as I placed his food on the table.

"You're not going to join me?" The look on his face registered disappointment.

"I'll drink a cup of coffee with you but I ate earlier," I explained. "I don't eat with my guests because I'm here to serve you."

"Well, I was thinking, Kate," he started, "I'd love to spend an extra day here and take you out for a nice dinner tonight."

I couldn't believe what I was hearing!

"I'll bet you rarely get treated like you deserve. I think we'd have a great time and would enjoy wonderful conversations together."

I was shocked into silence.

"You are a mighty fine-looking lady and I'd love to show

you off. You know, when I got home last night, I sure was disappointed that you had gone to bed."

"Oh, Mr. Heartling, I couldn't possibly do that," I said, delivering a gracious smile. "You are so nice to offer, but I don't think you realize that I am quite happy and content with my life as it is."

He looked even more disappointed than before.

"So, you have a boyfriend, do you?"

He asked his question like that must be the reason for my refusal. Be careful how you answer, a little voice whispered inside me. I tried to choose my words carefully. "I have many male friends that I enjoy being with, but I am not involved seriously with anyone."

"Well, I'd like to be one of those friends," he said, putting down his fork. "I asked some of the folks there last night if they knew whether you had a boyfriend. They all agreed that they had never seen you with anyone."

I got up to take some dishes into the kitchen and he stood and followed me. "I'm afraid you are pursuing the wrong person, Mr. Heartling," I said, shaking my head. "I'm sure there are a lot of nice ladies who would enjoy your company."

He looked sterner and came closer. "I know I'm old, portly, and bald, but I'm well-traveled and have a lot of spunk left in me, if you know what I mean." He winked at me, making my skin crawl.

I'm sure I did not want to talk about his sexual appetite. I walked back to the dining room.

"Did I embarrass you, Kate?"

His inclination to address me as if we were close friends was wearing thin on me. I took a deep breath. "Mr. Heartling, you need to be on your way," I said sternly, issuing him an even stare. "I don't like this conversation and I have a busy day ahead. Let's just say our good-byes."

"You are so uptight! I can see it," he said, coming close to me again.

What was he going to do next? I was about to reinforce my stance when I saw Cotton's pick-up truck pull in the driveway. It was Susie's day to clean! Thank goodness! "My work crew is here, Mr. Heartling, so can I help you with anything else before you leave?"

He looked angry as he turned to go to his room. He had only taken one or two bites of his breakfast.

I greeted Cotton and Susie at the door, wanting to give them a big hug. But instead, I tried to act normal.

"Have a good day, Ms. Meyr," Mr. Heartling said, carrying his luggage and moving toward the front door.

I was glad to hear I was once again Ms. Meyr. When I saw him pull out of my driveway, I went into the kitchen to sit down. I think I was shaking.

"Are you okay, Miss Kate?" asked Susie as she was pouring her own coffee.

"Yeah, sure. I am just glad to see both of you," I said, taking a sip of coffee. I did not want them to see me upset, so I made every effort to calm myself down and move on.

Cotton said he had to be on his way and Susie went to find her cleaning supplies. Susie was getting pretty big with her second pregnancy, but she never complained. It would be good for me to begin to plan what things will be like at the guest house in May when she delivers.

CHAPTER 27

I cleared the breakfast table and told Susie to help herself to any of the leftovers. I went up to my room to get my thoughts together for the day. My mind was in a whirl! Had I done something to create Mr. Heartling's behavior? Do other establishments with women innkeepers have the same problems? Should I be more cautious and not book single men? Married men, like Carson, could also behave badly. Was I making too much of this? Should my page of rules discourage conversation? Now I was getting silly. This may never happen again, so I needed to get back to my list for the day. The first thing I wanted to do was call Carla and check on her.

"Good morning, Carla. How are you doing?" I asked when she picked up her phone.

"Pretty good," she responded. "I have a doctor's appointment this afternoon to discuss more details about my treatment."

"I'm glad you are moving forward. Six weeks will be over before you know it."

"Has your Aunt Mandy returned?"

"No, not yet, but they are certainly making progress on her house! It is so interesting to see the progress made each day."

"I really enjoyed Maggie's visit last week," Carla mentioned. "She said no wedding date has been set for Jill and Jack. I'll bet the two of you are chomping at the bit to have that wedding."

"That's right, and I'll pester Jack again when we talk on Sunday. God help Maggie and me once we know a date! They won't have to do a thing with all the ideas we'll have!" Carla and I shared a laugh over that statement.

We chatted a bit more, and when we hung up I felt positive about Carla's mental state and sensed that she would have a good outcome from her treatments. Encouraged, I started a grocery list. While I was deep in thought, Ellie called.

"Hey, why not come out for dinner tonight?" she suggested. "Trout has asked about you, and Kelly is deep frying a turkey today."

"That does sound nice. I have something I wanted to talk to you about anyway, so dinner sounds like a good idea."

"Great. See you then," she said before hanging up.

Before I left to go grocery shopping, I gave Susie some last-minute instructions. Not having a lot of guests now gave me an opportunity to have Susie do some deep cleaning here and there. I honestly valued the work she did for me, and I particularly valued her trustworthiness.

"Miss Kate, this was on the dresser in The Study room," Susie said, handing me an envelope. "I didn't know whether you had seen it."

I took the envelope and went into the kitchen. When I opened the envelope and unfolded the note, it read:

Kate, I almost knocked on your bedroom door last night

when I returned home. I really wanted to experience more of your company. I decided against it and will never know what your response may have been. I would have likely been refused, for you probably have younger suitors pursuing you. If you ever feel lonely, please know I am available anytime. You already have my contact information. Ever so fondly, Edwin.

This was one for the books, I said to myself as I put the letter in my desk drawer. I took a deep breath and headed to the grocery store in Dresden. Perhaps it would do me good to get out a bit. I enjoyed the scenic drive and was grateful that the area was beginning to feel like home to me as I pulled a grocery cart from the racks, retrieved the list from my purse, and began to shop.

"Hey, welcome home!" Ruth Ann's voice greeted me from down the aisle. "I missed you!"

"Well, that's sweet," I responded. "What's new with you?"

"Things are good," she nodded. "I had the East Perry Rotary Club dinner meeting last night. They seemed to all be very pleased."

"I told you these things take a while," I reminded her. "I'm going to the winery for dinner tonight. Why don't you join me?"

She paused. "I think I can do that," she said, grinning. "Are we celebrating anything?"

"Nope. I'll pick you up at six thirty, okay?"

"I'll be ready," she agreed. "Say, have you had any word from Clark? I think I saw him pass by my place yesterday."

"I haven't seen him, but then he never tells me when he's returned, so that's just Clark." I said, feeling disappointment creep through me. I hoped I sounded more lighthearted than I actually felt.

CHAPTER 28

It was a lovely evening when I picked up Ruth Ann. She looked great and had a new reddish hair color that I had never seen on her before. "Your hair looks great, Ruth Ann," I mentioned as she tucked her hair behind her ears. "I really need another haircut, but I hate to bother Esther with all she's been through. I know she said to call her and set up a time, but I don't want to put one more thing on her right now."

"You always look great, Kate. Thanks for inviting me to come with you tonight."

We pulled up the hill to the winery, and I was immediately reminded of my last visit on New Year's Eve. I needed to pull myself into the present and enjoy this evening with my good friends. Ellie was glad to see us and was thrilled I had thought to invite Ruth Ann.

"I have a table for us," Ellie announced. "We have a band playing later, so I thought it would be quieter over here."

"Welcome back, Kate!" Trout greeted me with a wink. "Hey, Ruth Ann! So, what can I get you ladies to drink?"

"I'll have my same red," I responded.

"Anything red for me as well, so I'll have what she's having!" Ruth Ann said with a chuckle. I was pleased when Ellie pulled up a chair to join us. Our conversation was loud and immediate. We had so much to catch up on, starting with the subject of the house being built on my property. Ellie said it was the talk of the town. She said there was some confusion in the community chitchat about who would be the actual owner of the house.

"Kate's already got the workers wrapped around her little finger ever since she started feeding them those blueberry muffins," Ellie teased.

"Whatever it takes," Ruth Ann advised. "It's her signature bakery item and it works for her!"

"Speaking of her workers, Chuck Hopfer just walked in with his brother Kevin," Ellie noted. "Chuck comes in quite a bit on Friday nights."

I turned around and saw Chuck wearing a straw cowboy hat and his brother sporting a black one. "Is his brother married?" I asked, openly curious. "He looks a lot younger."

"He is, but I've never seen him with his wife," Ellie recalled. "He's not as cute as Chuck."

Each of us agreed with Ellie's observation.

"Kate, what did you want to talk to me about? I may get busy here and will have to help behind the bar."

I took a deep breath and started from the beginning about my experience with Edwin Heartling. The looks on both their faces were of concern. As I relayed my story, I could tell they were anxious to give their comments and advice. When I finished, they pounced!

"What a dirty old man!" Ruth Ann exclaimed. "What do

you really think he had in mind—a big smooch?"

We doubled over in laughter.

"I know it's not funny," Ellie said. "I get hit on at the winery by old geezers now and then. But I'm not alone here, so I don't feel as threatened."

"When I saw how his face changed when he realized I was turning him down, it did scare me a bit," I admitted.

"When I was in college, I had an older professor who continued to hit on me like that," Ruth Ann confided. "He stalked me to the point that I wondered all the time what would happen next. When I reported it to a counselor, she had a name for it."

"What did she call it?" I asked, genuinely curious and eager to put a name to what I had felt since the incident.

"Erotomania," she stated. "It's when a person is in need of something, like love and affection, and chooses someone to fill that need. And I mean anyone! They fantasize about what you may be like and what you mean by any words you say to them. Let's just say, for example, that you give him a compliment about something like his shirt, or that you're just plain nice to him. He will interpret that to mean that you really do like him. In his mind, you wouldn't say those things if you didn't. It's weird, I know, but it's very real to them and my counselor said to take it very seriously because when reality does set in, they can become angry and even violent."

This news was making me feel very weary and a little ill.

"Thank you for sharing, Ruth Ann," Ellie interrupted. "He probably festered in his anger all the way home and now he's going to come back for you, Kate."

While she smiled at her attempt at a joke, I shivered at

the thought.

"Ellie, don't tease about that," Ruth Ann cautioned. "I'm sure his ego is just a little bruised, that's all."

"Well, Kate, you're just going to have to stop being the 'hostess with the mostess,'" Ellie teased.

"It makes me want to exclude any single men as guests," I confessed. "How can I have them in my home, serve them food, and not be nice?"

"I would close off that stairway with some sort of thick, decorative roping or something when you don't have guests upstairs," suggested Ellie.

"Good idea," I agreed. I knew I had to create some parameters that worked to remedy the situation in order to feel safe in my own home in future situations. Clearly, written guidelines for guests were not sufficient deterrents for some folks.

"I put a sign on my kitchen door that says 'private' in order to keep them out," Ruth Ann shared. "I know you don't like customers in your kitchen, either."

I nodded. "They don't realize you are doing your job as a professional. You're not their Aunt Mildred entertaining them in her home."

Ruth Ann's face brightened. She piped up, "You should have called me with our pink flamingo code for help! This would have been the perfect opportunity to use it!"

We each chuckled, but I knew that beyond our laughter the situation still felt somewhat raw for me.

CHAPTER 29

The loud music started, just as Ellie had predicted, so it was very difficult to carry on a conversation. Chuck sent over a round of drinks for everyone before Ellie had to leave us and help Trout. As more people filtered in, Trout had gotten deluged with drink orders.

"I hate country music," I said rather loudly to Ruth Ann.

"You do?" she said, surprised. "I usually have it playing when I am alone at work. There are some pretty good local bands in East Perry. You'd better get used to it if you're going to be around here!"

Couples were drifting onto the dance floor at the small area to the side of us. I was beginning to feel like it was time to go home.

"You are the next hostess for Friendship Circle, right?" Ruth Ann asked in her loudest voice.

I nodded. "Yes. For lunch," I answered. "I have no idea what I'll be serving at this point." Suddenly, I felt someone grab my arm, and the next thing I knew I was being led toward the dance floor! When I turned to the person responsible for this extreme surprise, I could see Chuck laughing. He was clearly gleeful at succeeding at his effort, and he twirled me around handily before I landed in his arms. I could tell he was into this honky-tonk music. I was speechless!

"Ya' dance, don't ya'?" Chuck asked, looking down at me.

Until this moment, I hadn't realized how tall he was. "Not usually before someone asks for my permission," I retorted, half smiling at him.

"Well, Ms. Meyr, you seem to be pretty light on your feet, so may I have the rest of this dance?" he teased.

I grinned and didn't answer.

As the song progressed, he held me closer than I would have liked. His body strength was obvious and he smelled awfully good, like soap. He must have just had a shower at the end of his work day. Every now and then, he'd break away and twirl me again. I surprised myself by being able to keep up with his moves. I couldn't help but laugh out loud at times. I looked over to catch Ruth Ann's eye and saw that she was no longer sitting at the table. A quick glance around the dance floor revealed that she was dancing with someone I had never seen before. Some night this had turned into!

At the end of the song, Chuck gave me a slight dip, reminding me of the way dances ended in the fifties. When he brought me back up, there was Clark! Oh, Lordy!

"I'll take it from here," Clark said, expertly slipping his arm around my waist as the music started up for the next song.

"Hey, buddy! Good to see ya'!" Chuck said to Clark.

"You're back!" I confirmed as I adjusted to the beat of the music.

"Yeah, and I can tell you really missed me," Clark joked.

I gave him a puzzled look. "When did you get back?" I asked, suddenly feeling a little out of breath. I used to be able to dance and talk at the same time. Sheesh! Was it nerves?

"Yesterday," he mumbled, confidently turning me around in another spin. We didn't pursue any more conversation until the music stopped and he followed me back to the table. Ruth Ann was again in her seat.

"If it isn't Mr. Clark McFadden," Ruth Ann announced. "I thought I saw you drive by yesterday. Welcome back!"

"Do you ladies need a drink?" he asked, ignoring Ruth Ann's comments.

"No, we're fine. Why don't you join us?" I offered.

"Nah, I don't want to interfere," he said. "When did you and Chuck hook up?"

I couldn't believe he asked that question. "He happens to be working on Aunt Mandy's house which happens to be on my property," I answered sarcastically. He sounded jealous. Sometimes he completely infuriated me. The music started again and he took my hand, gently leading me to the dance floor. Thank goodness it was a slow and easy tune.

"You don't mind another dance to this country music, do you?" he teased, giving me an impish grin. "These slow songs are tearjerkers, aren't they?" he asked, pulling me very close.

"Are they?"

"Yes. They bring out the passion and love in everyday life," he whispered close to my ear, his tone suddenly serious.

"There's nothing wrong with that," I agreed, leaning in to his embrace. I had no idea Clark could dance like this. Why hadn't he shown me this side of him sooner? I loved this! I glanced over at Chuck and noticed he was watching us closely. We danced the remainder of the song in silence.

"Did you bring Ruth Ann?" he asked softly when the music stopped.

I nodded. "Are you okay?" I asked, looking into his eyes. "Have you had a lot to drink?"

He grinned and nodded.

"Would you like a ride home?"

"I'm good, but thanks," he said as he guided me back to the table. "I'd better leave you ladies now. It's past my bedtime, but you all have a good time." To my surprise, he gave me a peck on the cheek and walked out the door.

"Can you believe his timing? Walking in and seeing you dancing with Chuck?" Ruth Ann exclaimed, her voice near a squeak. "Was he upset that you were dancing with Chuck?"

I shook my head, still reeling a bit from the events of the past few minutes. "Who was the guy you were dancing with?" I asked quickly, hoping that focusing on Ruth Ann would slow my thoughts a bit.

"That's Bob Mueller from Dresden Bank," she explained. "He has helped me with some financial things. He's really a nice guy, never been married, and certainly not my type."

I wondered if she thought that Clark was really more her type. We were putting our coats on and preparing to leave when Chuck came over to the table.

"Leaving so soon?" he asked with a grin.

I nodded and gave him a polite smile. "You must have the day off tomorrow," I joked.

"I do, as a matter of fact, I do," he nodded back. "At least I guess I do—unless my boss objects." He winked. Then, his expression turned more serious and he asked, "Did I miss somethin' here? Do you and Clark have something goin'?"

"We're friends, that's all," I answered.

"Well, I don't want him thinkin' that I'm movin' in on him," Chuck assured me. "I was glad to see him here tonight."

Oh, how I wanted to move away from this subject. "Thanks for the drink, by the way," I said, deflecting.

"Nice to meet you, Ruth Ann," he said, looking her way. His attention turned back to me. "I come here once in a while on Friday nights. I hope I run into you again."

"Hey, Kate!" Ellie yelled through the crowd. I paused as she made her way toward us. "Thanks for coming out tonight and bringing Ruth Ann."

"Dinner was great," I added. "Please give my compliments to Kelly. His food is always great." In a matter of moments, Ruth Ann and I walked out the door, giving Trout a wave good-bye. When we got in the car, we immediately started to giggle. It was a fun evening that we could never have planned, even if we had tried.

"Okay, Katy my friend, did you notice that Chuck has the hots for you?" Ruth Ann blurted out.

"I just knew he liked my muffins," I said, laughing. And that's the way it went, all the way home, just like young teenagers.

CHAPTER 30

A week had passed with no word from Clark. The weather had been rainy, a sign of spring. It also meant there had been fewer days for the men to work on Aunt Mandy's house. However, I was pleased that Mr. Lottes, the distant relative of Josephine, was going to make his appearance tomorrow afternoon.

I spent most of the day taking care of paperwork in my office. My curiosity had me check the guest book to see where Mr. Heartling lived. His address was Hermann, Missouri, which I knew to be a lovely historic town. I then looked at the guest quilt and was astonished to see that his name was no longer on the quilt. I was certain he had chosen to sign on the corner block, but now his signature was gone! Josephine had removed names before that she didn't approve of, so this was likely no exception. It was one of the guest house ghostly moments that I had to keep to myself. My cell phone rang, so I retrieved it from my office. It was Jack.

"Hey, Mom! Guess who's visiting here this weekend?"

"It must be Jill. Am I right?" I guessed.

"You're right," he happily acknowledged. "She said to tell

you hello."

"Please tell her the same and let her know that her mother and I are waiting for that big date to be set," I teased.

"Yeah, we know, we know," Jack responded good naturedly.

"How long does she get to stay?"

"Just a few days," he answered. "She's taking me shopping today to get my reaction to some of her tastes in decorating."

"Oh, you mean like china and silver?" I asked, getting excited.

"No," he laughed. "We're not interested in things like that. She likes things made of natural products." I guess natural meant nothing traditional as in the usual wedding gifts. If that were the case, Maggie and I were going to be left with boxes of china, silver, and crystal instead of being able to pass them on to be used by the next generation. Well, at least they were making plans for the future. Before we hung up, we discussed Carla's recovery and ended the call by expressing our love to each other.

My stomach was growling and I realized that I had nothing to eat for dinner in the house. I knew Marv's was the place to go for a delicious take-out order. I combed my hair and put on a hooded sweatshirt before heading out. It was drizzling, so I pulled the hood over my head. I had just gotten into my car when a text came from John.

> I'm missin' you a lot, country girl! And txs for your email on the Dresden Plate quilt. Good reporting. I'm getting good stuff. Call me later. J

I smiled. I could hear his voice in my mind as I read the text. I suppose I missed him, too!

I got into Marv's without anyone noticing. I went to the end of the bar where I usually placed my orders. "What can I get for you, Kate?" Marv asked in a jovial voice. "We've got some good chicken and dumplings today with a side of slaw. How does that sound?"

"Perfect. I'll have some!" I responded eagerly. I tried to make a little small talk with the woman sitting on the barstool next to me, but her glazed-over look told me she had been there a very long time!

"Kate, there's a fella at the end of the bar who wants to buy you a drink," Marv said with a big grin.

I looked in that direction and saw Chuck. He wore a generous smile and tipped his hat in acknowledgment of me.

"Oh, I don't think so, but tell Chuck thanks for me," I replied.

After Marv gave him my message, Chuck left his seat and walked in my direction. I wanted to crawl under the barstool because of the way I looked.

"Hiding out, are ya'?" Chuck asked, giving me a wink.

"Yeah, kind of," I said softly. "It's pretty dreary out there, isn't it?"

"Yeah, but tomorrow they're predicting sunshine, so we'll be back to work," he reported. "I'll bet we'll be pretty hungry too, so maybe we'll get a visit from Little Red Riding Hood again."

"Aren't you the bold one?" I teased. "I'll see what I can do."

"Here you go, Kate," Marv said, handing me a take-out bag. "It's all paid in full, thanks to Chuck."

I immediately sent Chuck a look that communicated that he did not need to pay for my meal.

"I'm just kissin' up to the boss, that's all," Chuck teased.

After I expressed my thanks, I left before anyone else could recognize me.

Back at home, the signature German dish was delicious and the serving size was enough to feed a family of five. I remember that when I first moved here, Ellie had made chicken and dumplings for me. When I finished, I divided the remaining food into containers and placed them in the refrigerator to enjoy later.

Chuck was certainly an odd one. I had never known anyone who wore a cowboy hat, so I suppose I was a little charmed at the way Chuck tipped his hat. I wondered why a little country girl around here hadn't snapped him up.

CHAPTER 31

I was in the backyard assessing where to plant more flowers and looking forward to all the tulips and jonquils that would soon begin popping out of the ground. I loved spring so much and wanted to rush every good thing about it. A car came up the driveway. I was expecting Herman Lottes and was eager to meet him. When he got out of the car to greet me, he marveled about how much Borna had changed. He looked to be about seventy and was sharply dressed. Seeing me looking over my gardens, he also expressed a desire for an early spring. We went into the house and I offered him a cup of coffee. He walked around and admired the first floor before he sat in the living room where I had placed a plate of cookies to entice him.

He got out a pad of paper. He said he had jotted down some information that I might be interested in. He explained that as a distant cousin, he wasn't sure about the accuracy of his memory. He said that he sometimes remembered things and couldn't ascertain whether he had been present or if he was remembering details that others had told him.

"I called Sharla Lee at the museum as you suggested." His

voice was deep and he was very articulate.

"Good," I nodded, smiling. "They have been very helpful to me, including locating the Paulsons' graves, which are not far from here. You may want to stop by. They're in the Concordia Church Cemetery."

"That's convenient." His eyes slowly scanned seemingly every nook and cranny in the room. "I think it may have been a family reunion when I was here last. I was very young, of course, but I remember being very afraid of the doctor."

I chuckled.

"My dad, Eberhard, was in their wedding, I'm told. I wish I had a photo for you, but I don't. Did you know the doctor was a Catholic before he became a Lutheran? Perhaps he changed for Josephine."

"No, I didn't know that," I replied thoughtfully. "I find it hard to believe that he converted for her."

"They were married April 12, 1902," Mr. Lottes stated as he looked at his notes. "They were married in Dresden at Trinity Church by a pastor from Borna, I believe. My grandfather, Gabriel Lottes, owned a saloon in Dresden a long time ago. I'd really like to find where that may have been."

"It's such a shame that they didn't have children," I said. "That would've helped to clarify a lot of things about them."

"I agree. However, I can say that they certainly would be very proud of how well you have restored their homeplace."

"Thanks," I answered with a proud smile. "I just want you to know that Josephine's spirit is alive in this house."

He looked at me strangely. "You mean like a ghost?" he asked cautiously.

I nodded, smiling.

"Somehow, that doesn't surprise me. Interesting." He

paused and then added, "I also hear that the doctor liked his alcohol."

I chuckled. "Yes, that doesn't seem to be a secret," I acknowledged. "It amazes me that he got by with drinking like that. Please let me know if you learn anything more on your trip."

"Yes, I will," he said as he took a last sip of coffee. "Thanks so much for seeing me. You have my email, which may be the best way to communicate."

"I agree. Good luck with your endeavor."

Off he went. I was hoping for more information, but was glad he was interested in the fascinating couple. Talking about Josephine with Mr. Lottes encouraged me to once again visit the gravesites. It was a crazy idea, but I wanted to take Josephine's quilt with me. I had kept it in the upstairs hall closet since I showed it to my Friendship Circle group.

With a light March snow predicted, I wanted to take advantage of the sunny day. I cut some fresh greenery and a few of my early blooming flowers to put on the graves. Some of my holly still had some red berries, so I added some sprigs and wrapped a red ribbon around each bouquet.

I had to get the ladder to reach the high closet above the door. I could only hope that the quilt would still be there. When I opened the door, a musty smell engulfed the quilt which I had wrapped in a white sheet. Once off the ladder, I grabbed a jacket and put the wrapped quilt in a plastic bag. My bouquets were still looking fresh and bright.

When I started driving up the narrow road to the Paulsons' graves, I noticed the pile of dirt still left from Esther's mother's grave. The poor flowers left behind on the dirt were dry and forlorn. I was surprised no one had removed them by now.

Today, I was alone in this very small cemetery. I got out of the car and stared once again at the in-ground stone of Josephine Paulson. I placed flowers at each of their graves, giving them a smile. "I brought your quilt, Josephine," I said, getting it out of the bag and sheet, while talking to her like she was listening. "I thought it could use some fresh air so I brought it for you to see. I am so pleased to have it." I opened the very wrinkled quilt and gave it a shake. Then I carefully spread the sheet to protect the quilt. Gingerly, I placed the quilt right under her gravestone. I was pleased to see it displayed again after all this time.

I started to read some of the passages once again when it suddenly became dark, which was unexpected and somewhat scary. A very loud crack of thunder and lightning came next, which made me jump. In seconds, an avalanche of rain came pouring down. I quickly gathered the quilt in my arms, covering it with the plastic bag. I grabbed the sheet, holding it over my head until I opened the car door. I threw everything into the backseat in haste. I started the car but with the hard rain and such darkness, I wasn't sure I could see to get down the hill. How could this be happening? It had been so bright and sunny when I arrived! I couldn't just sit there, so I drove slowly along the narrow road that took me out of the cemetery and onto the road.

When I got back to the house, I pulled the car into the garage. I was so glad to be home! I opened the back door to retrieve the quilt and it was gone! The quilt was nowhere to be seen. The sheet and plastic bag remained crumpled on the back seat, both lifeless and empty. I looked and looked, knowing full well I had not left the quilt behind. I had to get in the house. This was maddening and mystifying. When I got in the house, I dried myself off with a kitchen towel. What had just happened?

CHAPTER 32

I sat on the porch watching the sun shining brightly once again. Still feeling bewildered about having no quilt, my thoughts replayed my visit to Josephine's grave. I distinctly remembered how I had crumpled the quilt and thrown it carelessly into the backseat. I made myself check the backseat once again, but to no avail. Josephine had taken the quilt from me once before, but this time it happened in my presence. I didn't think I should share this with Ellie. She would never believe this happened again!

The rest of the day was unproductive. I wanted to call John as I had promised, but I first had to relax with a glass of wine. That done, I knew baking would be relaxing so I started the process of getting things ready to bake a batch of muffins in the morning. It brought me comfort to know that Chuck and the crew would appreciate the delivery. I could tell Chuck liked me and appreciated my efforts. But why hadn't I heard from Clark? Maybe I should swallow my pride and just ask him to dinner. What was the worst that could happen? Before pursuing the idea, I called John. I knew he would welcome my efforts to stay in touch.

"How was your day?" I asked John when he answered.

"Well, would you believe that we got another snow?" he said in disbelief. "I'll bet you are having some nicer days in your part of the world by now."

"We are!" I answered, knowing the day's weather had been odd. "I'm curious about how your quilt research is going."

"It's going great! It's taken me by surprise. It's amazing what you learn if you just ask."

"Like what?"

"Have you ever heard of textiles in stone?"

"What? Textiles made out of stone? Is that what you mean?"

"Yeah, it's for real," he said, clearing his throat. "It's about how to research and date a textile that's carved in stone, as in gravestones. The lady I talked to at the museum said shrouds, fringe, and clothing that you see in cemeteries can tell you a lot about their history."

"But what about the subject matter of quilts in the cemetery?" I asked more pointedly.

"I'm getting there. From one angle, it's related. Quilts and funerals are entwined, according to some funeral directors I talked to. They have played a role way back to the time when bodies were laid out in people's homes. Even when undertakers took over and began to embalm and display bodies, fancy quilts were used. One director said it was more common for babies and children to be buried in quilts when they died. At a small funeral museum I visited, I was shown a fancy silk box that contained a small silk quilt with ribbons that you could purchase for your baby's funeral.

There was one in pink and one in blue. He said some babies are buried with the silk quilt, and some just use it for the funeral service. After the funeral, the family receives the quilt in the silk box. Today, the families usually bring in a favorite quilt or blanket to be buried with their little ones."

"How touching! I've never been to a funeral museum. You are really going all out here!"

"They had a lot of fascinating memorabilia," John said with excitement in his voice. "Now listen to this!" He paused. "One funeral director said you can choose quilt designs for the lining of your casket or you can have a casket chosen with a quilt design on the casket itself! He said the quilt lining patterns are very popular, especially if the person was a quilter."

"There are themes for everything, I suppose. Frankly, it sounds so commercialized, but it's a business like any other. Different strokes for different folks!"

John laughed. "I knew you'd be intrigued by this. I was blown away! I have a lot of reservations about the whole funeral industry, to be honest. I just didn't think they would go as far as offering quilts in their sales pitches, I guess."

"I couldn't agree more! I guess if it makes some families happy, who are we to say anything about it?"

John agreed.

I wasn't going to tell a soul about my experience at Josephine's grave, but this would fit our strange conversation, plus I trusted John's response. When I described in detail what had happened on my visit to the cemetery, he was silent and in disbelief. When I told him the quilt had disappeared once before, he was really shocked.

"Are you journaling any of these happenings?" John

asked.

I could tell he was taking me seriously.

"How does this make you feel?" he asked before I could answer the first question.

"Well, John, from day one I never took any of these happenings personally. They are what they are! There are always lessons to be learned, of course. I should never have taken that quilt out of the closet in the first place. I thought I had learned my lesson about not showing her quilt to anyone."

"It's that simple, huh?" he asked bluntly. "I still think the experience you had with Emily is so amazing and personal. It's a lovely story in itself."

"I agree. I'm having the Friendship Circle here at my house soon, so I hope to ask them some more leading questions."

"Before I forget to tell you, I got a phone call from Carla today," John announced. "She said she just wanted to know if she still had a job here when she completed her treatment."

"I hope you said yes!"

"Of course I did. I want to do something nice for her now, but I'm at a loss. Do you have any ideas?"

"I think I do," I assured him. "She isn't going to feel like cooking, so if you could have something delivered to her, I think she'd appreciate it."

"Good suggestion, and if I'm home I can certainly share some of my own cooking with her, which will be even better," he said, snickering. "Consider it done!"

CHAPTER 33

For only the second time, I spread out the beautiful linen tablecloth and matching napkins I had purchased some time ago from Imy. She had bought the matching set at an estate sale in Borna. I remember her describing the husband's grief when he saw his wife's handiwork being sold to the highest bidder. Imy bought most of the linens and told the husband she would see to it that the handmade pieces went to good homes. She knew mine would be one of those homes.

As I prepared for the Friendship Circle lunch, I knew they would appreciate the delicate fancywork as well. I planned a menu of hot chicken salad, cold pear salad, and popover buns. I knew my friends would expect something with blueberries, so for dessert I made a blueberry cobbler to serve with ice cream. I also had a silver dish of chocolate-covered blueberries which I knew would be a treat for most of them.

Ellen was the first to arrive with the excuse of coming early to help me. She sang praises about the china, silver, and my centerpiece of beautiful greenery. She said the contrast of the vivid greens against my white tablecloth was stunning. Thank goodness. She filled water glasses as I answered the door and welcomed my dear friends. Many of them admired some of the changes I had made to the house since they had been here last.

Since it was customary for the hostess to run the meeting, I passed out a simple agenda. It only took a moment for Charlene to whisper, "Do you mind if I make an announcement about my open house?"

"Oh, yes, we're all dying to know the scoop!" I encouraged her.

Charlene clinked on her glass of tea to get everyone's attention. "Most of you know about my new adventure, but I'd like to invite you all to the Coffee Haus opening next week."

Cheers and clapping followed.

"As per request, Mom's coffee cake will be available. I also want to announce that our friend Betsy here will be working part time for me."

There was more enthusiastic applause as Betsy blushed.

"That's great, Charlene," I stated. "It will be a great addition to Dresden and the whole county. I hope it will encourage others to explore different and exciting business options."

"Kate is right," Ellen chimed in. "That poor little bank has been vacant too long. You'll be going from one bank to another, I guess."

Everyone laughed.

"Here's a toast to the Coffee Haus!" announced Anna.

"Okay, ladies, now for some business to attend to," I stated. "Does anyone have her quilt block ready for the raffle quilt?"

Four ladies raised their hands.

"I will take them anytime."

"I'll be glad to help anyone," offered Ruth Ann.

"Thanks, Ruth Ann," I added.

"Remember the magazine article John Baker wrote on East Perry?" I asked, getting to the next topic.

They nodded.

"Now, John is doing research for an article on quilts and their continued uses until death."

They looked at me strangely.

"I told him I would ask all of you if you knew any stories about quilts and how they had managed to travel in their lifetime."

"I have a rather pleasant story to share that I think some of you know about," voiced Peggy.

Everyone got quiet.

"We like pleasant stories, don't we ladies?" Anna asked. "Tell us, Peggy."

"My husband's family lives in Illinois and they have a cemetery tradition, you might say," she began. "His family has their own cemetery plot right on their farm that's been in the family since the 1800s. They were finally able to get it certified. Every family member is buried there from way back. Since it's the family's responsibility to keep it maintained, they get together twice a year to accomplish that task. The men work on the grounds and the women set up a family member's quilt in a frame under a shade tree so it can be hand quilted on that day. Even the children put in stitches. Of course, there is a huge potluck with the best food ever! You should see all the dishes they serve on a long table they set up using sawhorses. We all look forward to it and it keeps the family close, if you know what I mean."

"Oh, my goodness," voiced Charlene. "What a beautiful sight that must be."

"I think we have some pictures that were taken through the years," Peggy mentioned. "I keep thinking that it would make a great painting. It's like sharing a family reunion with our relatives, both those who are alive and those who have passed on."

"Oh, Peggy, I know John will love hearing this story," I exclaimed. "I can just visualize it!"

"So, do they get very far on the quilt?" asked Ellie.

"You'd be surprised!" responded Peggy. "They try to finish it if the weather allows so it's ready for the binding."

"It seems as if food and stories are frequently shared in a cemetery," I observed. They all nodded in agreement.

CHAPTER 34

We were finishing dessert when Ellen announced that Concordia was planning a special Memorial Day service. "It's usually about those who have served in the armed forces, but this year we decided to honor anyone who belonged to Concordia Church in the past by bringing something of remembrance to share," Ellen explained.

"That's different," Peggy remarked. "Like, someone could bring grandpa's pocket watch?"

Ellen nodded and smiled at the thought.

"Yes, and since we were just talking about quilts in the cemetery, I think I'm going to bring one of my grandmother's quilts," Ellen added.

"That's really nice," Esther responded. "Quilts really represent the lives of so many women."

"Well, thinking outside the box, what if we did a cemetery quilt show?" I threw this idea out and was eager for a reaction.

"Kate, what will you think of next?" Ellen said with a chuckle.

"She is the creative one," Ellie boasted.

"Well, let's hear how she would describe such an event," Ellen challenged.

I had to laugh. They were all waiting to hear what I had in mind. "Okay. Think of all the good quilters that you've had at Concordia all through the years. I know one was Josephine Paulson. I could show her quilt, for example."

"Excuse me, Kate, but your Josephine was hardly a great quiltmaker from what I saw," teased Charlene.

Everyone chuckled.

"Now, let's not be critical of people's level of creativity here," Ellie cautioned. "Please finish, Kate."

"Well, I am visualizing rows of quilts that are shown by each person's gravesite. A family member could tell about the quilt. Or, I could also envision them all in one place, like perhaps on a clothesline. What a tribute to that person it could be and what cool information we might learn!"

"I can picture that," Esther mused. "They hang quilts on buildings in Sisters, Oregon, and they display them on church pews in Perry. So why not honor quilts from the deceased where their bodies currently reside?"

"Their bodies, but not their spirits," Ellen reminded us.

"I'm going to hang a nifty quilt on one of my walls in the coffee shop, by the way," Charlene chimed in. "I love what Ruth Ann did at Christmas with all the Christmas quilts."

"You girls are losing it!" chided Mary Catherine. "I always thought it would be a good idea for Anna to have a quilt show at Saxon Village."

"I have seriously thought about it," Anna replied. "If I added food to that, it could be a great event. Maybe I should just do an exhibit at the Fall Festival."

"Great idea, Anna," I agreed. "Ellen, back to the quilts in the cemetery. You could do this at the same time as the memorial service or when they have one of the church suppers."

By now, side-bar conversations had escalated and no one was listening.

"Kate, I'd better entertain a motion to adjourn before someone wants me to have a quilt show at East Perry Lumber!" Ellen teased.

Despite the clamor, that comment was heard and everyone laughed.

"You sure shook things up," Ruth Ann said to me. "You and your crazy ideas!"

"Yeah, and I'll bet you all wish that crazy gal from up north would go back home!" I said, chuckling.

"Not for a minute!" Ruth Ann objected. "You have fresh eyes that get everyone thinking. Didn't you just love Peggy's story of her in-laws' traditional gravesite visit?"

"I really did. I can't wait to tell John. I'm sure he'll want a photo from her."

"So, have you heard from Clark or Chuck?" Ruth Ann asked, clearly out of the blue.

"No, but I plan to deliver muffins to Chuck and the work crew tomorrow morning," I assured her.

Ruth Ann chuckled and shook her head. "Have you had any word from your aunt about when she'll arrive? I suppose she'll stay with you until she can move in."

"She will," I nodded. "I'm so glad I can help her with this big change. You can imagine how the decorator in me is just dying to get started decorating that place."

It was great to have Ruth Ann stay and help after

everyone left. I had to admit that I loved entertaining. Perhaps I would do more after Aunt Mandy's return. Later in the evening, Ruth Ann's question about Clark made me wonder if I should just call and ask him to dinner. That would be difficult for him to refuse. I wondered if he still fostered hurt by me not responding to his three magic words on New Year's Eve. He did show me affection when I danced with him, so perhaps I should just let sleeping dogs lie, as they say. I dismissed making a call to Clark and decided to email John instead. I couldn't wait to tell him about Peggy's story. He would be delighted.

As I went upstairs to retire for the evening, I was haunted once again about losing Josephine's quilt. Would it eventually show up as it had before? I really hoped that Josephine was not angry with me. To satisfy my bewilderment, I looked again in the hall cabinet and then in the upstairs attic. There were no signs of any quilt. I told her I was so sorry right out loud in the house in hopes that she would believe me.

CHAPTER 35

It was a beautiful spring morning and the builders were making great progress on Aunt Mandy's house. The roofers were ready to start, which was exciting to see. Chuck grinned from ear to ear when I got out of the car with muffins and coffee. Two other helpers nearby also came toward me, knowing there was a treat coming their way.

"This is mighty nice of you, Kate," Chuck said. "Say, are we ever going to meet the owner of this house?"

"Soon," I promised. "Is there anything I can help you with?"

"No, not really," Chuck said, shaking his head. "She has thought through almost every detail, and her architect has been checking with us on a regular basis."

"Oh, that's Wilson," I said with a smile. "I think he has taken a personal interest in my aunt and keeps her better informed than I ever could."

He grinned like he knew what I meant. "I hear you're from South Haven, Michigan," Chuck said, changing the subject abruptly.

I nodded. "Have you been there?"

"I like Michigan a lot, but I haven't been to your hometown. I have relatives in Birmingham."

"Oh, very nice," I responded. My cell phone was ringing. It was Ruth Ann. "Excuse me for a second, Chuck." I answered with a cheery good morning. "What's going on, my friend?"

"I'm calling on behalf of two sisters who are taking a quilting class from me today," she began. "They have decided to stay over for the night and I wondered if you had a room for them."

"Why sure!" I replied. "What time will they arrive?"

"We'll finish here around five," Ruth Ann stated. "They plan on going to Red Creek Winery for dinner tonight, so they will probably want to freshen up before they go."

"That's great. I'll be ready for them." I hung up and told Chuck to enjoy the muffins and bring back the basket as he had done before. I explained that I had unexpected guests coming and he understood. Many of the workers expressed their thanks and waved good-bye as I left.

When I arrived back at the house, Cotton was doing some cleanup work in the yard. "Making those deliveries again, Miss Kate?"

"Yes, and I checked on the house, of course," I said, grinning. "I'm glad you are sprucing up a bit here because I have guests coming at five today. Tell Susie she can come tomorrow and clean if she likes."

"I don't know how to answer for her these days," Cotton said as he stopped working. "She's getting bigger and bigger and complains a lot more. I'll bet that youngin' comes sooner than expected."

"Well, if she can't come, it's okay," I said, feeling badly

for her. "I think I can remember how to change the beds."

Cotton thought that was funny.

Feeling energized about my guests arriving, I got busy planning breakfast for the following morning. After that was done, I planned to pick a few early flowers and ferns for a bouquet for their room. Since no one was staying in the attic suite, I decided to place them there at no extra charge.

As I worked through the day, I thought about Susie having her baby and I still had no gift in mind. Too bad I was too busy to make them a baby quilt. Perhaps Ruth Ann would have one I could purchase from her. I also had to think of a housewarming gift for Charlene's new coffee shop. A plant would be easy to order from a florist in Perry. Someone in our Friendship Circle should open a florist or nursery here in Borna, I concluded.

I was picking flowers for the sisters' room when Chuck pulled in the driveway at the end of his work day. He saw me down on my hands and knees, working away at selecting flowers. Goodness knows what I looked like by this time of day!

"Someday, I'll put something nice in this basket as a returned favor," Chuck joked, putting the red basket on my deck.

"That's not necessary," I said, getting up and brushing my hair back. "It gives me an excuse to bake and check on the house."

He suddenly caught my eye and I could see he seemed more serious. "So, Kate, if you're not seein' anyone, would you have any interest in havin' dinner with some ole guy like me sometime?"

I smiled at him. "Thanks, Chuck, but we are enjoying a

great working relationship and I really don't want to pursue anything in my life romantically right now. Please don't take it personally. You are a very nice and attractive man and certainly not very old."

He grinned as if suddenly embarrassed. "Good enough, Kate." He nodded as he headed toward his truck. "You certainly know where to find me." He winked and drove away.

CHAPTER 36

Kelly and Shelley were redheaded sisters that showed up at five thirty. They appeared to be in their forties and looked very much alike, except that one was very thin. They were excited about their last-minute decision to spend the night in Borna. After they registered, I showed them the guest quilt that Ruth Ann had made for me. They seemed to know all about it.

"I'm so pleased that we get to sign this!" Shelley said, obviously excited. "Isn't she amazingly talented?"

I nodded and smiled. I watched as they carefully wrote their names close to each other. "What kind of class did you have today?" I was sincerely interested in what they had learned.

"Landscapes," Kelly reported. "There were six of us in the class and you should have seen what everyone came up with! Most of us have the embellishing left to complete. It's too bad everyone couldn't have stayed here tonight. It was really so much fun!"

"That sounds like a wonderful day," I agreed.

"Can we go casual tonight at the winery?" Kelly asked, brushing threads off her jeans. "We only have what we are wearing."

"Oh, sure. Everyone is casual there," I assured her. When we got to the attic, they giggled with delight as they saw their accommodations for the night.

"Aren't you glad we didn't bring the guys?" Kelly joked.

"Yeah, Carl never was one for B&Bs in the first place," complained Shelley. "Oh look, there's a robe for each of us so we can sleep in those if we need to."

"I love this bathroom!" Kelly squealed in delight. "Look! Our own bottle of wine. We can just stay here and drink!"

They laughed.

"Don't be silly. I'm starved," admitted Shelley.

We settled on a breakfast time before I left them so they could freshen up. Walking down the stairs, I couldn't help but conclude that it was much more enjoyable having women guests! After they rushed out the door to dinner, I poured a glass of wine and perched myself on the sunporch like I had all last spring and summer. I gazed out of the large windows and saw many shades of green trying to erupt on all the trees behind the house. It was staying light a lot longer now. I thought of Aunt Mandy and decided to give her a call.

"I think you're getting a roof tomorrow," I teased when she answered.

"Oh, I am so excited," she replied. "I hate that I'm not there. I've ordered quite a bit of furniture and accessories online. I have everything on hold while I wait for a closer delivery date. I hope it all works out."

"That's all part of the fun," I assured her. Before I hung up, I told her about the two delightful sisters I had for guests.

"It's so great that you get to meet such interesting people and never even have to leave your home," Aunt Mandy commented.

"Well, some are more interesting than others," I joked. As I nibbled on grapes and cheese, my mind went back to John and his article on quilts. Was I more into this subject than John? I got up and went to the rocking chair to write in the journal that Maggie had given me. I enjoyed writing goofy poetry every now and then. Perhaps if my poem made sense, I would email it to John.

After some time, I came up with a piece that held the simple title of A Quilt. It went like this:

A QUILT made for the living or A QUILT for the dead.
If there is a purpose, let it be said.
A QUILT can bring peace and A QUILT can bring sleep.
It's eternal comfort for those who weep.
A QUILT made in anguish or A QUILT of pure love,
When left behind, it's a gift from above.
I signed it: Your unpoetic neighbor.

CHAPTER 37

I was still awake and accomplishing some work on the computer when the sisters returned from the winery. They were surprised that I hadn't gone to bed and seemed happy to see me.

"Did you have a good time? How was dinner?"

"Wonderful!" Kelly exclaimed, clearly in a good mood. "We had the pork steak special which was delicious. Oh, and we met your friend Ellie!"

"Oh, good! She always appreciates any business I can send her," I added.

"Kate, if you don't mind, I think I would like a cup of coffee," Shelley said as she walked toward the kitchen.

"Of course. It's easy to pop in a cup. There's just about any kind of tea or coffee to choose from." I went to get them coffee mugs. After a few minutes, we were comfortably settled in the living room.

"Oh, it's so nice to be away from the kids," Kelly confessed as she laid her head back.

"I just wish we had more time to stay, plus I could use an

ego boost once in a while," Shelley said with a sheepish grin.

"What do you mean?" I couldn't help but ask.

They giggled.

"We tried to remember the last time we were hit on," Kelly revealed, still giggling. "It felt pretty good!"

Shelley looked embarrassed.

"I'll bet it did," I agreed. "Everyone needs to know, every once in a while, that we are still attractive to someone besides our mates." My comment seemed to surprise them.

"When the bartender found out we were staying here at the guest house, he asked if we had seen any ghosts," Kelly said. "Are we in for some paranormal activity tonight?"

I chuckled. "You're going to be just fine," I said with an assuring smile. "This old house has such a presence in the community, and there have always been ghostly rumors."

"Well, I don't mind a little excitement," Kelly boasted.

"Not me! I've had enough excitement for one evening and I'm ready to turn in," Shelley said as she got out of a relaxed position.

"Okay, sis, lead the way," Kelly said, dutifully following her sister.

"See you at breakfast," I reminded them. Seeing the two of them made me once again wish that I had a sister. I would settle for just having Aunt Mandy here with me. Actually, despite her age, she was quite fun and entertaining. It was getting late, but I was tempted to call Maggie. I missed talking with her. She was just like a sister to me. Carla would certainly be asleep, and if I texted John, he might take my attention the wrong way.

I went to my room and set the alarm for an early breakfast time. I could hear noises and voices above me. I had never noticed that when I had guests up there before. Surprisingly, it sounded like a big-time argument, but I couldn't understand any of the words. Perhaps they were discussing something that happened this evening. I suppose all siblings argue, but they seemed to be so happy and content when they went upstairs. By the time I was ready to crawl under the covers, things had quieted down.

I fell into a deep sleep. Unfortunately, a dream turned into a nightmare as I found myself desperately searching for quilts in a cemetery. I awoke with a start. What on earth was my dream telling me?

The next morning I felt like sharing my dream, but I was sidetracked by the behavior of the sisters at the breakfast table. They definitely were not speaking to each other, so I was the one trying to make a one-sided cheerful conversation. I gave them a generous breakfast of spinach and ham quiche, baby waffles, fresh fruit, and blueberry muffins. Shelley devoured everything I put in front of her, and Kelly just played with her food and kept drinking coffee nonstop.

"I hope you both come back again sometime," I mentioned as they were about to finish.

"Thanks, Kate. This place is lovely and breakfast was amazing," Shelley replied. "I can see why you are known for those blueberry muffins!"

Suddenly, someone knocked fairly hard on the front door. The sisters got up from the table as I went to see who was there. We were all surprised to hear from anyone at this early hour.

CHAPTER 38

Two sheriff's deputies were standing at the front door as the sisters lingered at the kitchen door. Their curiosity caused them to delay their exit rather than excuse themselves and complete their packing before leaving. I supposed that they didn't want to miss any potential excitement.

"Are you Ms. Meyr?" one deputy asked.

I nodded. "Yes. How can I help you?"

"Do you know anyone by the name of Susan Cantwell?"

I had to think for a moment, but the only Susan I knew was the runaway Susan that stayed here quite some time ago. "Possibly. Why?"

"May we come in and have a word with you?" the other deputy asked.

I was puzzled and opened the door to let them in. "Come into the living room where we can sit down," I suggested.

"Susan Cantwell was found deceased in a creek near New Madrid, Missouri," he began. "We have reason to believe she was murdered and then brought to the creek in order to hide her body."

"Murdered?" I said in disbelief.

They nodded.

I thought I was going to faint. "How awful!"

"The reason we are asking about her is because she was sighted in this area," one deputy stated. "Her husband was asking about her around here as well, from what we understand. She was driving a green Volkswagen. Do you know this woman?"

I nodded, feeling great sadness. "Oh, my God, her worst nightmare came true," I said, breaking down in tears.

Neither deputy spoke.

"Susan showed up unannounced and wanted a room for the night."

"What did she tell you?" they asked in unison.

"Well, it didn't take long to realize that she was running away from something," I said between sniffles. "I noticed she had a slight limp and then I saw bruises on her body. I finally just came out and asked her about them, once she felt a little more comfortable with me."

"Did she tell you what happened?"

"She told me about her abusive husband," I revealed. "She said he wanted to kill her. She felt horrible about leaving him because of their young son. I didn't tell a soul she was here. The poor woman was exhausted and frightened. You know, her husband came here not once, but twice, looking for her."

"That's what we've been hearing. Did she tell you where she was going, or had you heard from her?"

"No, she was very careful not to reveal any of that," I assured them. "Truly, I don't think she knew where she was going. I felt so sorry for her. I sent food, clothing, and a quilt with her because I sensed she might be staying in her car most of the time. I did hear from her twice, however. Once was a brief phone call when she was upset one evening, and then another time at Christmas when she dropped off a gift on my front porch with a note that said she was going home to her son for Christmas. I knew that was going to be a risky move for her. I think she mentioned wanting to live in this area someday. I had my doubts as to whether that would really happen."

"We have an arrest warrant out for her husband who is currently a suspect," one of the deputies offered. "Please call us if you see or hear from him."

I was handed a card with their names on it. My mind was thinking of so many things at once. "How did she end up in New Madrid? Did you find her car?"

"That's all we can share with you right now, Ms. Meyr. Just to make sure we have a positive identification, would you look at this photograph of her?"

I nodded as he pulled out a wedding photo of Susan and her husband. "Yes, that's Susan and the man that came by asking about her," I confirmed, my voice sounding weak.

"Thanks so much. We may need your help as this case evolves."

"I'll be happy to help," I assured them as we walked to the front door. "Her husband was a terrible beast."

When they left, I felt as if someone had hit me in the stomach. I had forgotten the sisters were in the kitchen listening to everything. They came toward me with ghastly looks on their faces. I had never known anyone that had been murdered, and it was turning out to be a sickening experience. Susan didn't deserve that. Despite trying to put on a brave front, I felt totally overwhelmed and dropped to my knees, crying for poor Susan and her failed struggle to find safety. Kelly and Shelley were both teary eyed as they tried to embrace me.

"This is horrible, Kate," Kelly comforted me. "Can we do anything to help?"

I was feeling embarrassed by my breakdown. I got up, determined to gather my emotions. "It is horrible and her horrible husband is still out there somewhere," I said angrily. "Thanks so much, but you need to be on your way. I don't want to detain you."

They knew I wasn't going to be fine, but before they left, they brought me a glass of water and I sat on the couch with my head between my hands. I felt badly for the sisters who were exposed to such shocking news after experiencing such a good time while on their quilting getaway.

CHAPTER 39

I sat down in my office chair feeling angry and horrified by the gory news of Susan's death. I had so many questions. I had no question about who did this to her, however. What was she doing in New Madrid? I wondered how long ago it was that they found her body. At least now I knew her last name for the first time.

I gathered my emotions and began a search on the Internet. How could there be so many Susan Cantwells? I finally found a press release about her body being discovered. The article said it appeared to be a homicide and that her body was covered in debris at the creek's edge. She was found by the county's police dogs. It went on to say that New Madrid was the home of her mother, Laura Montgomery, with whom Susan Cantwell had been visiting for a few days before her death.

I wrote down her mother's name so I could check for a phone number. I was pleased to find one listed under her name, so I added the number next to her name. I closed my laptop and immediately made a call to Mrs. Montgomery.

Her voice mailbox was full. I could only imagine how many calls she must be getting from the media, plus family and friends. I made a mental note to continue trying to contact Mrs. Montgomery.

The only person I remembered telling about Susan was Aunt Mandy. I felt I wanted to talk with someone about this, but wondered if I would upset her horribly. Somehow, I had to put this news aside and get on with my day. Charlene's open house was today, and that would be a good distraction for me.

I heard a knock at the back door. It was Susie and Cotton. I had forgotten that I had suggested that Susie clean today.

"You're expecting me today, aren't you Miss Kate?" Susie asked. "Are you okay? You look like you're upset."

There was no doubt that it had to show on me. Their timing was such that I simply had to share what was on my mind. We sat at the kitchen counter and I told them about Susan.

"I remember the lady in the green Volkswagen," Cotton recalled. "I also remember you were pretty closed mouthed about her visit. I can understand that now, and it was mighty nice of you to help her."

"She was so happy when I talked to her last. She left me a fresh pineapple in a basket at Christmas. Her note said it was a sign of hospitality, which was something she felt that I extended to her. It said she was going to face up to her husband in hopes of seeing her son for Christmas. I wonder if she got to do that."

"There are so many nice folks that die from mean people," Susie murmured.

"So he's on the run, it sounds like," Cotton confirmed.

I nodded. "I identified a photo of the two of them, which happened to be their wedding photo. Susie, are you sure you're up to working today? How are you feeling?"

"Oh, I might growl going up those stairs, but otherwise I can do most everything," she claimed. "This baby is so much more active than Amy Sue was."

"Is there anything you need for the baby?" I asked, hoping for a suggestion.

"You've done enough for us, giving us that new truck and all," Susie replied. "When they're little, they don't need much; and if it's a girl, we'll have a lot from Amy Sue that we can use. It's when they grow up that they get expensive."

"Please help yourselves to some of this breakfast. I always make too much, and I didn't have a chance to clean up much before the deputies knocked at my door. I should get ready for Charlene's open house in the old Dresden bank. Did you both know about that?"

They nodded and smiled.

"My mom told us about it," Susie mentioned. "That sounds so nice. I'll get everything cleaned up, Miss Kate. And don't worry. I sure feel bad you got this terrible news!"

I left them to eat their breakfast and I went to my office to try calling Susan's mother once again. Nothing had changed so I started to go up the stairs. As I looked at the quilt across the hall, I remembered how I couldn't get Susan to sign the quilt when she was here. I no longer had to keep that a secret, so I signed her name, and pictured her sweet face.

CHAPTER 40

The old bank in Dresden was drawing a large crowd outside. I had to park a good way down the road. I met up with Esther who had managed to snag a parking space near me. We commented that this gave every indication that Charlene's business would be a huge success.

When we finally managed to squeeze into the tiny place, I looked up to see a menu board of yummy coffee and pastry choices. East Perry County was joining the trendy hip generation that loved their coffeehouses. Charlene waved to me from behind the counter. Besides Betsy, Mary Catherine was helping, as well as some family members. The drinks were complimentary, so everyone seemed to be ordering fancy drinks that took extra time to make. It didn't take long for Esther and me to become separated from one another in the crowd.

"Hey!" Gerard's voice greeted me when I accidently bumped into him.

"Oh, I'm sorry, Gerard," I said with a chuckle. "This is the place to be, isn't it?"

"It's just hunky dory! Say, Kate, you're on my list to call

about a surprise party for Sharla Lee."

"How fun! It's sweet of you to do that. She is very deserving, and I'm glad you thought of me. I'll be happy to come!"

"I just hope we can pull it off so it's a surprise," he added, his eyes twinkling at the thought.

"That may be difficult," I agreed. "Can I do anything to help?"

"I think we're good, and we're having it at Ruth Ann's place so she'll be taking care of the food."

"Marvelous!" I responded. "How are you going to get her there?"

"She thinks it's going to be a birthday party for Carolyn, our part-time archivist," he revealed. "Have you met her?"

"No, but I'm looking forward to it." The line had shifted and it was my turn to order.

"What can I get you?" offered Mary Catherine.

"How about a mocha frappuccino?"

"You've got it!" she nodded. "Your plant is beautiful, by the way." She pointed to a windowsill that held a planter with a combination of red, white, and blue flowers.

"Thanks, Kate!" Charlene edged her way closer to me. "That was mighty sweet of you."

"The place looks great!"

She gave me a big smile as a thank you and returned to her work.

There were very few tables and chairs in the place and they were all filled, leaving standing room only. When I received my drink, I ordered some cherry crumb coffee cake to take home. I wasn't in the mood to socialize, so I said good-bye to some of the Friendship girls and made my way to the car. I was glad I had shown my support but I had other stresses filling my mind.

When I got home, Susie and Cotton had gone. I headed straight to my office where I had Susan's mother's phone number written down. I tried calling once again. This time, I was able to leave a message. I began, "Mrs. Montgomery, my name is Kate Meyr. I met your daughter some time ago when she stayed with me at my guest house. She told me about running away from her husband. I just heard about her terrible death from two deputies that came by the house. I am so sorry to hear this news. Please call me back at this number. I would really like to hear from you. Again, I am so sorry." The line went silent, indicating that my recording time was up.

I went to the kitchen and saw a note left behind from Susie. It read: *I had to leave early because I started to get contractions. I finished the attic but didn't get to your bedroom. Sorry, Susie.*

Contractions? That would mean the baby was on its way! I hoped that climbing those stairs didn't cause her to go into labor. I immediately called Cotton. He didn't answer. That wasn't like him. Did that mean he was at the hospital? Why was everything happening today?

As I sat down to think about Susie and Cotton, I thought about something Susie had said this morning. She mentioned that when babies are little they are more affordable, but not later as they grew. It was the perfect hint! I decided to give them a gift for the future. I would go to Dresden Bank and get Amy Sue and the new baby savings bonds. What a splendid idea!

CHAPTER 41

It was midnight and I was in a very deep sleep when my cell rang on my bedside table. I jumped and sat up as fast as I could.

"Kate, this is Cotton," he announced with excitement. "Carly Mae was born about fifteen minutes ago!"

"Congratulations!" I said, my voice pretty groggy. "That is great! How much did she weigh?"

"Seven pounds and eight ounces," he said proudly.

"How is Susie?" I asked, finally awake.

"She's just dandy!" he answered happily. "She was quite a trooper! This little gal came much quicker than her big sister."

"Please give her my love and tell her to come back to work whenever she's ready," I instructed. I was wide awake now and feeling happy for my little family. I got up and went downstairs to have a drink and snack before going back to sleep. However, I went straight into my office to check emails and voice mails first. Why was I always getting so many inquiries regarding rooms that translated into so few bookings? Ellen thought it was my location in this small town.

I was surprised to see an email from Carla. She claimed she was very tired from her radiation treatments but could not complain since she knew it was temporary. She mentioned that Maggie and John were sending food, so that was nice to hear.

Another surprise was an email from Max Harris, the older man that I went out with on a blind date in South Haven. He said he finally purchased a condo on the lake and hoped I would come to see it when I returned to that area. It was nice to be thought of, but Max needed a woman more his age and I didn't think it wise to encourage any kind of friendship. It did make me wonder when I would get back to South Haven again. The blueberry festival was always in August. If I went then, I could still be back in time for the East Perry Fair in September.

Since Maggie was in bed, I decided to email Maggie and pester her about the Beach Quilters coming to visit Borna. No matter how many would come, I would make it work somehow.

I was yawning heavily by now, so having a snack was out of the question. I looked down and saw where I had scribbled Susan's mother's phone number. It made me wonder if she would ever return my call. The whole thing was sickening to think about. Making myself concentrate on something else, I quickly responded to Carla's email and then closed my laptop.

I returned to bed hoping sleep would come fast, but it didn't. I wondered where Josephine's quilt had gone. I also couldn't ignore a gruesome mental picture of Susan sprawled lifeless in a creek. Why did awful thoughts often surface at night? I rolled over, trying very hard to think of pleasant things like Cotton and Susie's new baby, Charlene's new coffee shop, and Aunt Mandy's upcoming move to Borna. I could also include Clark and John, two friends who certainly could bring a smile to my face. Baking muffins was also a pleasant thought. Should I take some to the work crew tomorrow? I had to be careful not to give Chuck the wrong impression about my intentions. When I had turned down his invitation to go out, he gave me a wink right after I refused his offer. Men have such egos. They just can't imagine anyone refusing them.

Did I have to say my prayers all over again to get myself settled down enough to go to sleep? I put my pillow over my head and created total darkness. Sleep finally found its way into my bed.

CHAPTER 42

A week passed before I went to visit little Carly Mae. When I arrived, Susie was nursing her. She was a tiny, sweet thing. I had not seen a baby this small in a long time. She was the spitting image of her sister, Amy Sue. I was so out of the loop on motherhood that I wasn't certain mothers still nursed their babies anymore!

It was my first visit to their modest ranch-style house located on a gravel road. Despite Susie's additional duties with the new baby, her little place was quite immaculate. My gifts of the savings bonds were quite a surprise and were very well received. I was beginning to realize how much this little family depended on me. I depended on them as well. When Cotton walked me out to my car, he was curious to know if I had heard anything regarding Susan's murder. I told him I planned to keep trying to call her mother.

"I don't think Susan's husband is foolish enough to come around here again, but you must be very observant," Cotton warned me. "I know you have alarms and such, but your living alone is a worry to Susie and me, Miss Kate."

"I just want to talk to her mother and see that horrible man behind bars," I said, frustrated.

"You leave it up to the law," Cotton advised. "They have ways of smelling the tracks of a guy like that."

"I also want to know what happened to her son," I added. "She wouldn't have gone back at all if it hadn't been for him."

Cotton shook his head and we said our good-byes. I went on my way to Harold's Hardware Store to get some annuals to plant for the blooming season ahead and to purchase a couple of new cookie sheets to add to my inventory.

It didn't take Harold long to ask whether I was going to the big surprise birthday party for Sharla Lee. Of course, Harold would know about the party! Harold and Milly were invited to everything in town because they knew everybody.

"What in the world do I give someone like that?" I asked, hoping for a suggestion.

Harold thought for a minute while tapping his finger on his chin. "We got these nice lanterns in last week," he announced, walking down the aisle. "Milly took a couple of these for our front porch. We've got lots of nice colors to choose from, too. She may like one of those."

The display was eye-catching, and I knew Sharla Lee would like the brightest one Harold had. "Oh, this bright yellow one looks like her," I decided. "I think I'll take this black one for my front porch. Thanks, Harold! This will do nicely."

Harold gave me a big grin of satisfaction. Maggie

called while I was in line checking out.

"What's up?" I answered. "I hope you have good news for me regarding the Beach Quilters!"

"What is your occupancy on Memorial Day weekend?" Maggie inquired.

"Get real. I don't have a soul booked! Are you kidding?" I answered, my voice heavy with sarcasm. "Can you come then?"

"It's the best I can do!" she stated. "There may be only four of us with it being that weekend."

"That's wonderful!" I responded. "I'll take it!"

"Since we need a day to drive both ways, we'll arrive Friday night," Maggie informed me. "We'll spend most of the day at Ruth Ann's studio, from the way it sounds. On Sunday, we can sightsee and go home on Monday morning. I already checked with Ruth Ann about the date, and she's quite excited. Are you sure you have room for whoever decides to come?"

"I will sleep in a tent if I have to," I teased. "Everyone is welcome!"

Hearing this news was so energizing. It would give me something happy to look forward to. Somehow I had to include my Friendship Circle in on their visit, so perhaps a cocktail party on Saturday night would work. Maggie didn't mention including Carla, so I would have to check on that possibility later.

By the end of the day, I was mentally and physically exhausted. I was relaxing on my sunporch with a glass of wine when I had a brilliant, yet risky, idea. Why don't I ask Clark to go to Sharla Lee's party with me? He obviously had no plans to make the next move regarding our friendship, so I felt I had nothing to lose. What would I say to him? A text from John chimed in at that very moment. It read:

> So what's up with you, neighbor? Missing you!

I smiled. I did kind of miss him. Long distance relationships weren't easy, and I was finding that out with just my good friends in South Haven. Thinking of both Clark and John, I decided I was too tired to communicate with either one of them tonight!

CHAPTER 43

The next morning as I sat on the porch drinking coffee, I revisited the idea of asking Clark to Sharla Lee's party and decided to do it. I dialed his number and it went to voice mail. Maybe he is out of town. I left a message, saying simply that I had a request and left it at that. I decided to make a blueberry crumb coffee cake, something I hadn't made in a long time. The workers might enjoy a change from the muffins. While I let it bake, I showered and changed. As I got out of the shower and put on my robe, my cell phone rang. I hoped it would be Clark.

"Kate Meyr?" an older woman's voice asked.

"Yes, speaking," I answered.

"This is Susan's mother. Thank you so much for calling earlier."

"Thank you for calling back," I responded. "I was devastated to hear about Susan's death."

"It's been something awful," she answered, her voice shaky. "I had no idea she was in such danger. I'm sure she didn't want me to worry. When I didn't hear from her, I figured there was a good reason. When she came here for Christmas, she told me about staying with you and how kind you were to her."

"She was with you at Christmas?" I repeated.

"Yes, she was hoping it would be a way for her to see Devin, her son," she said, sounding as if she were about to cry.

"Did she get to see him?"

"No. He was out of state with Harper's parents," she said sadly.

"Harper is her husband that was looking for her?" I asked as I pictured him.

"Yes. Even with his son away, I'm certain he never stopped snooping around here in case she'd come home," she explained. "She went to the grocery store one day for me and never returned." She began to weep.

I hated upsetting her. Not knowing quite what to do, I waited for her to continue.

"They didn't find her until three days later. She loved playing in that creek as a child."

"Oh, how horrible," I responded. Tears flowed down my cheeks.

"We gave her a decent burial. He never showed up and neither did her son. It was the saddest thing. I couldn't have gone through it without the whole town's support. I thought of you and wondered how I could ever thank you for helping her. She loved that quilt you gave her and clung to it like a child does with their blanket. She said it gave her courage to be independent like you."

"Oh, I'm so glad to hear that," I said, feeling some sense of relief.

"I hope you won't be offended, but we wrapped Susan in that quilt before she was buried," she said softly. "She would have wanted it with her. Her body was so badly damaged that we had a closed casket for everyone except the family. That quilt made her look at peace."

I couldn't believe what I just heard. I broke down and cried into the phone. "Oh, I can't believe it would mean that much," I stumbled over my words. "I feel honored."

"I just hope and pray they capture this nasty human being soon and make him pay for this," she said sternly before we hung up.

I closed our conversation by saying I would pray for her and for little Devin.

I stretched back on my bed feeling complete sadness. Picturing Susan wrapped in my quilt was more than I could bear, but a much more pleasant sight than picturing her dead body in the creek. I had to believe that there would be justice in this whole matter. This entire story was so bizarre! Could I have made a difference in the outcome of things? Should I have insisted that she report her abuse? How do you force someone to do that?

I had forgotten about the coffee cake and I smelled the burning aroma all the way up the stairs. I rushed downstairs to retrieve it from the oven and opened the back door to let in some fresh air. It was the first time I could remember any of my baked delights ever going in the trash.

I poured myself some more coffee and realized I had lost my appetite after talking to Susan's mother. The news of my quilt being underground made me think of John. I couldn't wait to share this strange news with him. I picked up the phone and waited patiently for him to answer. I was about to hang up when I heard his voice.

"Kate, sorry. I just got out of the shower," he explained. "This is a nice surprise."

"Is this a bad time to talk?" My voice carried a serious tone.

"Not if you don't mind talking to me in the nude," he teased.

"Oh, John, put on your robe so you don't embarrass me," I responded.

He laughed. "Hey, go ahead. I'm all ears," he said seriously. "Is everything okay?"

I wasn't sure where to start because I had never told John about Susan's visit. To his credit, he didn't interrupt me and seemed to pick up on the seriousness of the situation. When I told him the gory details of the discovery of her body, I knew he was appalled.

"Oh, Kate. How sad for those who knew her and tried to help her," he replied. "I'm always amazed at these abuse stories and how hard it is to help someone. Are you okay?"

"Never mind me, but the reason I'm sharing this with you is because that quilt I gave her went in the coffin with her," I revealed.

"Are you serious?"

"Her mother said she clung to it because it gave her courage to hopefully be independent one day," I explained. "They just knew she would want it with her. She had a closed casket because of the condition of her body."

"Man, oh man, Kate. That is quite a tribute to you, my dear," John complimented me. "What you gave her was priceless and it gave her hope. I would love to use that story, with your permission, of course."

"I think it's so revealing about what quilts end up meaning to people," I said thoughtfully. "You never know where they'll end up in their lifespan and the meaning and comfort they may provide. Yes, I think you should use it."

We talked another fifteen minutes or so. He also shared that he had a call from Carla thanking him for the delivered food, and she asked him if she could return as soon as her treatments were over. He was pleased to hear from her and encouraged her to come back to work as soon as she felt able. It was nice to end our conversation with some good news.

CHAPTER 44

The morning of Sharla Lee's party arrived and made me rethink my invitation to Clark. Should I have just left well enough alone? I jumped when I heard my cell phone ring.

"Kate," Clark's said, "I was just making some scrambled eggs and found myself wishing I had a couple of those muffins that you make."

I smiled. "Well, it's nice to be missed for something, I suppose," I responded. "I called because I was kind of missing you and wondered if you'd go with me to a birthday party tonight at Ruth Ann's place." There was a lengthy silence on the other end. "I know it's kind of last minute."

"Is this a date?" he questioned. "Isn't that the question you asked me once? I guess I'd better ask who is having a birthday."

"It's a surprise birthday party for Sharla Lee from the museum," I answered. "Gerard and the staff are giving it, so it should be fun."

"You know I'm not much for crowds and parties," he said, sounding grumpy.

"I know, but you'll know everyone there. Plus, I thought we'd enjoy each other's company," I explained. Another pause. Was I begging him to go out with me?

"I can't figure you out, woman! And you say it's tonight? What took you so long to ask?"

"You!" I barked, feeling exasperated at his chiding. "I knew you would have this response. You're not going to hurt my feelings if you don't want to go."

"What time should I pick you up?" he asked, surprising me entirely.

"Good!" I answered, although after I said it I realized it didn't really match anything he had said. "How about seven?" I said, hoping to right my end of the conversation.

"Casual?"

"Clean and Clark McFadden style," I joked.

When I hung up, I still wasn't convinced it was a good idea. What would he be like in a party atmosphere? Even though he showed up at my open house, he left as fast as he could.

I spent the rest of the afternoon planning menus and making a list of things that would be needed when the Beach Quilters arrived. I sent an email to all the Friendship Circle members inviting them to a cocktail party that Saturday night. Cocktail parties weren't done in East Perry, so if folks were invited to your home that time of day, you'd better have a buffet of food they could call supper.

Getting ready that evening, I wanted to step out of my everyday jeans and put on something feminine and sexy that would put me in a party mood. These kinds of parties didn't happen often. I decided on a simple black dress that accentuated my curves. I chose only simple earrings, knowing

I would be with Mr. Casual.

When I came downstairs to wait for Clark, I decided to have a sip or two of wine to calm my nerves. I was pouring it into my glass when Clark arrived. He had arrived a little early. He came to the back door and what I saw was very pleasing. He had on a stylish sport coat that I had never seen him wear before.

"Hello, handsome!" I greeted as he walked in.

He responded with an appreciative whistle when he checked me out. "Hot damn!" Clark said, coming closer. "You look pretty sexy in that dress. I don't think I've seen you in anything but jeans for a long time."

I laughed, feeling a mixture of flattery and embarrassment.

"I'll have what you're having." He looked at my wine glass.

"I'm really looking forward to tonight," I said as I poured his wine. We took our glasses and I led us out to the sunporch.

"Yeah, if we weren't so hungry, we could just sit here the rest of the night," he teased.

"Oh, no! I'm not missing a party in Borna! They are truly a rarity!" I stated firmly, knowing he was teasing. "Harold and Milly will be there, and I bought a nifty lantern for Sharla Lee from his store." I proudly picked it up and swung it gently. It was adorned with a single big red bow on the top.

"It's bright enough, so Sharla Lee should like it," he said, grinning. "Say, how's the house coming along down the road?"

"The drywall was going up the last time I looked," I reported. "If Aunt Mandy doesn't arrive soon, the house will be done before she gets here. I hope she isn't going to change her mind."

"Is my buddy Chuck still hitting on you?" he asked, catching me off guard.

I smiled and shook my head. "I like him," I offered. "There are some things about him that remind me a lot of you."

Clark gave me a strange look.

"We should go, don't you think?"

"Well, I kind of liked having you to myself for a while, to be honest with you," he flirted.

So, Mr. McFadden's in a good mood! Feeling relaxed and attractive, I leaned closer to Clark and kissed him on the cheek to thank him for the sweet remark. As we stood to make our exit, I couldn't help but feel flattered seeing the boyish grin on his face.

CHAPTER 45

Lueder's Hall had been transformed into a party extravaganza with streamers and balloons of every bright color hanging from the ceiling. Everyone was awaiting Sharla Lee's arrival, and Gerard kept a watchful eye out as he waited for her car to arrive. To my surprise, a nice little string orchestra was playing in the background and professional waiters dressed in black and white tuxes were taking drink orders. It reminded me of New Year's Eve at the South Haven Country Club. Whoever planned this event knew Sharla Lee wasn't the honky-tonk style of person that preferred country music and cowboy boots.

In the center of the room, a giant round cake was decorated with "Happy Birthday Sharla Lee" in the center. Around the sides were the words joyful, giving, dear friend, loving, and happy. Each of those words described her so well. It was a great idea to express all those attributes on the cake!

Minutes after our arrival, Gerard excitedly retrieved the microphone and announced that the guest of honor was getting out of her car. The drummer played a light drum roll as she entered. When she saw all of us, we started singing Happy Birthday. She arrived with her loving, sweet husband who nearly had to hold her up when she realized the party was for her and not Carolyn, as she had been told. Carolyn greeted her and took the gift Sharla Lee had brought and gave her a hug in return. As Sharla Lee looked around the room, tears trickled down her cheeks. Just knowing Sharla Lee a short time, I already knew it didn't take much to create tears in her eyes. I looked up at Clark and saw that even he was touched by her emotions. I took his hand and gave it a squeeze, feeling so glad he was with me. When Sharla Lee came our way, she hugged each of us, just as she did everyone else in the room.

"I can't believe all this," she gushed. "Thank you so much for coming!"

We assured her that the pleasure was all ours. As we mingled in the crowd and enjoyed an amazing German buffet, I saw a side of Clark I had never seen before. He was talkative as well as charming, which I found very appealing. Finally, my date for the evening guided me to the dance floor. I welcomed the wonderful beat of the music and was amused to see townspeople dancing that I would not have imagined would dance. When we walked back to our table, I saw Gerard speaking to everyone, trying to be a good host. I impulsively grabbed his arm and drew him onto the dance floor. He blushed and didn't resist. To his credit, he kept the time of the music and even moved his feet. I had loved this guy from the very first time I met him at the museum. I fondly remembered his open heart and generous laughter that made me feel so welcome when I first arrived in Borna. When he seemed to be out of breath, I led him back to his table and he gave me an affectionate hug of thanks.

Clark had been watching us dance and handed me a drink when I returned to him. "I do love watching you move," he teased. "I don't think many men can keep up with you."

Watching Sharla Lee enjoy being Queen for a Night gave me chills. Every community needs a Sharla Lee. Her love and enthusiasm as she promoted East Perry bubbled over each and every day. It was nice to see her appreciated.

Clark and I left as many were still having a wonderful time. When we arrived in my driveway, Clark exited his car and walked me to the door. When we got in the kitchen, we joked about having had too much to drink.

"I don't want you driving home," I said, looking into his eyes. "Stay here, please."

He looked at me, rather surprised at my request. "Stay here or stay with you?" he asked, requiring more specific information.

"I don't know what you mean!" I said, skirting the question.

"You know folks will talk if they see my car here overnight," he said, backing away from me.

"It wouldn't be the first time," I shot back, sending a smile his way.

Moving right in front of me, Clark took me in his arms and gave me one of those passionate kisses like he gave me in front of Marv's place one night. I relaxed and fell into his embrace. I caressed the back of his neck and then kissed his closely-shaven cheeks.

"You feel so good," Clark whispered in my ear as my body melted into his.

He leaned me against the kitchen counter as he reached

for the back of my dress, pulling at the zipper. My shoulders were exposed and I didn't care. His lips moved down my neck, taking him to the front of my black lace bra. It felt so good to be this close to a man again. I felt brave and was enjoying each little pang of excitement.

Clark knew his way to the first-floor bedroom and led the way like a man in charge of his destiny. I knew I was vulnerable, but I also knew Clark loved me. It was my feelings I had to control. One touch led to another and I encouraged him each step of the way. I had fantasized about what sex would be like with this handsome man many times before, so I gave myself permission to enjoy his gentle affection. Neither of us uttered words of love. We were just enjoying the physical attraction and desire of each other. It was a perfect ending to a lovely evening. Neither of us worried about what the morning would bring.

CHAPTER 46

I made sure I was the first one to sneak out of the bedroom the next morning. Wearing only Clark's shirt, I began cracking eggs and stirring dough for blueberry muffins. I was wearing a grin, knowing our relationship would never be the same after last night. For the first time, I felt like a liberated woman.

It was Sunday and I had every intention of making it to church on time. I had hoped that Clark would be up by now, but when I checked in on him, he was sound asleep. I let his shirt drop to the floor and went upstairs to shower and change. I was also hoping Clark would wake up in a very good mood. When I returned downstairs, he was groomed, bright eyed, and wearing a big grin.

"Forgive me if I look like I just conquered the world," he teased.

I laughed.

"I would have preferred to have woken up with you next to me, but the smell of muffins and seeing you smile is the next best thing."

We sat at the dining room table and ate the breakfast I had prepared. He knew I wanted to leave soon, so he helped me clean up the kitchen, which was very endearing. When we went to the door, he pulled me close and thanked me for an incredible evening. I accepted his kiss and nodded as he left.

When I arrived at church, I spied Ruth Ann just as she was about to sit down. I made my way to her pew and seated myself beside her. "How can you be at church today with all you had to do last night?" I asked, curious.

"Hey, I'm good," she smiled. "Gerard and the crew did an amazing job of cleaning up. The place looks better than it did when they arrived. It was late, but boy do I wish everyone was like that! You wouldn't believe the condition some of these weddings leave the place in."

"We had such a good time," I reported with a whisper, just as the service began. After the service I wish I could've reported what the pastor's message was about, but I kept replaying the evening with Clark over and over in my mind.

Ellen was glad to see me at church, as I knew she would be. She knew who attended church in town and who didn't. Concordia was near and dear to her heart. She did everything in her power to make it survive and compete with the other county churches. When we filed out to the vestibule, I told Ellen about the cocktail party I was having for the Beach Quilters. She was thrilled and hoped all the Beach Quilters could come to the church's memorial service on Monday, but I told her they would be leaving to return home that day.

Ruth Ann and I decided to go to Marv's for his Sunday special, which usually featured fried chicken or chicken and dumplings. We were in good moods as we chatted. During lunch, I was surprised to get a phone call from Aunt Mandy.

"I have good news," she announced. "I'll be there to help you celebrate your birthday! Everything's arranged with the movers. Wilson thought the house may just be far enough along that I won't have to put anything in storage."

"That's wonderful!" I responded. "Yes, they are moving quickly. I'll check on the workers tomorrow. Is there anything I can do for you in the meantime?"

"I don't think so. Wilson's been a dear. You'd think it was his house he was moving into."

I knew that probably wasn't too far from the truth. Obviously, their relationship was blossoming. I should be relieved. "It will be great having you here for my birthday. I can't wait! Maggie and the quilters will be coming next week. I wish Maggie could still be here since we always celebrated our birthdays together." We visited a bit more, sharing details as we giggled with excitement. Ruth Ann knew what was happening just by listening to my side of the conversation. When I hung up, I told Ruth Ann that I was a little nervous about having the big city quilters arrive in our little town. I told her they were all advanced quilters, unlike me.

"I know. It makes me nervous, too," Ruth Ann shared. "Thank goodness they are all machine quilters, which is a common link between all of us. You can only do so much in one day, so I want to make it worth their trip."

I assured her they would go nuts seeing her studio and fabric stash.

CHAPTER 47

The day finally arrived when I would get to see Maggie and my former quilting buddies from South Haven. It was a smaller group than I had hoped, but I was happy to see Emily, Marilee, and Cornelia come with Maggie. I was surprised that Cornelia would leave her quilt shop, but there was no doubt that she needed a little vacation.

I booked Cornelia in The Study, Emily and Marilee in the upstairs suite, and Maggie in the Wildflower Room across from my bedroom. I didn't have Susie to help me prepare for their visit, but Susie assured me that she would be here after they left to help me clean up. I think the whole town knew about my visitors arriving from Michigan. Clark and John had both wished me a fun weekend.

It was around eight when Maggie's SUV pulled into the driveway. I flew out the back door to greet them. Maggie had a darker color put on her hair and looked a little heavier than when I saw her last. Cornelia looked the same, and Marilee and Emily looked too gorgeous to be my friends. After I gave everyone a hug, they eagerly went inside to check out the guest house. There were lots of compliments as they roamed the downstairs.

"I tried to tell them about everything, including your guest quilt in the entry hall," Maggie shared.

"Let's see, let's see!" cried Marilee, and they all headed in that direction. They didn't waste any time applying their own signatures and followed that by signing the guest book. There wasn't a registration process because they were my personal friends.

"We brought you some treats!" Maggie declared.

"Wow, thanks!" I said with excitement when I saw the basket of goodies. We went to the living room so I could explore the contents of the basket. I pulled out jars of blueberry jam, wine, and candy from Maggie, all of which she knew were favorites of mine. Cornelia brought me a pack of polka dot fabric that she had just received in the shop. It made me realize that I hadn't done anything with the last pack I purchased from her store. Marilee brought me a darling blue South Haven sweatshirt that came from her parents' shop called The Harbor. I loved all the pricey things at that shop! Emily made me a clever tote bag that had lots of colorful polka dots on it.

"This is like Christmas!" I gushed. "Thanks so much!"

"Thank you for having us," Emily said, excited to have finally arrived.

"Let me show you to your rooms, and then we'll have a little wine out on the deck," I suggested. "It's such a lovely evening."

"I'm ready!" Emily called out. "I'm dying to see Josephine's attic. I've heard so much about it."

"I'm glad I'm close to the kitchen. Plus, I'm scared of

heights," voiced Cornelia.

Everyone laughed. A few minutes later, it seemed that everyone was happy with their accommodations. Even though they were exhausted, we enjoyed some appetizers and wine on the deck.

"It's so dark out here," observed Cornelia. "I didn't know it could be this quiet anywhere."

"Yes, it took me a while to get used to it," I admitted. "I can sometimes hear the quietness, if that makes any sense."

My friends had so many questions about my new lifestyle, including some about my love life.

"Maggie told us that John Baker has a thing for you," teased Emily. "He's quite a looker. I met him at a friend's wedding. I have seen his articles here and there. He has to be an interesting kind of guy."

"We're just friendly neighbors," I explained, feeling a slight blush come over me. "He needs a pretty young thing in his life."

"Right, girlfriend," Maggie said sarcastically. "She also has a looker here in Borna. I've met him, and he looks just like Sean Connery." Cornelia seemed to be the only one who recognized the name. I guess it dated Maggie and me.

We sat on the deck until one in the morning, catching up with one another. Cornelia was silent about her shaky marriage and I didn't want to pry. I kept reminding them they all needed to be at Ruth Ann's studio by nine in the morning. The wine had slowed them down to a snail's pace. It was obvious they were officially on vacation.

CHAPTER 48

Everyone was pretty quiet and hung over the next morning at the breakfast table. They admired all the choices I had prepared for them, but there were not many takers. They did, however, make an exception for the blueberry muffins.

Cornelia seemed to be the most focused on Ruth Ann's class. She also took on the leadership of the group as she reminded them of the time and what to bring with them. I told them I had invited my Friendship Circle for cocktails that evening. I could tell they were too tired to even think that far ahead. Ellie was going to bring a few appetizers from the winery to accompany my beef and ham roll ups. I knew this would be everyone's dinner, so I wanted to have plenty of food on hand. I baked a cheesecake and some chocolate delights for dessert. I would also have a tray of fruit and cheese. I received an RSVP from every single member of our Friendship Circle. It was obvious that they were anxious to meet my northern quilting friends.

I used the antique tablecloth I had purchased from Imy

some time back. For my centerpiece, I picked some early blooms and arranged them with the wild ferns that grew so liberally under my oak tree. I wanted Ellen's approval, for sure! I didn't have the waiters that I had when I hosted my open house, so everyone would just need to help themselves.

At four, the Beach Quilters trickled in and went upstairs to change. I was anxious to hear about their class, but I knew that it would have to wait. Ellie was the first to arrive and offered to help me with everyone getting their first drink. She was definitely up for the job. I had been so busy lately that Ellie and I had visited very little. Of course, I wondered if she was still seeing Carson.

Maggie was a dear, making all the introductions. She was the socialite of South Haven, there was no question about that! There was instant gaiety as soon as everyone met. The Beach Quilters were very hungry, so they were the first to fill their plates. Maggie was looking forward to meeting Esther, who had cut my hair. All she could picture regarding Esther was the yellow mailbox and the chickens in her yard.

The Friendship Circle members had many questions about what it was like to live in South Haven. Maggie made a generous offer for everyone to stay with her if they ever made it to South Haven. Ellie said I should just ask John to move out of his downstairs condo for their visit so we could have the whole building. That would be a party! Everyone loved that idea. By eight, everyone had left except Ellie. She helped me clean up, even though my guests had offered. She was a gem and knew how important this occasion was to me.

Before everyone went to bed, we briefly planned the next day. I told them to sleep in and we'd have a leisurely, fun day. I went to bed with a great sense of accomplishment. I had my very best friend sleeping right across the hall from me.

Before I could go to sleep, I thought of Clark and John. I wondered what they were up to. Was Clark rethinking his overnight stay? How long would it be before I would see him again? I hoped Josephine would be kind to my guests while they were here. Emily and Marilee had asked more than once about any ghosts in the house. Maggie wanted to see Josephine's gravestone, so that was going to be our first stop tomorrow. It would be on our way to see Anna at the Saxon Village.

Every now and then, there was excessive laughter from the attic. It sounded like a pajama party was going on up there! I wanted everyone to have a good time. I had the best of friends from both of my worlds right now, and I could rest knowing that, for tonight, my heart was full.

CHAPTER 49

The next morning, Maggie was the first to arrive at the breakfast table. She complimented me on the great weekend she'd had so far. "Did you hear them giggling in the attic last night?" Maggie asked, smiling as she remembered.

"I did," I said, nodding. "What do you suppose was going on?" Before Maggie could respond, we were interrupted by the other three dragging their bodies to the table.

"So, did you get some sleep?" I asked as I poured their coffee. Marilee and Emily exchanged a knowing look.

"Well, I finally went to sleep after getting the bejeebies scared out of me," Emily said, shaking her head.

We responded with silence, waiting for an explanation.

"We got out the Ouija board we brought along," Marilee admitted, looking a bit sheepish. "Now understand, we'd both had a little too much to drink, but the board was definitely talking to us."

Oh, no. I was almost afraid to hear any more.

"What? What did it say?" Cornelia asked. "Why didn't you call me to come upstairs? I thought you had decided not to bring it."

"I didn't want to, but being in an old house and all, I decided why not?" Emily explained.

"So, what did you ask?" Maggie questioned as she drank her coffee.

Marilee gave a big sigh. "I asked if there was a ghost in the room. It took no time for our hands to move directly to the yes on the board."

"Oh, no," Cornelia said, nudging Marilee. "What else did it say?"

"I didn't really understand much of it," Marilee said, shrugging her shoulders.

"Yes you did," Emily argued. "You asked if it wanted to tell you something. The next thing it did was spell out q-u-i-l-t. That could mean a lot of things, of course."

I knew if it was Josephine talking, her quilt would be on her mind. I stayed quiet in hopes of learning more.

"Big deal. We are all quilters," Maggie said.

"Did you ask who the ghost was?" Cornelia wanted to know.

The women shook their heads.

"So, why were you scared?"

"Marilee asked if we were in danger," Emily confessed. "She should have never done that!"

"Oh, dear," I said, worried. "What did the board say?"

"It spelled out c-a-r, but then it went right to the word t-r-u-n-k, which didn't make sense at all," Marilee said. Why would a car and a trunk be dangerous? I'm not sure we got those words right."

"Go ahead and tell them the rest, Marilee," Emily requested.

"I asked if there was anyone else in the room. I thought there might be more than one spirit talking to us."

"Go ahead and say it, Marilee," Emily demanded. "It was very clear. We even asked it a second time and we got the same strange answer."

We waited in suspense.

Marilee took a deep breath. "It spelled out that c-a-n-c-e-r is here," Marilee said unwillingly.

We were taken completely aback.

"Are you sure?" I asked, my tone serious.

They nodded.

"Maybe the ghost had cancer when she died," Maggie guessed.

"Okay, friends. This is just a game and your breakfast is getting cold," I said as I filled their plates. "I want you to eat a good breakfast before we go. Let's change the subject."

"Well, Kate, where are we going first today?" Maggie asked, in an effort to help me out.

Before I answered, they each tasted some of the wonderful muffins which had just come out of the oven. "Since the cemetery is close and on our way to Saxon Village, we will stop there first," I explained. "After that, we can make a stop at Imy's Antique Shop. You won't believe the bargains you can get there!" The change of subject seemed to have cheered everyone up.

"I didn't get to go into the museum the last time I was here," Maggie complained. "Can we stop there? Sharla Lee is such a hoot. The others would enjoy meeting her."

"Okay, but we'll have to squeeze in lunch at some point," I reminded them. "We could stop at Marv's for a quick sandwich and then go to the winery for dinner."

"Sounds marvelous!" Cornelia agreed. "Can we invite Ruth Ann to dinner tonight? We really wanted to treat her to something before we left."

"What a great idea!" I said. "She would love that. I'll call her before we leave."

The busy plans ahead got everyone's mind off the Ouija board. Josephine's messages were still with me, however. What was she up to? I made the call to Ruth Ann, who gladly accepted our invitation and said she would meet us at the winery.

CHAPTER 50

The cemetery captured the hearts of my South Haven friends. They loved the incredible view and the quaintness perfectly displayed on the hillside. My flowers on Doc and Josephine's markers were gone. Ellen told me they pick up things every week that are placed on the gravestones. As we gathered around Josephine's marker, I said a few nice words about her and why I was so intrigued with knowing more about her. I bravely admitted I was sure she was the spirit in the house and said how much I respected her presence. My admission about Josephine brought out different expressions on each person's face. Marilee immediately asked if I ever felt afraid. I told her there were times that I was baffled or confused by some of her behaviors, but that I was never afraid. I said I felt we had an understanding and fondness for one another.

"Josephine was a good person and sacrificed a lot, in my estimation," I explained. "She was a quilter, in case some of you didn't know. It seemed to be a release for her, as it is for so many." I hoped that my characterization of Josephine would be helpful to my friends and not cause them to fear being in the guest house.

"Can we take some photos?" Emily asked.

"Sure," I nodded.

"Everyone, please stand behind her marker so I can see her name on it," Emily instructed. We all posed, but no one was smiling.

As the others headed back to the car, I touched Josephine's grave and told her I loved her.

Anna was waiting for us when we pulled into the charming grounds of the log cabin village. She motioned for us to come to the picnic table by the outdoor oven where she had just baked some bread. She had butter, honey, and her homemade blackberry jelly to accompany the bread. You would have thought we had not eaten breakfast by the way we dug into the heavenly combinations.

"We certainly don't need lunch!" Maggie announced as we finished up at Saxon Village. Everyone agreed. They thanked Anna for the tour and the delicious treats.

Sharla Lee and Gerard greeted us with open arms when we arrived at the museum. After I introduced my friends, Sharla Lee explained the new exhibit was East Perry County Farm Women. Many black-and-white photographs were beautifully displayed. She told us that many of the wives had to hold down regular jobs as well as cook, can food, clean, work on the farm, and rear their children. Everyone listened intently. Marilee then asked about their quilt-making.

"We certainly know that quilting was part of their daily lives," Sharla Lee stated. "Quiltmaking was a necessity, unlike today where it has become an art form. We've had quilt shows here at the museum and displayed some of the beautiful quilts that people have pulled out from their attics—quilts they had saved and tried to preserve." Sharla Lee moved us on down the aisle.

She explained another feature in the exhibit which was especially fascinating. It was a large photo of the Bucket Brigade. These were women who were professional maids and who migrated on the first ships from Germany and settled here in the county. They took the train or the river to St. Louis to work in fine homes. They were nannies, cooks, and maids. They soon included other women in the region. We couldn't stop talking about what their lives might have been like. The good news was that some of them married into wealthy families. The tour of the museum gave us so much information to think about! We thanked Sharla Lee and Gerard as we said good-bye.

Our next and last stop was Imy's, which was a good thing considering all the purchases they made! It took some convincing that there wasn't room for an antique chair that Emily wanted to take home with her. Maggie grabbed an Ocean's Wave blue-and-white quilt without even checking the price. I thought she and Marilee were going to fight over it, but Marilee settled on a colorful Nine-Patch quilt. Imy had just received some small paintings from her sister Pearlene, who is quite a talented painter. Emily fell in love with two of them, so she bought them both.

I was so busy encouraging sales that I walked away empty-handed, which was a first for me. We definitely made Imy's day with all the good purchases from her shop. She was truly grateful to have met some of my South Haven friends.

After a couple hours of rest back at the guest house, we changed clothes and were ready to head to the winery.

Ellie had saved us a table inside since it was about to rain. Trout immediately recognized Maggie and charmed the others. The surprise of the evening as we were eating was the appearance of Clark! He came directly to our table so I could formally introduce him to everyone. He was very sociable for a change and offered to buy us a round of drinks. They asked him a lot of questions, which I knew would give even more fodder for gossip. He quietly suggested to me that we have dinner together this week. I nodded without showing too much excitement. He politely said he was leaving and wished them a safe trip home. I was proud of him. All the way home, I was teased and warned about not letting this charmer of a guy get away.

"You're not going to convince Kate that she needs a man in her life to be happy," warned Maggie.

"Thank you, Maggie. You know me so well!" I chuckled.

When we arrived home, I squelched the idea of getting out the Ouija board to provide more entertainment. I encouraged everyone to get a good night's sleep to be ready for the day ahead.

I did some breakfast prep work in the kitchen before I went upstairs. Maggie's door was open, so I went in to have a short visit with her before she headed back to South Haven. She was reading but eagerly put her book aside and gestured for me to sit on the side of her bed.

"Kate, what is the real reason you keep your distance from Clark?" she asked.

I was really too tired to answer. "I am very attracted to him, so don't get me wrong," I started to explain. "Between you and me, I finally gave myself permission to have non-guilt sex with him."

Maggies's eyes widened and I thought she was going to fall off the bed.

I had to laugh.

"Seriously? Why didn't you tell me?"

"Well, I am telling you, and, after all, I'm human. I should probably have just experimented with Clay instead of thinking my hormones meant I should marry him."

"Kathryn Ann Meyr!" she exclaimed in a loud whisper. "I don't believe I'm hearing this! What if John wants more than friendship?"

This question threw me for a loop, but I smiled. "Well, just so you know, I've had the chance to take it a step further, but I didn't. I like things the way they are with John. He is a great neighbor and friend. He's so much younger than me, and I'm not nearly sexy nor savvy enough to be in his league."

We both had a good laugh about that comment. She knew better than to try to convince me otherwise. Maggie and I had enjoyed many of these kinds of talks growing up, sitting on our beds, just like tonight. It was just like old times. We hugged and said good night before I crossed the hall to my bedroom. I love that girlfriend!

CHAPTER 51

The house was quiet again once my friends hit the road back to South Haven. I was cleaning up the breakfast table when Susie and Cotton arrived. Little Carly Mae was in the carrier seat, sound asleep.

"I'm so glad to see you again," I said to Susie, giving her a little hug. "Is Amy Sue with her grandma?"

Susie nodded. "You have been so busy, haven't you, Miss Kate?" Susie said as she placed Carly Mae's seat on the rug.

I nodded and smiled. "It's been a little crazy," I admitted. "The Michigan girls just left, so I'll finish up here if you want to start upstairs."

"Well, I need to get started on the yard," Cotton said before I thought of a chore for him to do. His eyes were on the table where there were blueberry muffins.

"Help yourself. Aunt Mandy will be arriving here very soon, just so you know. I'm going to check on the house again today."

"Wow! That's good news!" Cotton said, scratching his head. "Is the house ready for her to move into?"

"It's close enough, from what I hear," I shared. "She seems to know better than I, so that's all good."

"Let me know what I can do to help," offered Cotton. "She is such a fine lady."

"I will," I nodded. "She'll need outdoor work done. I don't know whether she's made arrangements for landscaping."

We all got busy. I packed up some muffins and a few apples for the work crew. I went upstairs to get a jacket when Susie caught my attention.

"Miss Kate, the girls in the attic left a Ouija board behind," she said with a giggle. "Did you know about this?"

I shook my head in disbelief. "Oh, dear. Just let me put it in my room. I'll take it to them when I go back there." I put it on my dresser and grabbed my jacket, ready to be on my way.

When I arrived down the road, Chuck was about to get in his truck to leave. One guy was cleaning up a pile of lumber. The house looked amazing. I couldn't believe its progress each and every day.

"What do you think, Little Red Riding Hood?" he teased, referring to my red picnic basket.

"The house is looking great! Can I look inside?"

"Sure, go right ahead," he nodded. "They are finishing up the kitchen cabinets today."

The house sat back from the road far enough to have a circle driveway in front. I couldn't wait to walk in the front door for the very first time! Once inside, there were so many windows in the odd-shaped structure that I felt like I was standing inside a glass paperweight. Oh, how I would love to bring more of the outdoors into my house.

"Don't let me interrupt you," I said to the man in the narrow galley kitchen. The clever, modern-shaped kitchen would not work for me, but I knew it would be perfect for Aunt Mandy.

"It's quite a house, isn't it?" the man said as he put down his drill.

I nodded and smiled. "My aunt will love it!"

"It's time for some blueberry muffins," Chuck said, entering the kitchen with my basket.

"Gee, thanks!" said the worker. "I've had some before and they're delicious.

"We've had good weather, so we'll be able to get this wrapped up soon," Chuck said, his hands on his hips, mentally sizing up the place. "The trim on the screened-in porch will be painted tomorrow. She'll have a very nice view of the woods. If I may suggest, I would have her add a couple more lights outdoors. She'll be hearin' all kinds of creatures out there, so it would be nice to be able to turn on the lights and see what's goin' on."

"I see what you mean," I said, agreeing with his suggestion. "I think that's a good idea for safety as well. Would you see that it gets done? I'll pay for the extra expense. I don't want someone to have to come later to install them."

"Sure will!" Chuck eagerly agreed. "You know, there will be a lot of small honey-do jobs for someone to do. I thought Cotton might be helpful in that regard."

"Yes, we've talked about that."

"By the way, Clark was here yesterday checkin' everything out," Chuck disclosed. He paused, waiting for my reaction.

"Did he give his approval?" I asked, smiling.

"He didn't say a whole lot; but knowin' Clark, it meant he approved a whole lot!"

I had to laugh, knowing what he meant. I returned to

my car with an empty red basket. Chuck gave me a wink as I closed the door. I thought again about Chuck remaining single all these years. I wondered if he had ever considered asking Ruth Ann out on a date.

When I got back to the house, one of my tires made a funny noise. I got out of the car and saw that I had a flat tire. It was going flat quickly. Cotton saw me examining it and came my way.

"Yup, looks like you have a good-size nail hole there, Miss Kate," he surmised. "That's what you get for hanging out at a construction site!"

"Oh, dear, Cotton, can you fix it or do I need to call someone? I don't think I've ever had a flat tire in my whole life!"

Cotton laughed and shook his head. "Well, I guess you don't get too many nails on the road in South Haven," he said, shaking his head. "I'll get it changed for you. I hope you have a spare tire in your trunk."

"I have no idea, Cotton," I answered, feeling like a city girl.

CHAPTER 52

I was about to enter the house when Cotton called out to me. "Hey, you want this quilt inside or should I leave it here?"

"What quilt?" I said as I turned around to look.

Cotton walked toward me and in his hands was Josephine's quilt which had disappeared at the cemetery!

"Oh, my goodness!" I reacted, surprised. "Sure, let me take it inside." I couldn't possibly tell him I had no idea it was in my trunk. I was feeling grateful that Josephine had decided to return it to me. I quickly rushed into the house and up the stairs. I wanted to put it back in the hall closet where I had found it originally. After wrapping it in a sheet, I got my ladder to reach the upper cabinet. I felt a sense of relief when I accomplished the task of getting it back where it belonged.

Susie was wondering what I was up to, but she didn't ask any questions. I went about the chores of the day like stripping the linens from the guest beds for the laundry. I wanted to forget that the Ouija board had spelled out the word quilt and the word trunk.

I was glad to have some peace and quiet after Cotton, Susie, and Carly Mae left for the day. I liked having the house to myself once again. Maybe I wasn't cut out to be a guest house owner. It was cocktail hour in my mind, so I fixed myself a plate of snacks and a glass of wine, which I took to the sunporch. I was about to watch the evening news when Maggie called. Her voice was shaky like she was crying.

"What is it?"

"We had an accident on the way home."

"No! Where? Are you okay?"

"I feel so bad!" Maggie said between sniffles. "I think it was my fault. I didn't see this car coming and I pulled out right in front of him."

"So, are you hurt?"

"Not really, because Cornelia and I were on the other side of the car. Emily and Marilee weren't so lucky because that side of the car took the hit."

"Oh, dear! How badly are they hurt?"

"Luckily we were in a busy traffic area, so help came quickly. I don't know who called 911. Emily has a broken arm and left the hospital after being treated, but Marilee is hurt internally, so I know there will be lots of tests. I will never forgive myself!"

"Maggie, it was an accident," I stated firmly. "Accidents never make sense. They just happen for goofy reasons and we have to go on."

"We had such a good time, Kate. We laughed almost all the way home. When Cornelia and I sat in the waiting room waiting for Emily, she reminded me that the Ouija board said something about a car when we asked if we were in danger. That's pretty creepy!"

"Oh, forget that!" I said to comfort her. Of course, I wasn't going to tell her about the quilt in the trunk that had me alarmed. "I'll send them both something, and I hope they will be okay," I said, feeling sad. "Let's hope Marilee's condition isn't serious."

"She surely is in a lot of pain. Mark is here with me now, which is helping."

"That's good," I added. "Tell him I said that I'm glad he's with you."

We hung up and I felt terribly helpless. What a horrible ending to such a grand visit. I just sat there picturing what my friends were going through. A prayer for God's help was definitely in order.

CHAPTER 53

The next morning, Carla called as I was about to have my first cup of coffee. She knew all about the accident and wanted my reaction. "I think it could have been a lot worse," Carla surmised.

"Perhaps. How are you doing?"

"Decent," she stated. "I called to tell you that since I'm feeling stronger, I went over to John's to clean again."

"Well, don't do too much too soon!" I warned.

"He said he'd be calling you. He's all hyped up over some new quilt information. You two are something! He also said he was thinking of coming your way to visit again."

"I can't wait to hear about his discovery, but I surely don't need for him to visit," I said, concerned.

Before we hung up, I asked Carla if she would bake Emily and Marilee a Black Forest cake. I knew they raved every time they ate it at my house. I told her I was at a loss as to what to do for them. She gladly agreed and thought she'd also make one for herself and share it with John.

As I hung up, I saw Clark pull into my driveway. I rushed

to comb my hair and put on lipstick.

"It's about time you answered," he teased. "I knew you had to be here."

"Come in," I greeted him, smiling.

"No, I can't," he said shaking his head. "I'm headed to Perry to pick up some supplies. Do you have plans this evening?"

"No, not really," I answered.

"There's a nice little Italian restaurant outside of Jacksonville that I thought you might enjoy," he said. "Interested?"

"Sure, it sounds great."

"I'll be back for you around six then, if that works for you."

"Good! See you then!" I smiled.

I watched Clark get back into his SUV and admired his confidence and stature. It felt good to be asked out on a date, especially since our last encounter. I went to my office to check emails. There were some inquiries from people who might be interested in staying at the guest house during the time of the East Perry Fair in September. A phone call from John interrupted me.

"I just had to hear your voice. I haven't heard from you since your Michigan gang was there."

"I've been busy, plus I'm getting ready for Aunt Mandy to return," I explained. "She should come the day before my birthday. I can hardly wait! Her house is too cute for words, so I hope she'll be pleased."

"I can't wait to see it for myself," John admitted. "Tell her I'll make it to her open house if she has one."

"Okay, but I understand from Carla that you have some

additional information on some quilts."

"I'm telling you, Kate, I have enough to do a whole book, I think."

"Really?" I gushed. "Tell me more!"

"I was in Madison last week and I met a local funeral director who is also on Madison's tourism board. I had planned to interview him about their park system; but when we went to lunch, I told him about the article I was writing on quilts. He immediately opened up about what he referred to as funeral quilts."

"So, what new information did he have?"

"Well, for starters, he said many older women who are quilters are having their quilts displayed at their wakes."

"Sure. When Emma died, one of her quilts was displayed near her casket," I reminded him.

"Did they bury it with her?"

"I really doubt it," I answered.

"He also told me how popular the quilt design fabrics are for the casket linings. He said they can customize the casket with a quilt design as well. Did I tell you this before?"

"Yes, I think you mentioned it."

"He said they have a quilt-themed body bag for when they pick up bodies and bring them back to the funeral home. They said families really appreciate the personal touch rather than a cold, impersonal body bag. The power of a quilt design! Who would have thought?"

"Well, as long as it pleases all parties concerned, I guess," I responded, experiencing mixed feelings.

"There's more! As a quilter, I'm surprised you haven't shared with me that quilters are making their own quilt to be buried with. Weren't you going to ask your quilting friends about that?"

"I did. You know, that kind of information is so personal. I don't think it's something they would volunteer to tell you. My friend Ruth Ann has tons of quilts, so it would be interesting to know if she has thought about it."

"You should ask her," John encouraged me. "Since she makes quilts professionally, she may have had a request to make one for someone."

We chatted for another half hour, which certainly gave me plenty to think about. John was becoming obsessed with this topic. I supposed writers who do research really get into it. At the end of our conversation, he asked if I would like to have him visit for my birthday. My answer was absolutely not!

CHAPTER 54

Aunt Mandy couldn't arrive fast enough to suit me. She was determined to arrive the day before my birthday. She said she had a wonderful birthday surprise for me. She agreed to stay here at the house until things were settled at her new place. I planned for her to be in The Study so she wouldn't have to go up and down the stairs.

Both of our lives would be different with her here. I was pleased that she had her friendship with Wilson, the architect, so her entire social life wouldn't be totally my responsibility. She did, however, get to know my Friendship Circle when she was here and she adored Clark. In my mind, I was already forming a list of folks to invite to her open house.

I knew Jack was in New York to stay, so having family here was significant to me. Someday, Jack would bring his wife with him; and if I were lucky, there would be grandchildren that would visit as well. My mind was buzzing as I prepared for a dinner out with Clark. I wanted to look like it was indeed a special night.

When he picked me up, he seemed happy and talkative for a change. As we drove toward Jacksonville, he talked about his current challenge of keeping enough inventory for his gallery in Springfield as well as accomplishing what he was trying to do at his studio. It was a nice change for him to be doing most of the talking. When we arrived, the small and romantic restaurant was just what he had described. Since Clark had been there several times, he had wonderful menu suggestions.

I bravely asked Clark whether he had ever made a wooden casket.

He looked at me, confused. He had to clear his throat before he spoke. "I do know a wood carver in Arkansas who makes custom caskets. He said he is kept quite busy. Personally, I don't have any interest in making any. I don't relish the thought of my work going underground."

We chuckled at his remark. I'm glad he didn't ask if I wanted to order one! Of course, I didn't share with him that I was helping John do research for an article on quilts. John's was a sensitive name to bring up.

We lingered at the restaurant until they were showing signs of closing. I had two glasses of red wine, which was my limit. It was nice to have an evening with Clark that didn't have other people or circumstances to contend with. For once, it was just the two of us.

When we arrived back at 6229 Main Street, I asked Clark to come in for coffee. He looked at me, wondering if I meant more. I made us a quick cup of coffee while he waited in the living room. We both seemed exhausted. On the couch, we embraced and relaxed. In no time, we fell asleep like a longtime married couple. Being this relaxed with him was a wonderful feeling.

When I awoke at three, I was on the couch alone, covered by a quilt that had previously been on the rocker. I thought Clark may have gone to The Study, but when I checked he wasn't there. I suppose he just wanted to go home and didn't want to disturb me. Instead of going up to my room, I went back to sleep on the couch with a smile on my face. I was happy that we did not have any expectations about our relationship at this point. We were comfortable together and it had been a nearly perfect evening.

CHAPTER 55

It was time to make my Sunday call to Jack. I wished he would sometimes take the initiative and call me occasionally instead of the other way around. I caught him on the golf course, so our conversation was short. I wanted to inform him that Aunt Mandy was about to arrive. He wanted to know what my plans were for my birthday. When I told him just dinner with Aunt Mandy, he couldn't believe it. I told him it would be a different kind of birthday without my bestie Maggie here.

I decided to make an early morning check on my aunt's house because changes were happening so rapidly. When I arrived, I was surprised to see Cotton helping. It was great to see that he could make some extra money helping Chuck.

"I hear your aunt is arrivin' any day, accordin' to what Cotton said," Chuck commented when he saw me.

"Yes, I'm excited," I replied. "Chuck, the place looks awesome!"

"Well, here are the keys!" he said, handing them to me.

"I was goin' to drop them off today. Now you can come and go as you please; however, there is some trim painting still goin' on. I think you'll love the hardwood floors. I wasn't sure about her choice of slate on the porch, but it looks good. Want to take a look?"

I nodded and followed him inside. It was like seeing a dream home for the first time. We walked around the place as if I were doing a final inspection. I loved the smell of a new car and a new home!

"Now you have my number, so if she needs any changes done she can just call me. The same goes for you too, Kate." He gave me a wink, which I ignored.

"My aunt has her own ideas, so I have no way of knowing what her response will be."

"I hope I'll get an invite if she has an open house," Chuck hinted.

"I'll see to it!" I said, smiling.

"Miss Kate!" Cotton yelled from the kitchen. "I'll be at your place tomorrow to see if you need anything for the move," he assured me. "I'm not sure about Susie."

"I should be fine," I answered, loud enough so that he could hear me in the kitchen. "I still have to do some cooking and baking."

"Speaking of bakin', I'm sure goin' to miss those occasional blueberry muffins!" Chuck teased.

"Thanks. I love to bake, so it was fun sharing them with all of you."

"That coffee shop of Charlene's has sure taken off, hasn't it?" Chuck bragged as he continued to inspect the place. "You know, I think Charlene and I are distant cousins."

I laughed. "I think everyone in East Perry County is related in some way."

"Well, I'll be sure to stop by every now and then to check on you ladies," Chuck said as he prepared to leave. Maybe I'll get lucky and get a muffin or two from Red Riding Hood. I know she lives close by."

"Maybe!" Before I left, I told Cotton I was going to Harold's Hardware to get some potted flowers to put around the outside of Aunt Mandy's house. I wanted him to pick them up later with his truck.

Ellie called on my way to Harold's. "So, what are your birthday plans?"

"Well, since Aunt Mandy will be here and it's moving day, we haven't talked about it."

"I was thinking the easy answer would be for me to treat you both to dinner," Ellie offered. "You don't need to be cooking on your birthday, and you will both be exhausted. I checked the weather and it's supposed to be perfect for the deck, so how about we plan on that?"

"That sounds lovely and simple," I responded. "Thanks so much."

"I can't believe Clark hasn't asked you out!"

"We just went out, so it's no big deal. He knows I'm consumed by my aunt's move right now. You should see the place. It is so beautiful! I think I'm jealous."

"It's the talk of the town," Ellie claimed. "Has Ellen offered to decorate it?"

I had to snicker. "No, but I think we could use her help with the landscaping."

"Okay, so if I don't see you before then, come to my place around six," Ellie confirmed.

Harold was happy to see me and gave me a nice housewarming discount. Of course, he knew my aunt was arriving and that the house was very unique compared to Borna's standards. No secrets in this little town!

CHAPTER 56

Aunt Mandy called to give an update on her arrival. I couldn't believe the time was finally here. What a brave eighty-year-old lady! I fussed around most of the day, baking, cooking, and arranging flowers to make her arrival feel special to her. I took time in the afternoon to call Maggie and wished her a happy birthday. It was last year when she and Carla arrived as my first guests, ready to celebrate our birthdays. This year would be different. I also reminded myself that I could call this the first anniversary of Josephine's Guest House.

"Happy birthday, girlfriend!" I said when Maggie finally answered. "I miss you!"

She laughed. "The same to you, girlfriend!"

"So, are you and Mark celebrating?" I asked, feeling nostalgic.

"Nothing more than our usual dinner at the country club," she said softly. "I wish Jill could be here, but she's out of town on business."

"Oh, that's too bad. It was so great having all of you here

for a couple of days. How are Marilee and Emily?"

"They are both complaining, but the best news is that Marilee's condition is nothing serious," Maggie explained. "You know what a fashion plate Emily is, so the cast is cramping her style."

"I can imagine," I said, picturing Emily in a cast.

"Is there any word on Carla?" I inquired next.

"Not really, but she surely has handled everything well. She has even gone back to some of her cleaning jobs."

"I'm sure she's thinking of her finances. By the way, I wanted to tell you that Aunt Mandy should arrive this evening. I think I'm ready. I want her to stay here with me until we have everything just right at the house. Emily has invited us to dinner at the winery tomorrow night if we're still standing up from the move."

"That is all so exciting!" Maggie said, interested. "I'm sorry we have to be apart this year for the first time. Tell your aunt that I'm really happy for her."

After we hung up, I moved to the sunporch, where I felt sad and disconnected. Life was changing in many ways. I had to concentrate on Aunt Mandy. I was startled to hear someone knocking at the front door. From my seat on the sunporch, I didn't see any vehicle in sight. I rushed to answer it and saw a delivery man standing on the other side of the oval glass door. I opened the door, and he asked for Kate Meyr before handing me a long box of flowers. I was sure I had not received flowers from anyone since I moved to Borna. I thanked him and closed the door, eager to discover the mystery. Inside, I discovered many long-stemmed red roses. What a sight to behold! The fragrance was overwhelming. I folded back the tissue to find a card that read, "Happy birthday, sweetheart! J."

It was truly a surprise, but I was hardly his sweetheart! I quickly removed the card so no one else could read the message. I took the roses to the dining room where I selected a crystal Waterford vase from the cabinet to put them in. I clipped their edges and added water. I took them to the living room, where they lit up the room like there was a celebration. I had forgotten what it felt like to receive flowers.

I was about to succumb to a glass of wine while wondering why Aunt Mandy had not yet arrived. I thought about giving her a call to check on her progress. Low and behold, at that very moment she pulled into the driveway in her big white Cadillac.

I jumped up to go outdoors to meet her. I didn't wait until she got out of the car to blow her a kiss. She laughed, slowly making her way out of the car as if she were achy from the drive. I gave her a hug and didn't want to let her go. "I'm so happy you're here!" I said, looking her over. As always, she was smartly dressed wearing a starched white blouse and khakis. She had a pale blue cardigan sweater draped over her shoulders.

"You and me both," she said, keeping her arm around me. "It feels good to stretch."

"I'll get your things later," I said as we walked toward the house. We both noticed the pink, beautiful skyline that welcomed her.

"I'll bet you're ready for some Merry Merlot!"

She smiled. "Indeed!"

CHAPTER 57

We got comfortable on the sunporch. Aunt Mandy had admired the flowers upon her arrival and had approved of the changes made to my home since her visit last winter.

"I must call Wilson and tell him I've arrived," Aunt Mandy said, reaching for her cell phone.

I smiled. It was a sweet gesture.

While she made her call, I fixed a glass of wine for each of us. She loved a certain red wine I had that was called Merry Merlot. In the background, it was good to hear her voice that was soft and flirtatious at times, sprinkled with a giggle here and there. I loved it. When they finished their conversation, I presented her with a glass of wine.

"Oh, this is refreshing, Kate," she remarked. "It reminds me of the grand Christmas I shared with you."

"It was pretty special. Now, we have a decision to make. Do you want to see your house this evening or do you want to wait until morning?"

"Oh, sweetie. I don't think I can even get out of this chair right now. I think I'd like to see it for the first time in the daylight.

I've waited this long, and I'm just happy to be here with you."

I smiled, feeling warm inside. My earlier melancholy feelings had faded. "Well, you are going to love it," I assured her. "I love all the glass that you incorporated. The workmen have been very nice, and they said to tell you they are happy to correct or change anything that you want."

"That's good. I just hope the things I decided to keep from Florida will fit in nicely."

"How about I fix you a little something to eat?" I offered.

"Perhaps something light," she suggested as she took another sip of her drink. "I am anxious to catch up on things here in Borna. How is Clark, for starters?"

"He's just fine," I reported. "He works very hard."

"Now that's not what I meant, and you know it."

I laughed. "We went out to eat at a very nice restaurant recently. I also asked him to go with me to Sharla Lee's birthday party. We had a great time."

"Well, that's what I want to hear," she nodded, flashing a big smile. "I am quite fond of him. I also like John, that younger gent of yours. I haven't asked who those lovely roses are from, but I figure it has to be from one of them, am I right?"

I had to chuckle once again. "They're from John, but keep that a secret, okay?" I gave her a warning look.

"Oh, so there's still a bit of competition going on here, I guess."

I shook my head. "They are each so different. I really don't feel that I have to choose at all. I can have as many diverse friends as I want, can't I?"

"I concur," she said, resting her hand on her chin. "With that heavenly smell radiating from those roses, I don't think you can hide them too well."

I nodded, smiling, and decided it was a good time to change the subject. I filled her in on plans to have dinner tomorrow night at the winery. She seemed to love it when I made plans that included her. I told her to invite Wilson if she liked. I could see she was starting to fade from exhaustion, so I brought her things in from the car and got her settled in The Study.

I was feeling the effects of the day as well, so we parted ways and I went upstairs to my bedroom. I was so relieved to have Aunt Mandy settled here. I could hardly wait until tomorrow. When I propped the pillows on my bed, I sent John a text to thank him for the roses.

> Love the roses. You shouldn't have! Thanks so much! Kate

He must have been waiting to hear from me because his response was immediate.

> My pleasure! In one hour, you will be older! I wanted to be the first to wish you a happy birthday! J

> You were! Thanks! K

I preferred live conversations with John rather than sending texts. When we actually talked, our minds seemed to generate ideas and great conversation. That was something that lacked a bit between Clark and me. I checked the clock. June 17 was about to greet me. Happy birthday to me! Sleep and contentment took over.

CHAPTER 58

I was up bright and early the next morning so I could make Aunt Mandy a nice welcome-home breakfast. I knew how much she loved my veggie omelet with hot sauce, and, of course, my blueberry muffins. We could hopefully finish breakfast before her moving van arrived.

"Happy birthday, Kate," Aunt Mandy greeted, coming into the kitchen. I grinned as she gave me a peck on the cheek. "I had the best night's sleep that I've had in a long time. I love that mattress."

"Thanks, I've heard that before."

"This looks wonderful, and I'm so glad you remembered this omelet," she exclaimed, smiling. "I get so tired of my usual hot oatmeal each day."

As we were starting to eat, we were interrupted by Cotton knocking at the back door. "Come on in and have a cup of Joe," I encouraged him. "Look who's here!"

"Howdy, Miss Mandy!" he greeted as he removed his straw hat. "It's so good to see you again. We've all looked forward to your return. I first want to wish Miss Kate here a very happy birthday from Susie and me." He blushed. "I also wanted to offer my help today if you need it."

"Thanks so much, Cotton," Aunt Mandy replied sweetly. "First, I want to hear all about that new little baby! I have a little something in my suitcase for her."

"Oh, she's something!" Cotton replied proudly. "She's not sleeping through the night yet, so we'll enjoy her a little more after that happens!"

"If you want to check on us a little later over at the house, I'm sure we'll find something for you to do," I suggested.

"Okeydoke. I'll do that," he said, eyeing the muffins on the table.

"You want to take a couple of these to go?"

"Don't mind if I do!" he said, helping himself.

Half an hour later, we decided to drive over to the house and wait for the moving van. We had just closed the car doors when, lo and behold, the van slowly pulled onto the road. Aunt Mandy gave me a look of surprise.

"I can't believe this is happening!" Aunt Mandy said, her eyes watery.

"It's happening," I assured her. "We must remember to thank Oscar and Ellen for giving us this idea."

She nodded.

"We'll be neighbors now! I will keep plenty of sugar on hand in case you need to borrow a cup every now and then."

Aunt Mandy burst into laughter. When we pulled in front of the house, Aunt Mandy just stared. She seemed to be in complete awe. She got out of the car slowly and gazed at the front of the house. She noticed the potted flowers and tilted her head in admiration. She was speechless. When we entered the front door, she held onto me as if she would faint from the experience. She finally spoke when she saw the attractive galley kitchen.

"I've always wanted something like this," she said, caressing the countertop. "I think my choices here worked out, don't you?"

I nodded and smiled.

The last inspection was the screened-in porch, which was the main focus of the house. She said most of her evenings were spent having her evening cocktail on her screened-in porch at her previous home. She loved watching the changes of the seasons, no matter the temperature. She loved the slate floor and admired the view around her. I explained about the decision to add more outdoor lighting, and she seemed grateful that the lighting had already been installed.

"I think my personal things will do nicely," she concluded. "I can't wait to see everything in place."

"Well, I think they are unloading now, so I hope things are marked for each room."

"Yes, they are," she said as she got excited.

When Aunt Mandy saw the movers enter the house, she took charge. I was very impressed, and the movers were quite quick with their mission. One of them offered to put her bed together, which pleased her very much.

A little later, Cotton showed up and offered to get us some lunch from Marv's place. With the porch furniture in place, the three of us made ourselves comfortable for a quick lunch. It was Aunt Mandy's first meal in her new home. Her porch color scheme was yellow, green, and a touch of red. It was a lovely complement to the green plants I had chosen for her. It all spelled h-a-p-p-y!

As the afternoon went on, we made good progress.

Cotton surely came in handy with any lifting that needed to be done. Aunt Mandy became more and more certain that she wanted to spend her first night here tonight. She was determined, despite our advising her otherwise. I couldn't blame her. I would want to do the same. She told me in which box the linens were packed, and I got busy making up the bed. After I finished, I went home to retrieve her belongings from last night. When I returned, I set up the coffee pot and placed a small basket of muffins on her kitchen counter.

"Look, its four already and I'm going to leave so you can get a little rest before dinner tonight," I advised. "I will pick you up at six. I have things in place in your bathroom, so just relax. We do not have to do it all in one day."

She shook her head in disbelief. "I'll try to remember that. I surely don't want to be a drag during that great birthday party tonight," she laughed. "Thanks so much for all your help, sweetie. Cotton, I'll be expecting a bill from you and I'll give you a call for additional help, don't worry."

He nodded, pleased that his work was appreciated.

I left feeling good about all we had accomplished. My life in Borna would never be quite the same, and I would never be lonely here anymore.

CHAPTER 59

It felt strange to drive my car down the road to pick up Aunt Mandy. When she answered the front door, she asked if she could first give me her birthday present and I smiled in agreement.

"Did Cotton get these flowers watered today?" she asked as she went to get my gift.

"Yes, he did," I assured her. "You look wonderful. Did you get some rest?"

"Not really. I'm too excited," she said, handing me a large box.

"This is gorgeous wrapping paper," I remarked as I removed the green and purple paper and bow. I pulled the last bit of tissue away and saw it was a quilt. "A quilt," I said, surprised. "This is so beautiful! This must have a story. It's quite old, I think, but it's in such good condition!"

She smiled, knowing I loved the gift. "It was made by your grandmother," she shared. "She made it for our wedding and I just kept it through the years. She called it a Rose of Sharon. I know she loved to appliqué. I was really afraid to use it. I never wanted to part with it until I thought of you. It needs to go to the next generation. Your father never cared about such stuff from our mom and dad. It was the last quilt she made, to my recollection."

"I'm just overwhelmed!" I said, carefully unfolding it. "You may want to hang onto this for a while. We have some mighty cold winters here in Borna!"

"Yes, I remember," she chuckled. "It's perfect for you, and it was such a challenge to think of what to give you."

"Thank you! I will cherish this forever," I said, giving her a hug. "I love Grandmother's china! That is so wonderful to have as well!"

I took the quilt with me as we went off to the dinner party. It was starting to feel like a special day.

Ellie greeted us when we arrived. The sun was just about to set, making it a lovely time of day. The temperature was delightful. She had reserved a nice-sized table which was covered with a white tablecloth, and fresh flowers graced the center. Nothing said happy birthday, which I was pleased to see. We passed a few familiar faces, and I am sure they suspected it was a special occasion.

"There'd better not be any surprises," I warned Ellie.

She laughed. "I know better," she admitted. "I am planning to join you for dinner, if that's all right. I'm anxious to hear all about your impression of your new house, Aunt Mandy."

"Thanks, Ellie. This is quite lovely, isn't it, Aunt Mandy?"

"Yes, it certainly is!" Aunt Mandy agreed, sitting down.

"Just so you don't freak out, Clark said he was going to drop by later," Ellie divulged. "He had no clue as to what to do for you, so I told him it would be fine if he came by."

I nodded and smiled. "Aunt Mandy will be happy to see him," I added.

Trout came out with a birthday balloon and I wished he hadn't. He was so excited, though, that I had to be thankful. He took our drink orders and gave me a kiss on the cheek. From a distance, I noticed Ellen and Oscar having dinner. I caught her eye, so I went over to say hello.

After their birthday wishes, Ellen was anxious to hear how Aunt Mandy liked her new home. I filled her in on the day and told her we would welcome any suggestions regarding landscaping. I suggested that they should join us for a drink after dinner and they happily agreed.

I went back to Ellie and my aunt who were chatting away. The first course was being served. Kelly had prepared beef filets that melted in my mouth. Aunt Mandy was enjoying all the attention and the delicious meal. When Ellie told us to save room for birthday cake, along came Clark as if on cue and presented a lovely sheet cake with lit candles. Following behind him were Oscar and Ellen. They started to sing the Happy Birthday, which was so very embarrassing. Others on the deck joined in. As I knew so well, there were no secrets in this town. When they finished, Clark gave me a kiss on the cheek and instructed me to make a wish before I blew out the candles. He then greeted Aunt Mandy with a hug to welcome her back. I made a silent wish for health and safety before I gave it a successful puff of air.

Oscar got everyone's attention as he made a toast to my birthday and to Aunt Mandy, the new citizen of Borna. Ellen then clinked her glass with a teaspoon and made a birthday toast on behalf of the Friendship Circle of Borna. Despite the excitement, I noticed Carson standing at the door watching all the activities. Did he know I wouldn't be thrilled to see him here? Is that why he chose to keep his distance?

Oscar ordered a round of drinks and coffee as Wilson arrived. The look on my aunt's face was priceless. This was going to make her evening! She blushed something terrible when he kissed her on the cheek. Oscar and Ellen seemed to know he was going to stop by, which wasn't surprising since they were close friends with Wilson. I thanked him for his steadfast attentiveness regarding the house. He said he hadn't been there in a few days, but planned to stop by. I was certain it would be the first of many visits.

CHAPTER 60

Clark kept his distance until I approached him.

"You don't mind me crashing your party, do you?" Clark asked with a grin.

I smiled and shook my head.

"I have a little something for you, but I didn't want to embarrass either one of us by giving it to you here."

"How sweet of you, but it's not necessary," I responded quietly. "Why don't you stop by this week? I may be at my aunt's house most of the week helping her. I have to admit, I'm a little envious of her."

"I'm sure it will be yours one day," Clark said, which surprised me. "It will be a great cottage for guests and especially for an entire family."

"You're always thinking, aren't you?" I teased. "I remember when you first planted the seed about me opening the guest house."

"No regrets, right?" he asked, looking straight into my eyes.

"None, but reservations are not exactly flooding in,"

I remarked. "It's a good thing I don't have a vacancy sign hanging outside, because it would never change."

Clark laughed as he took a swallow of beer. "So, are you going to let me taste that cake or not?" Clark asked, staring at the others who were already enjoying a piece. Ellie was also passing pieces out to others sitting on the deck.

"Beer and cake?" I questioned.

"You bet!" he nodded, flashing me a confident smile.

"Happy birthday, Kate!" a voice said from the crowd. It was Chuck.

Clark gave him a strange look, like he was interrupting.

"Thanks, Chuck!" I replied. "Have you met Aunt Mandy?"

He looked her way and shook his head briefly. I interrupted Aunt Mandy's conversation with Wilson so I could make Chuck's introduction. Wilson then began to brag about how he had the best contractor in the state. Out of the corner of my eye, I noticed that Clark left and went inside to the bar. Chuck's timing was not that good, but I couldn't ignore him. After I excused myself from Wilson, Chuck, and Aunt Mandy, I decided to join Clark. This meant that I had to pass Carson who was still standing by the door.

"Quite a party you have going on there!" Carson teased, giving me his sleazy grin.

"Yes, very nice," I answered, trying to get past him. "How have you been?"

"Real good, thanks. I drove past that glass house of yours in the woods and it's quite something."

"Yes, it is, and today was moving day, so I'm exhausted!" I admitted.

He still wasn't planning to get out of my way. "Going in to see Clark?" he asked.

I nodded.

"He just can't quite close the deal on you, can he?"

I pushed him aside, ignoring his comment. I approached the bar where Clark was talking to Trout. At first, he ignored me. "Did you change your mind on the cake?" I asked to get a response.

He smiled into his glass. "I think I'll stick to beer," he said, not looking at me.

"I hear you approved of my aunt's house when you went to see it," I said, hoping to make conversation.

"I don't know who told you that, but I can probably guess," he said, sarcasm suddenly thick in the air. "The house is pretty modern for a woman of her age, which I commend her for."

"I agree," I nodded. "She knew right away what she wanted."

"You want a drink?" he finally asked.

"No, I need to get back to the dinner table," I said, looking toward the door and noticing that Carson was no longer standing there.

"I wanted to tell you that I'm going to be gone for a few weeks," he said, looking rather serious.

"Springfield?" I suggested, in hopes that this trip wasn't necessary due to medical troubles.

He nodded. "I'll stop by in the morning on my way and drop off your gift, if that's okay." He seemed to be moving past his sour mood.

"Sure. I'll have some muffins for you."

He finally gave me a relaxed grin. "Get back to your

party, birthday girl," Clark ordered. "I'll see you tomorrow."

I smiled and kissed him on the cheek before I went back to join everyone.

Aunt Mandy looked at me as if she needed to figure out why I had left. She was so savvy that way.

CHAPTER 61

When I drove Aunt Mandy home, I was reminded of how dark the country could be at night. I was glad she had dusk-to-dawn lighting to assist us as we arrived. She asked if everything was okay with Clark. I brought her up to date about him coming by in the morning to bring me my birthday gift before he went out of town. I got out of the car to walk her inside. The full moon was beautiful and helpful as we tried to see. We walked to her screened-in porch and sat down to enjoy the nice breeze.

"Were you expecting Wilson to join us tonight?" I asked her, teasing.

She smiled. "I like his spunk and creative energy. I don't know why he's taken a special interest in me, other than I think he's a bit lonely and perhaps a little bored in this small town. And, as you know better than most, unless you are a native, it's not the same."

I nodded. "Don't I know it," I said with a wry smile. "I'm okay with that, but I want them to like me for who I am. They certainly have embraced you, so I hope you'll be happy here."

"I'm going to love it here, I think," she said, looking around the room. "This fresh air will be good for me, and so far the folks have been lovely."

"This breeze makes me think about opening my windows on the sunporch."

"I'll bundle up out here until the snow blows in," she vowed, wearing a placid expression on her face. "I'm looking forward to having my first cocktail out here."

I laughed. "You'll have to bond to your fireplace, like I have. It is my refuge in the wintertime. Goodness knows, between us Cotton will need to keep us in plenty of firewood."

"Splendid," she nodded. "I shall look forward to that as well."

We said good night with contented hearts. I liked seeing the independent side of Aunt Mandy. I wanted her to include me in her life but not become too dependent on me. She hadn't considered living with me for a minute. She wanted her own place and lifestyle.

When I returned home, I went upstairs to review the moments of my first birthday without Maggie. If it weren't after midnight, I would have been tempted to call or text her. Did she even think of me as she dined and danced the night away at the South Haven Country Club? As I undressed, I stared at the Ouija board on my dresser. I wanted to touch it. I hadn't played with one of those since I was at a pajama party when I was fourteen. There were about six of us girls who managed to scare ourselves to death. We giggled just like Marilee and Emily did when they stayed here.

Curiosity got the best of me. I gently placed my fingertips on the guide. I hadn't even thought of what to ask it when it started to move! I figured it was just nervous energy coming from my hands. As I followed each letter, it spelled I-l-o-v-e-y-o-u. I pulled my hands back in surprise. Was it Josephine telling me she loved me? If not Josephine, then who? I stopped for a bit before placing my fingers back on the guide again. It did not move. Nothing happened. It had been a sweet message from someone, for sure.

Leaving the Ouija board, I brushed my teeth before crawling under the covers. The warm light greeted me once again. It was the best feeling ever. The light was so bright that I pulled the covers over my head. How could I ever be scared in this house with all the love I felt around me, even from a Ouija board?

CHAPTER 62

I had neglected to set an alarm, so I jumped when I looked at the clock the next morning. I had to get dressed quickly to look presentable for Clark. I set the table for two in case he could stay awhile. I wanted to check on Aunt Mandy, but I knew she was a late sleeper. When I opened the front door to get the paper, Clark pulled into the driveway. He came to the back door and greeted me with a big smile.

"Good morning!" I greeted, holding the door open for him. He had a small package in his hand.

"Any signs of a hangover today, birthday girl?" he teased.

"No, I was well behaved since I was the designated driver for my aunt."

"Have you heard from her today?" he asked as he poured his own coffee.

"She sleeps in, and I think the whole day wore her out. I just put the muffins in the oven, so can you stay for a bit?"

He saw the plate of fruit I had laid out. It looked fresh and inviting. "Don't mind if I do," he said as he took a chair.

I smiled, remembering a saying from Emma. "Emma

224

used to say, 'Will you take a chair?' I love that expression. I just hate that she's gone."

"She was a good lady," he agreed. "I have a little something for you. It's a late birthday present."

I smiled as I opened the simply wrapped box. It was a dainty necklace of an amethyst stone surrounded by tiny pearls.

"I have a friend in Springfield who is a jeweler, and he made this for me. I was thinking about your birthstones. Some claim it is an amethyst and some say pearls. It looked feminine and dainty, like you. I hope you like it."

"Thank you, Clark. It's quite lovely." I looked admiringly at the necklace.

"I don't see you wear much jewelry, but this might come in handy for a special occasion."

I touched his hand, feeling a rush of gratitude. "You have such great taste, and this is such a thoughtful gift."

He opened his mouth to respond when his eyes settled on the bouquet of roses that John had sent "Nice flowers. They must be from somebody special."

I was dumbfounded and couldn't think of how to respond. I didn't want to lie to him. "Yes, they're very nice. John, my Michigan neighbor, sent them."

The look on his face was solemn. "He definitely has good taste. I can smell them from here."

"So, how long will you be gone?" I asked, changing the subject as I poured more coffee.

"I'm not sure, but two to three weeks, most likely."

"I'm going to miss you, as always," I said, looking directly into his eyes. "I guess I always worry whether I'll hear from you again."

"What? Did I hear you right? I didn't think I'd hear anything like that from you."

Now I felt foolish. "I guess what I meant to say is that I sometimes fear the unknown."

"I think you know how I feel about you, Kate. I'm just waiting for you to catch up."

I smiled as he took his coffee cup to the kitchen.

"I have to get going," he said, setting his cup aside and pulling me close. "I'll be in touch. Enjoy that aunt of yours and the new house, okay?" He followed that with a big hug and a kiss on my forehead. He left and walked to his SUV without looking back.

As I watched him leave, I felt very sad. It was different when he was away. I went back to the table to look at my necklace. It was just like Clark to support his fellow artists. This gift was the most personal gift he had given me. I went upstairs to put it away. Clark was right in that this was something I wouldn't typically wear. I liked how he chose the gift so thoughtfully, however. I surely wished he hadn't seen John's roses. He seemed to be able to handle my relationship with John, which said a lot for Clark. I had to admit that I certainly wasn't prepared to tell John good-bye for good.

CHAPTER 63

It was close to noon when I went to check on Aunt Mandy. I had made her some tuna salad and I brought fresh tomatoes. She was unpacking dishes and was delighted to see me. She wasted no time telling me that Wilson had asked her to dinner that evening.

"I sense that he's a little lost in this community," Aunt Mandy shared. "I think he's used to being busy and having the conveniences of the city."

"Does being out of the city bother you?"

"Well, I might end up feeling the same as Wilson after some time passes. Who knows? I'm easily amused, however, and I like the quietness and charm I see here. The two of us always have so much to talk about. I think he'd like to take on more jobs. Perhaps it was too soon for him to retire."

"I'll drop a hint to Oscar about that," I replied.

"That was such a lovely evening last night. I hope you enjoyed it."

"I did, and Clark came by to have breakfast this morning. He gave me a beautiful necklace made by one of his artist friends."

"How nice. Will you miss him?" she asked as she set out plates for lunch.

"I might," I admitted, ready to change the subject. "I'm going by Ruth Ann's place after I leave here to turn in all the quilt blocks for our East County Fair raffle quilt."

"That would be so special to win. I can't wait to attend my first fair! Ellen said the Saxon Fall Festival is first. She called it a food fest."

I laughed and agreed. "Anna and her husband do a great job of organizing it year after year. As you can imagine, this county turns golden during the fall season!"

"I'll bet it does! It's my favorite season. It's so different in Florida. I'm hoping there will be less humidity here than back home."

I stayed another couple of hours to help get her organized in the kitchen. We agreed to go to church together the next day. I told her to report to me about her dinner date with Wilson. On my way to Ruth Ann's, I was thankful for the way things were working out for Aunt Mandy. I had to smile at the thought of her having an immediate dinner date upon her arrival in a new town!

Ruth Ann was expecting me and had a pot of coffee and a chocolate pie waiting. We laid out all the quilt blocks on her king-size bed. We had more than enough blocks to make a stunning quilt. She showed me a couple of options for setting it together. It was now all up to her.

When we went back to the kitchen for pie, she brought me up to date on her banquet schedule. She had some weddings on the books, and Harold and Milly had scheduled their anniversary dinner to take place one weekend. I loved hearing how the local community was embracing her business. When there was a pause in the conversation, I summoned my nerve and said, "John wanted me to ask if you've ever quilted anyone's funeral quilt."

She looked at me and smiled. "Are you still focused on that subject?" She poured us more coffee.

"Well, John has uncovered some interesting information and I have as well. It's something we've been sharing back and forth."

"The answer to your question is yes," she stated, surprising me. "This kind of information is not generally shared because it's personal and it is a private matter between me and my clients. I won't share any names, but recently two sisters brought me a wonderful embroidered top to quilt. It had violets all over it. They told me it was for their mother's funeral. They said she has always loved African violets, and they plan for the quilt to be used at her funeral. Their mother has been sick for some time. In the past, she had always made quilts for everyone else but hadn't made one for herself. She said she wanted one to take with her when she died."

"Oh! My goodness! Has the mother seen it? Is she still alive?"

"Yes, and she loves it! She has it on her bed and enjoys it every day."

"That is so special. John told me he had discovered that quilters were making their own casket quilts, which I thought was amazing."

"Yes, that's true. I know a lady who lives in Perry that is doing that very thing. She's not ill or dying, but she wants to be displayed in something beautiful at her funeral. I met her when I did a program for their guild there. She's doing a design of a cross using watercolor piecing."

"What is that?"

"It's when you use small squares of various shades of prints to create a watercolor effect in your design. She's been working on it for a long time. She said she detests the imported quilt look that so many folks are choosing for their caskets. She was a pretty classy lady, from what I could tell."

"Good for her!"

"But really, there are probably more baby quilts buried with people than any other types of quilts. I have quilted two that I know of. One baby was premature and one died of a brain tumor at eight months old."

"Seriously? How sad."

"I know. But, if you must bury a baby, it seems so much more comforting to wrap the body in a quilt. If not, the funeral home will just cover it up with a casket cover of some kind. You know how children gravitate toward their favorite blanket? Well, it's also true that some parents choose to keep their child's favorite cover because it may still smell like the child, and that gives them some comfort."

"It's so sad to think about how many parents have to deal with such things."

"If you share all of this with John, I hope you won't mention my name as the source."

"Of course not," I assured her.

I went home excited and yet sad about what I had learned. It's amazing what you discover when you just ask.

CHAPTER 64

I was anxious to share my new quilt information with John, but was worried about how to be discreet. Perhaps John, a professional writer, would know how to best handle that. I would have to give the subject some thought before talking to anyone. I would not want Ruth Ann feeling that I had betrayed a confidence.

I sat down at my office desk and opened the computer. Beside it was the information I had scribbled regarding Susan's mother. I had so many questions about the status of the case. Had they found her husband? I couldn't seem to get it off my mind, so I decided to email Susan's mother and request an update, knowing that I may hear nothing back at all. I'll have to admit, writing the letter made me feel better.

Emailing John was just like talking to him. It was so easy to pour my heart out to him and share what was on my mind. After I updated him on Ruth Ann's information, I requested that he ensure Ruth Ann's anonymity. I also asked about Carla and my neighborhood by the lake.

Just like that, his response was immediate. He must have

been on the computer. His response read: *This is awesome stuff, sweetheart! I'll honor your request.*

Why did he refer to me as "sweetheart" again? His email continued:

This has indeed been eye opening. Just so you know, I'm about to leave for dinner with a friend that's in from Minneapolis. You will be happy to know that she is my age and reminds me a lot of you. Keep up the good work! J.

He was having dinner with a friend who was a lot like me? Was this his way of telling me that he has a girlfriend? Would he be this open about it? Did he feel I was encouraging that? How could I not feel jealous, for heaven's sake? Was I naive enough to think this would never happen? He certainly knew Clark was in my life, so why was I surprised that he might be dating others?

Suddenly I had lost my appetite for dinner, so I closed the laptop and stood to get a glass of wine. I wanted to vent so badly that I grabbed my journal and began to write. My last entry had been about my sexual encounter with Clark. Reading my own words made it clearer to me how different my relationship with Clark was from my relationship with John. I wrote and wrote until the room became dark. The phone rang, and I could see that it was Maggie. I welcomed the interruption.

The first thing we covered was a report on our birthday dinners. We both played down any joy we may have had and agreed that we would never be apart on our birthdays again. When she asked if Clark had given me a gift, I told her it was a necklace that I would likely never wear. She got a diamond ankle bracelet from Mark that she had admired while they were on vacation. Mark was so good in that way. She really had her eye on a pricy sewing machine, but thought she'd better spring that on him later.

"How are Marilee and Emily?"

"Emily remains in a cast, and Marilee is still complaining now and then. I did get some news from Carla the last time I talked with her."

"Oh?"

"I think your downstairs neighbor has a girlfriend! Carla said she met her when she went there to clean. Has John said anything to you about her?"

I wanted to choke and could hardly answer. I swallowed hard. "As a matter of fact, he emailed me something about a girl being in from Minneapolis. They were about to go out to dinner. I guess we're talking about the same person."

"Interesting! How do you feel about that?"

I took a deep breath before I answered. "I'm jealous, okay? Isn't that crazy after I've kept telling him to find someone?"

"So, you don't want him, but you don't want anyone else to have him, right?"

"I suppose you spelled that out correctly."

"Oh, sister friend, you haven't changed a bit since high school! Do you remember Dennis Menard?"

I laughed. "Holy cow, sure!"

"You just had to go out with him until he finally asked you. Then you couldn't get rid of him fast enough! He only had eyes for you when all the other girls were dying to go out with him. I know because I happened to be one of them!"

"Okay, that's not fair. That was a long time ago. We were so young."

"I'm just sayin'!"

She knew me so well that it hurt. We talked for another

half hour. That was what was so great about our friendship. We had a long history that had survived the test of time. I trusted her implicitly. I loved Ellie, but our friendship wasn't the same as what Maggie and I shared.

I went up to my bedroom without dinner, feeling mentally exhausted. And, I was having a full-on pity party! My eighty-year-old aunt was out on a date, and I was home alone in my bedroom. My long-distance beau was even having dinner with someone his own age. I felt I was missing something, to be sure. My choices had me here in Borna, sitting alone on a Saturday night.

CHAPTER 65

I picked Aunt Mandy up so we could attend the later church service at Concordia. She wore a cute little mauve hat with a veil that added just the sweetest touch. It matched her suit perfectly and complemented her gray hair. Unlike South Haven, churchgoers here still dressed in their finest to attend Sunday morning services.

"I have so looked forward to this!" Aunt Mandy shared when she got in the car. "I'm curious to know if we will see Wilson and his daughter, Barbara. I think this church is where Oscar first met Wilson, if I recall correctly."

"I think you're right about that. I thought that while we're at the church, I'd show you the Paulsons' gravesites. The cemetery is quite charming, located on the hill by the church. After that, I could take you to Charlene's cute little coffee shop if you're up to it. They serve that good German coffee cake that her mother makes."

"I'm game! I have a feeling Borna is going to load me up on calories, but that's okay."

I chuckled. "I felt the same way, but after so many deprived years of trying to have the perfect figure, I succumbed and have been enjoying every minute of it."

When we entered the church, it was as if everyone knew that I would be bringing Aunt Mandy. We sat in the same pew where I had joined Emma on many occasions. It brought back sad memories of her, but I tried to shake them from my mind and concentrate on the present. Pastor Herman's message was to the point, as always. He had a way interpreting scripture and relating it to everyday life. I mentioned to Aunt Mandy that Lutherans sang every verse, no matter how many that added up to be. I was always touched by how many people voiced prayer requests during the time following his sermon. You certainly knew who had been taken to the hospital, who had birthed a baby, or who had just passed away. For such a little community, there surely was a lot going on!

My aunt and I did our best to look for Wilson, but with no luck. Oscar and Ellen were in the same front pew every Sunday. I saw Peggy across the aisle with Esther and her husband. The pastor had noticed Aunt Mandy's attendance during the sermon, and he was eager to welcome her as we entered the vestibule.

"Welcome to Concordia!" Pastor Herman said, shaking her hand. "I hear you have built quite a nice little place here in Borna."

"I'm sure it's quite the talk of the town, but I'm proud of it," she responded, smiling. "I plan to have an open house sometime soon, but feel free to stop by anytime."

"I might just do that!" He then turned his attention to me. "How are you, Kate?"

"I'm great and very excited to have my aunt here in

Borna, as you can imagine."

"Good morning," Ellen said, joining us. "How do you like our little church, Mandy?"

"It's very charming and welcoming."

"Oscar and I cannot wait to see the finished product of your new home," Ellen gushed.

"I'm happy to show it to you anytime," Aunt Mandy said, smiling. "I could use some of your good gardening advice."

"I'm glad it all worked out for you," added Oscar. "I hope Wilson followed through to your satisfaction."

"My, yes. Thank you, Oscar. He's been most helpful. I will be ever so grateful for you suggesting that location, too. It is perfect."

We finally made our way out the door. It was a perfectly beautiful day. I suggested that we drive to the top of the hill to the gravesite so Aunt Mandy wouldn't have to walk so far. She marveled at the view and the quaintness of the location. So many graves had flowers, which she thought was unusual.

When we got out of the car, I was shocked to see a yellow rose on Josephine's grave marker. My aunt quickly remarked that Josephine must have another admirer. I was speechless. Who would have put the fresh flower there? After a few moments at the gravesite, Aunt Mandy asked what made me so fond of Josephine.

I thought for a moment. "I think Josephine never had her own voice. She had to express herself in other ways, which she is likely doing today. It's strange how I feel her presence in that house."

"Did she die in the house?"

"No. After Doc died, she went to live with her sister, I'm told. I wish I had a picture of her. Isn't it odd that there doesn't seem to be a wedding picture or an anniversary photo?"

Aunt Mandy nodded in agreement. "So, in your mind, do you feel that she knows you're here?"

"Oh, I do! Some say it's their energy, but I refer to it as her spirit. I think she likes me. Isn't that crazy?"

"No, not at all! I think you are liked by just about everyone, and you have respected her memory, which is admirable, Kate."

We got back in the car to head to the coffee shop. That mysterious rose was preying on my mind.

CHAPTER 66

The coffee shop was packed full, but Charlene was very glad to see us. Gerard and his friends managed to squeeze in two places so we'd have a place to sit. I immediately made introductions, but they all knew about Aunt Mandy just moving to Borna. Of course, she basked in all the attention. We had just gotten our coffee when Chuck walked in. He must have gone to church because he looked pretty handsome in a sport coat. He saw us right away.

"Is that house of yours still standin'?" he teased, looking at my aunt.

"Yes, and I just love it," she responded.

"Say, I'm just curious. Do you get muffins delivered in the morning like I used to?" Chuck asked, sending a wink in my direction.

"Why, no! You must have been pretty special," she teased back.

"I'm not special enough, evidently," Chuck complained. "I think she's got another attraction in town."

Aunt Mandy laughed and I hardly smiled.

"You know, Chuck, I think I know the perfect girl for you," I stated, shocking him.

"You think so, huh?" he returned, tilting his head to the side.

"Ruth Ann. Do you remember her from the night at the winery?"

He grinned. "She's done a fine job with the place that she runs, but I'm not sure she's my type."

"I'm just dropping a hint, my friend."

"I wouldn't ignore that inside information," Aunt Mandy chimed in.

"Hey, do you women think I'm desperate or something? I'm kind of picky, and I know a good woman when I see one." He gave me another wink while flashing that wonderful smile.

"Don't believe anything that guy tells you," Gerard teased, overhearing our conversation.

"Well, Auntie, we need to get going," I announced. "It's been a pleasure, fellas." I stood and Chuck made his way to the line to place his order. I gave him a wave good-bye and received another wink from him before he turned to face the counter.

"Nice to have met you, Gerard," Aunt Mandy added. "You'll be seeing more of me at the museum. Do you still have the Bucket Brigade exhibit?"

"Better come before next week, because it's comin' down!" he warned. "Sharla Lee said we just got a donation of some really old dolls, so she's anxious to do a doll display of some kind."

"Well, I'm hoping to see them both!" Aunt Mandy said as we made our way to the door. Once outside, we shared a little chuckle about our visit there.

"Chuck is a little rough around the edges, but he's pretty handsome, don't you think?" Aunt Mandy teased, knowing she might get a reaction.

"He'll be a bachelor forever. He's never been married and Ellie said he's never had a steady girlfriend."

"Well, maybe there's a good reason for that."

I caught her drift but didn't respond. "I still think he and Ruth Ann would be a good match. She had her eye on Clark for a while, but then she saw us together. I was worried it might affect our friendship, but it didn't. She is a wonderful person."

I dropped Aunt Mandy off at her home, knowing she was ready for a nap. I was thinking that she might have had the same influence on me! However, when I got home, I answered a phone call from Maggie.

"Kate, I have some worrisome news." Maggie said, sounding stressed.

"About who? About what?"

"Well, I thought Marilee might be getting better, but in the process of her tests, they discovered that she has ovarian cancer."

"You don't mean it."

"She's had some of the symptoms for some time, evidently. She is so thin. They have surgery scheduled soon and then she'll follow up with chemo. She's not taking it very well. I'm sure the thought of losing her hair is part of it. You know her! Right now she won't see anyone, but the Beach Quilters are going to be there for her. Emily has some ideas about how we can help."

"I feel so badly for her."

"Of course, Emily didn't waste any time reminding me that the Ouija board read that there was cancer in the room. Remember?"

"Oh, for heaven's sake. It is crazy to think about that! Here we just got Carla back to normal. I hate cancer! I will email her instead of calling. I know that she has a lot on her mind right now."

"Please keep her in your prayers."

"I certainly will. I have Jack calling, so I'm going to let you go. We'll all get through this. Love you!"

"I love you too, girlfriend!"

CHAPTER 67

Feeling rattled from the news about Marilee, I somehow managed to talk to Jack without breaking down. He was full of news from work, so he kept the conversation going. For the first time, I didn't ask if he and Jill had set a wedding date. Jack wanted to know all about Aunt Mandy's arrival and her new house. Before we hung up, he did ask about Clark. I told him he was out of town. I tried to stay focused on our conversation, but it was difficult. When he said he needed to run, I was relieved.

I hung up and stared out of the window. My mind drifted to the subject of cancer. A person cannot help but wonder if he or she might be the next victim. My thoughts dipped deeper into negativity. Marilee may not be that lucky. Ovarian cancer didn't have a great survival rate. The Ouija board similarity had to be a coincidence; so did the word *car* and the word *trunk*. I had to put it out of my mind.

The rest of the day, I felt sad no matter what I did to keep myself busy. Aunt Mandy called to see if I wanted to join her on her porch for a cocktail. It sounded pretty good, so I told her I'd be there. She saw me coming and motioned for me to come around to the back screen door.

"Goodness, you've rearranged things already!" I noted, surprised.

"Do you approve?"

"Yes, indeed! This rug makes all the difference, and it brightens up the entire space."

"I was worried it was too much, but I like it!"

I sat down to join her as she poured Merry Merlot into my glass. I decided I needed to share the bad news about Marilee. Her pleasant expression changed to one of concern.

"Cancer has taken so many of my friends and relatives," Aunt Mandy admitted as she put down her wine glass. "So many people have to die in pain, which makes it extra brutal. I hope I go quickly."

"I think we all hope for a fast and easy departure for ourselves!"

"This may be the perfect time to share with you that when I went home, I changed my will," she said rather matter of factly. "I reevaluated my charity selections and also made you my executor and main benefactor. I hope my estate will not be a burden to you, but I am trying to simplify everything as much as I can."

"I'm overwhelmed! I don't know what to say. Are you sure about that?"

"You are my beloved niece and you are so wise!"

I tried to suppress a giggle. "Me? Wise?"

"You have enriched my life beyond measure."

"Well then, I accept. I want you to be happy. We will just grow old together, by golly!"

"I'll drink to that!" Aunt Mandy said, raising her glass as

we laughed heartily.

It was nearly eight, and I could see her becoming weary from a full day. I kissed her good night and told her I would pick her up the next day to go to Ellen's house for our Friendship Circle meeting. When I arrived home, I was pleased to see two reservations on my computer. They were both during the East Perry County Fair. One was a reporter from St. Louis and the other was a couple traveling on their honeymoon.

I never advertised a honeymoon suite, but Josephine's Attic Suite would be perfect. I booked The Study on the first floor for the reporter. In the back of my mind, I was hoping some publicity would come from the reporter staying here. He may be interesting, like John. Perhaps they even knew one another! Thinking of John made me realize I hadn't heard from him since his dinner date with his friend.

I closed my laptop and heard a knock at the front door. When I looked through the oval glass, there stood Carson. What in the world did he want at this hour? I opened the door slightly.

"What is it, Carson?" I asked, aggravated.

"I need a room," he said, grinning. "Your best friend just kicked me out. Can I please come in, for heaven's sake?"

I really wanted him to go away, but I let him in.

"Thanks Kate. I knew you'd help me out," he said, holding an overnight bag.

"Look, Carson, I don't want to get in the middle of anything between you and Ellie," I said firmly. "I'll check you in to stay in The Study, but I don't want to hear about your situation."

"Sure. Here's my credit card. I wish Ellie were more like you."

I didn't know what he meant, and I surely wasn't going to inquire any further.

"I'll leave early, so don't bother getting breakfast for me."

"That's fine, but it's included in the price, as you know. I'll leave this lamp on for you. I'll see you in the morning."

He looked at me sternly, as if he was both confused and disappointed by my behavior.

Without hesitation, I headed upstairs to my room. I heard him walk toward his room. I locked the two doors to my suite as fast as I could. I felt angry that he was in my house. I'm sure Ellie had a very good reason to kick him out. Perhaps I should have done the same. I wondered if she knew he was here.

CHAPTER 68

I was just getting settled into bed when I thought I heard something. It was the familiar stair creaking I heard when someone came up the stairs. I had that same creepy feeling when my elderly guest, Mr. Heartling, came up to see me one night. Thankfully, Mr. Heartling had changed his mind and wisely walked back down. I stayed perfectly still, listening intently. Then there was a soft knock at my door. Surely Carson wouldn't be so bold.

"Kate? Are you still awake?" he asked, his voice soft.

I didn't answer. I reached quietly for my phone and kept silent. He knocked again.

"Carson, I don't know what you want," I said, my voice measured and firm. "I am trying to get some rest. You are not allowed on this floor, so please go back to your room." There was a pause. I heard the doorknob turn.

"Now, Kate, don't be so huffy. I was just going to ask you for some aspirin."

"I can't and won't help you. If you don't go back to your room or leave this house, I am going to call someone for help."

He laughed, which only made me angrier.

"Okay, okay. Some hostess you are," he said sarcastically as I heard him walk further down the hall. If he made any attempt to get in that door, I was going to call 911. My thoughts began to race. Should I call Ruth Ann and Ellie and use the pink flamingo slogan we joked about to signal if we needed help? What should I do? I was listening intently for every sound he made. After what seemed like an eternity, I heard him creak back down the stairs. I drew a deep breath of relief. I was very awake and more determined than ever that he would never step inside this house again.

To be on the safe side, I got dressed. Now I would be ready, should I have any more trouble with him. I sat on the bed leaning against the backboard, willing myself to stay awake. After a while, I leaned into sleep. The next time I woke, it was three o'clock. I looked out the window to see if his car was there. There was no car in sight, so perhaps he had chosen to leave. However, if his car was parked at Ellie's house, I would have to leave my room and walk across the hall to see out The Wildflower bedroom window. I didn't want to risk that. I went back to bed and decided to wait until daylight. I also thought of Josephine and wondered if she was giving him any trouble in his room. I remembered how she had made a horrid night for one guest when she stayed here.

Finally, the sun was rising. With my cell phone in hand, I quietly made my way down the stairs, not knowing what to expect. Carson's door was closed. Was he asleep or was he gone? I wasn't going to open his door to find out! There was no car in sight as I looked toward Ellie's house from my office window. That was a good sign. That had to mean he was gone.

I fixed my coffee and opened the front door to get the paper. I put some English muffins in the toaster and got comfortable on the sunporch. It looked like it was going to be a beautiful day. About an hour later, I walked into the kitchen to refill my coffee when suddenly Carson said, "So where's my breakfast?"

I jumped a mile high and let out an ear-piercing scream. My coffee cup went crashing to the floor and coffee went everywhere.

Carson let out a cynical laugh as he enjoyed my reaction. "You didn't think I'd leave without saying good-bye, did you?" His delivery had an unmistakable flirtatious tone.

"I think you should leave, Carson," I said as I frantically tried to wipe up the coffee.

"You've got some serious problems. It's no wonder you don't have a man in your bed!"

"Just leave! I've had enough of your behavior. You are not allowed to come back here ever again!" I was shaking.

Giving me an even gaze, he slowly turned around and picked up his bag to leave. "My car was left at the winery, so I guess I'll have to beg a ride from Ellie."

"I hope she makes you walk there!" I shot back as I began picking up the pieces of my coffee cup.

He left and headed to Ellie's house. Should I call and warn her? I was almost as disgusted with her as I was with him. I wanted him out of my life and hoped Ellie would feel the same about getting him out of hers! The phone rang and I jumped to answer it, thinking it may be Ellie.

"Good morning, sweetie," Aunt Mandy's said. "How are you today?"

"I've had better, but I'll tell you about it later," I mumbled.

"I'm sorry to hear that. I'm just calling to see what time you'll be coming by for me today."

Oh, our meeting at Ellen's! I had nearly forgotten. "How about 11:30?"

"Jim dandy! See you then!"

CHAPTER 69

I began stripping the linens in Carson's room. I yanked them off the bed, wanting to burn everything he might have touched. Ellie threw him out for her own reasons, so perhaps I wouldn't have to do a thing. I had to remember to support her as a friend. I wondered if she would show up at the Friendship Circle luncheon. After a few chores, I dressed for lunch and picked up Aunt Mandy. She immediately came out of the door, so she had been watching for me. She looked so sweet wearing a beautiful teal outfit. I put all my grievances aside so we could have a pleasant day.

Ellen greeted us with open arms. We arrived at the same time as Peggy and Esther. Everyone was delighted to have Aunt Mandy join us. All of us were eager to see Ellen's gardens, which were in perfect bloom. Outside, we spent a while conversing about plant names and care before coming into the house. Aunt Mandy and I took note about what might work well in her new landscaping. By now, I knew Ellie would not be joining us. She would not have been this late to a meeting.

Ellen formally welcomed my aunt before we enjoyed a lunch of salad greens with cold salmon. She had freshly baked croissants right out of the oven, which was the perfect choice for a ladies' luncheon. I saw servings of crème brûlée cake with raspberries waiting to be served for dessert. Aunt Mandy was heavily engaged in conversation with some members that she did not know very well. When Ellen remarked about how unique Aunt Mandy's home was, my aunt graciously invited the group to have the next meeting there. I was astounded at her offer since she wasn't totally settled in.

"I may set us all up on the screened-in porch," Aunt Mandy suggested. "The breeze is quite lovely there, as is the view."

I pictured her glass table that only sat six people, but who knows what she had in mind?

"Ruth Ann has our raffle quilt put together, and she brought it with her today so we could see it before it's quilted." Ellen announced. All eyes were on Ruth Ann and soon compliments followed.

"Thanks, everyone!" Ruth Ann blushed. "Did you notice Charlene did a last-minute block to advertise her Coffee Haus? She did a great job!"

"I love the dark sashing," Anna commented. "I can't wait to see how you'll quilt it."

"I already have raffle tickets to pass out to each of you, thanks to Dresden Bank," Ellen announced. "It's not too soon to start selling them!"

"Now, Anna, do you have anything to report on the Saxon Fall Festival in October?" Ellen asked as she checked her agenda.

"Yes!" Anna answered enthusiastically. "We are having the Boxdorfer Boys for our musical entertainment on the stage this year. "If you haven't heard them, they're great! I am also taking coffee cake orders so we can bake them ahead of time in the outdoor oven. We usually run out, so it's a good idea to have them preordered. Let's see. Oh, yes! We have three more vendors than last year!"

"Thanks, Anna," Ellen responded.

"I would like us to follow up on an idea to have some quilts displayed around the grounds for next year," I reminded our group. "It would add such color and interest with the log cabins."

"I'm all for that, Kate, but we'll need a separate committee because I am really stretched with other things going on," Anna explained.

"Kate, would you care to take that on?" Ellen asked sweetly.

Everyone looked to me for an answer.

"I'll help you!' chimed in Aunt Mandy.

Everyone chuckled.

"See what happens when you suggest something?" Ellen joked. "It won't take very many quilts. Perhaps you can borrow some from your lovely South Haven quilters, like we did with the Christmas quilts."

"Let's do it!" cheered Charlene from the other side of the table. "Kate will do a great job."

Everyone clapped.

"Oh, before I forget, I want to announce Concordia's Apple Butter Cooking Festival coming up," Ellen said with a smile. "This year, to make it more festive, we're going to have colorful fall flowers on all the hillside graves. The men's club will have a lunch stand on that day as well."

I could just picture it. What a wonderful idea!

When we left Ellen's house, I teased Aunt Mandy about the trouble we both got ourselves into.

"Well, honey, you have to do your part in the community," she claimed. "You can hide or do your part to have a better quality of life. One needs to embrace life to its fullest!"

"I hear ya', Auntie!" I said, chuckling.

CHAPTER 70

I dropped Aunt Mandy off and noticed that Ellie had called on my cell. No doubt she had a lot to explain, and I wasn't sure how much I wanted to hear or tell. I just hoped she didn't blame me for letting Carson stay the night. It was starting to rain as I pulled into my driveway. Cotton was leaving after having mowed the lawn. I waved good-bye as he pulled away in his truck. There was also a text from John, which got my attention immediately.

> Hey neighbor. Hope you're ok. The quilt article has been rescheduled so I have time to add some more info. Have you learned anything more? Sure wish I could see you!

I wasn't sure how to take that message. Was he just using me as a resource these days? What did he really mean by wishing he could see me? I wasn't ready to respond—not just yet. I looked out of the window from my office and saw that Ellie was still home. I called her right away.

6626266

"Would you like some company?" I asked gingerly. "We missed you at the Friendship Circle meeting."

"Well, I had to do some paperwork here, and I'll be going to work shortly. Why don't I stop by on my way?"

"Sure, that would be great!"

I wanted to fill her in on more than the Friendship Circle meeting. How could I remain calm about her relationship with Carson and be there for her as a friend? I needed to find refuge in my kitchen. I longed for a lemon cream pie. I already had a pie shell baked, so I proceeded to accomplish the task knowing Aunt Mandy would love sharing it with me. In the back of my mind, I knew I had to respond to John. As soon as my lemon filling was done, I decided to call him instead of sending a text.

"Well, if it isn't my lucky day!" John responded.

"How are things?"

"Pretty good! I spent the morning on the lake. It's a perfect Michigan day, I'll have you know! I have an interview after lunch. How is your day going?"

"It's raining here. The lake sounds wonderful! I was wondering how your dinner date went with your friend from out of town?"

"Oh, with Robyn?"

"Is that her name?"

"Yeah, it was interesting, as always. She writes for the *Midwest Traveler* magazine. We know a lot of the same people in the industry."

"How nice. Another writer! I'm glad you're taking my advice about finding someone near your age."

"She is around my age and also happens to be happily married, I might add. Am I picking up on a tone of jealousy here?"

I had to pause out of embarrassment. "You might be. You didn't say anything about her being married."

He gave a hearty laugh. "Well, sweetheart, you just made my day! I may be getting somewhere here!"

Now I knew I had gone too far. "What do you mean by that?"

"Just when I think you've gone astray with the men of East Perry County, I get a glimpse of hope from you."

"I'm not going astray with anyone!"

"Well, when I offer to visit, you put me off, and you aren't willing to tell me when you'll be coming back here. What's a guy to do?"

He had me cornered, and I didn't know what to say.

"Just never mind," he laughed. "I remember that you have the East Perry county fair coming up. I could cover it and write it off as a business expense. I'm sure they would love the publicity, and it would give you an excuse for hiding me in your guest house!"

I had to chuckle.

"Okay, okay, drive on down. I do have other guests and it's a busy time for me, but I would love to see you again."

"The more the merrier! If you are too crowded, maybe I can bunk with the owner."

"John, you are too much!"

"Hey, don't stress out. I know you'll have to feed me at breakfast time. I'll settle for that if I have to."

I hung up with mixed emotions, as always. I was thrilled that he didn't have a girlfriend, but did I have any right to feel that way? I wouldn't let him be my boyfriend, so was I just leading him on to feed my ego? Oh boy, and what would Clark think about John's visit?

CHAPTER 71

At six, Ellie knocked at my back door. She looked tired and was not her usual cheery self. I offered her a drink, but she said she did not drink prior to going to work. We sat and I hoped that she could relax a bit.

She took a deep breath before she started to explain things. "Look, Kate, I'm sorry Carson imposed on you last night. There's a lot to explain, but I just want you to know that it's truly over between us."

"That's your business, Ellie. I just want you to be happy, and I especially want you to be treated properly."

"Ruth Ann was so right when she figured him out right away. He is a womanizer, among other things. Thanks for not judging me."

"Only if you promise not to judge me after I tell you that John is coming during the fair. He says he'll write up something for publicity, but it's an excuse for him to spend time with me. I don't know what it means, since I have a relationship with Clark."

Struck by the oddness of both of our romantic

relationships, we laughed.

"Men! As soon as you give them a little piece of your life, it gets complicated, doesn't it?" Ellie mused.

"You think you can get through life without them, but then you see Aunt Mandy still having a desire for male companionship at eighty years of age. Go figure!" I exclaimed.

We continued to chat for another half hour, trying to make each other feel better. I decided, under the circumstances, not to share Carson's aggressive behavior with her. She already felt badly about so many things regarding him.

After Ellie left, I called my aunt to see if she wanted some lemon pie. She declined, explaining that Wilson was coming over to play cards for the evening and he was bringing ice cream. It sounded perfect to me, so I couldn't be happier for her. I was feeling hungry for dinner, but with nothing prepared I decided to go to Marv's. I hadn't been there for some time, and I loved his daily specials.

Marv always stopped what he was doing to come say hello. "I haven't seen you for a while," Marv mentioned as he threw a bar towel over his shoulder. "I guess you're spending a lot of time at that fancy glass house down the road from you, huh?"

"Have you driven by to see it?" I asked, curious.

"You bet! It's the talk of the town. What can I get for you today? Our special is liver and onions."

"Oh, no. That's not going to work for me," I said, making a funny face. "Just give me a BLT sandwich with potato salad."

"Good choice! We've had the best tomatoes from the farmers here lately."

"I wish we had a farmer's market here in town."

"Well, most everyone has their own garden around

here, and we just don't get enough outside traffic to make it worthwhile. Now Harold has connections, and you can get any kind of produce you'd like from him."

"I'll remember that," I said, grateful for the helpful information. I was taking a sip of water while I waited for my order and noticed Chuck coming through the door. He looked pretty beat, but he smiled and made his way over as soon as he saw me.

"Why, I'll bet you'd like to buy me a beer, wouldn't you?" he asked with a wink.

"As a matter of fact, I'd be happy to! Marv, put his beer on my tab."

"Aren't you going to join me?"

"Thanks, but I usually get my food to go," I explained. "It's been a busy day."

"Okay, but I owe you a drink. Remember that!"

I nodded, smiling. I left enough cash on the counter to cover my food, the drink, and a tip. After giving Marv and Chuck a quick wave, I left. On the way home, I asked myself why I wasn't a bit more sociable. Chuck was really a nice guy, even though he wasn't my type. However, I was happy to arrive home and was perfectly content to enjoy my food all by myself. I checked emails as I gobbled away on my sandwich. It was especially good with the thickly sliced tomatoes Marv had described. Marv's prices were so cheap that I felt guilty at times.

The first email was from Carla telling me she had taken Rocky to the vet. She said they couldn't figure out what was ailing him. He was moping around the house and not eating. She hinted that he may be depressed about something. The poor baby was forced to live with Carla when I left South

Haven. It was Clay's dog, and I had never quite bonded with him. I told her I would be happy to pay for any expenses that she incurred for him.

Next, I sent an email to Maggie, asking about Marilee. I wasn't a close friend of Marilee, but she was part our quilt group and I certainly cared about her. At the end of the email, I made mention that John would be coming for the East Perry Fair. I knew that would get her riled up! I finally went to bed, wondering where Clark might be. He said he'd be in touch; but like so often, I had heard little to nothing from him. I guess I wasn't on his mind, and I had to accept that.

As I got undressed, I stared at the Ouija board that still sat on my dresser. Thoughts of throwing it away or putting it in the closet entered my mind. Unfortunately, it was not mine to dispose of. It certainly had been revealing! Maybe I should just see once again how quickly it responds. If it doesn't move right away, I'll forget about it. Sure enough, movement started quickly. It kept going and spelled out c-e-m-e-t-e-r-y. Why that?

"Are you asking me to go to the cemetery?" I asked out loud.

At first it was still, and then it suddenly spelled out y-e-s.

"Why should I go to the cemetery?" I asked again aloud.

It moved once again to spell out b-a-b-y.

I waited for more, but there was no further movement on the board. I went to bed trying to analyze what had just happened.

CHAPTER 72

I was glad I did not have breakfast guests the next morning so I could go directly to the cemetery. I put on jeans and a T-shirt before grabbing a quick cup of coffee. The rain had stopped, but the grass was moist when I drove up the hill to Josephine's gravesite. I parked in the road, not wanting to harm the grass due to the soft ground. I was once again shocked to see a perfect yellow rose on her stone. She must have a friend who is close by! My purpose was to find out what she described when she spelled out the word baby. Did she have a baby in the cemetery? The historical records showed no children, but what about miscarriages? I could only think of one person who would know anything about this cemetery, and that was Ellen. Despite the early hour, I gave her a call.

"Well, good morning, Kate," she answered cheerfully.

"Good morning. I'm sorry to be calling at such an early hour, but I'm at the church cemetery and I have a question for you."

"Well, if that doesn't beat all! How can I help you? I'm

on the patio having coffee with Oscar. I just told him earlier that you were checking out burial quilts. Are you discovering something? Wait until I tell him where you are!"

I could hear her chuckling as she let Oscar know that I was spending my morning at the cemetery. "I know he'll think I'm crazy, but have either of you noticed the placement of a yellow rose on Josephine's grave? They're always just as fresh as can be. Do you know who might be putting them there?"

"Well, no! That is peculiar. I suppose it could have come from a recent funeral, but I don't think we've had any burials up there since Esther's mom."

"There is something else I want to know. I have a clue that there might have been a baby of Josephine's buried here, even though the records show otherwise. Could that be possible?"

"The museum has our church records. I suppose if the baby wasn't baptized because of a premature delivery or miscarriage, it could still be buried there."

"It really does make sense. She would likely have been at home if such a thing happened to her. I feel like she is trying to tell me something."

"Now, Kate, don't get crazy here. Have you looked at the children's section down the hill from where her grave is? That's where it would be. Most of those stones are so worn that they may not tell you much."

"I have a small stone behind my barn at home. There is something engraved on it, but I can't tell what it is. Maybe it was a pet or maybe it was put there long before the Paulsons built that house."

"Who knows, Kate? Why is this so important to you?"

"I'm living with Josephine in her house, which has become my home. I want to know all about her, and I think she tries to communicate with me."

I heard Ellen sigh. "I'll tell you what—I will do a little snooping at the church and check the records again at the museum. I can also ask Arnie, our groundskeeper, if he knows anything about the rose."

"Oh, thanks so much, Ellen. Tell Oscar I haven't lost my mind."

We laughed. When I hung up, I walked down the hill on the very wet grass, feeling my shoes sink into the mud with each step. By the time I arrived at the section where babies and children were buried, my shoes were soaked. I looked at each and every little stone. Ellen was right. Most of the stones were worn or broken. On the very last rows near the trees, I discovered a small stone with four small letters. It had settled crooked in the ground from years of water washing down the hill around it. I brushed away the soil, and there was no doubt in my mind that it said the word baby and nothing else. Of course, it could be anyone's baby, but I was led to this little stone.

I felt suddenly overcome. I sat down on the wet ground next to the stone. Whoever's baby it was, seeing this grave made me sad. Women had so many secrets back in the olden days. Maybe it just wasn't in the olden days, come to think of it. What if the mother hadn't been married and she'd had to hide her dead baby? Speculating would not bring me closer to the truth. Maybe the church records would show who was buried in this tiny plot. I would just have to wait for Ellen to check.

Josephine herself was a secret. If she had birthed a

premature baby, she and Doc would likely have kept it quiet to avoid the embarrassment of not being able to have children. It was not a coincidence that I had found this stone. It was also no coincidence that we were told about Marilee's cancer and that I had a quilt in my trunk. Josephine had been channeling through me ever since I moved into her house, and it had all started with her quilt.

CHAPTER 73

I felt my mission was accomplished by going to the cemetery and finding the stone that said the word baby. I felt I had pleased Josephine in some way. I walked to my car, still not understanding where and why there was a yellow rose; but perhaps that would be determined in time. I had faith that Ellen and her connections would likely solve the mystery. Before I got in the car, I looked intently at the other graves to see which ones had flowers and which ones didn't. Was I missing a clue that might be right in front of me? A car pulled up behind me. I jumped, knowing I had to move my car on this single-lane road. I then saw it was Ellen. I burst into laughter.

"If you aren't a sight to behold!" Ellen teased, getting out of the car. "You had me so curious I had to come join you! I told Oscar I wanted to see that yellow rose for myself."

"I'm so glad you did! Come see the tombstone I found." Ellen followed me down the hill and stood nearby as I pointed out the crooked stone. "I think this is Josephine's baby," I said, stooping down to touch it. "Do you think you could find out anything about who put this here?"

"Well, I'll try, but there isn't a name, and I doubt if this even has a plot number. It looks so old, Kate."

"I know, but someone has to be buried here."

"Sure, but there is so much we don't know. I told you I would ask questions. Pastor Herman may know something, you never know. This rose is so perfectly beautiful, despite the hard rain last night."

"I thought the same thing!"

"Well, I have to be on my way to run an errand for Oscar, but I'll be in touch. You might check with Gerard at the museum about this. He loves a challenge when it comes to history."

"Good idea. Thanks for coming by. I think I'll stop by Charlene's coffee shop and treat myself to some breakfast. You are welcome to join me if you like."

"Oh, I wish I could, but I really need to run. I will be in touch."

Ellen left as I brushed myself off as much as I could before sitting in the car. Hopefully no one in the coffee shop would notice the soiled seat of my pants.

Charlene was very pleased to see me. The only other folks in the shop were Gerard, Warren, and Harold. I'll bet they had some great conversations here. "Don't mind those old geezers," Charlene teased. "They come almost every morning and cause trouble. Sometimes I have to throw them out."

The guys chuckled.

After I placed my order for a coffee and piece of cherry crumb coffee cake, I joined them. Harold got up saying that Milly would be calling him soon to tell him to get back to the store. I wished him a good day and sat next to two history buffs that could possibly help me.

When I told them I had just come from the cemetery, I

really got their attention. I didn't tell them my purpose, I but ended up describing the baby tombstone. They both agreed that, in the case of a miscarriage or premature baby, the child usually wasn't given a name. Warren said they didn't talk about such disappointments back then. Gerard had to insert his brand of humor by saying that they didn't talk about sex, either. Warren said people were so much more private back then as compared to now.

Unwise or not, I shared with them that there was a similar small stone behind my barn. When I suggested it might be for a pet, they dismissed that idea completely. They started teasing me about getting out there and digging for some results. They were so cute about crafting their own ways of making themselves laugh. I found humor in just watching them entertain themselves.

"I'll tell you what. I'll check on who owned that property before the Paulsons built there," Gerard offered.

"Thanks so much, you guys," I said, happy for their feedback.

"Next time, you're buying," teased Warren.

"You've got a deal!" I assured them as I got up to leave.

"Sorry, but everyone's got to go," Charlene announced from behind the counter. "I have to close at eleven."

I quickly told her I needed a coffee cake to go for Aunt Mandy. Aunt Mandy loved cherries, and I knew she would devour a couple of pieces of the cherry crumb coffee cake. Charlene was more than happy to make the sale. I had plenty to think about on the way home. I had made progress, but there was still so much to know.

CHAPTER 74

I went straight to Aunt Mandy's house with the coffee cake. I was anxious to hear how her evening went with Wilson. I called to let her know I was on my way. I never wanted to get in the habit of just dropping in on her without notice.

She was unpacking books and placing them on shelves when I arrived. Coming in with the coffee cake was a big hit. She thought it was the perfect option for lunch, so she poured us both a cup of coffee. It looked like it was going to be an old-fashioned coffee klatch. I described my purpose in going to the cemetery early in the morning and watched her face wrinkle into a look of concern. However, she was a good listener and didn't interrupt until I had shared the full story of my morning. Then she said, "Kate, maybe I shouldn't interfere with your thinking on this matter, but I can't believe you truly have faith in a silly Ouija board!"

"I know it's crazy, but I think Josephine is using it to communicate with me."

Aunt Mandy shook her head in disbelief.

"I may be crazy, but I think she wants me to know there was a baby. I'm going to have to examine her quilt again. I am certain there were names and dates that indicated miscarriages or early deaths of some kind."

"That's not unusual for that period of time. Lots of women went through miscarriages and even delivered stillborn. I'm just not sure what point you're trying to make by examining her so closely like you do."

I tried to put my thoughts into words. "It's like a puzzle or mystery, I suppose. I am living with a sprit that used to live in my house when she was alive. She was totally unrecognized, and there wasn't the next generation to tell the Paulson story. It's why I named the guest house after her."

"Well, that's fine, honey. I commend you for that, but her personal secrets or her unfortunate experiences are really none of your business. This may be a little harsh, but I think you must have too much time on your hands if you have the time to get into all this nonsense."

That was harsh. I swallowed hard and felt color creeping up my neck and onto my face. I blinked and said, "I never thought of it that way."

"I surely don't see very many guests staying at your place. Are you just enamored with the idea of owning a guest house but really don't want anyone staying there?"

Good point. "No one has ever asked me that before. I have to admit that I love having the place to myself most of the time, but I certainly don't regret having the business."

"Please don't take this wrong, but you don't advertise like most folks do in your kind of business. I'd think with your difficult location, you'd really have to concentrate on getting exposure. I know B&Bs that are so wonderful, they become the destination."

I was silent, not sure how to respond. She had never talked to me like this before.

"I guess I told myself not to expect too much in this little town, so I've accepted that. There aren't many people who travel through here."

"Well, when you don't expect much, you don't get much. Again, I'm not telling you how to run your business, but when I hear you are hanging out at a cemetery, I'm can't help but to call you on it!"

"Okay, I hear what you're saying. How about we change the subject to Wilson? How was last night?"

"I'd rather talk about that, too," she remarked as she shot me a big smile. "We played canasta. I haven't played canasta in years! We talked and laughed most of the night. He is such a fine man."

"I'm so glad you found each other."

"He is a real bonus when I think about having moved here. He is also quite proud of the design of this house. I hope Oscar will find more clients for him to work with. Wilson really likes being busy."

"I think it's time we start planning an open house, don't you?"

She smiled but protested, "I don't really know anyone other than some of the Friendship gals."

"You're wrong about that! I know that Chuck and his crew would love to attend your open house. I also know the husbands of the Circle members would love to see your house. Then there's Clark, Pastor Herman, Sharla Lee, and of course, Wilson!"

Aunt Mandy shook her head and laughed. "You do know

ANN HAZELWOOD

how to throw a party! I will need a caterer, you know."

"Kelly from the winery did a magnificent job when I had my open house. He also took on the role of bartender, so I could spend time with my guests."

"It sounds great, but I still have to do a bit of sprucing up around here, especially outdoors."

"Not to worry. I'll tell Ellen about our plan, and she'll be here with her crew."

"You are too much, honey. When you focus on something, look out! Maybe that guest house of yours will be next!"

Ouch!

CHAPTER 75

On my way home, I called Ellen and asked for her advice about landscaping Aunt Mandy's yard. She already had some ideas in mind and got extra enthusiastic when I told her there would soon be an open house. I went directly to my computer when I got home, wanting to check for any room requests. There were none, just like most of the time. What was wrong? Why did it take someone like Aunt Mandy to point out my problems with this business? I decided to call the best promoter East Perry had. Sharla Lee could promote and sell anything. She certainly had the contacts. I had to wait quite a while on the phone before she could break away from a visitor.

"I'm so glad to hear from you, Kate," she greeted me. "Tell that aunt of yours that I'd love for her to come by for a tour."

"Thank you. I know she hopes to visit soon. What I'm calling about today is advertising and promotion. I'm kind of stuck here as to what to do next. I'm really new at this. Is there any advice you could give me?"

"You are so kind to say that, but I don't have all the answers. Around here, it takes a village of contacts to make progress. I rely a lot on Trish from the Perry tourism office. She shares an office with the chamber of commerce. They do a lot of printed material that we don't do. Hasn't she called on you?"

"She may have, but I never know quite where to spend my money. There are so many options."

Sharla Lee laughed. "I'll give you her contact information. She's on top of everything. She needs to see your place, though. She schedules tours and promotes some events here free of charge. I think Ruth Ann has worked with her, and I feel like she could help you out."

"Thanks. I'll contact her." I said, ending the conversation. It was a start. Aunt Mandy would be pleased. Why didn't I do more of this before I opened my business? Did I think all I needed to do was put out a vacancy sign?

I went upstairs and put away the Ouija board. If I continued to play with it, I'd soon be checking it for the weather and my personal love interests. I would have to return it when I went back to South Haven or possibly send it back with John.

The prospect of seeing John again made me happy. Why hadn't I heard from Clark? He always says he'll be in touch, but he never follows through! How could we maintain any kind of relationship with that kind of behavior? I didn't even want to think about what it would be like to have John in town and Clark returning.

I went back downstairs to the computer where I received Trish's contact information. I didn't waste any time and sent her an email. I asked if I could set up an appointment. I didn't know much about Perry County other than its charming courthouse on the square. Having that done, I took a long look at my website to see what could be improved. I thought about using some testimonials from former guests. Some of my ideas wouldn't cost a dime.

I called Ruth Ann to chat with her about my mission. She admitted that she was lacking the same thing. She suggested that we do more joint advertising because that would save money. Unlike my guest house, however, her business was picking up. Her excuse for not focusing more on advertising was that she was too busy. That was certainly not the case with my business! Before I hung up, she let me know that she had completed quilting the raffle quilt. It reminded me that I had tickets to sell, or I would end up buying them all myself.

Ellen's name popped up on my cell as it rang. "I just wanted to call and tell you that I had a conversation with our janitor at church," she began. "He knew all about the yellow rose showing up, but was hesitant to say anything to anyone. He figures it must be placed there during the night."

"Who would visit a cemetery at nighttime?"

"It's mysterious, that's for certain. I guess it could be someone who doesn't want to be recognized. We'll figure it out one day, but in the meantime, Kate, I think we need to keep this quiet."

"You're probably right. Have you said anything to Oscar?"

"Oh, no. He doesn't want to hear anything about such things."

"Thanks Ellen. You're a trooper. I'm glad you don't mind helping out my aunt."

"I'm happy to do it, you know that!"

When I hung up, an email popped up asking about a room. I put aside my nonsense and tended to my real business.

CHAPTER 76

The next day, I told myself the day was going to be all about my business. I began by calling Trish in Perry and set up an appointment for the afternoon. She was delighted and suggested that we have lunch at a nearby restaurant called Mary Lou's. It sounded like fun, so I agreed to meet her at her office.

While I enjoyed a cup of coffee in the sunroom, I decided to quickly make some muffins and take them to Trish. It was a signature facet of my business that I wanted her to taste and smell. While the muffins baked, I got dressed in a navy-blue pantsuit and a white blouse. I had been so used to wearing jeans every day that it felt odd to dress professionally. However, after examining myself in the mirror and adding some accessories, I realized that I was glad to have made the effort to change my look and appear more professional.

Downstairs, I packaged the muffins and made sure I had business cards and brochures before I set off for Perry. It was a beautiful day to make the drive. I'd always wanted to explore more of the area; but with renovating the house and then building Aunt Mandy's house, I had felt committed to stick around Borna.

Perry was the county seat. It had over eight thousand people and was growing. I thought if there was time, I would visit some of the shops around the town square. Finding Trish's office was easy. She was on the corner of the square and there was plenty of parking. She was there waiting and was totally caught off guard when I presented her with some of my muffins.

Trish was an attractive blonde bursting with personality and ideas. As we sat in her office, she revealed that she knew all about my guest house. That put me at ease as I explained how naive I was in the hospitality industry.

"You can have the most beautiful place in the word, but if there isn't a soul to your business, it's just a house," Trish explained. "Because of your location, you must be good enough for customers to make it a destination. These muffins and your background in the blueberry world of South Haven make you very special! It's an image that you can use on your website and for your other advertising."

I smiled.

"Now, there are some other interesting historic places in your area, so have you thought about doing a package of some kind?"

"A package?"

"Yes, it's a bundle of goodies and opportunities at a better price, you might say. For example, you could include a night's stay with two tickets to the Saxon Village and a free bottle of wine from Red Creek Winery for one special price. You work deals with one another."

"I understand."

"I don't know if you've considered serving your guests a nice dinner, because there isn't a fine dining restaurant anywhere near Borna. If they wanted to celebrate a special occasion, a lovely dinner would be nice to include. Romance is a huge market. Do you have a honeymoon suite to advertise?"

"Yes, well sort of. I have a third-floor attic that I call a suite. As a matter of fact, I have a couple on their honeymoon staying there next week."

"That sounds perfect!"

We continued to bounce ideas around as we walked to the restaurant. Mary Lou's was a nice sports bar with lots of TVs. It was a high-end place for big hamburgers and anything fried that went with beer. They had just opened a brewery next door. Trish said a place like this was a much-needed business on the square and was doing well.

We both had the avocado and grilled shrimp salad. It was something different from my usual menu at home. It was just fun to be in a different atmosphere. Before I left, I invited Trish to come see my place.As she walked me to my car, I noticed a small, corner department store I thought I might visit. I said good-bye and walked across the street. I was immediately greeted by a friendly staff that was unloading some new fall merchandise. It was nice to see some trendy things and observe their excitement. It didn't take me long to select two black sweaters and a fall-colored scarf.

I saw there was a grocery store attached to the building, so I took the opportunity to pick up some things. The little grocery store in Dresden was limited in what it offered. Before I knew it my cart was full, but I was careful not to pick up anything frozen because of the length of the trip home.

The trip to Perry was very rewarding it and gave me the energy to promote more. I really owed this effort to Aunt Mandy. Family could get in your face with honesty sometimes. I wasn't used to that.

CHAPTER 77

I got home in time for cocktail hour, so I called Aunt Mandy to see if she was having some Merry Merlot while enjoying her screened-in porch. She was pleased to hear where I had been, and I told her I would stop by to tell her all about it.

When I arrived, I could see there were already some landscaping changes made to my aunt's front yard. She said Ellen and a couple of her grandsons had planted and mulched some things and would return tomorrow. She couldn't have been more pleased.

"I don't know how in the world I will ever repay that woman!" Aunt Mandy exclaimed, shaking her head.

"She loves doing it."

Aunt Mandy poured me a glass of wine as we discussed my day. She was pleased about my plans and was glad I took time for some shopping.

"I thought I'd drive over and see the museum tomorrow if I'm not needed here," Aunt Mandy mentioned.

"Sharla Lee will love seeing you."

"Oh, and another thing. Wilson thinks my car shouldn't be sitting out in the open. He thinks I need a garage. What do you think?"

"We talked about that in the beginning, but you were worried that it would take away some of your view. I didn't have a garage at first, but now I am so glad I do. The winters can be brutal."

"I agree, and he said we could easily get it done before winter. I think I'll give him the go ahead to hire Chuck and add that."

"Chuck will be delighted. I'd better warn you that he'll expect some of my muffins. I'd better teach you how to make them!"

We laughed. By the time I was ready to head home, we were sitting in complete darkness on her porch. It was so quiet and peaceful! We started on the invitation list and planned where her buffet and bar would be. If the nice weather held, some overflow could gather on the porch. I loved watching her get excited about it. This would verify that the whole community had welcomed her.

It was nine when I got home. I happened to look out the window and noticed that Ellie's car was in her driveway at a decidedly earlier hour than unusual. I hoped she was okay. I knew she was still pining over Carson. I went up to bed feeling the day had been productive on many levels. I kept thinking of ways to promote wedding guests, perhaps working together with Ruth Ann and Anna.

Suddenly, there were loud sirens going fast and furious by my house. I rushed to the street window to see what I could. Two fire trucks went by, followed by a police car. This was something I had never experienced since I had moved here. In this small area, it was likely that I would know the person they were going to assist. They weren't stopping near me, but there were many villages down the road. This must be one horrific accident. I went to bed praying as the sounds got dimmer and dimmer. Perhaps I would find out what had happened in the morning. When something happened, good or bad, it affected everyone in this community. I was not able to sleep, so I went downstairs to have some tea. I was starting to relax when another ambulance raced by the house. Please let this have a good outcome, I prayed.

CHAPTER 78

Ellie was the first to make the call the next morning regarding the sirens from the night before. She was quite worried about who it could have affected. She knew more people in the community than I did, so I could understand her concern. I told her I thought Harold would be a good person to ask. Ellie was heading to Perry to get supplies, so I told her I would find out what I could while she was gone.

Aunt Mandy's call was next. She, too, was awakened by the sirens and wanted to know if I knew what had happened. "Somehow these sirens are a bit more concerning out here in the country," Aunt Mandy noted. "In the city, they are just common everyday noise."

"I agree. I'll let you know after I make a few calls."

I wanted to venture out of the house today. I wanted to go to the bank, visit Ruth Ann, check in with Harold, and maybe stop at Imy's if I had time. I was about to get in the car when the phone from my landline rang. I thought it would be someone else curious about last night, but it was Mrs. Brueckner wanting to book a room during the fair like they had last year.

"As a matter of fact, I have one room left," I revealed. "I'll put you in the same room as last time. I'm so glad to have you back."

"We're glad to be coming back! My husband still hasn't stopped talking about those blueberry muffins of yours."

It made me smile. I could almost pinch myself in disbelief. All my rooms were filled for that weekend. It was exciting! Feeling energized, I headed to Harold's to see what I could learn about last night. While I waited for Harold to finish with a customer, I picked up two additional muffin tins. I knew I could use them when I had multiple guests.

"Well, Kate, did you find everything you were looking for?" Harold asked in jovial voice.

I nodded. "Have you heard anything about the commotion last night?"

He took on a serious look. "Yes, I heard about it late last night," he confirmed. "There was a fire at the Harold Mosely place on the north side of town. You probably don't know them, but they have a couple of youngsters that get in trouble all the time. Hector, the father, was taken away in an ambulance. Rumor has it this morning that he didn't make it."

"Oh, my goodness! What about Mrs. Mosely?" I asked, concerned.

Harold looked at me in an odd way. "She wasn't there. Hasn't been there for some time. Milly said she took off a good while back. She lives with her sister, somewhere."

I was relieved.

"Do you know those folks?"

"They were on our charity list this past Christmas," I

stated. I didn't want him to know any more.

"I never heard how the fire started," Harold said, scratching his head. "They must have all been asleep. I imagine they got burned pretty badly. They say there's hardly anything left of the trailer."

"It's all pretty sad. I'm glad his wife wasn't there anymore." I paid for my muffin tins and walked out with flashbacks of my experiences with the Mosleys. I met them almost as soon as I had arrived in Borna. The whole family invaded my house and demanded that I sell it to them. The next thing you know the boys started stalking my place, and Clark even got embattled with one of them. I tried to make peace by bringing them a basket of goodies at Christmastime, but that didn't work. The ham was returned to my back lawn. Hector's wife obviously felt badly about it and brought me a Christmas gift of a doily that her grandmother had made. She said it belonged in a fine home like mine. I will cherish it forever. It has a permanent home on my dresser.

I called Ruth Ann to see if she happened to be free for lunch. I wanted to discuss some promotional ideas. She had an appointment with a wedding client, so she couldn't meet up. I wasn't all that hungry, so I went on to Imy's shop. She was putting out some potted mums as I drove up.

"You're really on the ball. I can't believe you're already decorating for fall."

"Thanks. I get a lot of folks driving by here on their way to the fair, so I like to make the place look inviting. I have to get an early start to get everything ready."

"Good idea!"

"I was going to call you today, so I'm glad you stopped by."

"Did you get in something I would like?"

"No, not really, but I was going to ask if you'd like to go to an estate sale on Saturday. It's at the Homer Schmidt place. Mrs. Schmidt died some time ago, and Mr. Schmidt recently passed. They haven't sold anything until now. She always had nice things, they say. It's an all-day sale, so I didn't know if you would be up for it."

"I would love it!"

"They always have a good lunch stand, so there will be food and drinks if we need it."

"Sounds like a plan!"

We talked awhile longer about the commotion the night before. Time was passing, so I didn't take the time to go inside and shop. Somehow I wasn't in a shopping mood, so I went on home.

CHAPTER 79

When I got home, Cotton was working on the lawn. He stopped to speak to me. "Glad I caught you, Miss Kate. Susie wants to know if she should come in this week to clean."

"Sure, that'll be fine, but she'll have to leave the little ones. Are you sure she still wants to continue to clean for me?"

"For sure! She is dying to get out of the house. Her mom can watch the babies if she's feeling good."

"That sounds great."

"Say, did you hear about the Mosley trailer burning down? I heard Hector didn't make it. I guess there was a cigarette involved. Hector was in the bedroom and they couldn't get him out. Man, what a crusty old soul he was."

"Oh, it's all pretty horrific! I didn't know his wife had left him, so that meant she was safe. I wonder what will happen to the boys."

"I couldn't tell you, but it's a sad, sad, story."

"Keep me posted if you hear anything else."

Cotton nodded. "Sure will, Miss Kate. By the way, I got a call from Chuck and he asked if I could help him with a garage he's doing for your aunt. I'll just be the cleanup guy, of course."

"Good. Aunt Mandy really moved quickly on the garage idea."

"Well, if she wants it done before winter, we need to get moving on it."

"I'm glad you'll have the work. Tell Susie I'll see her soon."

"Thanks a lot."

I went inside to check emails. Once again, there were no requests for rooms. I decided I needed a decent dinner for a change, so I used some of the fresh produce I had purchased in Perry and made a veggie and pasta casserole. When I got it in the oven I whipped up some quick bread, which I hadn't made for some time. I loved making the house smell like home cooking and baked goods. I called Aunt Mandy and invited her to dinner. "I'll come get you if you don't want to drive."

"I'm not an invalid yet, my dear," she said, chuckling. "I need a few things from the hardware store, so I'll swing by after that. I appreciate the invitation, honey."

"Good. Just come when you can." I got busy setting a pretty table. It was nice to not eat every meal alone. The cell phone rang. I was hoping she hadn't changed her mind. To my surprise, it was Clark! "Is it really you?" I inquired sarcastically.

"Last time I checked! How are you?"

"I'm just fine. It's good to hear from you."

"What have I been missing?"

"Plenty, but the latest news is that Hector Mosley's trailer burned down last night, and I understand that Hector died. I don't know the condition of the boys, but the good news is that his wife had left him some time ago."

"Well, that's big news and also pretty tragic! I probably

shouldn't comment any further about that dysfunctional family. How is your aunt doing?"

"She's coming to dinner tonight, but what about your plans? Do you want to come for dinner when you return?"

"I can't commit right now, but I do want to talk to you about something that's come up. I don't want to commit to dinner."

"Oh, okay," I said, not able to hide the disappointment in my voice. "I have plans for most of Saturday. I'm going to an estate sale with Imy. I'm pretty excited about that."

"Do you have guests this weekend?"

"No, but I'm working on that."

"Good, I'll look forward to seeing your pretty face."

That was it! No commitment, as always! I wondered what he wanted to talk to me about. I hoped it wasn't regarding his health. Five minutes later, Aunt Mandy tapped at my back door.

"It's your neighbor! I took the liberty of picking up some pecan butternut ice cream for dessert."

"You are bad, Auntie," I teased as I put it in the freezer.

"Wilson told me about this little quick shop that carries unusual ice cream flavors. We had cherry walnut the other night. It didn't take him long to learn how much I love cherries." She smiled, obviously pleased that Wilson was so responsive to the things she liked.

"I'm telling you, Auntie, you've got that man under your thumb. It sounds so good. Do you want to start by pouring us some Merry Merlot?"

"My pleasure!"

CHAPTER 80

Aunt Mandy was pleased that I had heard from Clark and that I had visited with Trish about marketing ideas. When we finished dessert, I asked if she had any interest in going to the auction with me and Imy.

"Oh, sweetie, I just can't stand for long periods of time. It's still pretty hot out there for this time of year, too. It sounds interesting, but I need to get this place ready for an open house."

"I'm looking forward to spending more time with Imy. I wish she belonged to our Friendship Circle, but Ellie said she declined when they asked her to join years ago."

"Well, sometimes doing business and socializing doesn't always mix. This has been such a delightful and healthy meal, my dear. You are such a good cook. Have you considered Trish's idea of serving dinner here on special occasions?"

"I did think about it on my way home. Depending on the circumstances, I suppose I could be talked into it. They would have to book the whole house and be the only guests."

"Of course! You would have to have one price that

includes the room, dinner, and breakfast. You could also consider booking a dinner on a night when you don't have guests."

"I'm really not sold on the idea, but we'll see."

After we cleared the table and filled the dishwasher, Aunt Mandy got in her car and went home. I grabbed my journal near the rocking chair and went upstairs to my bedroom. I wanted to make some notes about attempting to turn my business around. If I put it in writing, it might serve as a form of commitment.

My mind wandered off about what the weekend might bring. When would Clark decide to show up? It was so like him to take his good old time and keep me guessing. It was around ten when I got a call from Maggie. Her calling at such a late hour concerned me.

"Are you still up?" she asked with hesitation in her voice.

"Of course! We country folk stay up late sometimes."

She laughed. "I'm having trouble sleeping these days. I haven't heard from you in a while, so when I heard some gossip today, I decided to call you."

"And what would that be, my friend?"

"Your former brother-in-law is going to marry that rich socialite from Grand Rapids!"

"You're kidding! Well, there must be a lot of money there."

"That's what they're saying. Maybe she can save Meyr Lumber."

"I guess that would be the good side. I never wanted anything to happen to the company. Clay and his father worked very hard to achieve their success. I can't help but think of poor Emily and her brothers. Does this woman have a name?"

"No one in my world has ever said. I heard they are going to build a gigantic home on the lake. It's all part of the deal, I guess."

"Thanks for the scoop, but I don't have anything as juicy for you. Nothing in that Meyr family surprises me anymore."

"Well, how's Clark?"

"I couldn't tell you. He's been out of town. I can tell you that John is coming to Borna during the East Perry Fair weekend."

"And what is that supposed to really mean, girlfriend?"

I laughed. "It means that he is going to write an article about the fair and that he'll be staying at my guest house."

"Why does this explanation sound fishy to me?"

We burst into laughter. When we finished our silliness, Maggie reported that Marilee was having a rough time with her chemo treatments and hadn't been to the quilting group for some time. Marilee did mention how much she enjoyed Carla's cake. Maggie continued, "The Beach Quilters made her a really neat lap quilt that was backed with minky fabric. We haven't given it to her yet, but it will be nice and soft for her to cover up with."

"That is very thoughtful. She will be thrilled."

Like always, a conversation with Maggie made me feel better. She never judged me, but encouraged me instead. That was a true friend!

CHAPTER 81

Imy picked me up at seven thirty in the morning so we'd have plenty of time to look over the sale items. When at estate auctions, she said she found it hard to bid on items when family members were also bidding on the same things. Imy said that dealers typically back off when they see that happening, but there are others who don't care or who don't recognize the other bidder as a family member.

"Oh, Imy, I can't imagine being a family member and watching your family treasures go to strangers."

"Sometimes you do see reactions afterwards. It's kind of sad, but most families have to face it at the end. If you need any advice about how to bid on things, just let me know."

"Thanks! What do you know about this estate?"

"Very little. Both parents have died, but the kids just let everything stay as it was for some time. I looked over the advertisement, and it appears that they have nice things. When I saw quilts on the list, I thought of you. They sold off all of the farm equipment yesterday."

We parked in the field along with what seemed like

hundreds of cars and pick-up trucks. We went straight to the lunch stand, run by the Trinity Lutheran Men's Club, to get a cup of coffee before we viewed tables and tables of merchandise. As we scanned the many household items, Imy said one could tell a lot about a family from the items they had for sale. It could show the good, the bad, and the ugly. As an example, she picked up a jar of buttons. She claimed that a jar of buttons could hold information about the lifestyle of a family. It might contain uniform buttons, fancy dress buttons, snaps, and extra garter hooks, but mostly it would hold mundane shirt buttons. I couldn't imagine all my personal things being strewn on a table for everyone to see.

I separated from Imy so she could concentrate on what she wanted to bid on for her business. I recognized some people in the crowd like Harold's wife, a lady from church, and a waitress from Marv's. I went straight to the pile of folded quilts stacked neatly on wooden tables. Most of them were very old and made with dark-colored fabrics. I knew most of the quilt patterns. No one seemed to be too interested in them, but the one that caught my eye was a Bow Tie quilt. It was pieced out of old neckties, and the bows were smaller than any I had ever seen. The piecing was precise and perfect. It appeared it hadn't been used or washed, which was what I usually looked for. I knew right away, with its masculine look, that it would be perfect in The Study guest room. When I picked it up and unfolded the beauty, folks gathered around to see more. I couldn't place it back on the stack. I knew I had to have it, but it wasn't that simple.

"That was made for Freddy, the oldest boy," a voice said to the right of me.

"Are you a family member?" I asked.

"Nope, just live down the road a piece," answered a hard-looking elderly woman. "We were neighbors with these folks a long time. Freddy and I grew up together."

"How do you know this was made for Freddy?" I asked, my interest piqued.

"His mama never let him forget it," she stated firmly. "Since Freddy never married, she'd say, 'Freddy, since you ain't got a wife to share this with, I want you to take this nice quilt to your grave.' Freddy ignored her as usual, but she was serious. She thought everyone ought to be buried with a nice quilt. It always had Freddy's name attached on it, but I guess they took it off for the sale."

"So, no one in the family wanted her quilts?"

"It don't look that way, does it?" she said coldly. "I'm sure they would rather have the money. Those boys don't live around here. They say Freddy owns a lot of land in Texas."

"Are any of the family members here today?"

"Don't see none," she answered as she looked around. "Are you gonna bid on that one?"

I wasn't sure how to answer. "I just can't believe the family wouldn't want some of these quilts," I repeated in disbelief.

"Oh, maybe they already pulled out the stuff they were interested in."

I continued clutching Freddy's quilt like it was already mine. The other quilts I could leave behind, but not this one. I eventually returned it to the stack and knew that I meant to secure it for The Study.

The auctioneer started with the tables and tables of glassware. That was Imy's specialty, and she kept busy bidding on numerous pieces. After the glassware was done,

Imy and I went to get a bite to eat while I kept an eye on the table of quilts. I ordered a sloppy joe on a bun that came with a big dill pickle and potato chips. There was a lot to choose from on the menu. Most everyone was eating the German bratwurst which I had never acquired a taste for. Imy had a fried catfish sandwich that she raved about. The homemade pies were so tempting that I had them hold two slices for me to take home. I selected the cherry crumb for Aunt Mandy and the chocolate with a mile-high meringue for me. When we got our food, we sat down under a shade tree and listened to the auctioneer get every penny he could from each item. I ate quickly so I could get back to the quilt table. Imy said she planned to bid on a couple of the quilts that she knew she could sell.

Before long, the assistants handed the auctioneer the Bow Tie quilt. It was held up for all to see. When the bidding started, it reminded me of an echo as I responded to each bid that came from the back of the crowd. As the bidding bounced back and forth, I felt that the price was getting out of my comfort zone.

Imy looked at me in amazement. "You know that quilt is going for far beyond what it's worth, don't you?"

I nodded. "A thousand dollars!" I yelled as loud as I could, getting everyone's attention. I thought Imy was going to faint. It was a big jump from the last bid of seven hundred dollars.

"Going once, going twice," the auctioneer said as the crowd maintained its silence. "Sold to the pretty young lady to my right," he pronounced as several people applauded.

I felt embarrassed as they handed the quilt to me. I couldn't believe what I had just done! Imy had warned me that this could happen.

"Congratulations, pretty lady," Chuck said, approaching me. "I was curious to know how far you would go to get that darn thing."

"Was it you that I was bidding against?" I asked, suddenly indignant.

He grinned in admittance.

"Why did you do that?"

"I'm kind of that way, I suppose. I like quilts, and that pattern was the best of the bunch. But when you bid a thousand dollars, I stopped. That's good earned money that I didn't want to spend on a quilt. I'm glad you got it."

I gave him a stern look and walked away to pay for my purchase. There was something I didn't like about that guy!

CHAPTER 82

Before I went home, I stopped by Aunt Mandy's to drop off her pie and show her my Bow Tie quilt. I wasn't about to tell her what I had paid for it! When I told her the story about my conversation with the neighbor, she was quite concerned that the quilt didn't go where it was intended. It did please her when I told her about Clark's phone call and that he had something to discuss with me. I told her I was disappointed that he refused my dinner invitation.

"Well, I got a nice dinner request that I didn't refuse," she teased.

"Is that so?"

"Wilson wants me to have dinner with him at his daughter's house tomorrow."

"That's interesting."

She grinned. "It's sweet, that's what it is. I feel like I already know her. He talks about her so much."

"This is getting pretty serious, if you ask me. I just hope you'll ask me to give you away at your wedding."

She shook her head and gave me a sarcastic look.

"You'd better get on your way, silly girl, and mind your own business!"

I did get on my way and smiled to myself about teasing her. I was quite intrigued as I watched this senior relationship develop. They didn't play games like I seemed to be doing with Clark and John. It made me so happy that she was truly settling here in Borna.

When I got home, I went straight to The Study to arrange the pretty Bow Tie quilt on a quilt stand. Just as I imagined, it was perfect and it added a nice accent piece to the room. I decided to call it FREDDY'S BOW TIE QUILT.

Tomorrow was the harvest festival at church. I didn't dare miss the occasion and I was anxious to see all the flowers on the gravesites. I had two small pots of yellow mums that I planned to place on each of the Paulsons' graves. I planned to take photos and send them to John.

I poured a glass of wine and nibbled on some of the summer sausage and crackers that I had purchased at the grocery store in Perry. It was delicious and just enough food to serve as my dinner. I made my way to the office and opened my laptop. There was an email from Jack saying he would be calling me at one on a conference call that was to include Mark and Maggie. With no explanation, I knew it had to mean that there would be a wedding date announced. I would love nothing more than to plan a wedding. I could hardly wait! I decided to send Maggie a text to see what she knew.

Did you get a request to accept a conference call from Jill and Jack at one o'clock tomorrow? Could it concern the big moment we've been waiting for?

I waited, but there was no response. Maybe I should have called her. I went upstairs to get ready for bed. I was too excited to fall asleep. I tried to imagine what the wedding would be like. Would Jill be a June bride? Who would be in the wedding? What would I wear? Would the reception be at the country club, like everyone would assume? How could Jack keep me waiting for answers?

As I chose my own answers to these questions, I realized that some of the Meyr family would attend the wedding—like my brother-in-law, James. Even though Jack was not happy about how they treated me when I moved to Borna, I knew I would have to accept that they were still his relatives. Oh, how I wished Clay could be here for all this excitement.

Finally my phone made a bing, indicating that I had received a text.

> Jill just texted us and gave us instructions for tomorrow's phone call. I hate waiting! What if they tell us the engagement is off?

> Oh, Maggie, be positive!

> Right. ;-)

CHAPTER 83

Aunt Mandy called early in the morning to tell me she wasn't feeling well enough to go to church. She'd had very little sleep the night before, claiming she was worried about the open house. I told her I would give her a good account of the festival.

The church's harvest festival was truly impressive. As I drove by the cemetery hill, it was completely embellished with fall flowers! No one was allowed to drive up the hill, so after I parked my car along the roadside I walked up to the Paulsons' graves to place my flowers on their gravesites.

When I saw their graves, flowers were already placed nearby. I added my mums, noting that there wasn't a yellow rose anywhere in sight. Perhaps the church volunteers removed it as they made room for their flowers. Curious, I walked to the side of the hill to see the tombstone with the word baby engraved on it. I was pleased to see that each of the infant tombstones was adorned with small fall floral bouquets as well. I took a couple of photos. Later, as I entered the church, Ellen was one of the greeters that welcomed me. "It's a beautiful sight out there, Ellen."

"Wait until you see inside!" She pointed to the display of harvest fruits and plants beautifully arranged on each side of the altar.

I quietly found a seat.

Pastor Herman's sermon was about all our bountiful blessings for which we should be thankful. It reminded me of Thanksgiving Day. The pastor made sure to acknowledge Ellen for her outstanding contribution.

After I left the service, I called Aunt Mandy to see whether I should pick up some lunch for her. She declined, saying she had eaten a late breakfast. I described the beautiful cemetery hill and encouraged her to drive by sometime soon to see it.

"Jack is calling today at one on a conference call with Mark and Maggie. I hope it's news about a wedding date."

"Oh, that would be wonderful! They are so smart to announce it to both sides of the family at the same time."

"I'll be sure to call you afterwards."

"Please do! You know where to find me."

"Is tonight your big dinner and when you get to meet Barbara?"

"Yes, and that's another reason for me not getting much sleep, I'm afraid. I want to make a good impression, you know."

"She is going to love you! If she doesn't, she'll be sorry!"

As I ate a small salad for lunch, I had to smile about Aunt Mandy having the jitters at eighty as if she were a young girl meeting her boyfriend's parents. I watched the clock as I waited for one o'clock to arrive. I jumped when the phone rang a little early.

"Mom, its Jill, Maggie, and Mark on the phone," Jack announced. "Can you hear us okay?"

"Hi, Kate," Mark was the first to say. "Hope you're doing okay. I haven't seen you in a while."

"Thanks, Mark. Jill, it's nice to have you on the phone for a change," I added.

"Well, I'm glad you were all available so we could tell you that we have set a wedding date!" Jill announced with much excitement in her voice.

Everyone cheered.

"We're all waiting!" said Maggie.

"It will be the thirtieth of June at our family church in South Haven at one in the afternoon," announced Jack.

"How wonderful!" I said before anyone else responded.

"Have you booked it already?" Maggie inquired.

"Yes, we're all set," Jill confirmed.

"Great news, you two!" I added.

"What about the reception?" Maggie asked.

"We booked the Hawk's Head," Jill said, clearly excited.

"Why on earth wouldn't you book the country club?" Mark questioned. "You could have booked that for nothing since we're members!"

"I know, but it wasn't special for us," Jill argued. "We've always liked the casual openness of Hawk's Head. We have our personal reasons, Dad. Jack and I are paying for everything, so don't worry."

"No you won't!" Maggie protested. "The bride's parents are supposed to pay for the wedding. We only have one daughter!"

"Mother, we are not children!" Jill fired back. "The reception is set for six, and we were lucky to get the band we wanted."

"Okay, daughter. We'll discuss this later," Maggie said, her voice firm.

"Well, I'm thrilled, to say the least," I offered. "You have a lot of time to do more planning."

"We will need invitation lists from both of you as soon as you can get them to us," Jill instructed.

We conversed back and forth for about ten more minutes. I was beginning to feel I was the third party in it all. As always, Maggie did her best to keep control of Jill, but it was pretty obvious that we were dealing with two adults who were planning their own wedding.

After our conversation, I wondered what the groom's parents did in all this planning. Weddings always seemed to be about mothers and daughters. I knew Maggie would get her hands on this wedding, one way or another!

With a smile on my face, I quickly reported to Aunt Mandy, giving her the wedding updates. "I hope you escort me to my son's wedding in South Haven on the thirtieth of June next year!" I announced.

"Oh, blessed be! I'm so happy for all of you. I wouldn't miss it!"

"I have a feeling there may be fireworks before it is all said and done, but the good news is that Jack is getting a wife and hopefully a family someday. I can't help but think how happy Clay would be."

"There's no question that he would be, honey. For all we know, he may know. Please convey to Jill and Jack how happy I am for them. God willing, I will be there!"

CHAPTER 84

I was absorbed with wedding thoughts the rest of the day until my cell phone rang, showing Clark's name.

"Will you be home the rest of the evening?" he asked quickly after I answered.

"Sure. Come on over."

It was good to see him when he walked in, although he seemed to be markedly thinner. He gave me a hug, but did not offer a kiss. He clearly had something on his mind. He agreed to have a beer, and we settled on the sunporch. I was determined not to ask any questions.

"You know, I wasn't going to share this news with anyone, but I'm not sure I can sort through this on my own," he began.

"Did something happen to you while you were gone?"

He nodded. "I got a very shocking phone call from a woman named Michelle who claimed to be my daughter." He gave me an even gaze.

"What? Are you serious?" I drew in a slow, deep breath.

"I can't remember every detail of the conversation,

but she had enough information that I couldn't deny the possibility that it could be true."

"Does she have proof? Who is the mother? Why did she choose to approach you now?"

He got up from his chair and started pacing. "I was married for a short time. We were pretty unhappy. I had a couple of encounters with a gal when I'd go out of town. She was a sweet bartender at a bar I'd frequently visit."

This was revealing. I am sure that my eyes were wide as he continued.

"The mother chose not to tell me she was pregnant, which doesn't surprise me. Now that her, or maybe our, daughter is pregnant, she decided to tell Michelle who her father is. She found out where I was living by asking the proprietor at the gallery in Springfield where she saw my work."

"That wasn't very professional of him."

He ignored my comment. "I honestly can't remember her last name, but everyone called her Lucy. She said her mom named her after Lucille Ball because she had red hair. She was beautiful and was friendly to everyone."

She was friendly, all right.

"At the time she was married as well, so the encounter was very casual."

"So, Michelle's dad isn't who she thought he was all these years."

"Lucy has been divorced for some time. I'm glad she never called me, but hearing about this has gotten my attention! Michelle was so polite and said she would feel terrible if she were mistaken. She wants some closure on this and asked if I would take a paternity test to know for sure."

"So, are you going to meet up?"

He sat down and put his head between his hands. "I suggested that we wait until we know the results."

"That makes sense. Where does she live?"

"Nashville. I think she said her baby is due in February. I didn't ask many questions, but I think she'll be raising this kid alone—just like her mother."

"So, Clark, you could become not only a father, but a grandfather!"

"Not so fast! None of this is certain, but I just had to tell someone."

"I understand. This must be quite a shock. What is your gut feeling from what you know so far?"

He got up to get his beer and took a swallow. "It's kind of bizarre, but it may be possible when I think about the timing. I simply had to respond."

"Of course you did! How old is she, by the way?"

"She'd be around thirty."

I couldn't help but think of my Jack who is around the same age. "So, did you begin the process?"

He nodded. "I just sent it off to the address she told me."

"When will you find out?"

"I have no idea."

"This reminds me of what I experienced once when I thought I was pregnant. I took a test in hopes that I wasn't pregnant; but when it was negative, I was disappointed."

Clark smiled. "I can see that." He closed his eyes and drew in a long breath. He slowly exhaled, opened his eyes, and looked at me. "I knew I would feel better sharing this with you."

"I'm happy to be helpful." I paused, thinking he seemed ready to end the subject. "I have a bit of news today. Jack and Jill set their wedding date for June thirtieth of next year. Maybe if I'm lucky I will be a grandparent in time, too."

He smiled. "Great! Will they be married in South Haven or New York?"

"In South Haven. It's where the bride and the mother of the bride will conduct the drama that's about to unfold. The bride and groom have made their own plans, and not everyone is pleased. It seems that the groom's mother is basically a nobody who doesn't have a role in all of the plans."

He laughed and we continued to hash out all the new information for another half hour before he had to leave.

"I'm glad you're back in time for the fair."

He laughed and shook his head. "You know I run and hide from such things."

"Well, I can't because I will have a houseful of guests. I'm booked up!"

"Well, that's great. Maybe we can have dinner soon, but right now I have a lot on my mind. I hope you've been behaving yourself."

What was that supposed to mean? "You know where to find me," I offered, suddenly not sure how to close the conversation. I walked him to the door.

Clark stepped closer. He wrapped his arms around me and held me close. We took several breaths and remained in the hug as if time had suddenly slowed. He released his embrace, gave me a brief look, and headed through the door.

CHAPTER 85

Days had passed and I hadn't heard a word from Clark about having dinner. I didn't want to violate his confidence in telling me about his paternity test, so I kept it to myself. I knew he was taking this seriously, and I was glad he showed confidence in me by letting me know. I did wonder how much thought he was giving to the remembrance of Lucy in light of recent events.

Fall was starting to show its early signs. Goldenrod was blooming everywhere and corn was being harvested in most of the fields. It was only early September, but businesses and homes were showing autumn and Halloween displays. It got me to thinking about what I could display on my front porch. I didn't like messy hay bales, but a lot of pumpkins and mums would be nice.

With Susie's help, the guest house was prepared to receive my East Perry Fair guests. I enjoyed planning the breakfast menus. John's recent texts caused me to be concerned about having him in town the same time as Clark. Would Clark even know John was here or would he even care if he did know? I had to admit that I was excited to see John after all this time apart.

Today was Aunt Mandy's open house and I wondered if Clark would be there. Aunt Mandy assured me that she had everything under control, but I knew Wilson was also at her disposal. I ordered some nice flowers from a floral shop in Perry to be delivered to her home. It was a perfect day for Aunt Mandy's party. I knew she would have a good turnout because folks would be curious about her and the unique house.

"I think my team is on the ball," Aunt Mandy claimed when I called. "Early this morning Kelly brought his equipment over, and even earlier one of Ellen's boys was here to spruce up outdoors! Your flowers are so beautiful, Kate. That was certainly unnecessary."

"I'm glad you like them. I'll come a little early to ease your nerves."

"Thanks. Wilson indicated that he'd do the same. He is bringing Barbara, so you'll get to meet her."

"Oh, that'll be nice. I'll look forward to it."

"Yes, she is so sweet. I know you will like her."

I decided to wear a brown polka dot dress with a white cardigan sweater. Any chance I had to get out of my blue jeans was a welcome event. Ellie called and asked if I minded her going to the party with me. She said she could get a ride home if I decided to stay later. I agreed, thinking it was a good idea.

When she arrived, she bragged about the delicious food Kelly had prepared for the event. "He loves to kick it up a notch for parties like this," she said with excitement. "He gets tired of making the same old BBQ and gumbo. By the way, Clark was at the bar last night. You didn't tell me he was back."

"He did stop by to see me for a little while. I hope he

comes today. Aunt Mandy thinks the world of him."

"Probably more than you, right?" she teased. "Have you told him that John is coming into town?"

I shook my head. "He'll probably never know. He never goes to the fair, and he knows I'll be very busy with my guests. I must admit, I'm anxious to get an update on John's research for the quilt article. Speaking of, did you get to drive by and see the fall flowers on the cemetery hill?"

"I did! It was quite a sight. I don't remember them doing that before. How long will John be here?"

"I'm not really sure."

Before we left, I showed her my auction purchase of the Bow Tie quilt. She really loved it and seemed to be envious. I told her to look at the quilts Imy had purchased when she went by Imy's shop sometime soon.

"It's my turn to have Friendship Circle, don't forget," Ellie said. "Your aunt can have it after me since she's having the open house."

"I love going to your place. Can I do anything to help?"

"No, not really. It's not the food that is difficult. But with working at the winery, I just don't have the time to clean and keep up with things."

"You should ask Susie to clean once in a while. She would welcome the extra money."

"I wouldn't need her on a regular basis; but if you don't mind sharing her, I may just ask her to help me."

"What are friends for, anyway?"

CHAPTER 86

Even though I had plans to arrive early for my aunt's party, Wilson and Barbara beat me to the punch. Wilson introduced me to his daughter who was surprisingly simple in appearance and very gracious in her mannerisms. I liked her right away. She loved Aunt Mandy's house, and I gave her dad credit for his unique design on the country road. "I've told her many times how much I envy her location as compared to my house situated on a busy main street," I said as Wilson went to join Aunt Mandy in the kitchen.

"Your guest house looks so inviting," she shared. "I would love to see the inside someday. I worried about how my dad would adjust to being here; but thanks to your aunt, he seems to be quite happy."

We laughed and nodded in agreement. Our conversation was cut short by the arrival of the first guests. Most of them knew me and not my aunt, so I greeted them near the front door. When Oscar and Ellen arrived, I couldn't thank them enough for being involved in the initial plan.

"I'm pleased to hear that Chuck will be building a garage

for her before the end of the year," Oscar stated. "He does such a fine job, and he loved the challenge of this design. If you ever want to develop this ground of yours any further, I would be happy to advise you."

"Thanks Oscar, but my aunt's house was truly an exception. I don't have any plans beyond that."

The Friendship Circle membership turned out in force. Those who had husbands joined them in the celebration. It appeared that most everyone showed up except Clark. Chuck brought his crew, along with their wives. Chuck cleaned up nicely, and I couldn't help but notice how he kept an eye on me. I continued serving and doing what I could to be helpful so that Aunt Mandy could visit with everyone. When the living room was filled with folks, Wilson tapped on his glass to get everyone's attention so Aunt Mandy could speak.

"Welcome, everyone," she began. "I'm overwhelmed by this community's hospitality. I would just like to thank a few special people who helped make this happen for me. Oscar, whom most of you know, recognized the perfect spot for me to build this home near my niece, Kate. Without her love and support, none of this could have happened."

There was a big round of applause.

"Now I'll have you know, the design of this house, which I only had in my head, could not have happened without the expertise of my clever architect, Wilson Schumacher. Didn't he do a magnificent job?"

There was more applause and Wilson beamed with pride.

"I was guided to hire a magnificent crew led by Chuck, whose last name I do not recall. Would you all give a wave to Chuck and his crew so they know who you are? Come to think of it, you all most likely know each and every one here today."

Everyone chuckled and applauded.

"Now, one more thing. No one in the county can put on the finishing touches like our friend, Ellen. Thank you so much, Ellen."

There was more applause as Ellen blushed.

"Thank you all once again for receiving me into your beautiful community. Please enjoy more refreshments, and thank you so much for coming today."

I couldn't have been more proud of the way she spoke. Surely the whole community would come to appreciate Aunt Mandy's charm and warmth as much as I did. Her open house was such a good idea and I deemed it an absolute success.

As I scanned the roomful of people laughing and talking, I was surprised to see Clark standing near the front door. I wondered how long he had been there. He made his way through the crowd and gave Aunt Mandy a big hug. She looked my way, giving me a quick wink and a smile. Clark then headed toward Kelly, who immediately offered him a beer. I watched them make small talk as I approached.

"Kelly, the food is awesome," I interrupted. "Welcome, Clark. Glad you could make it."

"Sorry I'm late, but my neighbor needed some help this morning," he explained.

I looked concerned. "Is everything okay?" I asked as we wandered away from Kelly.

He nodded. "It is now," he answered. "You look very nice."

I smiled, surprised and pleased by the unexpected compliment. "Thanks. So, how are other things going with you?" I asked, referring to his recent news.

"Good as can be expected. I've decided that I'm going to Nashville, regardless of the test results."

"You are?"

"It's complicated. I'll be back in a few days or so. It's a good time to leave with the fair going on and all."

"Do you want to come to dinner before you leave?"

"I really can't. I've got to finish a piece for a client before I go, plus I'm a little distracted, to say the least. I wouldn't be good company right now."

"I certainly understand."

CHAPTER 87

"Good to see you two," Harold said, approaching us. "This is such a fine occasion and your aunt is such a gem."

"Thanks, Harold," I responded. "Everyone has certainly made her feel welcome."

"Nice party," Ruth Ann said, joining our circle. "Good to see you for a change, Clark. Staying busy, I presume?"

He nodded, giving her a smile. "Yes, and it's been taking me out of town quite a bit," he explained.

"Well, we're just mighty proud we can say you're from around here," Harold bragged as he patted Clark on the back.

"Ruth Ann, did you notice that Chuck is here?" I hinted with a smile. "Gentlemen, would you excuse us?"

Ruth Ann looked at me with more than a little confusion on her face. We walked toward the screened-in porch where Chuck was talking with some of his crew. "Chuck, you remember Ruth Ann, don't you?" I said, gently cupping his elbow in my hand.

Ruth Ann looked at me with daggers in her eyes.

"Of course. It's good to see you again," Chuck politely

responded.

"You too," Ruth Ann blushed.

"Now that I see you here, I thought I might look into your place to have our work Christmas party," Chuck said. "I need to make a change from having it at my house. We have expanded, and my house is just not big enough anymore."

"That would be great," Ruth Ann said, looking more at ease. "Here's my business card. Just give me a call."

I started talking to Esther, who was standing nearby, so I could leave the two of them to discuss anything further. Esther looked at me strangely as I quickly moved us toward the other room. She giggled when I told her about my mission.

Little by little, the crowd began to disperse. Ellie got a ride home with Peggy. I noticed that Clark was still in the kitchen talking to Aunt Mandy, so I joined them. "I'm surprised you're still here," I said, looking into Clark's eyes.

"I think he's enjoying himself immensely, my dear," Aunt Mandy teased. "I was just asking about his brother. That was such a fun dinner we attended last Christmas."

"Yes, how is he doing?"

"I think he's smitten with a new relationship," he reported. "He's even mentioned the M-word a time or two."

We chuckled.

"There's nothing wrong with the M-word!" Aunt Mandy argued. "Changing the subject, I'd like the two of you to join Wilson and me for dinner one night when you return, Clark. It was actually Wilson's idea, and I would enjoy it so."

"Fine by me," Clark said quickly.

"Sure, anytime," I added.

Aunt Mandy then got busy cleaning up, leaving Clark and me alone in the kitchen. I felt awkward for some reason.

Clark looked into my eyes. "If I knew you wouldn't die from embarrassment, I'd pull you into my arms right now and kiss that pretty face of yours."

"Well, if I didn't think you were bluffing, I'd respond with a snuggly kiss on your neck, which seems to turn you on!"

We both burst into laughter.

"There you are!" Wilson said, approaching us with his daughter in tow.

"Clark, my daughter has heard so much about you. I wanted to make sure the two of you met," Wilson said as Barbara blushed.

I watched as Clark responded graciously. I left the three of them to their conversation as I began to pick up plates and glasses. My face was still red from Clark's unexpected compliments. Just when I think he never notices me, he throws me a line that makes me adore him!

"I don't think I have ever talked so much in my life as I have tonight," Aunt Mandy said, looking exhausted. "My goodness, I answered a lot of questions. Did you see the many hostess gifts they brought?"

I nodded and smiled in approval. "Well, they were happy to be invited. Everyone certainly was having a good time, and they loved your house."

"That's good to hear," she replied. "But I'm ready to have some peace and quiet again. By the way, did you notice that you may have had some luck playing cupid tonight?"

"What do you mean?"

"Chuck and Ruth Ann said good-bye to me at the same time and left the party together."

"I missed that! I'm glad it worked."

"I thought maybe you and Clark would have left together by now since he'll be leaving town."

"No, I made the offer for dinner before he left, but he said he doesn't have time," I said with disappointment in my voice.

"Well, he may regret that since he has competition coming into town," Aunt Mandy said as she plumped herself onto the couch.

"Oh, Auntie! You're full of mischief. We're both exhausted, so I think I'll go on home if that's okay with you."

"Good idea," she said with relief. "I'm sure that Clark, Wilson, and Barbara will be on their way in a few minutes. Oh, and Kelly left a lot of goodies in my refrigerator so I'm going to need some help eating them all this coming week."

"I'll do what I can!"

I kissed my auntie good night and went on my way.

CHAPTER 88

Susie and I worked diligently the day before my weekend guests were to arrive. We had thought we were ready, but there always seemed to be last-minute chores to be done. According to his last text, John would be the first to arrive. I continued to have mixed feelings about his visit. I planned a dinner for us in case he arrived in the late afternoon. The honeymooners Dave and Rose, the reporter Bill Larson, and the Brueckners, were all arriving closer to the fair opening. I had hopes that Bill and John would enjoy each other's company since they were both writers.

Ruth Ann called to ask if I could work a shift selling tickets at the raffle table during the fair. I begged off since I had a full house of guests for the weekend. However, the call gave me an opportunity to pry a bit for any information about Chuck. I was so sure that they would make a great couple.

"I was wondering how long it would take you to ask!" Ruth Ann kidded. "He is a pretty nice guy, but I could tell right away when we had a drink at Marv's that he is pretty self-centered."

"You had a drink at Marv's after the party?" I asked, surprised.

"Yes, it was kind of nice."

"Tell me more. Are you thinking that he can't handle a relationship?"

"I may be wrong, but our conversation was all about him. I don't think he had any real interest in me."

"Well that's not good, but maybe he was trying hard to impress you. After all, you are a pretty successful businesswoman."

"Look, it's no big deal. He hasn't called since, so he probably wasn't impressed with me in the least bit. I must say, he complimented you many times. He thinks you're the total package. Those were his exact words."

"You have got to be kidding!"

"I'm not! He thinks Clark is crazy for not closing the deal with you."

Where had I heard this before? "I think he'll call. He wouldn't have asked you out for a drink if he didn't think you were attractive."

"Maybe he wanted to make you jealous," Ruth Ann chuckled.

"Stop this nonsense! Why would I try to get you two together if I were interested in Chuck?"

"I'm just pulling your leg, girlfriend!"

After our conversation, I sent Susie home with leftover open house cookies and started making a cheesecake. The process was calming to me, and the dessert would come in handy over the weekend. It was nice to enjoy some peace and quiet before tomorrow arrived.

When I went upstairs to bed, I remembered to pull the Ouija board out of the drawer so I would remember to give it to John. It needed to go back to South Haven. It was very tempting to ask it questions about the upcoming weekend, but I advised myself against it. I crawled into bed wanting to fall asleep early, but instead rested there, completely awake, for what seemed like hours. There were so many questions on my mind. How close would I get to John this weekend? Would our relationship become more physical? Would I even have any time alone with him? Was he truly serious about coming here to cover the fair? I had to quit thinking about it. I was glad he was coming to visit, and I needed to let that be that!

I finally got out of bed to find a magazine or book to read. When I turned on the light, I heard water running. I went to the bathroom and water was running from the faucets in the sink and in my shower! It was alarming. What kind of sign was this? Was Josephine trying to tell me something again?

I turned everything off and decided to forgo the reading materials. I headed back to bed. I pulled the covers over my head until I saw pure daylight taking over the room. I pulled the covers down and once again felt the warm light that had comforted me many times. It had such a loving feel to it, and I knew it was from her. It gave me great comfort and I suddenly felt relaxed enough to sleep, which I welcomed.

CHAPTER 89

Fully rested the next morning, I was ready to welcome John and the others to the guest house. He could arrive as early as lunchtime. It was a beautiful fall day, so after I finished a day-old muffin for breakfast, I went out to pick flowers to place in each guest room. The black walnut tree was already shedding its tiny leaves and green walnuts were dropping everywhere, despite Cotton's diligence in keeping up with the mess.

Ellie saw me outdoors as she was driving by, so she pulled into my driveway. "Good luck with your weekend," she called as she rolled down her window.

"Thanks, but I have to admit I'm a bit nervous. John will likely be here about noon."

"What will the two of you do for dinner? Why don't you come out to the winery?"

"Oh, I don't know. We'll see. I have a lot of things to do."

"We'll likely be slow this weekend, and I'd love to see you."

"I don't know if I'll even get to the fair. I really want

Aunt Mandy to see the parade. She can't do all that walking, however."

"She would love it all! By the way, Trout told me to tell you he has the perfect Jeep for you to buy. It's only one year old and it's bright red. Doesn't that sound cool?"

I smiled at the thought. "Boy, I really would like to get something better for the coming winter, but I just haven't had the time to look around. I plan to keep the Mercedes even if I get a second car. Oscar said the Mercedes should be my going-to-church car."

Ellie laughed. "You'd better contact Trout soon. Maybe you could talk to him tonight."

"Thanks, Ellie."

"Oh, I also wanted to tell you about a ghost walk that Concordia is doing this year. You may want to check that out."

"Really? I hadn't heard."

"It's right up your alley. I saw the flyer at Harold's. It said they stop and visit some of the graves that have a story. Maybe they'll stop at Josephine's or Doc's gravesites."

"I can't believe Ellen hasn't said something to me. Go ahead and tell Trout I'm interested in the Jeep."

"Okay, I hope I'll see you later. You'd better take advantage of Clark being out of town!"

"You are bad! Go away!"

We burst into laughter as she drove away.

As I gathered the cut flowers, I envisioned myself in a bright red Jeep. When I got inside the house, I called Aunt Mandy to see about parade plans and her interest or ability to attend.

"Oh, Wilson has offered to take me to the parade. Is that

okay?"

"That's great. I was just trying to plan accordingly. I didn't want you to miss it."

"Sweetie, you have such a busy weekend. You don't need to fuss over me. Is there anything I can do to help you?"

"Everything's under control. John should be arriving anytime."

"Please give him my love and bring him over to the house. You know there are always cocktails on the porch every night."

"That's great. I know he wants to see you and your house."

We had no more than ended our conversation when John pulled into my driveway driving a silver convertible. My heart sank. After all the anticipation, I didn't feel ready! I ran to the mirror in the hallway to view my appearance before running out to him.

"Welcome!" I shouted. "Look at this!" I exclaimed, eyeing the car.

He took me in his arms and gave me a tight squeeze and a kiss on the cheek. "It's great to be here! What a beautiful drive. The colors are barely turning, unlike what I left behind."

"I love your car! It's so good to see you again!"

"I thought the drive would be a lot more fun with this car, and the weather is perfect with a jacket. I'll put the top up later tonight." He got his suitcase out of the tiny trunk and followed me into the house.

"Have you had lunch?"

"I'd just like something to drink, thanks. Iced tea would be great if you have it."

"Sure. You really look great, John. How are things back at the lake?"

"Colder, that's for sure."

"Oh, how I remember. Come, sit down and fill me in on Carla and everyone."

We settled on the sunporch and we couldn't talk fast enough. I had so many questions.

CHAPTER 90

As the afternoon went along, the early darkness of fall was evident.

"Where can I take you to dinner tonight?" John finally asked.

"I'm happy to make dinner here, or Ellie suggested that we might want to come out to her winery."

"The winery sounds good to me. You have plenty of other things to do."

"I'm fine with whatever," I said, feeling a bit concerned about folks seeing us together. In the end, I made a quick decision to go to the winery. "Let me change and freshen up before we go."

I went upstairs to change while John got settled in The Study. Going to the winery was risky. I dressed slowly knowing that no matter how I tried to spin this in my mind, it was a date with John. However, since Clark and I didn't have any formal commitment to each other, I shouldn't feel guilty about having dinner with my South Haven neighbor. When I came down the stairs, I saw John gazing at the guest quilt on the wall.

"Do I get to sign this quilt one time or as many times as I visit?"

"No one has ever asked me that before, but I think only once. The names do not have dates. The guest book will reveal the number of visits. I have to make sure I have space on the quilt as time goes by."

"Understood. Are you ready to go? You look very nice!"

"Just let me get my jacket out of the closet."

Off we went in John's convertible. I could not remember the last time I had ridden in a convertible. I think I may have been in high school when Jim Davis, a classmate, flaunted his vintage convertible. Tonight the breeze was swift, despite us driving at a slow pace. I felt so carefree. I wanted to raise my arms as if I were riding a roller coaster.

The winery was surprisingly busy when we arrived. We took the last parking space on the top of the hill. Before we went inside, John took the time to put the top up. Folks were already watching us. I dreaded how Trout might react when he saw us together.

"Hey, welcome!" Trout greeted as we approached the bar.

"Do you remember meeting John Baker from South Haven?" I asked innocently.

"Sure do! You're the travel writer, am I right?" Trout recalled. "That was a nice article you wrote. We were glad to see the winery included."

"I'm pleased to be back," John said, smiling.

"Here for dinner?" Trout asked, raising his voice to be heard above the noise.

"Yes. Is there room?" I asked as I looked around the

room for Ellie.

"There's a table by the kitchen, if you don't mind that, or there's plenty of room on the deck, if you like," Trout offered.

"Whatever the lady would prefer."

"Yes, the deck will be great," I decided. "Where is Ellie?"

"She'll be back shortly," he responded as he handed us a one-page menu.

John gave it a quick look. "Oh, I'm all for the gumbo and a light beer."

I quickly decided on a Philly beefsteak sandwich and a merlot, trying to keep it simple. "Thanks for the tip on the red Jeep that's for sale," I said to Trout. "You can tell the owner that I'm interested."

"Great. I will," Trout responded as he continued to prepare drinks. "I think it will be just what you're looking for."

"Are you sure you'll be okay out here?" John asked as we walked toward the fire pit.

I nodded. I felt John's arm around my shoulder as we found a place to sit. It was likely normal for him, but I felt self-conscious. So far, I didn't know any of the other people sitting on the deck. In no time, Trout brought out our drinks and explained that they were a little behind in the kitchen.

"That's what happens when the boss is away," I teased.

Trout nodded and smiled.

"So, John, how is the article coming along?" I asked after my first sip of wine.

"I'm just waiting to finish it off," he said. "I've been slammed with other work, unfortunately. I'll have it ready by next week, most likely. Do you have anything new to add?"

"Not really, but I must admit that it has been very

interesting for me to think about," I said thoughtfully. "All the quilts you and I talked about had another original purpose, but ended up providing something else at the end."

I could see John considering my words. "It's like they ended in a permanent resting place of sorts," he concluded.

"Yes, exactly!" I agreed as our food was placed before us.

"I think you just summed up the article, my friend!" John boasted as he took his first spoonful of gumbo.

"Do you like it?" I asked, observing his reaction.

"Man, this is great!" he exclaimed.

CHAPTER 91

As we continued our chatter, the fall air got cooler. I loved hearing about John's assignments and the research he was doing. His face lit up each time he described his adventures. Ellie finally joined us and explained that they had supply issues that she had to take care of earlier in the evening.

"John, I hear you are going to the fair," Ellie commented with a grin.

"Me and my faithful camera," he boasted. "I've been reading up on it, and I'm especially interested in seeing the mule-jumping contest. I know one magazine in particular will love that! I hope to get there several hours before it starts in order to interview folks."

"It's been going on for some time," Ellie added. "Folks here think nothing of it. We really take pride in our parade, too. I hope you'll get to see it."

"Absolutely!" John nodded, assuring her that he would not miss it.

"Hi, you guys," a familiar voice greeted us.

I turned around and saw Ruth Ann. Much to my surprise, she was with Chuck.

"Hello, you two!" I responded.

"Who's your boyfriend here?" Chuck asked. An undeniable bit of sarcasm accompanied the question.

"I'm her brother from Michigan," John spoke up quickly. "And you are..."

"Just call me Chuck," he responded, suddenly confused.

"I'm Ruth Ann, a neighbor of Kate's down the street," Ruth Ann said, offering her hand to John.

"Nice to meet you both," John said kindly as he shook Ruth Ann's hand. He looked at Chuck and explained, "I'm actually Kate's neighbor at her condo in South Haven. I'm writing an article about the fair."

It was clear from his expression that Chuck was still trying to figure everything out.

"Have you two had dinner, or are you here for drinks?" Ellie asked the two of them.

"Chuck was at a dinner party we had at my place tonight, so we just decided to come out and get a drink," Ruth Ann explained.

"Join us," John politely offered.

"No, thanks. We just wanted to say hello," Ruth Ann answered quickly, speaking for both of them. "It's too chilly out here for me!"

"Well, nice to meet you both," John said politely.

Chuck nodded and smiled, his look still one of hesitation and consternation.

"Take care, you two," I added.

Ellie followed them inside, and when they were out of sight I laughed aloud. "I sure love you, brother," I teased as I gazed impishly at John.

"You love me? I can only wish!" he teased back. "I knew what that guy was trying to insinuate, so I thought I'd throw him off."

"You had him pegged, all right. He's been trying to get me to go out with him, and I haven't complied. What's interesting is that I have been pushing him and Ruth Ann to go out in hopes that they might work out as a couple. Seeing them here tonight tells me I may have had some success."

"I guess it's quite a challenge being the town's most eligible single lady."

I responded by playfully punching his arm. "It's so difficult and demanding," I said, mocking his comment.

After another half hour, we decided to leave. There were never any dull moments with John. When we got back to the house, I told John I needed to prepare a few things in the kitchen.

"I'm looking forward to those muffins," he said as he smiled at me. "How about I make us a fire?"

"I would love that. Thanks!" After a short while, I joined him, bringing a cup of coffee for each of us. The fire was a wonderful addition to the evening. I was beginning to relax.

"Will I be seeing Clark this weekend?"

The question caught me off guard. "He's out of town."

"Ah, perfect timing." He winked.

"I'll have to admit that I was glad to hear it myself when he told me. But I think the world of that guy, John, so don't pick on him."

"I wouldn't think of it! I'm glad you just think the world of him and haven't fallen in love with him."

I got up to refill our coffee cups, hoping that he knew not

to pursue the topic any further. My cell phone rang which startled me, given the late hour.

"Kate? This is Bill Larson." His voice had a tone of urgency in it.

"Yes?" I answered.

"I hate to ask you this, but if it's okay I'd like to arrive tonight instead of tomorrow. I know it's kind of late, but I can be there within an hour."

"Why, sure. I'm still up. Do know how to get here?"

"I do! Thanks a lot. I'll see you soon."

CHAPTER 92

"Are we getting company?" John asked, looking disappointed.

"Bob Larson is arriving tonight instead of tomorrow. He's the reporter I mentioned."

"Pity. I thought I'd have you to myself tonight."

"I don't want the other guests to think that there is anything between us, John."

"Why is that?"

"It's not professional."

"I beg to differ with you, but I'm glad that you admit there is something between us. That's the most encouraging thing I've heard since I've been here!" He chuckled to himself.

I shook my head. "More coffee?"

"Come here and sit next to me," he said, gently patting the couch.

I hesitated but complied, sitting gingerly beside him.

"I know you're attracted to me, as I am to you. So I'm patiently waiting for any encouragement on your part."

"You scare me a little bit, to be honest."

"How so?"

"I shouldn't be attracted to you at all with our age difference. Don't try to tell me otherwise, you hear? I like you and want to keep you as a friend. Aren't you seeing anyone at all?"

He smiled and thought before he spoke. "I occasionally do go out, mostly on a business basis, if I'm honest. Some of these women are beautiful and can be somewhat aggressive. That's not my style. I'll never forget the first time I laid eyes on you, Kate. I never for a moment wondered how old you were. Remember that cookout we had at my condo? All night long, I wondered if I would be ever able to kiss you. When I learned that you were a recent widow, I made myself back off. I realized that you were dealing with a lot of hurt and possible bad feelings about men in general. I really admire how you picked up the pieces and started a new life for yourself. That's the kind of thing I look for in a woman."

I stared at him, trying to digest it all. "That's so nice of you to say. As time goes on, I'm sure things might become clearer to me."

"Maybe I can help." He pulled me close and gently kissed me on the lips. It brought back memories of the first time he kissed me. I couldn't help but respond. Neither of us felt the need to speak. It felt comfortable and natural.

Out of the corner of my eye, I could see headlights pulling into the driveway. I pulled away, and John looked surprised. "We have company," I announced, standing up.

John grinned, knowing he had succeeded in making the point that I do have some interest in him. He got up and put another log on the fire while I opened the door for my guest.

"You made good time, Mr. Larson. I'm Kate. Welcome to

Josephine's Guest House."

"Glad to meet you," he said, accepting my handshake. "Please call me Bill. I hope I didn't keep you up too late."

"Not at all," I assured him. "Come on in and meet another one of our guests, John Baker."

The two exchanged niceties before I escorted Bill to the office to register. John remained in the living room, checking his phone. After Bill signed the guest book and quilt, I showed him the Forest Room upstairs. There, I asked if he would like some wine, coffee, or beer and he requested a glass of wine.

Bill then joined John in the living room and their chatter began. They had many questions for one another, which I found interesting. I could see, however, that my services and presence were no longer needed, so I excused myself for the evening. I had to admit, Bill's arrival was perfect timing.

I locked my bedroom door, undressed, and crawled under the covers. I couldn't help but repeat in my mind all the sweet things John had confessed to me. Knowing my guests were well taken care of, I accepted the beauty of sleep.

CHAPTER 93

I was up early preparing a veggie and bacon quiche, fresh fruit compote, and blueberry muffins. I predicted the guys would be showing up late for breakfast after having a long evening. Today was the big East Perry Fair that folks around here look forward to each year. The weather was sunny and cool, which was perfect for everyone.

"Good morning, Mr. Baker," I said in a professional manner. "You're up earlier than I expected."

"It's an important day, so I wanted to get started early," John replied as he poured his own coffee. "Do you have any plans tonight?"

"If you're back in time for cocktail hour, Aunt Mandy would love to see you," I suggested.

"Absolutely!" He grinned and nodded. "I'm anxious to see her place, and I hope the invitation includes you! The main event today is the mule-jumping contest, and that doesn't start until four, so I'll get back as soon as I can."

"I'll tell her," I said as I poured myself a cup of coffee.

"I love the bow-tie-looking quilt in my room," John

mentioned. "Is that the one you bought at the auction?"

"Yes. I love it too."

"I love wearing bow ties myself, but there are fewer and fewer occasions to do that."

"You would look quite dapper wearing one, John."

John and Bill sat down at the table and began indulging like two little boys who were starving. It made me feel good to watch. I kept their coffee cups filled. Bill was not only in town to report on the fair, but was also involved in a murder investigation in Jacksonville. It was fascinating to listen to the conversation between the two men.

"Kate, at some point I'd like to hear the story about how you landed in Borna from South Haven, Michigan," Bill said.

"It's nothing to write home about, as they say," I replied as I refilled my cup.

"Don't let her get by with that response, Bill," John interjected.

"How do you two know each other?" Bill asked, surprising me.

"Now that's a story you don't want to write about," John teased.

I gave John a stern look. I think Bill assumed we were a couple. The topic was dropped. Ten minutes of conversation later, they were both off to track down their individual stories. Traffic was already heavy, slowly streaming by my house for the parade. I was so glad someone else was taking Aunt Mandy. I gave her a quick call telling her we would likely be by for cocktails. I had just turned on the dishwasher when I saw the Brueckners pull into the driveway. "Welcome back!" I greeted as I met them at their car.

"Thanks, Kate," Mrs. Brueckner said, stretching her

arms and legs. "We planned to be here earlier, but traffic is horribly slow."

I helped them inside and offered them a cup of coffee before taking care of registration. As soon as they dropped off their luggage in the Wildflower Room, they were off to the fair. The Brueckners had relatives in the area, so they reminded me that they wouldn't be back until late.

As soon as my honeymoon couple arrived, I had plans of getting a glimpse of the fair myself. My favorite feature was the exhibit hall where ribbons were given in many categories. My cell phone rang and I could see that it was Maggie.

"Am I calling at a bad time? I know you have guests," her familiar voice asked.

"No, I'm fine. I'm just waiting for one more couple to arrive."

"Did John get there?"

I knew that was why she was calling. "Yes. He's already at the fair."

"I hope he's behaving himself."

"Everything's fine. Don't worry. What's new there?"

"I really called to tell you that at yesterday's Beach Quilters meeting, Cornelia announced that her quilt shop is up for sale."

"Oh no! She's hinted about that before."

"She said that it's just time. She plans on keeping some machine quilting customers and wants to work from her home."

"I hate to hear that. Are any of the girls interested?"

"Not that I'm aware of."

"How is Carla doing? John paints a pretty positive picture when I ask him."

"Yes, I agree. She's doing really well; however, Marilee is really having a difficult time."

"That is awful. I'm sad to hear that," I replied. Changing the subject, I asked, "Anything new with the wedding that I need to know about?"

"I'm sorry to say that they have every detail worked out on their own. Jill seems to be really enjoying the process, so I don't interfere. The Beach Quilters decided yesterday to give Jill a little luncheon shower. The bridesmaids are planning one, too."

"Oh, how nice. I don't want to miss all of that."

We chatted until I saw a young couple pull into my driveway.

CHAPTER 94

"Welcome!" I said as they got out of their cute little Volkswagen. For a second, it reminded me of Susan.

"What a beautiful place you have here," the wife marveled.

"Hi, I'm Kate. Let me help you with your things."

"Call us Rose and Dave," they suggested with big smiles.

Once inside, there were many distractions for Rose, but Dave and I went into the office to take care of registration. When Rose saw the guest quilt on the wall, she told us about a wonderful wedding quilt they had just received from her mother. When it came time to sign the guest quilt, Rose and Dave each wanted a separate block to sign. They certainly were an example of an independent couple!

Their faces were beyond happy when they saw Josephine's attic, which to them was the honeymoon suite. Our small talk revealed that they had been on the road for a few days since their wedding. They were heading south to see friends and relatives. I suggested that they may enjoy the Red Creek Winery for dinner. Meanwhile, as I tried to explain breakfast, the two of them could not keep their hands off each other. I knew they would be pleased when I left them alone.

Feeling like my responsibilities were taken care of, I left for the fair. Traffic was moving better. I was hoping to squeeze into the museum's parking lot, but it was full, leaving me to park on the side of the street. As I walked toward the fair, I passed businesses and homes that were crowded with friends and relatives. Beer-filled coolers were placed on porches and lawns. I was sure that many traditions were taking place as families and friends gathered to enjoy the festivities.

"You need a ride, little lady?" a man's voice yelled from a passing vehicle.

It was Chuck. "Thanks, but I need the exercise," I responded, continuing to walk. He waved and went on. Before I entered the exhibit hall, I purchased some iced tea to quench the thirst I had earned from my walk.

I was immediately greeted by Peggy, who was minding the table for the Friendship Circle raffle quilt. There was a crowd around her, indicating that sales were brisk. Ladies were praising the workmanship and guessing which buildings were which. "I'll take ten dollars' worth, Peggy," I requested. "I would love to own that for the guest house."

After my tickets were filled out, I began looking at the many quilts on display, hoping Ruth Ann would be one of the makers like last year when she won a blue ribbon. This year's blue ribbon went to someone I didn't know. It was an amazingly intricate quilt made entirely of six-inch blocks. They were each different and the name of the quilt was DEAR JANE'S BEAUTY. It must have taken her forever to make. I couldn't help but wonder if this was a quilt the maker would want to take with him or her to the grave. The other quilts were very nice, but they didn't hold a candle to the winner.

I moved on to the crafts area and then to the plants and flowers. Ellen's name was by some of the ribbon winners, which did not surprise me. It brought back memories of last year's entry from the Friendship Circle which was called PLANTS OUT OF THE POTS. It was so unique. I still had my little African violet plant blooming in the nest, which was the piece I entered. This year, there were more baked goods entered than last year. This was right up my alley.

"You should have entered your blueberry muffins," Ellen's voice said from behind me.

"Well, thanks." I smiled. "I did win a prize one year at our blueberry festival."

"I met one of your guests today," Ellen mentioned.

"Oh, who?" I asked.

"John Baker, the guy who wrote the article," she stated. "I was pleased to see him taking so many photos."

"Yes, it'll be great publicity."

"Oscar said that when he spoke with him, Mr. Baker said you were a special friend, which is what really brought him here."

"Oh, he's just a nice neighbor from my condo in South Haven," I explained.

"Well, he's charming. Has he met Clark?"

I wanted to tell her to mind her own business, but I nodded, smiled, and told her that they had met. I moved on to the jars of canned goods that were neatly arranged in rows. There was artistry in the way they packed the fruits and vegetables. I saw that Esther had won a ribbon for her dilled green beans and her bread-and-butter pickles. The day was passing quickly, so before I headed to my car, I bought a toasted white cheese sandwich, which was a fair favorite. Ellie said the more cheese sandwiches they sold, the more beer sales they made.

CHAPTER 95

Walking back to my car, I met up with Dave and Rose who were walking hand in hand. I also noticed that the Dresden Inn property across from the museum was packed with cars, and there seemed to be a large family celebration taking place. I couldn't help but feel a bit envious.

As I passed some residences, I saw quilts on the ground where children were playing and rolling around. One quilt was covering lawn chairs to create a tent for them to hide under. Maggie would have been appalled seeing such quilt abuse, but it made me smile knowing quilts had so many uses in life for all ages of people. I could only hope that the makers of the quilts would be happy as well.

I was hoping to run into John somewhere; but knowing him, he was either investigating animal abuse or interviewing some of the many locals who hung around the beer stands. He was so inquisitive sometimes that it made me nervous.

I made my way home in snail-paced traffic. It was a good feeling that the fair had been successful and that I had found some time to participate in it. As I arrived at the house, there was a red Jeep in my driveway. A man was getting out of it and was walking toward my back door. When he saw me arrive, he paused and waited for me to come closer.

"Are you a friend of Trout's, by any chance?"

He smiled. "You must be Kate Meyr," he said with his hands on his hips. "I was at the fair, so I thought I'd drop by to show you the Jeep I'd like to sell. Trout says it would be perfect for you. Since you're pretty busy, I thought I'd make the effort to bring it to you."

"I appreciate that. And you are…"

"Oh, I'm sorry. My name is Cole Alexander. I live in Dresden, but my business is in Jacksonville. I just bought a new Jeep that is bigger and has four doors. This one is a little too small for my purposes. I was hoping to sell it outright to get a little more for it. The Jeep Wrangler Unlimited is popular. It's got all the bells and whistles on it."

"Well it's pretty darn cute and a nice shade of red, which I like."

He chuckled as a man would, thinking I only cared about the vehicle color.

"I know nothing about cars in general, so I have put off this task," I admitted. "I refuse to go through another winter with my Mercedes."

He laughed and nodded. "You may want to drive it today, if you have time."

"As much as I would love to, it'll have to be another time. I have a houseful of guests this weekend. Can you come by on Monday?"

"It would have to be quite early, if that's all right."

"Great. If it drives okay, we have a deal!"

He laughed again and became quite attractive with his

different kind of smile. I liked him right away. East Perry County surely had its share of good-looking men.

"I've always liked this house. I'm glad it was saved and restored. You've created a good use for it."

"Thanks. I'm a transplant from South Haven, Michigan. I fell in love with the house and the community. How do you know Trout? From the winery, I guess?"

"Pretty much. Plus, we go fishing together quite a bit. Surely you know that he's an avid fisherman."

"Yes," I replied, nodding vigorously. "What is your business in Jacksonville?"

"I'm in real estate development. Senior living housing is my area of expertise."

"That's interesting. Folks are certainly living longer these days, and there's a huge need for that type of housing."

He nodded. "Say, I don't want to keep you any longer. I hope I didn't offend you by just stopping by like this."

"Not at all. You did me a big favor. I'll see you Monday morning. Perhaps you'll have some of my blueberry muffins with me."

"Now that's a deal. Perhaps we can barter somehow."

I had to chuckle. "Thanks for coming by," I said as I went into the house. What a great guy, I thought. I wondered how old he was. He had a few gray streaks in his dark hair. He looked to be about Clark's age. He was probably happily married. Why do I even care? I couldn't handle another man in my life!

CHAPTER 96

I knew John would be back anytime, so I quickly prepared a French toast casserole that needed to set overnight. I reset the table. Dave and Rose arrived and didn't bother coming to say hello before they headed upstairs. I could only imagine what their urgency was all about. It caused me to smile and reminisce. Aunt Mandy called to verify that we planned to come by for a drink. I told her to stand by as I didn't know the exact time that John would return. She reported having a wonderful time with Wilson and mentioned how impressed she was with the parade. She said she had made lunch for the two of them when they returned. That was so like her, and I hoped he appreciated everything about her.

I was upstairs freshening up when I looked out the window and saw John returning in his handsome convertible. He should have been in the parade with all the attention he was getting driving around in that car!

"Hey, there!" I said, coming down the stairs.

"I'm ready for that cocktail as soon as I change. I'm afraid I got a little close to the mules and pigs. I not only look bad, but I think I smell!"

I laughed.

It wasn't long until he returned, all fresh and neat. We got in his convertible and headed down the road. Needless to say, John's reaction was pleasing when he saw the house location and its unique shape.

"This is amazing! This needs to be in a decorator magazine."

Aunt Mandy greeted him with a big hug. John didn't waste any time telling her what a beautiful place she had and that he had connections to magazines who would want to feature it.

"How would you feel about that, Aunt Mandy?" I asked.

"No," she quickly responded. "I don't want to be discovered here in this little town. It's nice and quiet, which I enjoy."

John had many questions for her while I fixed us each a drink. I prepared a plate of olives, cheese, and crackers for us to nibble on. I couldn't get a word in as Aunt Mandy told him about the new garage, which was nearly finished. I couldn't help but wonder what project she'd have for Chuck next.

The early darkness of fall reminded John and me that our evening was slipping away. We offered to take Aunt Mandy to dinner, but she said she was really tired from the day's activities. John took photos before we stepped out the door, and he promised he would send a copy or two to her.

On the way back to the house, I told John that I needed to stay put for the rest of the evening since my guests would be returning. I said I could prepare an easy dinner, which I knew he would enjoy since he ate out so much.

Dave and Rose were sitting side by side in the living room

when we walked in the house. John immediately engaged in conversation with them. He was curious about what they thought about the fair. I had to admit, I was curious as well. While they talked, I took a pan of lasagna out of the freezer and put it in the oven. I thought of Jack and how it was his favorite. I offered to share our dinner with Rose and Dave, which delighted them. I sipped on some wine while I made a salad and prepared garlic bread.

"Miss Meyr, is there a ghost in this house?" Rose asked as she came into the kitchen.

"Why do you ask?" I tried to suppress a grin.

"I can't really describe it, but there have been times when I felt like Dave and I were not alone in that attic. In the middle of the night, when I got up to go to the bathroom, I thought I saw a lady standing by our door. I may have just been half asleep, plus this is an old house, after all. I guess most folks expect a ghost, right?"

"You have a good point there. Everyone has their own expectations here, I suppose."

"Need some help?" John asked, joining us.

"No, I'm good," I replied, giving him a wink. "Would you start a fire for us?"

"Consider it done!" John said, moving toward the back door.

Rose and Dave had no plans other than to cuddle for the rest of the evening. They were delighted to have a free meal. I think they thought of John and I as couple, judging from several of the comments they made. I just left it alone, thinking that I may never see them again. All in all, dinner was delicious and we had plenty of conversation. I really wanted to ask Rose some details about her having seen a lady, but I simply couldn't. We were about finished when the Brueckners returned for the day. They reported having a good time. Shortly after, Dave and Rose headed upstairs with their wine glasses full. It left John and me alone as we did the dinner clean-up.

CHAPTER 97

"This is a little bit like being husband and wife, isn't it?" John teased as we loaded the dishwasher.

"Is that a good thing? And how would you know about that?"

He laughed.

"I meant to tell you all evening that I may be the owner of a red Jeep very soon. The owner brought it by for me to look at and I hope to test drive it on Monday."

John thought it was a good idea, but then he started asking car-related questions that I couldn't answer.

"I trust Trout's recommendation, and the owner seemed like an honest and genuinely nice guy. He has purchased a four-door model. This one is just a two door, which is the perfect size for me."

"Be sure to text a photo, okay?"

"I will. This fire is especially nice tonight. Every night I hate putting it out before I go to bed. But I worry if I just let it die down on its own."

John looked at me with concern written all over his face.

"Do you ever find yourself lonely at night? From what you tell me, you seem to be home alone every night and you seldom have guests here."

"I'm fine, and I'm working on stepping up my marketing. Evenings are usually the time I set aside to communicate with family and friends, so I don't think of myself as lonely."

"I understand. I feel that as long as I have a computer keyboard nearby, I'm perfectly fine as well. Does that sound strange?"

"Not really. I'll bet you were like that as a little boy too, right?"

"I was! I was never bored if I had a pen and some paper."

I smiled at that thought as I poked the fire. "Having Aunt Mandy here has given me a stronger sense of home. I'm no longer the new woman in town. I actually have more friends here than I did in South Haven."

"I wish we could have met sooner than when we did."

"Why is that?"

"Things may have been different between us."

"I wouldn't be the same person. I was married and had a son. You may not have been attracted to me at all back then." I smiled, thinking how much things had changed.

"Why do you suppose we have this special friendship?"

"You filled in some blanks for me at the time. And, I like having a male friend."

"But not as a lover?"

"I wouldn't want to change a thing. Don't be silly. If I slept with you, our relationship would be over. I admire you so much and feel like I can talk to you about anything."

"I don't know if I should be happy with your assessment or not. But, I feel close to you as well."

"Let's not analyze this to death. I don't want commitment, and I don't think you do either. When I meet or if I meet someone to love again, I want it to be fabulous. I didn't have that with my husband."

"I think I'm going to remember this talk for a long time," John said, squeezing my hand.

We ended our evening with a peck on the cheek before we went to our rooms for the night.

Settling into bed, I was thankful to have a friend like John. I thought of Clark and how different the two men were. Clark did give me a spark of womanhood, which I hadn't experienced since dating Clay. I missed Clark, but I'd have to respect the private man that he was. Perhaps that was the attraction.

Tomorrow, everyone would leave. Then I'd have the guest house to myself again, except for Josephine, of course.

CHAPTER 98

It was exciting to have all my guests come to the breakfast table at one time! There was a lot of chatter and some signs of exhaustion from the weekend. John was on his cell phone arranging his next trip. Dave and Rose were excited about continuing their journey and eventually going home to their new apartment. They still had wedding gifts to unwrap. Rose was also busy dictating how she wanted to decorate, and Dave simply nodded his head like a good husband. The Brueckners were sharing happy and sad news about their weekend visit. There was a new baby in the family, but Mrs. Brueckner's sister was dying from cancer. In the end, Mr. Brueckner had the record for having the heartiest appetite. He loved my blueberry muffins and hinted that he'd like to take some home. Bill Larson, like John, was on his phone between courses of food. He was still grilling John for magazine sources that John could help him with. Bill found the Brueckners interesting since they were native to the area. He asked them why they never missed an East Perry Fair, and lively conversation ensued.

Cotton and Susie were scheduled to come for the day when everyone was gone. Cotton had leaves to collect and Susie had bedrooms to clean.

John waited for everyone else to leave before he prepared to be on his way. When he was ready, I stood in front of him with mixed emotions. We were definitely close friends, and he was a little piece of South Haven that I missed.

"I'll text you when I get home. I hope I don't run into snow along the way."

"Be safe, and give Carla a hug for me."

"Everyone will want to know when you'll return again, including me."

"I know. There will be bridal showers for Jill that I will try to make if I can."

With that, John gave me a big hug and a gentle kiss on the lips. I was struck that it seemed we were still little more than just buddies. I sensed that he didn't want to leave. Perhaps he had expected more from me during this visit.

After I waved to John from the deck and he sped away, I went inside to pour myself a cup of coffee. In all the flurry of the morning, this would be my first cup. I sat down for a moment to enjoy it. I finally felt like a successful businesswoman. I had filled my guest house to capacity. I may even have made some money!

Ellie called on my cell phone. She said she saw all the cars leaving. "Are you exhausted?" she asked with a chuckle in her voice.

"No, I feel somewhat energized. They surely were a diverse group of folks!"

"I don't know if you've heard about the quilt winner."

"No. Who was the winner? Is it someone I know?"

"Esther! Our own Esther!"

"How did that happen?"

Ellie laughed. "Well, she bought tickets just like the rest of us. Thank goodness we had some little girl pull the winning ticket, or some folks may have thought it was rigged."

"Well, good for Esther! I'm so happy it was a local person instead of someone from out of town."

"That's what I thought."

"Tell Trout that I plan to test drive the Jeep tomorrow. I met Cole, the owner, and if all goes well, I'll be writing him a check."

"Terrific! I've seen his Jeep. I can see you driving around in that."

"I really appreciate Trout's help."

"Do you know if your aunt is still planning on having the next Friendship Circle meeting?"

"I think so. I was about to call her to see if she needs anything from the grocery store. I need to buy some things after this busy weekend."

"Well, have a good day, my friend. Maybe we can meet for coffee one day this week."

"Sounds great."

After I hung up, I called Aunt Mandy to see what she needed from the grocery store. She always kept a running list by her phone in case I was going. She wanted to know if everyone departed okay, and she especially hoped that I wasn't exhausted.

CHAPTER 99

After I got groceries, I stopped by Imy's shop. I hadn't seen her since we went to the auction together. "I'm so happy with the Bow Tie quilt that I bought at the auction! My guest this weekend even commented on it. Have you gotten anything new in the shop?"

"Now that's a silly question," Imy teased. "There's always new stuff coming in every day. I already sold a couple of the quilts that I bought at the auction."

"Wow, that's great! Are you going to open your shed up for Christmas again this year?"

"I sure am!"

A unique set of items caught my eye. "Those fireplace tools are gorgeous. Are they new or old?"

"They are very old, but have never been used. I traded some glassware that wasn't selling for that set of tools."

"I think you have a buyer! Mine look horrible. I'll be happy to replace them."

"You're such an easy sale, Kate."

I laughed, knowing she was right.

"It was nice to have some new customers this weekend. Some were staying at your place. They were a cute young couple, and they bought some picture frames."

"Oh, Dave and Rose. They were on their honeymoon. Did they tell you?"

"It wasn't hard to figure that out!"

We laughed heartily together, and a few minutes later I walked out with the fireplace set and a very old *Good Housekeeping* cookbook. What was one more cookbook on my shelf?

When I got to Aunt Mandy's house, she seemed tired and listless. It wasn't like her, and she wasn't wearing makeup. She always wore makeup. "Are you okay?" I looked at her, wanting to discern the problem.

"Just the sniffles, but it has taken the wind out of my sails."

I put her groceries away and left so she could get some rest. It had been a busy couple of days for her, and I hoped that some rest would do the trick.

Susie and Cotton were nearly finished when I returned. Susie filled me in on the status of the laundry. Cotton said he'd return in the morning to fix a loose gutter and do some scraping on the barn, in preparation of painting it soon.

I replaced my fireplace set and the difference was amazing! The cookbook went on the shelf with the many others in my collection. Through the years, it had been suggested to me that I should do my own baking cookbook.

My dinner consisted of leftover quiche. A text came from John while I was eating, telling me he was ready to get back to his SUV. The convertible did not do well in the snow. He once again said he had a good time. He signed the text

"Hugs, J."

It was Sunday, so I made my weekly call to Jack. He was pleased to hear about my houseful of guests.

"So, how are the wedding plans coming along?"

"You have to ask Jill about that. She's in charge and seems to know what she wants."

"So, what can I possibly get you for a wedding gift? Do you have any good ideas?"

"Jill and I have talked about that, and Maggie has asked the same question. We decided it would be helpful if you could contribute to our honeymoon trip to London. It will be quite expensive, and we would appreciate the help."

"Why London?"

"London is similar to New York. I've always wanted to go there, and Jill hasn't even been out of the country."

"Well, consider it done. You will love London."

Jack asked about Aunt Mandy, which I thought was always so sweet of him. He once again said he was glad we were here together.

After the call ended, I stayed in front of the fire writing in my journal about the big weekend. As the flames died down, it reminded me of the late hour. Upstairs, as I began to undress, I thanked God for my many blessings and gave Josephine some credit for behaving herself with my guests.

CHAPTER 100

I kicked off my shoes and laid out my nightgown. At that point, I realized I hadn't set the house alarm. I had gotten so used to leaving it off while my guests were here that it had slipped my mind. I grudgingly went down the stairs and immediately felt a presence of some kind. In a shocking moment, I saw someone sitting in my swivel office chair! I let out a gasp, feeling my body jump in fright. It was Susan's husband, Harper! How could this be? He sat there with a nasty grin on his face, his eyes glaring at me in the near darkness.

"What are you doing here? How did you get in?" I shrieked in fright as my body began to shake.

"Remember me, little lady?" he asked, waving a gun so I could see.

I held onto the bottom bannister to steady myself. "Susan's killer, right?"

He chuckled and leaned back leisurely in the chair. "I have a score to settle with you. I don't like being lied to—not once, but twice," he growled. He got out of the chair and came toward me. "I'm not quite sure what all I'm going to do to you, but for starters, why don't you have a seat in that comfy little chair of yours."

I refused to loosen my grip on the bannister, but he yanked my arm and dragged me until I fell into the chair with a jolt. "You don't scare me with that gun. You have no business breaking into my house and ordering me around like you did Susan!"

He didn't like that comment. Without warning, he hit me hard across the jaw and the impact was so extreme that I almost fell to the ground, taking the chair with me. I knew he meant business now. If he would kill Susan, he would kill me. It was noticeably dark. If my porch light had been on, I could have seen him better. The only light came from the upstairs hall.

Without another word, he placed his gun on the desk and pulled out a roll of mechanical tape. He forced each of my wrists to the arms of the chair and wrapped them tightly. I could only wiggle my fingers. Next, he moved to my ankles. He forced them together and sturdily wrapped them with the tape. It hurt terribly and made movement impossible.

"There are no words to describe what a lowlife you are! What will your son think of you when he learns that you killed his mother?"

I saw anger rush to his face. "You don't know my son, so shut your damn mouth!"

"Susan told me everything about you. I saw her bruises! I told the police everything. You'll never get away with this!"

"You talk too much, bitch!" he said as he pulled a red bandana from his back pocket. With a determined look on his face, he pushed the rough, filthy fabric into my mouth.

I gagged and thought I might throw up. I wasn't sure I could still swallow.

"In case you think you have phone service here, think again!" he said, holding up the pulled phone cord.

Was it a good thing my cell phone was upstairs? Would he think to go find it?

He gave a yank at the shade by the office window that faced Ellie's house. He lit a cigarette and blew smoke directly in my face.

I couldn't breathe for a second and tried to cough.

"You know, no one will think anything about this place catching fire and burning to the ground. The volunteer fire fighters around here are a joke! By the time they get word of a fire, get dressed, and get to their little fire engine, you'll be toast." He let out a gust of laughter. His body moved around me and he grabbed the back of my hair. He then began running his fingers through it. "This head of hair would burn pretty fast, the way I figure. I'd like to take care of you first, just in case this house survives, so maybe I'd better start there."

Everything he said was ugly. The way he said it was ugly. I was frightened by this monster. As I desperately prayed to God, I glared as hard as I could into his eyes so he wouldn't think that I was afraid like Susan. I was certain that putting fear in women's eyes gave him a great deal of pleasure.

A car went by, and Harper quickly hid in the nearest corner so there wouldn't be any movement seen from the oval glass window of the front door. "You know, I didn't think you'd ever go upstairs to bed. I was gonna come up there and take care of you until I heard you come down the stairs." He shook his head and snickered, revealing a hideous brand of glee. "You look pretty helpless, Kate Meyr!"

Another laugh from him made me cringe. I wanted cry, but didn't dare. Was I going to die? Was I fooling myself into thinking someone would barge in the house and save me like Clark did when Blade attacked me? This guy had already killed one person. I could be next!

Suddenly, Harper jumped and looked up the stairs. He pointed his gun, ready to shoot. "Who's that? You wanna get shot?" he yelled loudly at the stairs. He paused. He moved closer to the stairs to get a better look and fired the gun. The noise was deafening! What was he shooting at? He backed up, moving closer to me with a frightened look on his face and recklessly fired again!

I closed my eyes, thinking I would be in the line of fire eventually. I heard a terrible commotion. I opened my eyes and saw Harper running out the back door as fast as he could! What on earth did he see on the stairs to shoot at? Was it Josephine? I was alive and he was gone! Thank you, God. Thank you, God, I repeated quietly.

I had to let someone know what had happened. I feared that he would change his mind and return, so I felt I had to work fast. My voice was muffled by the distasteful bandana. I worked and gagged until I could work the bandana out of my mouth. I could breathe again, and my anxiety lightened. Tears of relief streamed down my cheeks. My body was helpless, but if I pushed with my bare feet I could slightly move my chair. Thankfully, it had rollers on it.

If I could scoot to the kitchen, the wall phone may still be connected. Very slowly, inch by inch, I made it to the hall and then barely over the rug before I got closer to the kitchen. I reminded myself that I couldn't think about him coming back, but I knew I had to move as quickly as I could just in case. In the darkness, I finally found my way to the wall phone with its long cord dangling close to my fingers, which were free. I pulled and yanked until it fell to the floor. There wasn't a sound. It was obviously dead as well. Now what?

CHAPTER 101

I noticed that when Harper ran out the back door, it hadn't closed completely. With it slightly ajar, it would be possible for me to push it completely open with my feet. If I could push the door open, I could start yelling. Who would hear me? If two gunshots hadn't brought help, would my yelling bring anyone? It would be hours before morning. Surely Cotton or Cole would show up at some point!

Inch by inch, with pure determination, I used my feet to scoot closer to the door. Having the door open at all would draw attention, and it would allow anyone to hear me better. The first time, I barely moved it. I got closer and gave it everything I had and was able to push it open completely. Cold air rushed in. I forgot how cold the nights had gotten. My bare feet were now exposed to the air, as was the rest of my body. It filled me with the urgency to yell as loudly as I could. Where were the boys who seemed to run across my yard during the late hours? I yelled help three times as loudly as I could. It felt good, despite no one hearing me. Even if someone drove by, they would never hear me calling from the back of the house. So much for living in a quiet little town!

Shivering from the cold, I had to back away to a warmer part of the house. Once again, using my bare feet, I turned and pushed, making very little progress. I saw the quilt hanging over my rocking chair by the fireplace. I would make that my goal in hopes of pulling the quilt down on top of me. It seemed like the distance was too far, but I would have to try. I kept getting snagged and caught on things that slowed me down. My teeth were starting to chatter and my feet were like ice.

When I finally made it close to the quilt, I turned the chair so that my fingers could grab an edge. My weak attempt made the quilt fall to the floor instead. Now the quilt was in my way as I tried to maneuver my chair. I did discover that I could get my feet under the folds of the quilt as I struggled. The protection was worth the effort. That was it. I knew this was where I'd have to remain until someone discovered me. I could see the moon from the window. It provided a bit of light. I was exhausted. I heard another car drive by. With the back door open, I could hear the sounds from the outdoors much better. I took a deep breath and started praying, hoping to feel some level of calmness. I was not going to die. I had survived and was so thankful that Harper was gone. I was in one piece and had lived to tell about it. I had to be patient. Pain from my jaw had turned into a throbbing headache. What a monster he was! To think that he was considering setting my hair on fire! Susan was so right when she kept telling me that he was going to kill her. Physically exhausted, my head finally collapsed to the side. With the help of God, I dozed off until very early in the morning when I heard some big trucks pass by. I told myself that the worst was over. Now I just had to wait for the first person who would pull in my driveway. I wondered where Harper had gone. Would he regret not shooting me and come back at some point?

About a couple of hours later, I heard someone pull into my driveway. From where I was tangled up, I couldn't see who it was. I heard the closing of a car door. I hoped that it was Cole coming up the deck. I could hear footsteps.

Now was the moment I had waited on for hours upon hours. "Help, help, come help me!" I yelled as loudly as I could.

In a flash, Cole rushed inside. The look on his face was like he had seen a ghost. He quickly started asking me one question after another as he worked to remove the tape from my wrists. My voice was shaky, both from relief and from the cold air. I was likely not making any sense. The sting was horrific as he yanked the tape as quickly as he could from my wrists and ankles. He apologized as he tried not to hurt me. When I was completely free, he took the quilt from the floor and draped it around me. It felt so good. He led me to the couch as I tried to stretch my body. It hurt and felt good at the same time. My explanation of what had happened was all jumbled.

"I'll call 911," Cole said, reaching for his cell.

"Wait, Cole," I said, trying to compose myself. "There are detectives looking for this guy. I have their number on my desk. That's who we should call as soon as possible. I'm fine, but the longer I wait to call them, the further away this guy will get."

He looked at me strangely, but got up and went to look for the number on my desk. When Cole got the detective on the phone, I took it from there and went through the chain of events that happened. Cole looked and listened in disbelief. The phone conversation continued, and I pointed to the fireplace as I talked so Cole would get the hint to light a fire. He finally did so with frustration and confusion written all over his face.

"The detectives said it would be half an hour before they get here," I said after I hung up.

"Kate, how do you feel?"

"My head is throbbing, my jaw is aching, but I'm slowly getting warmer. I can't feel the warmth of that fire soon enough!"

"I'll make you something hot to drink as soon as I get this going."

"I'm so glad to see you Cole, but I'm so sorry to put you in the middle of this," I said, knowing I was about to break down in tears. "I was so scared." I wanted to cry all over again, but now was not the time. That was when I told him that I had harbored this guy's wife at the guest house while she sought a safe place to stay once she had left him.

Cole kept shaking his head in disgust.

"Cole, I need you to get my cell phone that I left on my bedside table upstairs. It's the first bedroom on the left. Thank goodness I didn't have that on me, or he would have destroyed that, too."

"I can get it. You sit here and rest. Don't get up until you feel steady on your feet. I called you this morning and wondered why you didn't answer. I decided I would just drop by anyway, since we had discussed it."

"Thank goodness you did! Come to think of it, I think I'll go up and get the phone. I'll take it slowly, but I need to move." It felt weird to even try to walk. I think the blood circulation had been cut off from my feet. I took it slowly as I glanced toward my office and headed carefully up the stairs with Cole right behind me. It didn't take long to find the first bullet hole. There was plaster dust everywhere. I reached my bedroom and pulled on some heavy socks as I sat on the side of the bed. I could tell that Cole didn't know what to do next. Picking up my phone gave me a feeling of being in control again. Yes, there was a dial tone.

CHAPTER 102

As I floated carefully back down the stairs, I could feel the warmth circulating throughout the entire house. All was well, I said to myself. In the kitchen, I put the kettle on for tea. I got out tea bags and cups as Cole appeared helpless and in shock.

He grabbed my shoulders, asking me again if I was all right. He questioned my decision not to call for any further help. "Kate, I still don't quite understand what made the guy run out of the house. You say he looked up the stairs and fired his gun? Twice?"

I nodded.

"He saw something on the stairs that truly frightened him. I'll never forget the look on his face. He thought we were alone. It really freaked him out when he fired and nothing happened."

"So, what did he see?" Poor Cole was trying to picture the scene.

I tried to explain. "Josephine occasionally appears. Her spirit still resides here. I have never seen her, but others have.

I have always sensed that she protected me somehow and now I'm convinced of it."

Cole just listened. He didn't know what to say. "He was shooting his gun at a ghost?"

"I think so. She either disappeared, or he saw the bullets go right through her. Please keep this all to yourself, Cole. It's all good. If you don't believe in ghosts, I understand. This scare hasn't been my first rodeo since I moved into this house. I refuse to be scared here, and I don't want my guests to be afraid."

"I understand, I really do. I will keep it all confidential. I just hope you're okay. Can I get you some aspirin for that headache?"

"Yes, in the hall bath you'll find some." He was so sweet as he tried to help.

"Oh, here comes Cotton to do some work." I got myself to the door, and when Cotton got out of the truck I told him I was visiting with Cole about the Jeep. He nodded and went about his work. He probably thought it was strange that I didn't offer him coffee like I usually did.

"So, when would you like me to come back to talk about the Jeep?" Cole asked out of concern. "I'm not leaving right now, so just think about it."

"I'm sorry, I don't know. I can't seem to think about that right now. I feel badly that you got involved here, and if you have someone else interested in buying the Jeep, I understand."

"Oh, no, I'll hold it as long as you like. Just call me when you feel up to taking it for a drive. Here's my card. I'm sorry, but I'm not leaving you until the detectives come if that's good with you."

"Thanks. I'd appreciate it. They will likely have a couple of questions for you as well. Would you like something to eat?"

He snickered. "No thanks, I'm fine. Are you always this hospitable, even when you've had an intruder in your home?"

I snickered as well. I had to admit, my behavior was most likely strange.

"Tell me, Kate, how did you end up living here in Borna? Trout said you're from Michigan."

I took a deep breath and gave him the short version of my arrival here. It was actually good to talk about something else. He listened so intently. It was like he really wanted to know.

"Cole, what about you? Do you have children?"

He smiled, which gave me the answer. "I have a daughter who lives in Perry. I see her when I can. She and her husband just found out that they're going to have a baby. That means I will be a grandpa!"

"That's wonderful! I have a son getting married in June. Perhaps I'll have the same news one day. What does your wife do?"

He paused. "Oh, I'm going through a very long and complicated divorce right now. I thought Trout might have told you."

"No, he didn't. I'm sorry to hear that."

"Thankfully, I'm very busy with my business and I relax by going fishing with Trout when we can get away. My dad is living alone in Perry, so my daughter and I make sure we check on him."

I was about to respond when I heard the detectives arrive. I'm sure Cotton would observe all the activity. I was pleased that they arrived in an unmarked car. Perhaps anyone driving by would assume the car belonged to one of my guests.

After I explained to the detectives why Cole was there,

they took his contact information and told him he was free to go, if he liked. He hesitated, but I insisted that he go. I walked him to the door and gave him a big hug. I was surprised when he hugged me back. I think it was a very scary and unsettling experience for him.

For the next hour or more, I went over every detail with the two men. One of them began taking fingerprints at various places. I was settled on the couch. I was pleased that they didn't react oddly when I told them Harper had seen Josephine. I'm sure they had heard everything at one time or another.

Before they left, they cautioned me about Harper still being in the area. They wanted to know if I had any firearms in the house for protection. I immediately responded by assuring them of my dislike for such things.

"You need someone to contact nearby that you can trust. Would you like to stay with someone until he's captured?"

I took another swallow of tea. "Heavens, no," I said, shaking my head. "I have friends and family close by. I'll be fine. By the frightened look on his face, I don't think he'll be coming back here anytime soon."

"Be observant when you go out," one of the men cautioned. "He stalked you once, and he may do it again. He is very angry with you, and some folks don't use common sense to get even!"

CHAPTER 103

After the detectives left, I went upstairs to rest. I was totally exhausted and relieved that my drama was over. Now, I just had to keep a lid on all of this. Who could I trust to share this with? I had to tell Ellie at some point because I may need her help in the future. It would be hard to keep it from Cotton and Susie, but I knew I had to. Maggie, John, Carla, and those in South Haven were not going to be told. I was sure about that! Thank goodness that Clark was not around. Once Harper was caught, I could be less cautious and free from worry.

I would have to get someone to repair the gunshot holes in the plaster. Thank goodness the shots didn't go through me. God had truly been with me. Josephine did everything she could to protect me. If news of this incident got out, who knows what they would say about the house having a ghost? I couldn't risk any of that and still be in business.

My body relaxed enough for me to fall into a light sleep. It was later in the afternoon when my cell phone rang and woke me up. In a groggy state, I looked at my phone and saw it was Aunt Mandy. I knew I had to answer.

"I just wondered if you wanted to come to dinner. I was hungry for a pork roast, so I have one in the oven."

"Oh, that does sound wonderful! Did you invite Wilson? You must be feeling much better."

"No, I didn't invite Wilson. Do you think I should have? And yes, I am feeling just fine again."

"That's up to you about who to invite, but I wouldn't mind having you to myself. Can I bring anything?"

"Not unless you want dessert. I'll leave it to you."

I hung up and realized this would be the perfect time to tell her what had happened. A glass of her Merry Merlot would certainly make it easier. I slowly got dressed, trying not to aggravate my aching head. I still had some cheesecake left from the weekend, so I wrapped up a couple of pieces to take with me.

When I arrived, Aunt Mandy was on her porch enjoying the chilly weather. She was wearing a sweater, and I had a feeling that she would enjoy her porch until the first snowfall arrived.

"We'd better have a hot toddy," I said, joining her.

"This Merry Merlot is keeping me nice and warm, thank you. I hope you brought your appetite."

"I'll do my best, and I brought dessert."

"So, tell me all about your guests. Did John behave himself?"

"Everything went fine, but I did have a little problem after they left," I said, hesitating.

She looked at me oddly.

"I wish I didn't have to tell you, but I don't want there to be any secrets between us. I had a break-in last night."

"Oh, good heavens, no! Are you okay?"

"I'm fine, now." I took a deep breath and started from the beginning about forgetting to turn the alarm on and going down the stairs. I left out some of the horrible details like the blow across the jaw and that he wanted to set my hair on fire. I could tell it was upsetting her, so I didn't want to drag it out with details. When I got to the part about Harper seeing someone on my stairway and shooting, questions and concern poured from her.

"You mean to tell me he saw your Josephine?" she asked with fright in her voice.

"He asked me who she was. Of course, I couldn't see anyone. It had to be her. You know, it's not the first time someone has seen her. Rose, who stayed here just this weekend, said she saw a woman standing by the door."

"This is unbelievable! You could have been killed!" I could see her starting to fall apart.

"I know, but whoever he saw saved my life. Josephine has always protected me in some way."

"So he ran out the back door? Aren't you afraid he'll return?"

"Not really. By the look on his face, I don't think he'll ever set foot in my house again."

"My heavens, child, he doesn't have to come into your house to hurt you! He could shoot you on some street corner!"

"This creepy human being is not going to ruin my life like he did Susan's. I've had a little experience with bad men before, if you recall."

Aunt Mandy had so many questions and concerns. It certainly ruined our nice evening together. She was a strong woman, or I never would have told her. I knew she would worry something terrible until this man was caught.

When I got home, I knew I couldn't possibly share this story with anyone else. It was too painful. I surely hoped Cole would be able to keep it quiet. Walking up the stairs, I saw the bullet holes once again. To think that one of them may have gone through me was horrifying. I crawled into bed repeating the many prayers of thankfulness I had already said. Somehow, I had a feeling that Harper would be caught. I had to think positively. As so often before, warm daylight filled the room. More than ever, the warmth was comforting and loving. I now could rest in peace.

CHAPTER 104

I called Cotton first thing in the morning to see who he knew that did drywall work. He started to ask why, but I cut him off by telling him to let me know if he thought of anyone. As I fixed myself some breakfast, I was feeling lucky and quite energized. I was looking ahead to planting some more bulbs, starting on a Jack and Jill's wedding quilt, and visiting South Haven. I dreaded the winter nights ahead, especially without visitors in the guest house. I was surprised when my cell phone rang and it was Cole.

"I'm just calling to see how you are doing. I hope you don't mind."

"Not at all. I'm glad you called. If you'd like to swing by today and bring the Jeep, I'm available."

"Are you sure? There's no hurry."

"I want to get it taken care of. Would you like to come for lunch? I owe you so much."

"Why, sure. Can I bring anything?"

"Just bring that cute little Jeep of yours!"

He laughed, and after we hung up I realized that my

day's plans had just changed. What would a macho man like Cole prefer for lunch? That was easy. I knew that every man's favorite food was meatloaf. I could also make a quick tomato bisque and serve the rest of the cheesecake. Having this to do would occupy my mind.

At one, Cole arrived. He looked pretty handsome in that red Jeep, but that would soon change. When he walked into the kitchen, the aroma of food impressed him. He couldn't believe I could make such an appetizing lunch that quickly. "You should open a restaurant, Kate. Even a fancy tearoom would be nice to eat at occasionally."

"You make a good point and I wish someone would, but I don't think it'll be me."

We sat down and Cole's eyes were as big as his appetite. It was he who brought up the intruder first. I told him how difficult it was to tell my aunt. "I simply cannot let this incident get out, Cole," I emphasized once again.

"My lips are sealed," he said, zipping his mouth shut. "Now keep in mind, I may try to blackmail you a time or two," he kidded.

"Ah, very clever! Did you bring the car title with you?"

"Signed, sealed, and delivered."

We continued to have great conversation as Cole enjoyed seconds. We talked about his daughter and my son, which was nice for both of us. Time was passing, but it was nice talking to a man about so many things instead of only chatting with my steady influx of girlfriends.

Cole helped me clear the table before we went outside to get in the Jeep. With me in the driver's seat I sat higher than in the Mercedes, and it felt like driving a large toy truck. Cole kept giving me information about the vehicle

ANN HAZELWOOD

as I concentrated on the completely new feel of the vehicle. Cole suggested that we drive toward Red Creek Winery and surprise Trout with a visit. I agreed, knowing my day was completely shot with the purchase of this Jeep anyway. When we arrived on the hill, Cole looked at me with a big grin and complimented me on my driving skills.

"Well, look who's here, Ellie," Trout yelled across the room.

"I think I just bought myself a Jeep!" I announced.

"Well, we need to celebrate. The drinks are on me!" Ellie cheered.

"So, do you like it?" Trout asked as he poured our drinks.

"I do, but I'm not used to all the extra bells and whistles this has."

We enjoyed a couple of drinks, and it was nearing the dinner hour when we left. It was a little more celebrating than I had planned.

"This was really a fun day, Kate," Cole said when he walked me to the door. "You are quite the lady, and I think you and Red are going to get along just fine."

"Red? Is that her name?"

"Red is really a he, but if you want it to be a she, that's fine."

I laughed. "Red! I like it! Mirty is the name of my Mercedes. What will you call your new Jeep?"

"Stallion, because she's black and beautiful!"

I nodded, giving my approval.

"Well, I guess I'll deliver Red tomorrow. What time is good for you?"

"How about first thing in the morning? I'll have some warm blueberry muffins and coffee ready."

"That's a deal."

The rest of the day was occupied with my upcoming purchase. Before I tried to go to sleep that night, I sent John, Maggie, Carla, and Jack a photo of Red. I wished I could send something to Clark, but I thought it required too much of an explanation. If I took complete ownership tomorrow, I would first drive to Aunt Mandy's.

John sent a text immediately.

> Congrats! Now you have no excuse not to drive to South Haven. The article is finally done and in print. I will mail you a copy. Thanks for all your help. J

I didn't respond, but I was anxious to see the article. It was fun to share in his research.

Jack sent a text, too.

> Cool, Mom!

There was no word from Maggie. I missed my bestie and hoped I would see her soon.

Tomorrow was Josephine's birthday. She would be 137 years old. Maybe I'll bake a little birthday cake in her honor. It may be just the two of us enjoying it, but I owed her so very much.

CHAPTER 105

I woke up after a night of tossing and turning. I kept seeing Harper's face as he shot his gun up my staircase. I tried to think of other pleasant things like my new Jeep, but it was difficult. I finally got up early and made my way downstairs to make muffins and to say happy birthday to Josephine. It was a beautiful fall day, and I was going to make the best of it.

After the muffins came out of the oven, I went into the office to check emails. Finally, there was an email from Maggie responding to my photo of Red. She loved it, as I knew she would. I still had not firmed up going to see her on Thanksgiving.

Josephine's birthday cake ended up being a pound cake. I could serve it with blueberries from my freezer with a topping of whipped cream. As I was cleaning up the kitchen, Cole and Red arrived in my driveway. I guessed I would have to be the one to take Cole home. "Good morning!" I said as I opened the door. "Red looks like it's just been washed. Did you do that for me?"

He blushed and nodded. "I smell something great!"

"Are you ready for coffee?"

"You bet! What time do you get up?"

"It depends if I have guests or not. By the way, today is Josephine's birthday. She would have been 137 years old."

"Well, it appears that she is living on to be even older!"

"Good point. Do you think I'm being silly about her?"

"You are addressing the reality. Who cares what other people think?"

"Thank you. I needed to hear that right now."

We sat down and I took great pleasure in watching Cole enjoy the warm muffins. I also had a plate of fruit to offer him. "I assume I'll be taking you home, but would you mind us swinging by my Aunt Mandy's house first? I'm anxious for her to see Red."

"Is she the lady with the octagon-shaped house that Trout told me about?"

"She is. I'm pleased that she has recently moved here from Florida. It's a win-win for both of us. She is quite chipper for her age."

"I would love to meet her. Say, Trout tells me that you have a relationship with Clark McFadden."

I smiled, but didn't answer.

"I've met him and really admire his work. How did you manage to get him to do work on this house?"

"It was odd, because he refused at first. He had always admired this house, which I guess made it tempting. He was here a lot, so we got to know each other pretty well. As you may know, he is a very independent sort, so we're just good friends." I wasn't sure I convinced Cole.

"Hmm, interesting," he said with a grin. "So without me

getting too personal, are the two of you committed to each other?"

"We've never had a conversation like that. We both like our lives pretty much the way they are."

"Hmm," he repeated.

"I'm going to give my aunt a call to let her know we're coming."

"Sounds good. Here is a folder with everything you will need to know about Red, including the title."

"And you, Mr. Alexander, are a little richer today," I said, handing him a check.

CHAPTER 106

Aunt Mandy and I were anxious to go to Ellen's for the next Friendship Circle meeting. I cautioned Aunt Mandy that no one knew about my incident, including Ellie, and I intended to keep it that way. It felt good to drive my Mercedes again. I didn't want to flaunt my new purchase. Those who were close to me had already met Red.

In the end, Ellen was gracious enough to host the meeting that had been previously scheduled at Aunt Mandy's. With her recent open house and catching the sniffles soon after, it was determined that Aunt Mandy could be a hostess at some other time.

Ellen loved entertaining, especially when it was our Friendship Circle. She was a good cook as well as a creative decorator. She chose a happy sunflower theme to honor the fall season. We were encouraged to gather around the table for lunch before we tackled the business of the day. Everyone was excited about going home with one of Emma's quilts, which was the focus of the meeting, but the chatter varied at the lunch table as we enjoyed the beautiful gardens outside

ANN HAZELWOOD

Ellen's windows. The menu was delicious taco soup, ham salad sandwiches, and a choice of pumpkin pie or carrot cake for dessert.

"How is Wilson?" Ellen asked my aunt. "You two must join Oscar and me for cards sometime."

"I would love that," Aunt Mandy responded. "I hadn't played cards since I left Florida, then Wilson and I played canasta last week and it was quite fun, once I remembered a few things."

Ellen smiled.

"Who is Wilson?" Peggy asked.

Ellen took over and answered for Aunt Mandy as my aunt smiled in approval. We eventually made our way to the living room where Ellen had had stacked Emma's quilts. She had a clipboard with notes about some of the quilts. We all got comfortable on the cushy pastel living room chairs that complemented her decor.

"We have more quilts than members in our group, so whatever is left will go to the Lutheran Family Children's Services, an organization which Emma was quite fond of," Ellen announced. Her sons have already chosen the quilts that they want to keep. I think we need to hear the family's comments about each quilt as I show them. If there is more than one person interested in a particular quilt, we will draw straws."

"I don't think I have ever drawn straws before, have you?" I whispered to Aunt Mandy. She snickered and shook her head.

"I won't take one of Emma's quilts since I didn't know her," Aunt Mandy stated. "I would like mine to go to the charity."

I smiled, feeling that Aunt Mandy had made a good and generous decision.

"Most of these are quilts that Emma made in her lifetime, but there are some made by others like this Nine Patch made by Emma's mother," Ellen explained. "It's pretty tattered, which was probably why her sons passed on this one. The note says that this was one of Emma's favorites because it was made from scraps of clothing that Emma wore as she grew up."

"Oh, that would be special to have," I whispered to Aunt Mandy. "How could the family pass that one up?"

"This one was actually Emma's baby quilt," Ellen announced. "This little Four Patch is pretty faded; but as you know, these were handed down to other siblings and really used."

"Did she have siblings?" Ellie asked.

"Yes, but I don't think most of them are living," Ellen responded. "This Dresden Plate was the last quilt Emma made," Ellen mentioned as she unfolded it.

"I remember seeing this in her quilting frame," added Esther. "I think she was making it for someone because she was concerned that she wouldn't have it ready in time. It's so beautiful."

"Well, that's a shame," said Ruth Ann. "I wonder who she was working on it for?"

"Her sons would have known, I suppose," Ellen replied as she moved on to the next quilt. "Her amazing handiwork really shows on this one. As some of you know, this quilt pattern is called Drunkard's Path."

Chuckles sprinkled throughout the room.

"She did this all by hand, of course. And, it's never been

used or washed. The blue and white is most striking in this one."

"That pattern is not fun to make," Ruth Ann commented. "I hope I get my hands on that one."

"The next quilt is the ever-popular Double Wedding Ring quilt," Ellen announced as everyone raved. "The note says it was made for Emma's wedding. She kept it "for good," this says. This is a much smaller ring than we normally see in this pattern. Since her mother was a quilter, I think we can assume that it was made by her mother."

"That's always been my favorite pattern," Mary Catherine mentioned.

"The note on this Fence Rail quilt says the maker is unknown," Ellen read. "The boys noted that they loved sleeping under this quilt because it has a flannel backing."

"Well, wouldn't you have thought one of them would have wanted to keep that one?" Esther asked, puzzled. "That is sad, if you ask me!"

CHAPTER 107

"Here's one that you will either love or dislike," Ellen said humorously. "This is called a crazy quilt. They are fascinating. Some are very intricate and fancy while some are not. This one is outlined in what they call feather stitching, but it doesn't have all the bells and whistles like silk ribbon embroidery and hand painting. You can see on this one that the velvet fabrics are holding up, but the silks are falling apart. The son said that his mother referred to this quilt as a "parlor throw." Their use was more for looks than for warmth. I hope this gets a good home."

I thought of Maggie and knew she would die to have this.

"That would never hold up in my house with my two dogs," Peggy commented.

"This fan quilt is made with handkerchiefs," Ellen announced above the chatter of the crowd. "The note says this was never used. It was kept in her cedar chest all the time. As you may know, Emma loved handkerchiefs."

"Oh, you can do so many things with them," noted Ruth

Ann. "This has Emma's name written all over it."

Ellen continued to show us another eight or nine quilts that belonged to Emma. We were attentive as we pictured them in Emma's life. The afternoon became very long as we shared more coffee and dessert. When Ellen finished with the quilts, everyone gathered to determine their favorite quilt and took time to look at all of them closer. I held back to make sure I didn't step on anyone's toes with my choice.

"So, honey, which one best suits you?" Aunt Mandy asked quietly. "I think Ruth Ann has already claimed the handkerchief quilt."

"I know you may think this odd, but my heart goes out to Emma's baby quilt," I admitted. "To think it brought Emma into this world and is not staying in the family is really sad. No one is even looking at it."

"You have such a tender heart, my dear."

I first got closer to the beautiful Dresden Plate, which Emma had just finished. I couldn't believe the perfect workmanship that she could achieve at her age.

"I can't decide between the Dresden Plate and the Double Wedding Ring," Ellen said as she held up both.

"Pick the one that tugs at your heart," I suggested. "I'm going to take her baby quilt."

Ellen looked at me, surprised by my advice. She took a brief moment to consider her two choices. "Well then, it's the Double Wedding Ring for me," Ellen decided. "I've always wanted one, and no one in our family has ever made one to pass on."

Aunt Mandy and I watched as everyone excitedly chose their favorite quilt.

"There will be some quilts left if you'd like another,

Kate," Ellen offered. "The baby quilt isn't really useful."

"If no one ends up taking the Dresden Plate, I would love to have it," I confessed.

"I'll let you know," Ellen said.

"Thanks for doing this for Emma," I said to Ellen. "This was better than her boys just picking one for each of us."

"She was the senior member of our group and was dearly loved," Ellen recalled. "I hope she will be pleased with the outcome."

Aunt Mandy and I left. We were exhausted from the long day.

"Are you up for an early cocktail?" Aunt Mandy asked when we got near her house.

"No thanks, Auntie," I said with a sigh. "I don't know about you, but I'm seeing nothing but quilts!"

She laughed.

"Do you realize that those quilts have begun a new chapter in their lives?"

"Maybe that's what quilts are for," Aunt Mandy responded with a big smile.

"You have a point there," I said with a nod. "I always think it's nice when their story goes with them, but that doesn't always happen."

"You're right."

"I am going to label Emma's baby quilt so no one thinks it was mine. I just want Emma to know it's in good hands. When I first met Emma, she tugged at my heart just like this baby quilt."

"Have a good evening, Kate, and don't forget to turn on your alarm before you go upstairs."

I smiled and nodded to confirm that I would indeed

remember to set my house alarm. It was good to get home to peace and quiet. I looked at my cell phone and realized that I had it turned it off during our meeting and hadn't turned it back on again. To my surprise, there was a message from Clark! I listened to it right away.

"Hello, busy lady! I'm planning to be home tomorrow and look forward to catching up soon!"

That was it? Well, I guess I should look forward to that as well, but it sounded like another wait and see from him.

My other message was from Maggie. She said she missed me and wanted to extend a formal invitation for me to have Thanksgiving with them. I knew I'd have to answer her soon.

I then went to the office to check for any reservation activity. I looked at my office chair and decided I never wanted to sit in it again. I pulled it out of the room. It was going straight to the dumpster!

CHAPTER 108

"Hey, Maggie Moo!" I greeted when Maggie answered.

"Hey, Katy Girl! What's going on with you? I got the picture of that snappy red Jeep you just bought. I like it!"

"Thanks. I love it! I bought it practically new from a really nice guy here in town."

"Was he cute and single?" Maggie teased.

"Funny you should ask, because he was! Well, cute and almost single!"

"Oh, no. What's the guy's name?"

"His name is Cole Alexander, and I find him to be very interesting."

"I don't know how you do it in that bitsy town of yours, but you've definitely got the touch!"

I laughed. "Tell me about Marilee and Carla. I am also curious to know if the quilt shop sold."

"I'm worried about Marilee. She looks awful, and she doesn't want to talk about it. Emily says it's all bad news. I don't know what to make of it."

"Oh, no," I said, feeling helpless and sad.

"Carla is fine. She has bounced back very quickly. There's no buyer yet for the quilt shop. I worry that Cornelia will become impatient and just close."

"Did you get Marilee's quilt done?"

"Yes, and when we gave it to her, she barely responded. She's just not herself."

"Please keep me posted. I'll keep praying for her."

"So, will you come Thanksgiving or not?"

"I won't promise, but I think I can. I'll be taking Red this time."

"Who's Red?"

"My Jeep! Cole said that was her name."

Maggie got a chuckle out of that. We chatted for another half hour about Mark's work, Jill's secrecy about her wedding dress, and the latest country club gossip. I told her about my wonderful afternoon with the Friendship Circle and how we divided up Emma's quilts. I was happy that she did not ask me about John or Clark for a change.

It was still early in the evening, so I decided to make a fire. I retrieved my journal so I could record the unusual day at the Friendship Circle. I jumped when I heard a knock at the back door. I usually hear if a car pulls in the driveway, but I hadn't heard anything. Out my bay window, I could see it was Ruth Ann.

"Hey, what are you doing out here?" I asked, surprised.

"I was going for a walk and saw your lights on, so I thought I'd stop by."

"Come on in, girlfriend," I said with a smile. "Interested in a drink?"

"I am! I was actually going to keep walking down to Marv's."

"So, have you had any events lately?" I asked as I poured her a glass of wine.

"I have one this weekend. Ed Mueller's granddaughter is getting married, and the reception is at my place."

"How nice! That's more than I can say for my business. I guess everyone has a place to stay, because I don't get many calls. The problem of housing is usually solved when people have so many relatives in town where they can stay instead. Have you seen Chuck lately?"

She gave a big sigh. "I don't know what it is with me," she said with disappointment in her voice. "I never get past one or two dates with anyone. One can't be too available, too eager, or too successful. The answer is no, I haven't seen him."

"Well, you don't have to beat yourself up over it. Chuck is a confirmed bachelor and would likely never change for anyone."

"Fine, fine, fine, but couldn't he still have a relationship? I'm not looking for a husband! What's wrong with me, Kate? Never mind, I think I know the answer."

"How can you insinuate that there's something wrong with you and not him?"

"Because I know I'm overweight, don't wear tight-fitting clothes, never show any cleavage, and have a strong personality."

I tried not to laugh. She was being silly. "Is that what you think he wants?"

"I think it's what most men want. I'm too comfortable and lazy to reinvent myself. I want to stay on the professional side with this business I have. It's another reason why Carson is not my rep anymore. I can't stand womanizers like him!

I'm just too picky to put up with any nonsense."

It took me another hour of giving a pep talk and serving another glass of wine for her to quit whining. She was convinced that she saw this pattern of behavior in herself and was convinced she'd never find a man. I convinced her to be herself, but told her that it also didn't hurt to try a few changes that she herself might be happier with. If finding a man was not a priority with her, then she need not worry. Men could surely become a time-consuming entity in our lives!

CHAPTER 109

The next day, I kept thinking about the late-night visit with Ruth Ann. That morning, I kept shivering as I worried about the first freeze of the year. It was hard to bear the thought of another winter coming. Susie arrived for her day of cleaning as I was making a fire.

"I sure love your red Jeep, Miss Kate. It really suits you."

"Thanks! I'm sure I'll appreciate it when we get our first snow."

"I don't think there's much to clean here today. Is there some project you'd like me to do?"

"I have a baby quilt that I'd like you to wash in the bathtub like we did once before."

"Oh, sure. Did you buy this at Imy's shop? It looks pretty old."

"No, it was Emma's baby quilt. Everyone in our Friendship Circle got one of her quilts."

"The family didn't want it? Didn't she have two sons?"

I shook my head. "Sad, right?"

When I left her to check my computer, I had two

potential reservations! One was around Thanksgiving, so I needed to decide about going to South Haven. My cell phone rang and I saw it was Cole. What could he possibly want?

"Hey, I wondered if you were free for lunch today. I'm driving to Perry to drop off some things at my daughter's house. I thought we could find a nice restaurant somewhere."

I didn't know what to say. This was too much, like he was asking me out on a date.

"Oh, Cole, I'll have to pass. I have Susie here cleaning today."

"I just thought you'd like a drive in my new Jeep. I'm anxious to show it off. Would you give me a rain check?"

"I suppose. Thanks anyway. Enjoy your Stallion!" I hung up thinking about how close I came to saying yes. The last thing I needed was an introduction to any of his family members!

"Miss Kate!" Susie yelled from the kitchen. "Your friend Ellen is at the back door."

"Good morning, Ellen," I rushed over to greet her. "Come on in."

"Sorry I didn't call first, but I just wanted to drop off this quilt."

"What quilt?"

"The Dresden Plate quilt that you loved so much," she explained.

"No one else wanted it?"

Actually someone changed her mind about taking it, so it's all yours!"

"Are you sure?" I noticed Susie trying not to eavesdrop.

"I know Emma would have wanted you to have it," she said, smiling.

"Well, I'm thrilled to take it off your hands."

"I'm on my way to Jacksonville, so I need to run. Enjoy!"

Out the door she went, and Susie glanced at the quilt. "I wish someone would knock on my door and hand me a quilt," she teased. "That is so beautiful!"

"It is! It was the last quilt that Emma made."

"I don't know how anyone manages to get those quilting stitches so small!" Susie said, looking closer.

At that very moment, I knew who the quilt should really belong to. Susie and Cotton would never own anything this beautiful. "I think it would be perfect for you and Cotton."

"What? You don't mean that, Miss Kate. I know Emma was a friend of yours. I can't accept that!"

"Yes, you can! Emma gave away her quilts to folks who appreciated them. I've seen her do that. I don't need another quilt, and I know you will take care of it."

"Oh, Miss Kate, this is too much!"

"It's mine now to give away, and I know Emma is smiling on me."

Susie beamed with happiness and ran her fingers across the tiny stitches.

With a smile on my face, I went back to the office to pay bills as Susie floated off to finish the laundry.

CHAPTER 110

Cotton Picked up Susie around four as I was starting to plan my evening. My cell phone rang and there was Clark's name, bright and clear.

"Well, my eyes must be seeing things, because I saw a bright red Jeep parked at your house on my way home today," he teased.

"That's right. I am the proud owner! When you leave town for such a long time, you never know what you may have missed!"

"I guess so. Would you like to tell me all about it at dinner tonight?"

"I would be happy to."

"Trout told me he's doing prime rib tonight at the winery, so I thought you and I should help him out."

"That sounds wonderful."

"See you around six then." Just like that, Clark resurfaced

without excuse or explanation.

I made my way up the stairs to begin a quick makeover. I had to admit that the thought of seeing Clark again was exciting.

When he arrived, he took a few minutes to walk around my Jeep and check it out. He patted the hood like he approved. "I like it," he said when I opened the door. Stepping inside, he looked into my eyes and drew me into a warm, sweet hug.

After a moment, I pulled away and exclaimed, "You've grown a beard! You look so different!"

He looked sheepish. "I hope you like it. After all, I recently became a father and will soon be a grandfather!"

"Well, you look the part. Tell me what you've learned since you left."

"I'll tell you on the way to dinner," he insisted as we got into his SUV.

The air was very chilly. It reminded me of the night I sat taped in my chair, freezing from the cold air coming in from the open door. I had to put those thoughts out of my mind. "First, tell me that your checkup went okay."

"It went well, which encouraged me to meet up with Michelle, my new daughter."

"You did?"

He nodded. "She's a smart, good-looking young woman; but then, why wouldn't anyone expect anything otherwise?"

I smiled in approval.

"She majored in art and teaches art at a middle school."

"How appropriate. Another artist!"

"She'll be quitting soon because her baby is due in December."

"Does she look like you?"

"I think she favors her mother. She's rather shy, and she had a lot of questions for me. I didn't meet her husband. His name is Jim. She probably wanted to check me out first."

"So, did you go to Springfield?"

"Yes, I made a delivery and did a little socializing."

I wondered what that meant.

"How about you? I'm sure no grass grew under your feet while I was gone."

"I don't know what you mean," I responded as we got out of the car.

"I took your advice and picked up Kate," Clark said to Trout as we walked in.

"Did you see her new Jeep?" Trout asked, giving me a wink.

"I did, and I think it suits her very well." He put his arm around my shoulders.

"Did she tell you she bought it from Cole Alexander?" Trout asked with an impish grin on his face.

"No, she didn't!" Clark responded as he looked at me oddly. Keeping his gaze on me, he asked Trout, "Did he sell her on anything else?"

"She'll have to answer that," Trout said, walking to the other end of the bar.

I wasn't going there, so I just gave Clark a big smile. We sat down at the bar, and Ellie joined us. To my surprise, Clark shared with Ellie and Trout that he met his daughter for the first time on this trip. He seemed proud and quite comfortable talking about it as I remained silent.

Our meal was delicious, and the conversation was quite fun until right before we left. Ellie asked me if two detectives had been around my place asking questions about a killer they were looking for. I played dumb and yet showed concern. "No, perhaps I missed them somehow," I said calmly.

"Well, a killer on the loose in this area is not a good thing," Clark warned. "Did he kill someone around here?"

"Not that we've heard," Trout chimed in.

I changed the subject to the idea of going home. Of course, I should have known the detectives would be searching around the area. I didn't want to think about it after such a pleasant evening.

CHAPTER III

When we arrived at my house, Clark said he'd picked up a gift for me. He reached in the back seat and handed me a coffee table quilt book with a large red bow around it. "I know how you love quilts, and I happened to meet the author of this book at her signing in Springfield. I had it autographed for you."

"How sweet of you to think of me, Mr. McFadden." I gave him a peck on the cheek. "Would you like to come in?"

"You know, it's been a long day and I've had more than my share to drink, so maybe I'd better pass," he said with a yawn.

"I can tell, which is all the more reason that I think you shouldn't drive home tonight. If you recall, I have many empty beds in this house."

"Don't I know it," he grinned as he pulled me close. "You are a convincing woman."

Clark followed me into the house and offered to build a fire. I liked the idea and proceeded to put my quilt book on the dining room table to examine later. I took my jacket off as I made my way to the office to check for any messages. I saw a flashing light on my answering machine, which was odd. Everyone who knew me would call on my cell phone. I pressed the button and recognized the voice of one of the detectives that had been at my home. He said that they had important news to share, and that I should call them back as soon as possible. My heart skipped a beat and I began to feel dizzy. Calling them back on a night that I had enjoyed up to this point was not going to be easy. What would I do about Clark? What if they were calling to warn me about Harper? I sat down on my new makeshift chair borrowed from The Study to think about what to do.

"Are you okay? Did I hear you talking?" Clark asked from the other room.

"I was listening to my messages, and…" I was unable to finish my sentence. I burst into tears. Why couldn't I control myself? Now I would have to tell Clark after all. He had entered the room and was waiting patiently for an explanation.

"What is going on, for heaven's sake? Did you get bad news?"

I tried to gain control of my emotions before I spoke. "I don't know where to start." I took a deep breath. "I have to make an important phone call, I'm afraid."

I started from the beginning. Clark's eyes widened as I went along. He kept interrupting me and asking questions. I could see his anger rise when I got to the part about being taped up and threatened with fire. At that, Clark punched the wall so hard I thought there would be another hole in my plaster like the gunshots had made! Part of his anger was the fact that I hadn't told him. I couldn't convince him it was my problem and that I didn't care to share it with the whole world. With Clark now completely sober and extremely angry, he said I needed to make the phone call. Clark staring at me made making the call even more difficult.

"Elliot Carver here, Division 1," the man answered bluntly.

I recognized his voice. "This is Kate Meyr returning your phone call," I said meekly.

"Yes, Ms. Meyr," he acknowledged. "We wanted to let you know as soon as we could that we located Harper near Chicago, Illinois, at a local hotel."

I felt the dawning of a sense of relief.

"Fire was exchanged between Harper and the local police, and he was killed at that location."

"Oh, thank goodness!" I said, my voice breaking. "Did he have his little boy with him? Is his boy safe? Did he hurt anyone else?"

"Calm down, Ms. Meyr," he said firmly. "We'll be able to answer all of your questions as this evolves. We haven't located or notified the next of kin, but we just wanted you to know that you are safe."

"Thank you, thank you," I said as I hung up.

Clark watched as I became overwhelmed with tears of relief. He stood by in silence, knowing what this must have been like for me. He must also have realized what he had missed by not keeping in touch with a friend who needed him.

Needless to say, the evening didn't go as planned—but for me, it was a gift from heaven. We went into the living room to bask in the comfort of the fire. We sat close to one another in an embrace, sharing very few words as the late hour turned into morning.

CHAPTER 112

Before Clark left early the next morning, he reassured me that I would be safe and that I needn't worry about him. He vowed to keep the whole ordeal a secret. I certainly knew I could count on Clark. He had always been there for me since I had arrived in East Perry. When he said he'd check on me later, it gave me a sense of security. Right now, that was what I needed most.

I picked up the beautiful quilt book that Clark had given me, along with my coffee, and perched myself near the fire that the two of us had kept going during the night. I untied the big ribbon and saw that the title was *Everlasting Quilts.* I opened the cover and noticed that the author had signed it saying, "To Kate, a special lady who has love and warmth, like a quilt." That was telling in itself, but the powerful photos of antique quilts that followed were breathtaking. As I scanned the pages, each quilt had a story to be told containing details of how it had traveled through its life span.

It made me reflect about how I discovered Josephine's black embroidered quilt during the first week of my arrival in this house. Its powerful messages affected me in many ways, as it still does today. The quilt encouraged me to learn more about Josephine.

Researching the lives of quilts for John alerted me to unfamiliar quilt practices like the family that picnicked in the family's cemetery while they quilted a new quilt in a frame under a shade tree. That became such a vivid, pleasant picture in my mind. Future generations could tell about their quilt being quilted in the cemetery!

Discovering my niece, Emily, sitting by her mother's tombstone was so touching. I learned that at every visit, Emily dutifully brought her mother's favorite quilt along to honor her mother. Emily said it had been her mother's wish to be buried with the quilt, but Emily's father chose to do otherwise. Love and respect prevailed.

Watching the farm auction where participants bid on and received someone's private possessions, like their quilts, is a reality that many families face. I could only hope that Mrs. Schmidt, the maker of the Bow Tie quilt, approved when I took it to my home. I will always cherish where it came from and will preserve it. Did her other quilts get spread out across the country or did they stay near the farm where they were crafted? Did it matter in the eventuality of things? It mattered to me!

Seeing sweet Emma's quilts get divided among her friends was a sad and yet joyous time. Who would have guessed that her very own baby quilt would find its way to a guest house in the same town where Emma lived? Would the next owner feel the connection and love that I felt at that moment when I knew I had to have it? Would the next owner care, or would they throw it away?

When I passed the Dresden Plate quilt on to Susie and Cotton, I knew it was the right thing to do. It would have been exactly what Emma would have done! Susie will give the quilt the care it requires. More importantly, this young couple will pass on the love as they enjoy that quilt during all the seasons ahead of them. That new Dresden Plate's life was just beginning!

When Aunt Mandy gave me Grandma Meyr's Rose of Sharon quilt, I knew its new life in East Perry County would change once again. Its dormant years of being saved "for good" were at an end. As the next generation to have the quilt, I wanted to give it life and purpose. I'm sure that would have been Grandma's intent when she made it. I wanted to show it off and would therefore think of her more frequently. It will truly to be admired for many generations to come.

Just like the quilts in the lovely book that Clark so carefully chose for me, the quilts in my life have proved to be amazingly resilient as they have traveled through their life spans. They soften the rough edges of our lives. If they could talk, they would tell us of their travels and we would be intrigued by their journeys. They are so forgiving as they get passed from one owner to the next. Their purposes of comfort, love, and joy have proven to be everlasting!

Cozy up with more quilting mysteries from Ann Hazelwood...

Wine Country Quilt Series

After quitting her boring editing job, aspiring writer Lily Rosenthal isn't sure what to do next. Her two biggest joys in life are collecting antique quilts and frequenting the area's beautiful wine country. The murder of a friend results in Lily acquiring the inventory of a local antique store. Murder, quilts, and vineyards serve as the inspiration as Lily embarks on a journey filled with laughs, loss, and red-and-white quilts.

The Door County Quilt Series

Meet Claire Stewart, a new resident of Door County, Wisconsin. Claire is a watercolor quilt artist and joins a prestigious small quilting club when her best friend moves away. As she grows more comfortable after escaping a bad relationship, new ideas and surprises abound as friendships, quilting, and her love life all change for the better.

Want more? Visit us online at ctpub.com